DEAD MAN'S LIST

TITLES BY KAREN ROSE

Dirty Secrets (enovella)

BALTIMORE NOVELS

You Belong to Me
No One Left to Tell
Did You Miss Me?
Broken Silence (enovella)
Watch Your Back
Monster in the Closet
Death Is Not Enough

CINCINNATI NOVELS

Closer Than You Think
Alone in the Dark
Every Dark Corner
Edge of Darkness
Into the Dark

SACRAMENTO NOVELS

Say You're Sorry
Say No More
Say Goodbye

NEW ORLEANS NOVELS

Quarter to Midnight
Beneath Dark Waters
Buried Too Deep

SAN DIEGO CASE FILES

Cold-Blooded Liar
Cheater
Dead Man's List

KAREN ROSE

DEAD MAN'S LIST

BERKLEY | NEW YORK

BERKLEY
An imprint of Penguin Random House LLC
1745 Broadway, New York, NY 10019
penguinrandomhouse.com

Book design by Elke Sigal

Library of Congress Cataloging-in-Publication Data

Names: Rose, Karen, 1964–author.
Title: Dead man's list / Karen Rose.
Description: New York: Berkley, 2025. | Series: The San Diego Case Files; 3
Identifiers: LCCN 2024029855 | ISBN 9780593817179 (hardcover) |
ISBN 9780593817186 (ebook)
Subjects: LCSH: California—Fiction. | LCGFT: Romance fiction. |
Thrillers (Fiction) | Detective and mystery fiction. | Novels.
Classification: LCC PS3618.O7844 D43 2025 | DDC 813/.54—dc23/eng/20240708
LC record available at https://lccn.loc.gov/2024029855

Printed in the United States of America
1st Printing

The authorized representative in the EU for product safety and compliance is
Penguin Random House Ireland, Morrison Chambers, 32 Nassau Street,
Dublin D02 YH68, Ireland, https://eu-contact.penguin.ie.

To the memory of Loretta Barrett. Unlike Sam's mom, you made banana bread that was a delicious treat to whoever was lucky enough to receive it. I miss you, Mom.

And to Martin, my rock. I love you.

DEAD MAN'S LIST

PROLOGUE

I t was, Kit thought as she drew her jacket tighter, too cold to be sitting out in the barn. But McKittrick House, despite its homey warmth and delicious smells of apple pie and clean laundry, was not where she needed to be right now.

There were too many people in the big house. She loved them all. Her parents, her brothers and sisters—foster kids, all fifteen of them. It was the first Friday of the new year, and they'd gathered to celebrate.

They were one big truly happy family.

They were one big truly *nosy* family. Everyone wanted to know if she'd had her date with Sam Reeves yet.

She had not. And she might not. Their second date, which had been hanging over her head for more than a month, was now upon her. She'd spent six months during the spring and summer avoiding the police psychologist. *Because I was scared.*

She'd known that she'd hurt him eventually because she was shit with relationships. And Sam deserved better. But then she'd agreed to go on one date and, in a moment of weakness, asked him on a second. That had been over a month ago and life had interfered. But now it was time to face the music. *And I'm still scared.*

"Cold feet," she muttered to herself. "It's just cold feet."

She shifted on the hay bale, glad she'd had the presence of mind to throw a saddle blanket over it before she'd sat down. Hay bales looked like perfect seats but they were prickly as hell.

Like me, she thought with a sigh.

Her sigh echoed back to her, and Kit stiffened. She'd thought she was alone.

"Hello?" she called. "Come on out, whoever you are."

One of the stall doors opened, revealing a teenage girl with pink and blue streaks through her sandy blond hair.

"Rita? What are you doing out here?"

Her foster sister—soon to be legally adopted sister—stepped into the dim light. "I needed some quiet."

"Wanna sit and be quiet with me? Or I can leave."

Rita's smile was wobbly. "I'd like to sit and be quiet with you."

She sat on the bale, Kit's arm wrapping around Rita's thin shoulders. "You're not wearing a coat. You're going to freeze out here."

"I'm *fine*," Rita said with a condescending huff. "It's not that cold."

But Rita was trembling, so Kit tightened her hold. "Mom and Pop know where you are?"

Rita nodded. "I didn't want them to worry."

"Thank you." Kit would say no more, giving Rita the quiet she'd requested. If the girl wanted to talk, Kit would listen.

Rita sighed again, long and loud. "Cold feet, huh?"

Kit frowned. "Did you hear me say that?"

"Yep. You're going on that date tomorrow, Kit."

Kit's frown became a scowl. "Says who?"

"Says me. And Mom and Pop and all the others back at the house. You're meeting Sam tomorrow for your date in the desert if we have to tie you up and drive you there ourselves."

"That's kidnapping," Kit said lightly, wishing she were certain the family wouldn't do such a thing. But they just might. They liked the psychologist who, for some reason, still seemed to want to date Kit. "I could arrest you."

"It would be worth it."

Kit let go of Rita's shoulders to cross her arms tightly over her chest. "Damn, girl," she grumbled.

Rita laughed, a sweet sound that they were all hearing more often these days. "You will go, right?"

Kit shot Rita a sour look. "I don't know."

Rita shook her head. "Kit, what are you afraid of?"

Kit exhaled quietly. "I don't know."

Rita put her arm around Kit's shoulders, and Kit's heart cracked a little. She loved Rita so very much, even though the girl could be a little shit when it came to Kit dating Sam.

"You wanna know what I think?" Rita murmured.

"I don't know," Kit said again.

"Too bad. I'm going to tell you anyway. I think you're scared you'll like him too much. That you'll have too good a time and he'll want a third date. Am I close?"

Yes. "Maybe."

"I also think you've had too much time to build this up in your mind. You were supposed to have this date over a month ago, but things happened and it got drawn out and out and out."

Defensiveness coiled in Kit's gut. "Not my fault."

It really hadn't been.

"No," Rita said, speaking carefully now. "You had a case and

Sam understood that. He had an emergency with one of the teens at the shelter, and you understood that. Then you had another case—which, by the way, I don't think you *had* to work that weekend. I think that was you having cold feet."

She was right again, Kit thought. It rankled, being called out by a fourteen-year-old. "How would you even know that?"

"I asked Connor when he came last week to bring Christmas presents for Mom and Pop. He said the case was important, but not so much that you couldn't have investigated the next day. He was peeved that he had to cancel his date with CeCe because you got scared of your date with Sam."

Kit blew out an irritated breath. Her partner in the homicide department had a big mouth. "Connor Robinson told you that?"

"He did." Rita chuckled. "Then he begged me not to tell you that he'd said that because he was afraid you'd get even with him."

"He'd be right," Kit said darkly. "Besides, Sam canceled most of the dates. Not me."

"Well, yeah. His father went into the hospital."

Sam's father had had a small stroke and, while he'd be okay, Sam had spent most of December in Scottsdale. Kit had meant to drive to Arizona, to be there for Sam, but she'd lost her nerve.

She hated herself for that. But Sam's father's stroke had made her paranoid about leaving Harlan and Betsy. They were about the same age as Sam's dad. That something could happen to them was terrifying.

"You know too damn much, kid," she said, sounding petulant to her own ears.

Rita tightened her hold on Kit's shoulders. "Kit. You like Sam. I know you do. What's the worst that can happen?"

That I'll fall for him. That I'll come to need him.

That he'll come to need me.

And *that* was too much responsibility. "Since when are you a therapist?" she asked, a little more nastily than she'd intended.

"Since you needed one," Rita shot back, unfazed. "Look. You can talk to me or not. But don't cancel your date. Please. I think you need him."

Kit's chin came up. "I don't need anyone."

"That's a lie," Rita said softly. "And you promised that you'd never lie to me."

Kit sighed. Once again, the kid was right. "Why are you doing this to me?"

"Why are you doing this to yourself?"

Kit's lips twitched. "You've been picking up techniques from Dr. Carlisle."

Rita's therapist was Sam's boss, and the woman made Kit nervous. She—and Rita—saw far too much.

"Yes, I have. I'm thinking about being a therapist, too."

"I thought you wanted to be a cop."

"Maybe I do. I'm fourteen. I've got time to decide."

Time. That was the one thing Kit wasn't sure that she had. She *did* want this date with Sam and she *was* scared. But time was passing and, as so many helpful people had reminded her, someone else might snap Sam up.

Because he was a good man.

Too good for me.

"Why are you out here?" Kit asked, desperate to refocus their conversation. "What's bothering you?"

Rita studied her, her gaze cagey. "I'll tell you if you promise to go on that date and not stand Dr. Sam up."

Kit closed her eyes. "Why is this so important to you?"

"Because I love you," Rita said, so softly that Kit nearly missed it.

"Shit." Kit's eyes burned. "No fair."

Rita shrugged. "I calls 'em like I sees 'em."

Which was one of Kit's favorite phrases. *Using my words against me.*

"Brat."

"Promise me," Rita murmured.

"*Fine.* I promise. I will go. I will try to have fun. I just . . ." She trailed off, swallowing back the words.

Rita met her gaze. "You what?"

"I don't want to hurt him," she confessed. "I'm shit with re-lationships. And why am I getting dating advice from a fourteen-year-old?"

"Because I'm wise beyond my years," Rita said dryly. "You said so yourself, just last week."

"Brat."

"Just . . . breathe, Kit. It's what you always tell me to do."

"You have thrown way too many of my own words back at me tonight. *Fine.* I promise I will go on the date. Now you spill. Why are you here?"

Rita bit her lip. "Drummond's trial is in two weeks."

Kit brushed a lock of hair from Rita's forehead. "I know, honey."

Christopher Drummond had been arrested for murdering Rita's mother. Rita had found the body and had known her mother's employer had killed her, but no one had listened because the man was richer than God and, in San Diego, nearly as powerful.

Kit had gotten the case reopened, recusing herself because of her relationship with Rita. Connor Robinson had investigated the case and made the arrest. And, while it was not a slam dunk, the prosecutor was confident he could get a conviction.

But Rita would have to testify. And Christopher Drummond would be there, staring at her.

The worst part was that Drummond had sexually assaulted

Rita as well. None of the family knew the details, and Rita wouldn't talk about it. They knew only that it had been one of the times her mother had brought Rita to work with her, cleaning Drummond's house. Rita had refused to press charges and they'd respected her decision. But that assault had to be dealt with at some point.

Rita's apprehension about Drummond's trial made perfect sense.

"I'm scared," Rita confessed. "What if he gets off, Kit? What if he goes free?"

"Joel isn't going to let that happen." Joel Haley was the prosecutor, a friend of Kit's, and Sam's best friend. He knew what he was doing in a courtroom.

"You can't promise that," Rita said, staring at their feet.

"You're right. I can't. But I can promise Joel will do everything in his power to see Drummond put in a prison cell for the rest of his life."

Rita lifted her gaze to Kit's, her fear clear to see. "If he goes free, he'll come after me. I'm the one who accused him. Even if I didn't press charges on the . . . on the other thing."

Kit's jaw tightened, fury burning in her chest. "He may try, but to get to you he will have to go through me. And Mom and Pop and every single McKittrick. And we are formidable."

Rita smiled, but it was forced. "We are."

"I'll be with you in the courtroom. Mom and Pop, too."

"Promise?" Rita asked, sounding like a very young child.

"I promise. I've already told my boss, and he knows I'm taking vacation days for the trial."

Rita's eyes widened. "You're taking *vacation*? You never take vacation."

"I am this time." Kit booped Rita's nose. "For you."

Rita's eyes filled with tears. "I do love you," she whispered.

Kit couldn't stop her own tears. The words were hard to say back, even though she felt them keenly. She'd only just learned to tell Harlan and Betsy that she loved them. But Rita needed the words.

"And I love you. I will keep you safe, Rita. Always."

"I know. Thank you."

"You never have to thank me," Kit said fiercely. "You deserve to be protected."

"Because you couldn't protect Wren?"

Kit flinched, because Rita was right once again. Kit's sister Wren had been murdered when they were only fifteen, and Kit had never recovered. They'd never found the doer, either. It was a bitter pill to swallow, knowing Wren's killer was out there somewhere, walking free.

Kit didn't want Rita to live her life knowing that the monster who'd assaulted her and who'd killed her mother hadn't paid for his crime.

"Partly because of Wren," Kit admitted. "But mostly because of you. You are good and kind and you deserve the best life. A safe life."

Rita smiled, and this time it was real. "You really do love me."

Kit rested her forehead on Rita's. "Even when you're a brat who's wise beyond her years."

"Thank you." Rita straightened. "We should get back in there. There won't be any food left." She rose and pointed a finger at Kit. "Tomorrow. You and Snickerdoodle are meeting Sam and Siggy."

"Dogs and desert," Kit said dutifully. "I promised. I won't back out."

Sam loved the desert, and Kit let herself remember that she'd wanted to know why. She let herself remember that Sam was good and kind and deserved a fun date.

Maybe I do, too.

"Thanks, Kit." Rita hugged her, then skipped out of the barn before Kit could react.

Before she could hug her back. Kit wasn't great at giving hugs.

Kit wasn't great at too many things.

Sam was good at everything. He was a caring therapist, he volunteered his time with teens and the elderly, and he had the patience of a saint. He'd never pushed her or made her feel bad for needing her space or for being prickly. Sam was a good man, plain and simple.

With a big sigh, she folded the saddle blanket, putting it away. Then she walked out of the barn, only to see two glowing lights off to the side. Two lights that illuminated a man's big hands as he carved a block of wood.

"Pop? What are you doing out here? You'll catch cold."

He looked up from where he sat on a bench, a flexible flashlight hanging from his neck. Kit had gotten the light for him for Christmas and she didn't think she'd seen him without it since he'd opened the box. It provided enough light for him to get all the details right on whatever he was creating.

"I wanted to make sure you two were okay. I didn't listen in."

Kit settled next to him on the bench. "Rita was making me promise not to cancel my date with Sam."

Harlan smiled. "Good for Rita. That girl is somethin' else."

"She is. She's also nervous about the trial."

Harlan's smile faded. "I know. We'll stand with her."

"She's afraid if Drummond gets off, he'll come after her."

Harlan's jaw tightened. "I'm getting better security."

There was something in his tone that gave Kit pause. "What's going on, Pop?"

Harlan exhaled quietly. "Someone sent a letter to Rita. Unsigned."

Kit tensed. "Tell me."

Wordlessly, he pulled a folded paper from his pocket and handed it to her.

Kit unfolded the single page with trembling fingers.

I see your school is doing *Alice in Wonderland* this spring. Have fun being in the ensemble. It's not a huge role, but I know you'll do it brilliantly. I'll be in the front row.

New rage bubbled up. *Son of a fucking bitch. Drummond.* But there was no signature. No evidence it had come from the disgraced former city council member. The man had been released on two million dollars bail and was freely walking the streets until his upcoming trial. Now Rita's fear made even more sense. "When did this arrive?"

"Right before Christmas."

Kit drew a breath, trying not to sound angry with her father. "Why didn't you tell me?"

"I'm telling you now," Harlan said. "Rita didn't want you to know. She was afraid you'd go after Drummond. Get yourself in trouble."

How Kit wanted to do just that. *Get Drummond. Not get into trouble.* But they'd be one and the same if she allowed herself the vengeance she craved on Rita's behalf. "Do you think this is from him?"

"Don't you?"

"Yes, but I imagine he's smart enough not to have left any evidence. Did you report this?"

"Joel knows. That letter's a copy. He has the original."

"Okay." The prosecutor on Rita's case would do the right thing. "That has to be enough for now. And it shows that Drummond is scared. That's positive."

"Yeah." Harlan's throat worked as he tried to swallow. "I hate him," he whispered.

"Me too. What security are you having installed?"

"Cameras along the property line and around the house. An alarm system on doors and windows. Cartridges for my shotgun."

"Anson?" Kit ignored that last one.

"Of course."

Anson was one of the fosters who'd passed through McKittrick House the year before Kit had arrived. He owned a security firm up in Anaheim. He'd do an excellent job.

"You might also consider a dog for Rita and the other girls." Emma and Tiffany were the newest foster children at McKittrick House, and they and Rita had become best friends. She lightened her tone, needing to lessen the tension on her father's kind face. "They might feel safer with a dog. And then they won't always be 'borrowing' Snickerdoodle from me."

Harlan lifted a bushy eyebrow. "Did the girls put you up to this?"

"Nope." Kit forced a grin. "All my idea. Every girl needs a dog, Pop."

He chuckled, but it was also forced. Still, it was a chuckle. "I'll take the kids to the animal shelter this weekend. We'll see if we can find a dog who'll suit."

Kit rested her head on his broad shoulder. He was the strongest, safest person she knew. He'd been her rock since she and Wren had snuck into this very barn as twelve-year-old runaways. Harlan and Betsy McKittrick had found them hiding and given them shelter. And so much love.

"Thanks, Pop. For everything. For me and for Rita and all the others. Love you."

"Love you too, Kitty-Cat." He kissed the top of her head. "Have fun on your date."

She sighed, letting the Rita problem go for now. "I'll try. But if there's a murder, I'll have to cancel."

Harlan snorted quietly. "You sound almost hopeful."

She kind of was. But wishing for a murder was wrong, and Sam deserved better. "I'm not hopeful. I'm just . . ."

"Scared," he supplied gently.

"Yeah."

"It's okay to be scared, Kit. But other things scare you and you push through. You'll be okay. I know it."

Kit wished she were as confident.

And she still wished for a murder. Just a small one.

CHAPTER ONE

Be careful," Sam said, pointing to a shrub next to the trail. "That's a catclaw. Its thorns are sharp."

"Okay," Kit said, giving the bush a wide berth and tugging on Snickerdoodle's leash to make sure that she kept her distance as well.

Their hike so far had been filled with similar safety callouts from Sam and not much else. It was . . .

Awkward, Kit thought with a wince. This date was not *bad* but just so awkward, and she had no idea what to do about it. The desert itself was beautiful in a stark way, and Sam had chosen a less traveled trail. They'd had complete solitude, not having seen another hiker for miles. The weather, while unforgiving in the summer, was perfect during the winter. The skies were clear, the cool breeze refreshing.

But as pretty as the landscape was, this day had been uncomfortable as hell.

Sam had picked her and Snickerdoodle up that morning and right away Kit had known something was wrong. Usually sweet and calm, Sam was tense and overly polite.

It was like they were strangers.

I've messed things up already, and I don't even know what I did wrong, she thought sadly.

The drive to the park had been quiet, their minimal conversation stilted. Sam had asked her a few questions in a cautious tone, and she'd replied equally cautiously in sentences that never managed to be more than a few words.

They'd started their hike in a muted mood, with Sam pointing out landmarks and plants like he was a tour guide. Brisk, efficient, but impersonal.

I have to fix this. Because not only did Sam sound impersonal, he seemed sad, which she couldn't stand. Especially if she'd caused it. Abruptly she stopped on the trail, Snickerdoodle obediently sitting at her side.

Sam had taken a few steps forward before realizing she was no longer beside him. Carefully he turned so that he and Siggy faced her. Sam's expression was blank, and Kit's heart dropped to her stomach. "Kit? You okay?"

"No." Her voice shook and she drew a breath. "I'm sorry."

His shoulders sagged, disappointment unmistakable in his eyes. "I know."

Panic flared, and she realized just how much she'd wanted this date to go well. How much she'd wanted to see Sam happy. "I did something. Ruined something. You're not happy. We're here, in the desert, and you're supposed to be happy."

He frowned. "What are you talking about? I thought . . ."

She took a step closer. "What?"

His throat worked as he swallowed. "I thought that you were going to say that this date was a mistake."

Her mouth dropped open. "What?"

He studied her face. "You're not thinking this was a mistake?"

"No. Just . . ." She kept her gaze focused on his. "I was scared of today."

"I figured you would be. I thought for sure you'd find a reason to cancel on me."

"I almost did."

One side of his mouth lifted in an almost-smile. "Not a shock. Who talked you into coming?"

"Rita," she said dolefully. "And Pop. Called me out on my bullshit. Is that why you've been so distant all day? You thought I was about to call this a mistake?"

He nodded warily. "Were you?"

She did look away then, taking in the desert around them. It really was beautiful. "I don't think so. I wanted to come here. With you. Wanted you to show me the desert and why you love it. But it's been more than six weeks since I asked you on this date. Enough time to second-guess myself. And maybe to second-guess you. You could have anyone. Everyone tells me so. I still don't know why you seem to want to be with me."

And that was the honest truth.

"Kit." He waited until she met his eyes again. "My feelings haven't changed. I want to be with you, but I don't want to rush you into anything you're not ready for. I can wait. You're worth waiting for."

She took another step forward, now so close that she could see the thick dark lashes framing his green eyes behind his Clark Kent glasses. Could see the freckles sprinkled across his nose now that he'd gotten some sun.

She could see his sincerity, the very thing that had originally drawn her to him. And suddenly she wasn't afraid anymore, because this was Sam. Other than her father, Sam was the kindest, gentlest man she knew. He would respect her limitations. And he'd protect her heart.

She needed to protect his as well.

"I'm ready for this date." She reached out, gripped his jacket, tugging him closer. "I want to know you better."

His chest expanded with the breath he drew. "Thank God," he muttered, his hands coming up to cup her face, sending a shiver down her spine and over her skin. "I've tried to give you space."

"Don't," she said simply, releasing her hold on his jacket and sliding her hands around his neck. "I . . . I missed you," she admitted.

His smile was pure delight. "You did?"

"I did. It's been too long since we went on our fishing date." She rose on her toes. "Too long since you kissed me good night."

His swallow was audible. "Thought about that, did you?"

"I did. Did you?"

"Yeah. Every night. Every morning. And maybe a few times during the day."

"Same," she whispered, their lips now brushing. An almost-kiss. If she leaned up just a little, she could kiss him for real. She closed the distance between them and then his mouth was finally on hers. His kiss was sweet and undemanding, but his hands, still cupping her face, trembled.

He wanted more.

And so do I.

Dimly the sound of barking intruded. Two different barks. Two different dogs.

Dogs.

Snickerdoodle.

Kit no longer held her leash.

Shit.

They pulled away at the same time, each looking around for their dogs because Sam had dropped Siggy's leash, too.

"Siggy!" he called.

"Snickerdoodle!" Kit shouted, then huffed a relieved breath when Snick came trotting around a cluster of small boulders, her tail wagging. But she was alone. No sign of Siggy.

Sam left the trail, taking off at a jog. Kit grabbed Snickerdoodle's leash and followed him.

Then stopped dead in her tracks.

"Dead" being the operative word.

Siggy had a shoe in his mouth. A man's wingtip, size eleven or thereabouts. The shoe's mate was half buried in the sand on a man's foot.

A very dead man, lying faceup in the desert sand.

What was left of his face, anyway. The animals of the desert had been snacking.

So gross.

The body was positioned in a hollow beneath the boulders, sheltered from the wind. Still, the sand had swept over the body, covering the legs, one foot, and part of one arm.

Accident or murder? She took a few steps closer and had her answer. The man's neck was an open gash, now home to dozens of flies. His throat had clearly been slit, ear to ear.

Be careful what you wish for, she thought, remembering how she'd hoped for a murder the night before.

Kit glanced at Sam, whose gaze was fixed on the man's face, his eyes wide, his face slack with shock. "Sam? You okay?"

He cleared his throat roughly. "Well, shit."

She nodded once. "Shit indeed. I need to call this in."

"Wait." He edged closer, gaze still fixed on the victim. "Look at his face."

"I did. There isn't enough left for a clear ID. The ME will likely have to use dental records or DNA. He—"

"No, Kit. *Look* at him. I know him."

Startled, Kit crouched at the dead man's side. And then she recognized him, too. Or at least the tribal-style tattoo that wound up his neck, ending behind what had been his ear. "Well, shit."

Sam huffed a mirthless laugh. "Shit indeed. That's Councilman Brooks Munro."

Of the San Diego city council.

Kit scowled down at the body. "This is not gonna be fun."

"Our second-favorite local politician," Sam said, his tone dripping with disdain.

Kit looked up at him in surprise. She'd never heard him use that caustic tone before and wondered what his experience had been with the councilman, who had a reputation of being very charismatic and charming. At the same time, Kit had heard rumors of impropriety, but nothing had ever been proven.

"Who's the first?" she asked, although she thought she knew.

He met her gaze. "Drummond."

Drummond had resigned his seat after being charged with murder, but Kit took Sam's point. She still wondered why Sam hated this councilman. "Munro has been missing for a few days," she said.

"I know," he said flatly. "I saw it on the news."

"He was reported by his wife, who's been out of town. Two officers did a welfare check and found blood on his garage floor. Enough that they assumed that he'd been seriously injured."

Sam grimaced. "I'd say he was seriously injured. Oh shit. Kit. His hands . . ."

Kit sighed. The victim's fingers were missing, as were the toes on his exposed foot. "Could have been animals."

"God, I hope so. But you don't think so."

"No, I don't." Because now that she was closer, she could also see the stab wounds in the man's chest. She counted at least twenty at first glance. Someone had really wanted this man to suffer. "But the ME will tell us for sure. Let me call it in."

She pulled her phone from her pocket, but she had no signal. "Dammit."

"Wait." Sam dropped to one knee and began rifling through his backpack, piling its contents on the sand until he found what he'd been looking for. "Here." He held out a phone. "Sat phone. You'll get a signal with that."

"Do you always carry a sat phone?"

"Yep. It's a safety thing. Siggy and I hike in remote areas. Cell signals are never a given."

She glanced down at him while she searched her phone for her boss's contact information. "Are those . . . Sam, do you have night-vision goggles?"

He looked up, expression slightly embarrassed. "Christmas present from my parents. I promised I'd carry them with me, just in case. I also packed a picnic lunch, but I don't think I have any appetite anymore." He loaded everything into his pack and stood, his expression now pained as he turned his back on the body. "Please call Lieutenant Navarro, Kit. I want to get away from here as soon as we possibly can."

Kit hated to tell him that it would likely be hours before they could leave. So she merely dialed Navarro's number.

"Navarro. Who is this?" her boss answered brusquely.

"It's Kit. We've got a situation here."

Connor Robinson stuck his head in Lieutenant Navarro's office. "So you two just happened to find the one missing body in nearly one thousand square miles of state park?"

Kit and Sam were in her boss's office, waiting on Navarro to debrief them. They'd dropped the dogs off with Harlan and Betsy, and Kit had picked up her own car, knowing that her day was far from over. Hopefully Navarro would let Sam go home as soon as they'd reviewed his statement, but Kit had the awful feeling that her boss would keep her far longer.

Don't assign me this case. Please.

"I'd bet a week's pay that it's not the only body hidden in the park," Kit told her partner.

Sam made a pained sound, and Kit patted his hand. "You okay?"

"No," Sam grumbled. "Day's ruined. Date's ruined. And I'm never going to get the sight of his face out of my mind."

Connor made a sympathetic face. "That sucks, man. Sorry your date was ruined."

Sam made another grumbling sound that was cuter than it should have been.

"We'll have another date," Kit promised. "A no-dead-body date. I promise."

"Okay." But he still frowned, and Kit felt bad for him.

Munro's body really had been a gruesome sight, and Sam had handled it better than a lot of people would have. She knew that he'd seen bodies before, but Munro's was . . . extreme.

Even for me.

"What are you doing here today anyway?" Kit asked Connor. "It's Saturday. Did we catch another case?"

"No. I heard about the body and that it was discovered by an SDPD cop. I knew you'd headed up that way so I wanted to find out if you were the ones who'd found it."

It was Kit's turn to frown. "How did you hear about the body?"

Connor grinned. "Baz called me. He'd heard it through the station's grapevine. I have to say I'm miffed that you didn't at least text me."

Kit rolled her eyes. "Baz has been surgically grafted to the grapevine, I think." Her former partner had retired after having a heart attack nine months before. She missed him terribly, but she and Connor had found their stride together. "And I didn't text you because you were supposed to be with CeCe today."

"Her mom twisted her knee and CeCe took her to the doctor." He shrugged. "So I came in. Oh, sorry, sir." He abruptly moved to one side of the doorway, making room for Navarro, who looked unhappy. "See you later."

"No," Navarro said. "You stay."

Connor winced, and Kit had to swallow a groan. If Connor was staying, it meant they'd be working Munro's murder investigation.

Which sucked, because this was going to be a bitch of a case. The suspect list was already a mile long. His constituents seemed to love him, but few people in law enforcement liked Brooks Munro. In fact, too many people hated his guts.

Navarro pointed to her and Sam. "You two. It's always you two."

Kit bristled. "Sir?"

Sam's mouth fell open. "I beg your pardon?"

"Trouble just seems to find you," Navarro muttered, sitting down at his desk. "And you can't even deny it."

Sam sighed. "No, I guess I can't, but it's not like we found the body on purpose. It spoiled our entire day. And my appetite for the next week."

Navarro's lips twitched. "It was pretty bad." He shifted his attention to his computer. "Good initial report, Kit. All the particulars are here. Brooks Munro, age fifty-one, city councilman. Was last seen alive on Wednesday by his office administrator. He didn't show up to work on Thursday, didn't return his wife's calls. Wife, who was out of town, requested a wellness check. Cops found blood on his garage floor. Car was missing." He looked up, brows lifted. "It wasn't just a car, Kit. It was a goddamned Ferrari. Do we have footage from his home security cameras?"

She shook her head. "Not yet. I figured the lead detectives would request it." *Please don't make us leads.*

Navarro just looked at her. "Request the footage, Kit."

Dammit. She sighed, and Connor slumped in his chair. "Fine," she muttered.

Navarro cleared his throat, and both Kit and Connor straightened.

"I mean, yes, sir," she said. "Of course, sir."

Connor rolled his eyes. "Suck-up."

Navarro shook his head. "Was he killed in the desert or his own garage?"

Kit opened the Notes app on her phone. She and Sam had stayed at the scene until both SDPD's CSU and ME teams had arrived and had begun processing the scene. "From what I saw, there was blood in the sand under the body after the ME removed it. I don't know yet how deep it went. But that alone indicates he was likely killed there in Anza-Borrego. ME's initial opinion was that he died from the wound to his throat."

Beside her, Sam shuddered but said nothing. She wanted to

pat his hand again, but she was acutely aware of Navarro's gaze. So she soldiered on.

"I don't know where the stab wounds were made. I counted at least twenty. Alicia says she'll give me an exact count when she gets the body on the table." Dr. Alicia Batra had arrived on the scene about forty-five minutes after CSU had trudged in from where they'd parked their van. "Sand covered part of his lower body, so there could be more. Or wounds on his back."

"Will she be able to give us some idea as to the murder weapon?" Navarro asked.

"Maybe. The wounds looked different, one from the other. Some looked deep, others looked shallow. Some were just slices through his skin. My first impression was that someone had wanted him to suffer."

"I wish I were shocked," Navarro said dryly.

"That man made a lot of enemies," Connor said. "This is gonna be fun."

From his tone it was clear that he meant the opposite.

Sam had begun to frown, and Kit quietly murmured, "Sam?"

Sam blew out a sigh. "I met him only once and instantly hated him."

"Join the club," Navarro said. "What did he do to you, Dr. Reeves?"

"Back in August, I was tasked by the New Horizons board to meet with the city council members because they were about to vote for a funding package."

Navarro leaned forward, brows knit. "New Horizons, the teen shelter?"

Sam nodded. "I've volunteered there for several years now. I did a presentation to the whole council, but a few members were absent, so I made one-on-one appointments with them. Munro was my last appointment. Only about half of the members had been receptive to the funding and Munro might have been a tie-breaker. He seemed on board, at first. But as I was packing up my materials to leave, he said that he expected I'd be 'grateful' for his vote."

Kit tensed. Sam was the nicest guy, and Munro pulled that shit with him?

"Did you ask what he meant?" Navarro asked.

"Oh yes. I was . . . stunned. I wasn't expecting it and I should have. I'd heard the rumors, but he'd been so agreeable up until that moment." His cheeks darkened. "I'm embarrassed to say that he caught me off guard."

"Don't be," Navarro said. "He was a smooth character. Oozed charm when he wanted to. We've suspected him of taking kick-backs for years but haven't been able to make anything stick."

"Still is embarrassing. I'm supposed to be able to read people. Anyway, he said that he heard that I was responsible for the psychological exams on defendants currently up for trial, and *then* my guard went up. I asked him which defendant, in particular. He said, 'Ronald Tasker.' I'd just been assigned Tasker's exam the day before."

Navarro whistled softly. "Tasker tried a mental illness defense for the murder of his wife. He slit her throat and chopped her into pieces."

"Munro's throat was slit," Kit said. "And before that, he'd been sliced and diced. Connection?"

"Maybe," Navarro allowed. "Put it on your list, Kit. At least Tasker's defense didn't work. He's doing life without parole. You didn't do his psych exam, did you, Sam?"

"No. I was so shaken when I left that I didn't know what to do at first, but then I called Joel."

Sam's best friend, Joel Haley, was one of San Diego's lead

prosecutors. Kit was glad he'd had someone to turn to. Still, she wondered why Sam hadn't called her first.

And then she got it. He'd met with Munro in August, when she'd been actively avoiding Sam Reeves at all costs.

You could have helped him, but you were too chickenshit to admit you liked him.

She swallowed her sigh. She couldn't change that now. She could only be there for him in the future.

"Joel said there wasn't anything we could do," Sam went on. "That it was my word against Munro's. But he got me pulled from the case. Joel gave the new psychologist a heads-up that he might be approached to alter his testimony, but that didn't happen."

"Did Munro say anything more to you?" Navarro asked.

"No. But he voted against the New Horizons funding proposal. Luckily I'd garnered enough support from the other council members that he wasn't a tiebreaker."

Luck had nothing to do with it, Kit thought, pride warming her from the inside out. Sam was good with people, and he could convince a rock to dance.

He'd gotten through to Kit, after all, when she'd been determined to fight her attraction.

"I wonder if there are any other cases Munro tried to influence," Kit murmured.

Connor groaned. "It's not like there weren't enough suspects already."

"You keep saying that," Navarro commented dryly. "Make a list. Start asking questions. If you need backup, I'll call for someone. I want an update in four hours. I can hold the captain off that long. I'm sure he's already heard from the mayor. Also, I heard that the wife is now home. Go talk to her." He made a shooing motion at the door. "Off with you."

Kit gathered her things and followed Connor and Sam out of Navarro's office, hearing the door click loudly behind them.

They'd been dismissed.

"Can you sign out a car so we can notify the widow?" Kit asked Connor. "I'll meet you downstairs."

"Sure, if you'll take lead on the notification. Bye, Sam. Don't be a stranger."

Kit turned to Sam with a sad smile. "I'm sorry our date was ruined."

"You promised me another," he said in a low tone that sent shivers over her skin.

She swallowed. "I did. I'll think of something good."

He brushed his finger over the back of her hand, discreetly enough that no one would have noticed had they been watching. "I think it's my turn."

She drew a breath. "You're on. And, for the record, you have nothing to be embarrassed about. Munro was a snake."

Sam's brows lifted. "What did he do to you?"

"Nothing directly to me, but I've heard rumors of his dishonesty. Accepting bribes on building projects, mostly. But no one ever comes forward to file a formal complaint, and I've also heard that many of his constituents gush about how wonderful he is. Especially his female constituents. He was a good-looking man." *Before the animals ate his face,* she thought, but kept that to herself because that seemed to have bothered Sam the most. "Like Navarro said, he was a charmer when he wanted to be. Particularly if he needed something from you. His expectation of quid pro quo from you didn't surprise me, but I'm still so mad at what he did to you."

Sam's mouth curled at the corners. "Aw, shucks, ma'am."

She laughed. "Go on. Enjoy what's left of your day off. I have to go to work."

He started for the door, then turned. "I can bring you supper. I'm going to your folks' house to pick up Siggy and I'm sure your mother will insist on feeding me. She'll make plates for both you and Connor. I have to come back this way, anyway."

"Thank you," she said, touched. *This man. He's too good for me.* "Text before you leave Mom and Pop's house, just in case we're out interviewing someone."

"I will. Be careful, Kit."

"I will. And Sam? I had a good time today. Before the dogs found Munro, anyway. We should go back to the park sometime."

He grinned. "I knew I could get you to like the desert." He turned for the door, a distinct spring in his step.

I think you could get me to like too many things, she thought. Then she straightened her shoulders.

It was time to find out who'd killed Brooks Munro.

Rancho Penasquitos, California
Saturday, January 7, 6:30 p.m.

"Whoa." Sitting in the passenger seat of their department car, Kit stared at the monstrosity that had been Brooks Munro's home. She didn't think she'd ever get used to the lives of the wealthy. It was a totally different world.

Based on what she could see from the base of his driveway, Munro's home was impeccably landscaped with perfectly sculpted trees and a lawn without a single crooked blade of grass.

Unlike their owner. Munro had been as crooked as they came.

Kit was still angry about what Munro had tried to do to Sam. Sam Reeves was a good man who'd never compromise his ethics.

"You're grinding your teeth," Connor commented. "Still mad about Munro trying to trade favors with Sammy?"

She sighed. "I used to be more inscrutable."

Connor chuckled. "And meaner. You're nicer now. You're also taking lead on this notification, in case you've forgotten."

"Yeah, yeah." It was her turn anyway, so Connor wasn't getting away with anything. "Wilhelmina Munro is the surviving spouse. She's sixty-one, ten years older than Munro. They were married for five years."

"She's also old money," Connor said. "Really old."

"How do you know that?" Kit asked, reviewing the background she'd run while Connor drove. "All I found was that she's a twice-married retired yoga teacher without even a parking ticket. I figured it was Munro's money that financed this place."

He lifted a brow. "That, Kit, is sexist."

She snorted a laugh, because she'd schooled him on his patriarchal attitudes many times in the past. "You're right. I'm sorry. So how do you know she's old money?"

"The background check should have shown her maiden name was Cliff."

"It did. So?"

"She's the granddaughter of Jonas Cliff. You know, the founder of Cliff Hotels."

"Oh. Even I've heard of him. So her money comes from a hotel empire?"

"It does. But this house is actually in Munro's name, which is why you assumed he'd financed this place. Wilhelmina bought it for him. Gave it to him as a wedding gift."

"How do you know that?"

"I asked my mom," Connor said smugly. "She keeps a list of all the rich people so that she can hit them up for donations whenever her club's doing a fundraiser. She knows all the gossip about everyone. I remembered her saying that she'd gotten money from Wilhelmina for one of her charities, so I called her when you were saying goodbye to Sammy. I figured we'd need a little inside information."

Kit studied the mansion. It was easily ten thousand square feet. The detached garage alone was nearly the size of her parents' farmhouse. "Hell of a wedding gift. I wonder if the widow knows that Munro was a slimeball?"

"According to my mom, Wilhelmina's been living on her family's estate near Boston for the past month. The gossip's been all over the country club. Everyone thinks she finally found out he'd been cheating on her."

"She owns an estate in Boston? That didn't come up on her background check, either. Only a bungalow she used to own in Mission Beach."

"The estate may be owned by a trust, but as the last surviving Cliff, it's hers."

"I wonder what Wilhelmina will tell us about him." Then his words sank in. "Wait. Your parents hobnob in the same country club as Munro?"

"They're members, but no hobnobbing with Munro has ever happened. My folks didn't like him because he bragged about everything."

Kit hesitated. "Your mom knows to keep this under her hat for now, right?"

Connor nodded. "You can trust her, Kit. She inferred that Munro was dead from my question about his wife and wished us luck with our suspect list."

"Then let's get busy notifying Wilhelmina so we can start building that list."

Connor started up the long driveway. "There's someone on the front porch."

An elderly man stood at the front door, weary resignation on his lined face.

"They knew we were coming," Kit said logically. "The guard at the front gate had to have called them after we drove through. I wonder who he is."

Connor released his seat belt. "Let's get this over with."

Together they approached the front door, eyeing the man with wary curiosity. He looked to be somewhere in his seventies.

"Good evening," Kit said. "I'm Detective McKittrick, and this is Detective Robinson. We're here to talk to Mrs. Munro."

The man sniffed. "To tell her that her sonofabitch husband is dead. She already knows."

Kit shouldn't have been surprised. They'd suppressed as much information as they could, but a lot of people had been aware of emergency vehicles and police gathered in the park. It hadn't made the news yet, but it was just a matter of time.

"How did she hear the news?" Connor asked.

"A reporter called, asking for a comment. Miz Wilhelmina hung up without saying a word."

"Your name, sir?" Kit asked.

"Jake Rafferty. I'm Miz Wilhelmina's caretaker."

Kit kept her expression neutral, despite her surprise. "Caretaker? Is she ill?"

Rafferty shook his head. "I take care of her house in Boston. I came with her. Just in case."

In case of what? Kit wondered. In case Munro was dead? In case Wilhelmina needed the older man? In what capacity might that be?

"When did you arrive in San Diego?" Kit asked.

"This afternoon. We took the first flight out. She was *worried* about that lying SOB."

They'd have to check this man's alibi. Hopefully he'd been

where he claimed. They didn't have a solid time of death, but Munro had been dumped in the desert no later than that morning. Probably the night before.

"Did you know Mr. Munro well?" Connor asked.

Rafferty laughed, a rasping sound. "Are you asking me if I killed him, Detective? The answer is no. I did not. But I'd like to buy a beer for whoever did. I knew him well enough. I know he lied and connived and got Miz Wilhelmina to marry him so he could get at her money. I know he was catting around on her before the ink was dry on the marriage license. I know that he was a cheating, boozing, abusive SOB. I know I had to put Miz Wil back together when she finally came home. He'd all but broken her. For that alone, he needed to be dealt with. But I did not do it."

"Raffie," a voice gently admonished. "Ask the detectives in, please."

Wilhelmina Munro stood in the doorway, her face in shadow. She was a tall woman, her back straight, her shoulders stiff. She exuded exhaustion.

Kit wanted to yawn just looking at her.

Rafferty motioned to the door with a gnarled, arthritic hand. "Go on in."

Wilhelmina led them to a living room decorated in chrome and black leather. It was a masculine room, and the chair the woman had chosen dwarfed her slim body. "Please sit, Detectives. Can I offer you a drink?"

"No thank you, ma'am," Connor said, sitting on the sofa closest to Wilhelmina. Kit took a chair that allowed her to watch both Wilhelmina and Rafferty, who'd remained in the room's arched doorway. "You know why we're here?"

Wilhelmina nodded once, a regal dip of her head. Her hair was an ash blond with a liberal sprinkling of gray. She was a classically beautiful woman with a bone structure most models would kill for. No wrinkles marred her skin. She had either great genes or an excellent plastic surgeon. Other than the gray in her hair, she looked no older than forty.

"My husband is dead," she said, her voice shaky. She was genuinely distressed or a reasonably good actress. Maybe a bit of both. "His body was found in the desert this afternoon."

"We're sorry for your loss, ma'am," Kit said respectfully.

"No loss," Rafferty muttered loudly.

Wilhelmina sighed. "Raffie, please."

Rafferty grunted. "Sorry."

Kit was pretty sure he wasn't sorry at all. "If we might ask, who told you of your husband's death?"

"A reporter called a few hours ago," she said. "Told me that my husband had been murdered, his body dumped in Anza-Borrego. That hikers and their dogs had discovered his body." She swallowed. "That his throat had been slit."

That reporter had a damn good source. At least Mrs. Munro didn't know it had been Kit and Sam who'd done the discovering.

"Did you get the reporter's name, ma'am?" Connor asked, no happier about the leak than Kit was.

Wilhelmina's lips thinned. "Tamsin Kavanaugh."

Kit tried to shove down the growl that rose in her throat. Tamsin Fucking Kavanaugh. That woman had been a thorn in Kit's side for as long as she'd been a cop.

Wilhelmina's laugh was mirthless. "I agree, Detective McKittrick. I was no happier to hear from her than you are when she hounds you for a story."

Startled, Kit met the woman's eyes. Apparently, she hadn't hidden her reaction as well as she'd hoped. "Excuse me?"

"I read the paper, Detective. I know who you are. Who you both are," she added, gesturing to Connor. "I've read Kavanaugh's articles about you, and she's a sorry excuse for a reporter." She looked away. "She also had an affair with my husband."

Oh wow. "Recently?" Kit asked, managing to keep her voice level.

Wilhelmina shook her head. "A few years ago. It was a mutually beneficial relationship for both of them, other than the obvious, of course. Kavanaugh got an in at city hall and Brooks got good press coverage. Again, I have no proof, and my husband denied it, but I figured it out."

Kit blew out a breath. "Of all people, I'm sorry that you had to hear it from her."

"So am I. What questions can I answer? I'm truly exhausted."

"We'll be as quick as we can," Kit promised. "You were the one who reported your husband missing. What prompted you to do so? Did you speak often?"

"No, we did not," Wilhelmina said with ill-concealed derision. "We separated a month ago, and we rarely spoke on the phone. I called him on Wednesday evening because my bank had informed me by email that he'd withdrawn a large sum of money from our joint account. It was the account we used for this house—to pay the taxes, upkeep, that kind of thing. We were overdrawn, and I always get notified when that happens."

"How much did he withdraw?" Connor asked.

"Fifty thousand dollars. He transferred it from the joint account to one of his personal accounts."

Kit wondered what Munro had done with the money. "So you called him and he didn't answer?"

"Yes, but that didn't surprise me. I figured he wouldn't, given that he'd taken that money without informing me. He did that sometimes, took money from that account when he'd spent his allowance."

From all Kit had heard about Munro's arrogance, being on an allowance must have steamed him. She made a mental note to subpoena Munro's bank records.

"Do you have access to his personal accounts, ma'am?" Connor asked, on the same page.

"No, I do not. He didn't answer my call on Wednesday, so I called his office admin on her cell phone, because it was after hours at city hall. She said that he'd left for a meeting and had gone straight home afterward, but she'd relay my message the next morning." She hesitated, then shrugged. "She'll tell you when you interview her, so I might as well tell you now. I told her to tell him that I would put no more money in that account." She sighed. "I might have called him a philandering ass. I was angry."

"I can see that," Kit murmured, wondering just how angry Wilhelmina might have been. Angry enough to hire someone to kill her husband? It wouldn't be the first time an angry wife arranged for a hit on her cheating husband. The woman certainly had the money for a hit man.

"What is the name of his assistant?" Connor asked.

Wilhelmina's expression grew frosty. "Veronica Fitzgerald. She may have known him better than I did. They'd known each other longer."

Okay, Kit thought. There was ill feeling here. "How long had they known each other?"

"She worked for him for fifteen years, long before he became a city councilman. Back when he was in real estate."

"They were fucking," Raffie said bluntly.

Wilhelmina's sigh was less than patient. "Raffie."

"It's true," Rafferty said, unrepentant.

Kit cleared her throat. "Did you know this or only suspect?"

"*Suspect*," Wilhelmina said firmly. "I never had proof that he cheated with any of his women, but I know that he did." She lifted her chin, twin flags of embarrassed color on her cheeks. "As long as he kept it discreet, I didn't rock the boat."

Kit didn't think Munro had kept it discreet at all, not if what Connor's mother had said had been true. Wilhelmina and Munro had been the subjects of country club gossip.

"When did you call to report him missing?" Kit asked.

"Thursday, a little after noon Pacific time. I'd called Veronica again at nine a.m. and she said that he hadn't come in to work. She sounded truly worried, and I knew he was alone here in the house. I thought maybe he'd fallen. He sometimes drank too much and . . . well, I despised him, but he was still my husband."

"He didn't *sometimes* drink too much," Rafferty inserted. "He *always* drank too much. *Sometimes* he got violent. He hit Miz Wil. Gave her a black eye."

Wilhelmina closed her eyes. "That's true. That was what made me leave a month ago. I just packed my bags and left."

"If he drank, cheated, and got violent, why didn't you divorce him?" Connor asked softly.

Wilhelmina's slim shoulders sagged. "Initially, it was because I was humiliated. Rafferty had tried to get me to see that he was a lying philanderer before we got married, but I refused to see it. Brooks had me utterly charmed. He always denied sleeping around, and I wanted to believe him. I finally decided to divorce him this last time, when he hit me. I had the papers drawn up, but I didn't get a chance to sign them before this happened."

"Would he have gotten much of your personal fortune?" Connor asked.

"Fuck no," Rafferty snapped. "At least she listened to me on that."

"He would not have," Wilhelmina answered calmly. "And I never would have married him without a prenup, Raffie. You know that."

"Maybe. But he was trying for an insane payoff in the case of divorce and you were looking like you were going to give in. The prenup her lawyer drew up kept Munro on a short leash." He looked at Kit and Connor. "He wanted a million bucks in the event of divorce, but I threatened to put my foot up his fucking ass. He signed the prenup because he thought I was crazy enough to follow through."

"Are you?" Kit asked. "Crazy enough to follow through?"

"Hell, yeah. I would have messed up his pretty face. I hated that man. He hurt my Wil. And nobody hurts my Wil."

"How long has he been your protector?" Kit asked Wilhelmina.

"Since I was ten years old. Raffie was my father's caretaker. He and his wife were like second parents to me, so you have to understand Raffie's feelings about Brooks. I had to beg him not to get on a plane to California when I arrived in Boston with a black eye. I hated my husband for cheating on me and using me, but I didn't kill him. Neither did Raffie."

"So what prompted you to report him missing?" Kit pressed. "Why didn't you assume he was avoiding you, instead of thinking he'd fallen in a drunken stupor?"

"He missed a meeting with the mayor on Thursday morning," Wilhelmina said. "This was according to Veronica. I figured something bad had to have happened to keep him from going to that meeting. He was so proud of his access to the mayor. Bragged like he was the mayor's BFF or something. He never missed an opportunity to flaunt his influence."

There was something the woman wasn't telling them. Kit could see it in her eyes. She'd come back later and ask the question again once she'd learned a little more about the players.

"Mrs. Munro, who do you think killed your husband?" she asked.

"I don't know. He got hate mail every day from angry constituents. Maybe one of the construction firms he double-crossed."

"That's specific," Connor noted.

"Yes, because that was what led to him hitting me. It's been in my mind for the past month. Brooks thought it was hilarious, taking their money as bribes, then not following through on his promises. I heard him talking on the phone, saying things like, 'What're they gonna do? Report me? They'd be confessing.'"

Connor's head tilted. "You knew he was accepting bribes?"

"I knew that he bragged about it to someone—and I don't know who he was talking to. I didn't report him because I had no proof. I tried to get proof, but that was when he hit me. He caught me going through his office files and he was very angry." She touched her eye, now healed. "I left that evening. I'd planned to come back for divorce proceedings, but this happened first."

"Will you be in town long?" Connor asked.

"I'll be here until he's in the ground. Then I'm selling this awful house. Do you want to see the blood in the garage?"

Kit and Connor rose. "Yes, ma'am," Connor said.

"I'm going to ask Raffie to show you. I can't tonight. He'll show you out. Raffie, let them search Brooks's office, too. Whatever they want to take, they're welcome to. Good night, Detectives."

Kit shook her head. "Ma'am, you can't stay here. At least not for a few days. Before, this house was the scene of a possible abduction. Missing Persons searched and released the scene, but now we have a homicide. I'm afraid you'll have to stay somewhere else until we've done our searches."

Wilhelmina sighed. "Then it's a good thing I haven't unpacked yet."

"I'll show them the garage," Rafferty said with a huff. "Then I'll find a place for us to stay, Miz Wil."

"Thank you, Raffie."

CHAPTER TWO

Kit rubbed her eyes. They'd gone through only a fraction of the papers they'd taken from Munro's home office, and her head ached. She was hungry and over-caffeinated.

She turned to the whiteboard, where she and Connor had started compiling names of suspects. They'd both agreed that Wilhelmina Munro would remain on the list for the time being. She might have an alibi for the time of her husband's death, but murder for hire was still a possibility.

Kit pointed to the folders stacked on the table. "We've got two dozen unhappy contractors who claim that he cheated them and at least three unhappy husbands who believed their wives were cheating with him. Plus, constituents who hated him for various reasons."

Munro had kept printed copies of the threatening emails he'd received. A few were highly detailed about what the sender would do to Munro. Kit wondered what kind of threats he'd received over the phone or in person if these were the kinds of threats people had felt comfortable enough to put in writing.

Connor nodded. "We've also got anyone who wanted him to influence the justice system on their behalf—like he tried to do with Sam—but who got sentenced to jail anyway. So far it's only Ronald Tasker, but I figure there have to be others."

At the moment, Tasker was at the top of their list of suspects, given the way he'd sliced up his wife after killing her. He was in prison, but again, he was rich enough to have hired it out.

Kit tapped the articles they'd found on the local newspaper's website. "Plus the guy he beat in the last election, whose life was ruined after Munro spread the rumor that he was a pedophile."

"Why is it always a pedo? That's the rumor people trot out whenever they want to make someone look bad."

"Because it's one of the worst things we as a society can think of," she said quietly.

Connor glanced at her sharply. "Kit. Did you . . . ?" He shook his head. "Never mind. None of my business. I'm sorry I asked. Forget it."

She knew what he was asking. "No, not me. Almost happened once, in one of the foster homes before McKittrick House, but no."

Connor's jaw tightened. "How did you stop them?"

Kit smirked. "I stabbed him with his own letter opener. I was only eleven, so I didn't stab him very hard, but I drew blood."

"Good." The word was filled with dark satisfaction.

Kit hadn't liked Connor when they'd first met, but she'd grown fond of him over the nine months they'd been partners. He was a frat boy with a heart of gold.

"He claimed I'd stabbed him for no good reason, but it was

in his groin, so it was tough explaining why he was alone in my room with his pants down." She sighed. "But I was still labeled a violent troublemaker because I'd stolen the letter opener from his desk and had hidden it under my pillow."

"Unbelievable."

"But true. I got moved to another home that was worse. But that's where I met Wren, so it was worth it." It had been nearly seventeen years since Wren's murder, but not a day went by that Kit didn't miss her sister. Not a day went by that she didn't renew her promise to find whoever had killed Wren and tossed her body into a dumpster. "That foster father liked girls who looked like Wren, and she was terrified. I wasn't going to let her get hurt, so we ran away."

Of course, there had been much more to it than simply running away, but Kit wasn't going to tell Connor that she'd nearly killed the foster father the night they'd fled. She'd been only twelve and hadn't known how many of his wife's sleeping pills to put in his evening whiskey.

The McKittricks knew. She'd finally shared it with them when she was sixteen years old, expecting them to turn her away, but they hadn't. They'd loved her anyway. They'd adopted her anyway.

"Where did you run to?"

"A barn," Kit said with a smile. "It was cold out and we snuck in there to get warm. We took a blanket from one of the horses and huddled under it. And then this big man came into the barn and caught us. I was so scared. But . . . that night changed my life."

"Harlan McKittrick," Connor murmured.

Kit nodded. "My origin story. Harlan and Betsy McKittrick saved my life." She realized she'd reached into her pocket for the small carving she never went anywhere without—the cat with a bird sitting on its head. A gift from Harlan, made with his own hands. Kit was the cat and Wren was the bird. It had become her good-luck charm.

"I'm glad you found that barn," Connor said, his voice catching.

"Me too. But those foster fathers really were pedos. This guy who Munro accused wasn't."

"William Weaver." Connor taped Weaver's photo onto the whiteboard. "His wife left him and took his children. He lost his job and his home, and vowed retribution against Brooks Munro. Who denied he'd spread the rumor, of course."

"Of course. But by the time Weaver had been proven innocent, the damage had been done."

"Hell of a thing to do for a city council seat."

"Had to have been lucrative for Munro. The council salary isn't that high, and Wilhelmina paid for the house, but he bought the Ferrari himself."

That information had come from Rafferty, who'd also disclosed the amount Wilhelmina had given Munro as allowance. It hadn't been enough to finance a Ferrari lifestyle, so money had to have been pouring in from somewhere else.

"That model Ferrari isn't all that expensive," Connor said.

Kit coughed. "Um, for those of us who don't have trust funds, a quarter mil is a helluva lot of money."

Connor winced. "Sorry. I meant there are far more expensive models. He got the bottom-of-the-line Ferrari. Top-of-the-line is twice the cost. So it was more about image than quality."

"Rich people," Kit muttered.

Connor chuckled. "I drive a Toyota, y'know."

"I know. It's why no one has keyed your car in the parking lot."

"My strategy is working." He spread out the photos CSU had taken of Munro's garage after Wilhelmina had reported him missing. "His Ferrari is gone."

There'd been a pool of blood where the sports car should have been parked.

"I know. But why? Was Munro injured when he discovered someone stealing his car?"

Connor wrote it on the whiteboard under *Theories*. "It's possible, considering they dumped his body in the desert. I'm thinking they didn't expect it to be found."

"He wasn't buried, though. Not well, anyway." That bothered Kit. "Why didn't his killer at least try to bury him?"

"Are we sure he didn't and the wind didn't shift the sand away?"

"No. But the park rangers didn't think that was the case because of where the body was positioned. It was behind some boulders." She found the photo and grimaced. The body truly had been a mess. Poor Sam. He wasn't used to such things. Not yet, anyway. If he continued as a police shrink, he'd see more.

A soft knock on the open door had her whipping her head toward the sound.

And speak of . . . well, not the devil. Sam Reeves could never be a devil.

But there he was, holding a familiar warming bag. It belonged to her mother and had "McK" written in bold Sharpie on every side.

"Sam?" Connor asked. "What're you doing here?"

"Dinner," Sam said.

Kit was starving. And whatever her mother had made smelled amazing. "I thought you were going to text to make sure we were here."

"I did. Six times."

Kit checked her phone. Sure enough, there were six unread texts. "I'm sorry. We lost track of time."

Sam smiled, but it looked forced. His face was pale, his eyes stricken. He must have still been upset over finding Munro's body, so Kit turned the photo over so that he wouldn't have to see it again. "I figured as much," he said. "Can I come in?"

Connor gestured him to the table. "Of course. Is there food for me, too?"

Sam set the bag on the table. "Of course. It's a whole chicken pot pie."

Connor groaned. "Gimme. Gimme now."

Sam took a step back. "Don't bite my hand off. There's enough for a small army in there."

"Or just me and Connor, who can put away as much food as a small army," Kit said dryly, opening the bag and pulling out the plates and serving containers. No paper plates for Betsy McKittrick. She'd sent her best Corelle, the cheerful blue and pink flowers on the plates making Kit smile. "Ooh, and candy bar cake." She took a sniff. "Snickers."

"Oh my God," Connor moaned. "Food now. Please."

Kit rolled her eyes and served him a plate. "At least you're quiet when you're stuffing your face." She glanced at Sam and paused, her hand on the serving spoon. He still looked upset. "What's wrong?"

Sam looked away. "I . . . I'm sorry, Kit. I didn't mean to listen in."

She frowned, then understood. "Oh. My origin story." He'd overheard. She wasn't sure how she felt about that, but she needed to wipe that guilt from his expression. "I probably would have told you at some point anyway, so it's fine."

His shoulders relaxed. "Thank you." He took a look at the whiteboard, his eyes going wide. "That's a lot of names."

"We're not close to being done," Connor said with his mouth full. He swallowed. "Munro's Ferrari is also missing."

"The killer stole it?" Sam asked.

"Maybe," Connor said. "If it *was* the killer, why do you think they would have done it, Sam?"

"To sell it? Why does anyone steal a Ferrari?"

Kit agreed. "It could be as simple as that."

Connor shook his head. "Logistics," he said, then stuffed more food in his mouth.

Kit looked at the photo of Munro's garage, startling when Sam took the spoon from her hand. He served her some pot pie and gently nudged the photo back into its folder.

"Eat, Kit. Your mother made me promise that I'd get you to eat."

Kit tucked in and sighed happily. "Mom's food is the best."

"Five stars," Connor said, mouth full once again.

"Manners," Kit snapped. "At least I wasn't born in that barn. You might have been, though."

Connor only grinned, waiting until he'd swallowed to speak again. "What are the logistics? Did the killer hide in Munro's garage? Did he stab Munro at least once there in the garage? There's enough blood for one good gushing wound, but not twenty."

"He definitely slit Munro's throat in the desert," Kit said. "We were wondering why he didn't bury him."

"Depends on when he dumped him," Sam said, taking the chair beside her. "There were high winds the day before we hiked. I was watching the weather, afraid that we'd have to cancel if it didn't die down. It did die down, of course, but if it was that windy when he was dumping the body, he was either fighting the wind and the sand or he figured the wind and sand would do his burying for him. Or some of both."

"Okay." Kit paused, her next bite on the fork. "That makes sense. Next question is, why did his killer choose that spot in that park to hide a body? I've asked the park service for a list of names of people who entered the park for the last three days, but the park has open entry, so they'll only have names of people who used the areas they charge for."

Sam made a face. "His killer didn't drive a Ferrari in that sand, I can guarantee."

"So what are the logistics?" Connor asked again. "He enters Munro's garage—how and from where? He stabs Munro at least once. Does he put him in the Ferrari? That's not smart if he intends to sell it. Blood's a bitch to get out of the stitching on the leather seats."

"Where did he take the Ferrari?" Kit started a new list on the whiteboard, a marker in one hand and her fork in the other.

Sam took the marker from her hand and gently pushed her back into her chair. "Eat. I'll scribe."

Connor snickered. "Eat, Kit. Or he'll tell your mommy."

"Then I'll tell her never to feed *you* again," Kit shot back.

Connor mimed zipping his mouth shut.

"I thought so," Kit muttered. "The detectives that responded to the initial missing-person call put out a BOLO on the Ferrari but got nothing. They tried to trace the GPS, but again, they got nothing. It appears to have been disabled. The last location was the garage itself."

Sam noted that. "So whoever took it knows cars. I wouldn't know how to disable a GPS."

"It's not that hard," Connor said. "I did it once or twice in my misguided youth when I didn't want my folks knowing where I was. My dad figured it out and put another tracker on the undercarriage, and I was busted. But I was able to disconnect the GPS that came with the car."

Kit shook her head. "Mom would have grounded me and taken away dessert for a month if I'd tried that."

"I was grounded for two months and my allowance cut to just enough to buy lunch at school," Connor said morosely. "Anyway, I think it's interesting that Munro didn't have an auxiliary tracker on his car. Or that his wife didn't put one on. If he'd cheated on me, I'd want to know where his ass was at all times."

"And if she did and hasn't told the cops?" Kit mused. "Still not sure I bought her innocent act."

"You notified her?" Sam asked.

"She already knew," Connor said.

"Tamsin Fucking Kavanaugh," Kit muttered.

Sam grimaced. "Not her again."

Sam had been on the receiving end of Tamsin's poisoned pen the spring before when someone he'd cared about had been murdered.

"Tamsin and Munro were bumping uglies," Connor said.

Sam grimaced again. "Good God, man. First Munro's dead face and now the image of him and Tamsin doing it? Now I'm wishing I hadn't had dessert. Have you talked to her yet?"

"No," Kit muttered. She wasn't looking forward to that interview. Tamsin Kavanaugh would want some quid pro quo of her own, and Kit would rather eat her own foot than owe the woman anything. "But back to the Ferrari. If the wife is involved, she could have had the Ferrari towed somewhere."

Sam jotted that on the whiteboard. "It also could have been a souvenir. Especially if his killer wanted some financial retribution."

"Good point," Connor said, filling his plate again. "Write that down."

Sam did so and stared at the board. "Did you get the footage from the security cameras around Munro's house?"

"We did," Kit said, "but they're pretty useless. You see someone in a hoodie and a face mask—like a Halloween hockey mask, not a medical mask, and then they spray-painted the camera lens."

Sam studied the photo, frowning. "I don't guess you can trace the mask."

Kit shook her head. "The party store sells thousands of the things every year."

"Spray-painting the camera lens is old-school," Sam commented. "It would have been safer to disable the cameras, but the killer didn't do that."

"The weird thing," Connor said, "is that the Ferrari doesn't show up on any of the cameras around the neighborhood that day. I'm thinking that whoever took it had an enclosed trailer of some kind, like they use for transporting race cars. They could have driven the Ferrari in and closed the back door."

"Does a trailer show up on the security cams?" Sam asked.

"Haven't had a chance to look yet," Kit said, pushing her empty plate away. "It's also possible that there were two different doers. One stole his car and the other grabbed and stabbed him."

Connor shrugged. "For now, let's assume there's just one or if there were two, they were working together. He could have gone there to steal the car and was interrupted by Munro. He stabs him, grabs him, then . . . what? Takes him to the desert to slit his throat?"

"That seems extreme," Sam said. "The wounds on Munro's torso indicate either rage or some kind of torture. Or both. The missing digits on his hands and his one shoeless foot seem to point to the latter."

Connor's expression was disgruntled. "True. So he goes there planning to steal both Munro and the car? He had to have planned ahead for the car. That sounds more like a revenge scenario. He kills Munro and keeps his car, like you said, Sam, as a souvenir."

Kit checked her phone. "The video from the guard shack and three of the neighbors' camera feeds have been uploaded to the department server by the detectives who took the missing-person report." Who'd been more than delighted to hand their files over to Kit and Connor. Nobody wanted this case. "Let's establish the existence of the trailer before we go off in that direction." She eyed the list of suspects they'd assembled so far. "If we know for sure that there was a trailer, access to one is something else to check each suspect for."

"I can check the feed," Sam offered. "I've got nothing else planned tonight and I took Siggy home on the way to bring you your dinner. That would leave you free to continue strategizing how you'll talk to all these people."

"We'd appreciate that," Kit said. "Depending on who we interview, we might ask you along for the ride."

Sam's nod was immediate, if not a little grim. "Absolutely."

San Diego PD, San Diego, California
Saturday, January 7, 10:30 p.m.

Sam hit the rewind button with a silent sigh. He'd gotten lost in thought again and missed about two minutes of footage from the security camera on the guard shack at the entrance to Munro's gated community.

It wasn't because the work was tedious—even though it was. It wasn't even that Kit was at the end of the table, talking animatedly with Connor, her blue eyes focused and intelligent as they explored more of Munro's life for investigative direction, even though it was that, too.

It was the knowledge that she'd had to stab her foster father with a letter opener to keep from getting assaulted.

Sam had been standing outside the door, his fist raised to knock, when he heard Connor's stumbling question. Had Kit been raped as a child? Or sexually abused in some other way?

Of course Sam had wondered. How could he not? But he would never have asked her.

Hearing her tell her "origin story," as she'd called it, had been devastating. She'd been eleven years old, for God's sake. *Eleven.*

Then when she was twelve, running away with Wren . . .

There'd been something in there that she hadn't shared. He knew the cadence of her speech well enough to figure that out. Plus, there'd been that little pause after he'd confessed his eavesdropping. She'd been freaked out at first, and then her eyes had narrowed, just the slightest bit. As if replaying everything she'd said.

And the look of relief in her eyes had been unmistakable.

Something else had happened when she and Wren had run away. But he wouldn't ask. Someday she'd tell him herself.

Or she wouldn't. Either way, it didn't change how he felt about her.

She'd just been a little girl, and his heart ached. But she wasn't a little girl now. She was a grown woman who'd made something spectacular of her life, and he was in awe of her.

But fantasies of punishing those sons of bitches who'd tried to hurt her in the past would have to wait. Sam needed to help her in this moment.

He concentrated on the camera feed once again, staring at the monitor Kit had set up for him. And finally watched a trailer driving in and out of Munro's gated community.

"I think I've got it," he called to the two detectives, who instantly stopped talking and came to look over his shoulder. "The trailer is pulled by a Ford truck. The sign on the side of the trailer says 'Norton Landscaping.' I don't know if it's a real company or not."

Kit was already googling the landscaping company on her phone. "It is a real company, owned by David Norton. From their website, it looks like they employ at least twenty people."

"Seems bold," Sam said, "using their own trailer. I wonder if Munro's killer stole it."

Connor was typing on his own phone. "I'll look up the owner and we can pay him a personal visit at home first thing in the morning."

"We should check the stolen property reports first. They may have already reported it missing." Kit smiled at Sam. "Thank you. You saved us a lot of time and aggravation."

Sam's cheeks heated, but he was pleased. He liked doing things for Kit. She was so self-sufficient, she often made it difficult to help her. "No problem. I wish the camera had gotten the driver's face."

"Hopefully the gate guard got a description," Connor said. "We've already got the guard on our interview list, but now we know what to specifically ask him. We can ask the neighbors, too. Hopefully someone saw this guy before he put on his mask."

Sam wasn't so sure. "People tend to ignore manual laborers. My mother is an exception. She bakes banana nut bread for whoever does even the smallest job, then sits and chats with them. But even she can't tell me what they looked like. She does know the name of every spouse, child, and pet of every plumber and electrician who's ever come to her house. But she couldn't describe them."

"That's so nice," Connor said. "Banana nut bread is delicious."

Sam grimaced. "Not Mom's. Unfortunately for the workers, my mom is a terrible cook and an even worse baker, but her heart's in the right place. My point is, I'd be surprised if anyone really noticed this guy's face if he was posing as a worker."

Kit nodded. "You're probably right. But most neighborhoods have at least one super nosy person who watches from the window. Maybe Munro's will have one of those."

"I wonder if Norton Landscaping has existing customers in Munro's neighborhood." Sam opened the company's website and clicked the testimonials tab. "If they were there often, the gate guard might have just waved the driver through, and no one would have thought twice about the trailer."

"Good point." Taking the chair beside him, Kit tapped her phone and began to read. "Sam. Look."

Sam jerked his attention away from her profile. He'd been staring at her like a lovestruck teenager, but it was hard not to. She had a girl-next-door kind of face, her strawberry-blond hair pulled back into a sensible ponytail. That such a sharp brain lurked behind such a sweet face turned him on like nothing else. But he was here to work.

He saw Munro's name on the screen and sucked in a breath.

"Brooks Munro was a client," Kit told Connor, showing him the testimonial. "He gave them a nice recommendation."

Connor took the chair beside her, turning it around so that he straddled it. "'Gifted and professional,'" he read. "'They've been caring for my lawn for three years. Their work is exceptional.' Well, I guess that question is answered. Either someone from the landscaping company is bold, careless, or they're missing equipment. When did you clock it?"

"It left at five forty-five on Wednesday evening."

Kit nodded. "Is that consistent with your theory about the windstorm in Anza-Borrego?"

"Not Wednesday night, no. But Thursday, the wind started to get bad and there were wind warnings through Friday night."

"Okay, then," Kit said. "If he drove out there Thursday or even Friday night, he could have dumped the body in the dark, hoping it would be covered by sand."

"And that park's famous for stargazing, right?" Connor asked. "So it would have been really dark. Nobody would have seen him. Or her."

"Or her," Kit murmured. "Did you see when the trailer entered the neighborhood, Sam?"

"At six a.m. It was there all day. I checked the feeds from the neighbors and the only place the trailer could have gone was Munro's house. His is the only one on a dead-end street and that's the way the trailer turned."

Kit frowned. "That's super early to be entering the community. Why so early? And why did they stay all day?"

They were all quiet for a minute before Connor shrugged. "Those are good questions. For now, let's focus on the trailer itself. Maybe one of the neighbors will remember seeing it parked in front of Munro's house or—more importantly—remember seeing the driver. He was there for nearly twelve hours. Plus, the trailer's twice the normal length."

Otherwise, Munro's killer wouldn't have been able to fit a Ferrari inside.

Kit checked her phone for the time. "It's too late to talk to the neighbors tonight. Tomorrow, we can talk to the woman who lives closest to him."

"But that's still a fair distance," Connor said. "She might not have seen anything. They're both on five-acre lots, but her house is even bigger than Munro's. Maybe not as ostentatious, though."

That was a better opening than Sam had hoped for. "Munro's

house *is* ostentatious," he said, bracing himself for their question. Because he hadn't mentioned this detail earlier, and he should have.

Her blond brows shot up. "You went to his house for your meeting?"

"I did."

"Why didn't you say so earlier?" she asked.

Sam winced. "I guess I didn't want Navarro considering me a suspect again."

Kit coughed to hide a laugh. "Yeah, I can understand that. Weren't you suspicious that Munro asked you to his house?"

"Not really. Not at the time, anyway. When I called to ask for an appointment, his admin said he wasn't coming into the city that day and if I wanted to meet with him, I'd have to go to his place. Afterward, I was annoyed at myself for not being suspicious. I should have brought a tape recorder. When I told Joel, he just sighed and told me to stop trusting people so much."

Kit's expression softened. "I think that makes you you. Don't change."

Sam felt his cheeks heating yet again. Every time she paid him a compliment, he wanted to shout from the rooftops. *Tone it down before you make an even bigger fool of yourself.*

Because he *should* have suspected Munro. "I didn't think I had anything he'd want. Now I know differently. That was the first time I'd been approached to tamper with my evaluation of a defendant. I won't make that mistake again."

Kit squeezed his shoulder briefly, and he missed her touch when she pulled her hand away. But they were working right now. He didn't like it, but he understood.

"Where did he take you? In his house, I mean?" she asked.

"His study. I have no doubt that it was set up for recording.

If I'd agreed, he could have used that against me. I realized that as soon as he asked me about Ronald Tasker. So I clearly said no and immediately left. I took a selfie of myself at the guard shack so that I could prove the time of my escape."

"Smart," Connor murmured. "What a sleazebag Munro was. We need to ask CSU to check for microphones and recording equipment."

"Yes," Kit said with a sigh, "because we have interviews to do." She gestured to the whiteboard. "So many interviews."

"What time should I meet you tomorrow for these inter-views?" Sam asked, half expecting Kit to have changed her mind.

"Meet us here at seven a.m. First stop is David Norton. I want to be at the front door of his house by eight."

Sam nodded once. "I'll be here."

Linda Vista, San Diego, California
Sunday, January 8, 8:00 a.m.

Kit got out of the department car, closing the door quietly. No need to wake up people who had the luxury of sleeping in. Sam got out of the passenger seat and Connor emerged from the back, grumbling that he hadn't had enough beauty sleep.

David Norton, the owner of the landscaping company, lived in a two-story house in a tidy, quiet middle-class neighborhood. A trailer was parked in his driveway, the graphics identical to the one that had likely been carrying Munro's Ferrari. The trailer was only about half the size, though.

"Hopefully he has a good explanation for why his company's trailer was at Munro's house all day on Wednesday," Kit said. "I'd like to cross a few names off our list today. Let's go."

Once they were on the front porch, she knocked at the door, then stood back to wait.

The door was opened by a boy, maybe six or seven years old. He was missing three of his front teeth. "My parents don't want to buy anything." He looked over his shoulder, then leaned closer. "Unless it's Girl Scout cookies. Mom'll let me have those as long as we don't tell Dad."

Kit cleared her throat to hide a laugh. "Sorry. Not selling anything good like that. Can you call your mom or dad?"

His lip stuck out in a pout as he walked back into the house, leaving the door wide open. "Mom!" he yelled. "Some lady's selling something that's not cookies."

"Oh, for heaven's sake. David! Come and watch the sausage. I gotta get rid of whoever's at the door." A forty-something woman approached, her eyes widening as she took in the three people on her doorstep. "Can I help you?" she asked warily.

This would be Carla Norton, David's wife. They'd done a records check before leaving the precinct that morning. No outstanding tickets and neither had any registered firearms.

Kit produced her badge. "I'm Detective McKittrick, San Diego PD. These are my colleagues, Detective Robinson and Dr. Reeves. We'd like to speak to you and your husband. It's important."

Carla's back went ramrod straight as the color drained from her face. "Who's dead?" she demanded in a whisper. "Davy or Danny?"

Kit blinked, caught unprepared. "Um, neither, ma'am. Not to my knowledge, anyway."

She sagged. "Oh God. I thought you were here to—" She shook her head. "Come in." She led them to a living room. "Please sit down. I'll get my husband." She turned but paused. "You're not here about my sons?"

"No, ma'am," Sam said kindly. "Are they missing?"

She nodded jerkily. "Ran away a month ago. I keep expecting . . ." She forced a smile. "I'll be right back."

Kit eyed Sam as they sat on the sofa while Connor took a wingback chair. "Have you seen them?" she asked Sam softly. "At New Horizons? Or heard their names?"

"I don't think so, but kids often give fake names. I'll ask around later to see if any of the other kids have seen them." His smile was sad. "Poor mama."

The mother in question reentered the room, followed by her husband, a tall man who, according to his driver's license information, was forty-nine. His expression was closed as the two sat on a love seat. "What's this about?" David asked, his tone harsh.

"We're homicide detectives, sir," Connor said. "We're investigating the murder of Brooks Munro and we're hoping you can help us."

David Norton frowned. "Brooks Munro the councilman? He's dead? Are you sure?"

Oh yes. Kit thought about the gaping maw that had been Munro's throat. *Very sure.* "He is," she confirmed. "When did you last see him?"

David stared at them. "I haven't. I don't know why you're here."

"He's one of your customers, isn't he?" Connor asked.

"Uh . . ."

"He is," Carla said quietly. "He gave a recommendation and we put it on the website."

"Oh. All right. Well then, yes. He's one of our clients. But I've never personally met the man. I'd have to check our records to find out when we last serviced his lawn. Why?" he asked, sounding genuinely confused.

Connor pulled a folded paper from his pocket. He'd printed screenshots of the trailer leaving Munro's community. "Is this your trailer?"

David took the paper, Carla looking over his arm to see. Both frowned, then looked at each other. "David? What's going on?"

"I don't know," he muttered, then met Kit's eyes. "This is our logo, our artwork, but we don't own a trailer of that size. Where did you get this photo?"

"It left Brooks Munro's community the day he disappeared," Kit said, watching their reactions. She had no intention of answering his question. At least not until she was sure that he wasn't somehow involved in Munro's murder.

Carla's hand flew to her mouth. "David?"

David shook his head, looking confounded. "This is *not* our trailer. I don't know whose it is, but it does *not* belong to me or to my company. Do I need a lawyer?"

"Would you allow us access to your service records?" Connor answered, dodging the question about lawyers. "We'd like to see when your company serviced Mr. Munro's property."

"Yes," Carla said firmly. "David, we have nothing to hide."

"Famous last words," David muttered, then shook the printed screenshot. "How did this happen? How did someone get a trailer with our logo?"

"We don't know, sir," Kit said honestly. "We were hoping you could tell us."

David slowly exhaled. "Sorry, guys. I'm calling my lawyer."

"David!" Carla exclaimed.

"We're not guilty, Carla. We're smart. I'll have my lawyer contact you, Detectives. I assume you have a business card. If he says it's okay, I'll give you access to my service records."

Kit handed him a business card, annoyed and trying hard not to show it. "Can you answer one question for us?"

"Depends," David said cagily. "What's the question?"

"Are your trailers painted or wrapped?"

"Wrapped," he said readily enough. "We use a body shop in Mission Valley. I'm happy to give you their information."

If the trailer truly didn't belong to Norton Landscaping— and it was easily enough checked—then Munro's killer had to have gotten it somewhere else.

Kit opened the Notes app on her phone. "Whenever you're ready."

"Jennifer's Body Shop," David said.

Kit looked up from her phone. "Seriously? Wasn't that a movie? *Jennifer's Body*?"

"A horror movie," Carla said. "But this Jennifer is a real person and she runs a body shop. She's . . . dramatic. But she does good work and we always get a discount."

"Okay," Kit said. "Did she also design the graphic for the trailer wraps?"

"That's two questions," David said, grunting when Carla elbowed him.

"Dammit, David," she hissed. "This is serious."

"So am I," he snapped. "We need to let our lawyer handle this."

Carla shook her head. "Jen's boyfriend is the graphic designer. I think his name is Bran. Like the cereal."

David's lips thinned. "Whatever."

"I want the cops out of our lives," Carla said quietly to him, then looked at Kit. "No offense."

"None taken." Kit rose. "Thank you for your time."

Connor handed Carla one of his business cards. "Call either of us if you change your mind. And if you could have your attorney contact us as soon as possible, we can get the information we need and be out of your hair."

From the corner of her eye, Kit saw Sam slip Carla one of his business cards, the one from New Horizons. The woman's eyes filled with tears as she clutched the card to her chest.

"I volunteer at New Horizons," Sam murmured. "It's a shelter for teen runaways. If you send me their photos, I'll pass them around and keep my ear to the ground for word of your boys."

David sucked in a breath. "Carla."

She lifted her chin. "They're my sons, David. I will find them."

David closed his eyes, but not before Kit saw the pain there. "I want to find them, too. But they don't want to come home."

Carla's jaw twitched. "And if they did?"

"They'd have to obey the rules of the house," David said wearily.

Carla looked like she wanted words with her husband, but she just promised to email Sam photos of her sons before showing Kit, Sam, and Connor out.

"Well," Kit said when they got back to the car. "That was different."

"What was that at the end, Sam?" Connor asked.

"Seems like David made some rules that Davy and Danny didn't like and they ran away. David has given up on them coming home, and Carla refuses to do so."

Connor squeezed into the back seat with a grimace. "Chances of finding those kids after a month suck."

Sam sighed as he slid into the front passenger seat. "I know. I'll make some calls, just in case. And the kids that come through New Horizons hear things. A few of them trust me enough to tell me the word on the street."

Kit started the car. "Next stop, Jennifer's Body Shop?"

Connor snickered. "I wanted to laugh so bad." He waved his hand. "Drive on, Jeeves."

"That's Detective Jeeves to you," Kit said lightly. "Run checks on Jennifer and her boyfriend Bran."

"Like the cereal," Connor deadpanned. "On it."

Sam was already on his phone, sending texts. "New Horizons?" Kit asked.

Sam nodded. "If I can help them find their kids, I will. Carla Norton's already emailed me the photos. I'm passing them on to the staff on duty today."

Kit's heart squeezed. The kids passing through the teen shelter were lucky to have a man like Sam on their side. "I know you will. Okay. Jennifer's Body Shop, here we come."

CHAPTER THREE

Sam winced as Kit brought the car to a stop in front of the apartment building where the owner of Jennifer's Body Shop resided. He'd just finished reading the plot of the movie the body shop was named for. "This is horrible."

"Duh," Connor said. "It's a *horror* movie. You haven't seen it?"

"Ah, no. No horror movies for me. They give me nightmares."

"Me too," Kit said. "I figure I see enough on the job. I don't need to be watching films about murder, too."

Sam figured that was true enough. He'd already seen more death than he'd ever wanted to see, and that was before he'd become their criminal psychologist.

Sam looked up at the apartment building. "What do you know about Jennifer Porter?"

"She's full owner of Jennifer's Body Shop," Connor said. "Forty-two, no criminal record, one registered handgun. She specializes in wraps but also rebuilds muscle cars. The photos on her website are amazing. If I had a hot car, I'd get her to wrap it."

Sam twisted around to look back at Connor. He felt a little guilty for taking the front seat when Connor was so clearly uncomfortable in the back, but they'd done rock, paper, scissors, and everyone knew that was sacrosanct. No takebacks.

"Why don't you have a hot car?" Sam asked. "You drive a Toyota, just like I do."

"I had one," Connor said morosely. "But CeCe said it was a death trap."

"It was," Kit inserted. "She was one hundred percent right."

Connor huffed. "Maybe. So I sold it."

"Poor baby," Kit drawled. "What about the boyfriend? Bran? Did you find anything on him?"

"I did. Bran Reynolds is thirty-five and has a graphic arts degree. He has a website showing his designs and Norton Landscaping is one of them. He lives here with Jennifer."

"Cozy," Kit said. "Let's see what they have to say about David Norton's trailer."

The elevator was broken, so they hauled themselves up four flights of stairs to Jennifer Porter's apartment.

"We can skip leg day today," Sam muttered.

Connor chuckled. "I never skip leg day."

Sam just sighed. He knew that was true. He now played squash with Connor a few times a month. Connor was fast and strong. Sam was still skipping leg day.

Kit knocked briskly, then stepped back, pulling out her badge.

Jennifer opened the door and scowled. She had bright red hair with a line of dark roots. It shot out in all directions, probably not having seen a brush yet that morning. She was medium height, solidly built, her arm muscles defined and covered in tattoos.

"Not interested," she said and started to close the door.

"Ma'am?" Kit interrupted. "We're with SDPD. I'm Detective McKittrick. These are my colleagues, Detective Robinson and Dr. Reeves. We'd like to ask you a few questions."

Jennifer's eyes narrowed. "What kind of questions?"

"About your business, ma'am." Connor pulled the screenshot of the trailer from his pocket. "Did you make this trailer wrap?"

"Yes. Why? I do lots of wraps for David Norton. We finished that one this past week."

"He says he didn't order this one," Kit said. "That it's not his."

Jennifer frowned. "Well, he's lying. I saw his name on the invoice. What's this about?"

"We believe the trailer was used in the commission of a crime," Connor said. "We're trying to track it down."

Jennifer pulled her phone from her pocket and began to type. Eyes wide, she looked up at them. "McKittrick and Robinson. You're Homicide."

"Yes, ma'am," Kit said. "I hope you can help us track down the customer of this wrap, if it wasn't David Norton."

"I know I saw his name on the invoice," she said, clearly rattled. "Come in. I'll check my records. Bran? The cops are here."

A younger man stepped out of the kitchen. "What's going on? Is it Shelley?"

"No. It's about that wrap we did for Norton Landscaping. Please, Detectives. Sit down." She left the room for a moment, returning with her laptop. She sat in a recliner, and Bran perched on the arm. "There has to be some mistake," she said as she typed. "David Norton and I have been doing business for years."

"Was this a new design?" Connor asked.

Bran nodded. "It was. He emailed me about it."

"Did either of you talk to him?" Kit asked.

Jennifer shook her head. "Not recently. Bran set up online ordering and it's made dealing with customers so much easier."

"Everything's in writing and the designs are approved online," Bran explained. "Much less stressful than dealing with them face-to-face or on the phone. David approved this design himself. It was for a much larger trailer, so everything had to be resized."

"Did you see David Norton when he picked up the finished trailer?" Connor asked.

Another shake of Jennifer's head. "I didn't."

"Ask Shelley," Bran said quietly.

Jennifer shot Bran a glare. "She's not answering my calls or texts. You know that."

Bran sighed. "I know. But I was hoping that she might be back from wherever she went by now."

Jennifer pointed to her screen. "I don't have to call her. There are special instructions on this order. He dropped off the trailer the night before we were due to start. It was picked up the same way—after hours. He was to call the office with his credit card to pay the balance before he picked it up since we'd be closed." Her mouth fell open. "Wait a minute. He never paid for the wrap. Sonofabitch. Norton always pays his bills at the time of pickup."

Bran made a frustrated sound. "That email address is one letter off his normal."

Jennifer gasped softly. "You're right." She met Kit's eyes. "Were we cheated?"

"We don't know," Kit said. "When was it dropped off and picked up?"

"Dropped off on Monday after hours and picked up Tuesday, also after hours. We never do pickups after hours unless the client has paid in full in advance. I need to talk to Shelley, because *I* didn't authorize this. Norton is a good client, but I never would have let him take the finished trailer without paying for it."

Sam believed her. It looked like Kit did, too.

"Miss Porter, wait," Kit said when the woman started to dial a number on her cell phone. "Tell me about Shelley. How well do you know her?"

"She's my sister's kid," Jennifer said, visibly upset. "She's nineteen and kind of a screw-up, but she's really trying to get her life back on track. She's an addict but she went to rehab and she's been clean."

"For two weeks," Bran muttered.

Jennifer gave him a warning glare. "I gave Shelley a job several months ago. Before she went into rehab. She did steal some money before rehab, but she's been okay since she came back. I don't know what happened here."

"Don't call her yet," Connor said. "We'll get to the bottom of this. Where does she live?"

Sam didn't have a good feeling about Jennifer's niece. From the look in Connor's eyes, neither did he.

"Fifteen minutes away, with my sister. But I haven't seen her since Tuesday afternoon. She sent me a text on Tuesday night, said she was taking off the rest of the week. That she'd be back on Monday. I wasn't happy about it, but there wasn't anything I could do. She never answered my calls or texts. I'm going to read her the riot act when she comes in tomorrow. But if she met the guy who ordered that wrap . . . You said he killed someone?"

"We don't know for sure," Connor said. "But it looks like it."

Jennifer wrung her hands. "If he hurt her . . ."

"Give us her address and we'll go check on her," Kit promised.

Jennifer's chin lifted. "I'm going to follow you in my car. Bran?"

"You know I'll come with you. Let me put away the eggs and we can go."

Kit wanted to argue with them. Sam could almost see the words she wanted to say. But in the end, she only nodded. "Of course."

Wordlessly they descended the four flights of stairs, the three of them getting into the department car. The mood was heavy as they drove to Jennifer's sister's small house, Jennifer and Bran following behind.

Kit stopped Jennifer and Bran when they started to accompany them up to the house. "Wait here on the sidewalk. Please."

"Fuck," Connor muttered as he, Sam, and Kit approached the house, and Sam knew exactly what they'd find inside. The stench of death was unmistakable.

Kit gave the house a visual once-over. "How come nobody reported this? They had to have smelled it."

The neighborhood wasn't great. Sam imagined that most people minded their own business here.

Connor pulled a handkerchief from his pocket and covered his nose and mouth. "You might want to wait outside, Sam."

"I'm with you," Sam said, even though he thought he'd throw up any moment.

Kit shrugged. "Your call. It won't be pretty."

Sam looked over his shoulder at Jennifer, who stood with Bran at the bottom of the driveway, a hand clasped over her mouth and horrified tears running down her cheeks. It appeared that they understood the significance of Connor's handkerchief. "Let's get this over with. She's going to need support."

Kit pulled on a pair of disposable gloves and twisted the door handle. It opened with no resistance, and Sam gagged.

"Fuck," Connor said once again.

Fuck indeed.

Because lying on the living room floor was a young woman of about nineteen and an older woman who bore a resemblance to Jennifer Porter. Both had their throats slit, just like Brooks Munro.

"He killed them, too," Connor said. "Goddammit."

"I'll call it in," Kit said heavily. "Connor, let's check the house. Whoever did this is probably long gone, but we need to be sure."

"I'll see to Jennifer," Sam said. It was what he knew best. Comfort and support. Jennifer Porter was going to need a lot of both.

San Diego, California
Sunday, January 8, 12:30 p.m.

"Lunch delivery," Kit said as she dropped the sandwich on Alicia's desk.

Dr. Alicia Batra looked up at Kit. "You're turning into your mother, always feeding me."

Kit grinned, even though her heart hurt. The sound of Jennifer Porter's sobs still echoed in her mind. She'd heard those sobs before. Sometimes out of her own mouth.

It was a shock, losing someone to a violent murder.

Luckily, Sam had been there. The man had said and done all the right things, making sure that Jennifer and Bran had gotten home safely.

"If I grow up to be Betsy McKittrick, I'll die happy."

Unwrapping the sandwich, Alicia gestured to the chair next to her desk. "Where's Connor?"

"He'll be up. We were trying to interview the security guard from Munro's community about the trailer when you called. He wasn't home, so we have to go back later, plus a million other interviews. Connor's calling his girlfriend to let her know he won't be coming home for dinner."

"Neither am I," Alicia said dryly. "I now have two more bodies in my morgue. And don't ask me for their time of death because I haven't started their exams. I just finished Brooks Munro's, which was why I called you in." She paused, frowning. "You okay, hon?"

Kit gave herself a shake, unable to erase the memory of Jennifer's sobs. "The victims' relative followed us to the scene. She was . . . well, you know."

"I know," Alicia murmured. "It's hard when the families come in to identify bodies. I guess I'm lucky in that it doesn't happen with every exam I have to do."

"Sam was with us. He was so good with the victims' family. It left me free to do my job."

"That's sweet. So . . . what did you find at this newest scene?"

"A lot of blood. Signs of a struggle. The younger victim— Shelley—had sent a text to her aunt at eight p.m. on Tuesday night, so she was probably alive then. *If* her killer didn't send the text himself later. Knowing the actual time of death will be helpful."

"I'll get you TOD as soon as I can, but it's not going to be as precise as you want it to be. I can only give you facts about Munro for now. His killer used a sharp, thin blade. But only on his throat and legs."

Kit narrowed her eyes. "What does that mean?"

"Yeah," Connor said, closing Alicia's office door as he entered the room. "What does that mean?"

"Come and see." Alicia led them into the exam area, where Munro's body still lay on the steel table. A sheet was draped over the lower half of his body.

"I always think they're going to look better after you've cleaned them up," Connor murmured. "But they don't."

"Not my job, thankfully," Alicia said. "I leave that to the morticians. Although Munro's going to have a closed casket. Y'know. His face. Plus, his head."

Kit had expected the ravaged face—*thanks, cute desert creatures*—but there was damage to his head that hadn't been apparent when she and Sam had found him.

The sides of his head were dented in.

"Holy shit," Kit said. "What did his killer *do* to him?"

"Smashed the hell out of his head," Alicia said. "The wounds on either side of his head are similar in area and depth. This wasn't an assault with a blunt object. Constant and heavy pressure was applied."

"A vise?" Connor asked.

"That was my guess," Alicia said. "Someone tortured this victim."

"I figured that from the slices in his skin," Kit said.

"Let's talk about those. He's got twenty-five stab wounds in addition to the slit throat. Twenty in the chest and abdominal areas, two in the back, one on the back of each leg, and one in his groin. He's missing all his fingers and toes. But the groin wound is grisly. Connor, prepare yourself." She pulled the sheet back, and even Kit winced.

The man's genitalia had been mutilated.

Connor cleared his throat. "Premortem or post?"

"Definitely premortem. This guy was alive for everything that was done to him. Whether he was conscious for all of it is another question, but he was conscious for at least part of it. The abrasions at his wrists and ankles indicate a struggle. But the abrasions are deep. He was tied tightly. But that's not why I called you two in. Each of these wounds is different. Different size, depth, and angle. There appears to have been at least four weapons used." She pointed to one of the shallower wounds. "The blade went deep enough to hurt, but not enough to cause real damage. The blade used was nonserrated and sharp. I'm thinking a box cutter or a utility knife. The cuts are uniformly deep."

"Okay," Kit said. "And the others?"

"Not so fast. These cuts are uniformly deep, but they are all angled differently, just like the deeper wounds. In addition to the utility knife, you've got a serrated blade, a super thin blade, like a stiletto, and finally a thick blade, like a survival knife. I'm estimating it was about a quarter inch thick, which is hefty for a knife. But all the wounds, no matter what blade was used, are all angled differently."

"Different hands," Kit murmured. Which was a complication. How many hands? How many doers?

"That's what I think," Alicia agreed. "There are also indications of hesitation on a few of the cuts. The slices on the legs were done with the stiletto-style blade that cut his throat. They severed the victim's tendons. He couldn't have run away, even if he hadn't been tied."

Kit fought a shudder. "I mean . . . we know people hated Munro, but . . . wow."

"Yeah." Alicia sighed. "I think his fingers and toes were removed with the thick blade. It would have been hefty enough to slice through bone and cartilage."

"Fucking hell." Connor cleared his throat again. "How many stabbers are we potentially talking about?"

"Could be up to twenty."

Kit didn't want to think about that. "Or one guy deliberately making it look like there were multiple hands."

Alicia shrugged. "Maybe. I think, at a minimum, the same hand cut his throat and sliced the tendons in his calves. There was bandage residue around the deepest cuts. And the severed digits. He was given first aid, at least enough to keep him alive.

The deepest wound in his gut had sand in the tissues, deep down. Like the sand was on the knife when he was stabbed."

"So that wound was made at the scene of his death," Connor said.

"I'd say so. That wound alone would have been enough to kill him, but the slit throat was the mechanism of death. None of the other wounds had sand at the deepest point, so I don't believe they were done at the same time. The sand was nearer to the skin surface, probably blown in after his body was left behind."

"Can you tell over what time period the stab wounds were made?" Connor asked.

Alicia shrugged. "At least a day. Maybe two. His fingers were first, I think. That's all I got. The rest is your job."

"Yay," Kit said sarcastically. "So his killer arranges for a wrap to be made for a large trailer, kills the body shop assistant who was likely there when he picked up the trailer—"

"And her mother," Connor interrupted.

"And her mother," Kit confirmed. "He then drives to Munro's neighborhood the next day posing as a landscaper, grabs Munro and his Ferrari, does some damage to Munro there in his garage, then . . . what? He takes him somewhere else where a mob goes all *Murder on the Orient Express* on him?"

"Don't forget the money," Connor said.

Kit nodded. "Munro took fifty Gs from the account he shared with his wife the same day that he was nabbed."

"I have no idea how much it costs to wrap a trailer big enough to fit a car," Alicia said, "but maybe Munro's killers used the money he took out of his account to pay the body shop."

"Nah," Kit said. "They stiffed poor Jennifer."

Alicia frowned. "Rude."

Kit laughed. Outsiders might be offended, but this was how

they dealt with the darker aspects of their job. "My point is, this was an elaborate setup. It took planning. If it was a mob, someone's going to talk, sooner or later. They won't be able to help themselves. Either they'll want to confess or they'll want to brag."

Connor made a face. "Hope they break sooner versus later. We're late for the deadline Navarro set for today's update. He's probably getting all kinds of questions from the higher-ups."

Kit sighed. "I know. I've been putting it off, but it's time to bite the bullet. Let's go talk to the boss. Let us know if you find anything important when you autopsy the newest victims."

"Will do." Alicia waved. "Thanks for the sandwich."

San Diego PD, San Diego, California
Sunday, January 8, 1:45 p.m.

"Where did he get the trailer to begin with?" Navarro asked.

Kit had a headache and was craving a quiet moment. "Good question. We need to check the reports of stolen vehicles. We also need subpoenas for Munro's bank records. He transferred fifty grand from his and Wilhelmina's joint account to one of his personal accounts on Wednesday. That was the last day he was seen alive. We need to know where that money went."

Navarro frowned. "What do you think about Dr. Batra's theory of more than one killer?"

Kit shrugged. "It's certainly possible. We've already got a suspect list a mile long. A lot of people seemed to have loved him, according to the printed-out emails we found in his home office. Lots of fawning and gratitude for things he'd done for them. But a whole lot of people hated him, too. There were nearly as many threats as thank-yous. We're assuming that if Munro was stabbed by multiple people, at least one person was in charge. Someone needed to plan for the trailer and for the stab fest, if there was one."

"You sound skeptical," Navarro noted.

Kit shrugged again. "No, just . . . I'm afraid to pick a path this early. We don't have enough information." She glanced at Connor, who appeared deep in thought. "What?"

"Why Anza-Borrego? Why not leave him in the trailer and park it somewhere? He wasn't worried about someone finding Shelley and her mother. Why try to hide Munro's body? He couldn't have believed we wouldn't trace the trailer."

"You're right," Kit said. "I don't know."

"Well, find out," Navarro snapped. "And quickly."

Kit had to bite back a retort. Navarro was their boss, after all. "We could use some help running down leads and shortening our suspect list. You said that you'd give us some help."

"Marshall and Ashton just finished a case. They're yours for now. Have them do the paperwork. Background checks of your lead suspects, subpoenas of Munro's accounts, that kind of thing. I want you two interviewing witnesses. Figure out if it was one guy or a group. But quickly."

"We got that part," Kit muttered. "Can we get a subpoena of Wilhelmina's finances, too? She had motive and means. She has more than enough money to hire this done."

Navarro grimaced. "You'll need to get more evidence, I think. She was the one who called it in."

"Because—" Kit stopped, a thought popping into her mind. "Because she got that email about Munro overdrawing their joint account. What if he did that on purpose?"

Connor's eyes narrowed as he nodded. "You could be right. Let's say whoever entered his home on Wednesday wanted money. He could have forced Munro to move the funds."

"And Munro chose their joint account, knowing his wife

would raise a fuss," Kit finished. "That suggests he was forced to move that money, and that his communication had somehow been cut off. No 911, no call to his admin, no shout for help. Not that any of his neighbors would have heard him. They're all too far away. What if drawing Wilhelmina into this was his only way to call for help?"

"Or what if Wilhelmina planned it?" Connor squeezed his eyes shut. "We need to eliminate Wilhelmina as a suspect."

Kit agreed. "Let's go back to the Ferrari. It's a big thing to steal and required a lot of preplanning. Why the Ferrari?"

"Did his killer take anything else?" Navarro asked.

"We asked Rafferty when he was showing us the garage," Connor said. "So far, nothing obvious was taken, and Wilhelmina took her jewelry and valuables with her when she left him. We'll have to figure out what else Munro owned that was valuable."

Kit's mind was still on the Ferrari and the logistics required to steal it. "I wonder what Munro's killer offered Shelley in exchange for the trailer."

Connor nodded. "Good point. She broke the rule by not getting the guy to pay for the trailer when he picked it up. She was an addict. Jennifer said she'd been clean, but Bran, the boyfriend, said that it had only been for a few weeks. Shelley could have been using without Jennifer knowing."

"He might not have offered Shelley anything," Navarro said. "He might have just taken the trailer at gunpoint."

Kit shook her head. "But he killed her in her home. If he'd stolen the trailer at gunpoint, wouldn't he have just killed her there at the shop? He let her go home."

"He could have forced her at gunpoint or with his knife," Navarro said, still playing devil's advocate. "Could have made her go home and killed her there."

"Maybe," Kit allowed. "We'll check it out. If he communi-cated with her beforehand, arranging for a pickup outside of the shop's rules, we might be able to track him that way."

"Whatever you do," Navarro said, "do it—"

"Quickly," Kit interrupted with a sigh. "We know, we know. We'll add it to our list. That might be something Sam can find out for us. He developed a rapport with Jennifer and her boy-friend Bran while we were securing the scene."

"Is the security guard on your list?" Navarro asked. "The one at the gate to Munro's community?"

"He is," Connor said. "His name is Marco Valdez. He and the other guards work a twelve-hour shift. He would have just ar-rived when the trailer passed through the gate, and he would have been off-duty fifteen minutes after its exit. So he was the only one who would have seen the trailer. He's twenty-six years old and lives alone. We'd just knocked on his door when Dr. Batra called us to the morgue. He wasn't home and his neighbors haven't seen him in a few days, but he normally keeps to himself and they said that wasn't unusual."

"Still doesn't sound good," Navarro muttered. "Any sign of forced entry into his house?"

"Nope," Kit said. "But on the bright side, we didn't smell any-thing dead. He's due back at work tomorrow morning, so hope-fully he'll show up."

"Hopefully." But Navarro sounded as grim as Kit felt because the guard was a loose end. "What else?"

"I've been thinking about how long that trailer was in front of Munro's house," she said. "He was there from six in the morning until almost six that evening. What did he do all that time? And why did he arrive so early?"

"Good questions. Figure it out. But do it—"

"Quickly," Connor said with a sigh.

A knock on the door had the three of them turning. Sergeant Ryland of CSU stood at the door. Navarro motioned him in.

"Glad you're all here," Ryland said, taking a seat next to Navarro at the table. "We hit the jackpot at Munro's house. Missing Persons didn't know to look for recording equipment, but Munro had his office wired for audio and video."

"Did he have bugs in other rooms?" Navarro asked. "Or just his home office?"

"Only the home office," Ryland said. "And we did a very thorough check."

"I wonder if Wilhelmina knew about the bugs?" Connor murmured.

Kit shook her head. "If she knew, I think she would have used that feed against Munro versus searching through his files for proof of his bribery. Did you find anything on the feed?" she asked Ryland.

"Oh yes. We made a copy of the recording from the day he disappeared. I uploaded it to the server. You're going to want to see this."

Navarro moved his laptop to the table and brought up the recording.

Munro was sitting at his massive desk, clearly inebriated, a half-full bottle of whiskey at his elbow. He was looking at his phone, frowning, when the office door flew open. Munro fumbled for the drawer, but a man in a hoodie and a Halloween hockey mask beat him to the punch, racing across the room to hold his gun to Munro's head.

"Drop the phone," the intruder said, his voice deep and raspy. He wore the mask they'd seen in Munro's security footage.

Munro did as commanded, the phone clattering to the desk.

"Turn off the cameras," the man demanded.

Munro's jaw tightened. *"And if I don't?"*

"I'll kill you where you sit."

"What do you want from me?"

"What you owe me, you sonofabitch. Fifty grand, for starters."

Munro looked startled, then slurred, *"Oh, I know who you are."*

"Shut the fuck up and turn off the cameras."

Munro grabbed his phone, but the intruder took it from his hand. *"I have to use the app,"* Munro insisted.

The man held the phone in front of Munro's face. The phone's home screen must have unlocked because the intruder put it on the desk and began tapping.

The feed went dark.

"That's all we got," Ryland said. "But the time stamp on this recording is three minutes after the garage camera was painted over and twenty minutes before the trailer was captured leaving Munro's neighborhood. It's also consistent with how long the dried blood was on the garage floor."

"Was anything else missing?" Connor asked.

Ryland nodded. "Munro wore a Rolex watch in this video, but it wasn't on the body and it's not in the house. Brand new it retails for forty grand."

Connor looked at Kit. "Between the Rolex and the Ferrari, sounds like a job for Goddard."

Detective Bruce Goddard was in the robbery division and had helped them in the past. "Let's call him."

Ryland rose. "I'm headed to the lab. We've got more video to review. Munro had multiple servers that appear to hold up to six months of footage."

Connor followed Ryland to the door. "Kit?" he asked when Kit stayed seated.

"I'll be out in a minute." She waited until Connor had closed Navarro's door. "They're going to find Sam on Munro's footage."

Navarro's brows went up. "What? When? Oh." His face settled into its resting scowl. "He went to Munro's for that presentation about New Horizons, didn't he?"

"He did."

"And he didn't tell me because he's still antsy about being a suspect."

Kit nodded. "Exactly. Just wanted to give you a heads-up. He said he clearly said no to Munro, just in case he was being recorded, then reported the whole thing to Joel."

"Thanks for telling me. Tell Dr. Reeves that he doesn't need to worry about it."

Kit had to admit to being relieved for Sam's sake. "Thanks, boss." She pushed away from the table. "We'll work quickly, and I'll call Sam right now and ask him to find out what he can about Shelley's movements in the days before her death. Hopefully we can find out if she communicated with her killer about the trailer."

"Thank you. Kit? Be safe."

"Always."

CHAPTER FOUR

Sam parked in front of Jennifer Porter's apartment and took a moment to clear his mind.

Because Kit had called and asked for his help again. He wasn't sure if his sheer delight was pathetic or normal. But that didn't change the fact that he'd tingled all over as he'd driven away from New Horizons.

Sam was a helper. He'd known that about himself for most of his life. It seemed seared into his DNA. Helping serve lunch to the teens this afternoon? No big deal. Showing the photos of Davy and Danny Norton to the teens at the shelter? He considered that part of his job.

But helping Kit was different. And helping Kit because she'd *asked* him to? It gave him hope that things might eventually work out between them.

That was what he needed to clear from his mind, at least for now. The hope. Because he was here to do an important but difficult job—talk to a grieving family member about the person they'd just lost.

He'd checked Shelley Porter's social media posts before he left New Horizons and had noticed a change in her posts over the past six months. They'd become dark and brooding, the photos taken in shadow. Her surroundings had become less tidy, candy wrappers and other trash littering the floor of what appeared to be her bedroom. There had been a thirty-day gap while she'd been in rehab, but in the most recent photo, he thought he'd seen the base of a syringe on the nightstand beside her.

Kit and Connor wondered if whoever had arranged for the trailer wrap had made a deal with Shelley. Offered her something to entice her to break her aunt's policy of always getting the money upfront.

That might or might not have been the case, but Sam would bet that Shelley had started using again. It hurt his heart. A young life wasted.

And her mother had suffered the consequences as well.

Sam climbed the four flights of stairs and knocked quietly on Jennifer's door. The door opened, revealing Bran, Jennifer's boyfriend.

"She's asleep," Bran said quietly.

That might be for the best. "I have some follow-up questions that could help the police solve her murder. Can I come in?"

Bran stepped aside. "Of course. Thank you, by the way. You were so good with her earlier. She's . . . well, she likes to seem tough, but she's a marshmallow inside."

Sam smiled sadly. "I know the type." That was Kit, through and through. "They don't make it easy for you to take care of them."

"That's God's honest truth. Have a seat."

Sam sat on the corner of the sofa. When Bran sat at the other end, Sam said, "I need to ask you more about Shelley. Was she using again?"

"Yes. Jen didn't want to hear it, but I saw the signs." He shook his head. "I tried to tell her that Shelley was using again, but Jen shut me down. We actually fought about it, and we never fight. Jen didn't mention this, but Shelley took two hundred dollars out of the register two weeks ago. She was right out of rehab. I told Shelley that I knew she'd done it, and she got nasty with me. Said if I didn't back off that she'd tell Jen that I'd made a pass at her. Which I never would have done. Jen's it for me. I don't cheat."

"Did you tell Jennifer this?"

"I tried. She said that I must have misunderstood. I did *not* misunderstand."

"It's hard to accept the failings of people you love."

"I know. So I let it drop. Jen saw Shelley as the little girl she'd helped raise. She lived with her sister Carol and Shelley up until she and I got this place two years ago."

"Did Carol and Jen speak often?" Sam asked.

"Not every day. I guess you're wondering why we didn't go over there before today. To check on them."

"I did wonder that, yes," Sam admitted.

"Jen was furious when Shelley texted Tuesday night. She left Jen high and dry, which meant Jen had to do her job and Shelley's, too. Jen was working late every night this past week and when she came home, she was tired and so mad that she didn't want to see Shelley's face. She said it was a good thing that Shelley wasn't answering her phone, because she'd say stuff she couldn't take back. She was letting herself cool down." Bran sighed. "And now there's the whole trailer thing. That trailer job was worth a lot of money for Jen. For Shelley to allow someone to take the trailer without paying, and then she's killed?" He shrugged, not finishing his thought.

"What are you wondering?" Sam asked gently.

"I'm wondering if the guy offered to pay Shelley in cash on the side, some percentage of the total. Shelley would have kept the cash, then would have thrown a tantrum about how mean Jen was and would have denied everything when Jen discovered the money was never paid. Any amount of cash would have gone straight into Shelley's arm."

"What prompted Shelley to go to rehab?"

"She got arrested for possession. Carol and Jen begged the DA to cut her a deal that included rehab."

"Who would Shelley have confided in? Who might know if she'd made a side deal on the trailer for the cash?"

"Her good-for-nothing boyfriend. His name is Ace Diamond," Bran said with disdain. "I don't think that's his given name, but it's the only name I know. He's a thug and he was stoned every time I saw him. He works for Jonesy's. It's a butcher shop."

Sam barely managed to control his flinch. He knew the list of injuries inflicted on Brooks Munro. Kit had brought him up to speed when she'd asked him to get more information on Shelley.

That Shelley's boyfriend worked for a butcher might just be a bad coincidence. Sam hoped so.

"Got it, thanks. Anyone else besides the thug boyfriend?"

"She also had a best friend. Her name is Julie Sparks. I don't have her contact info, but she works in a clothing store at the mall. The one where all the mannequins wear neon-colored miniskirts."

"I think I know the one." The clothes made Sam wince every time he passed by. The colors were so bright. "Thank you, Bran. I know the words seem empty, but I am sorry for your loss."

Bran nodded soberly. "Thank you for taking care of Jen. It was . . . more than I expected."

"I'm happy to help," Sam said as he walked to the front door. "Make sure she sees a therapist. Either the one I recommended or another of her choice. Murder is a trauma. There's absolutely no shame in asking for help."

"I'll take care of her," Bran vowed.

When Sam was back in his RAV4, he dialed Kit and brought her up to speed. "Should I talk to the best friend or the thug boyfriend?"

"Both," she said. "But I'll go with you. Connor is working with the two detectives Navarro assigned to help us. Let's talk to the best friend first. I'll meet you at the mall. If she's not at work, we'll visit her at home. Give me a second." There was a pause and a sigh. "Bran's right. Ace Diamond is not the thug boyfriend's real name. The best friend might know it, though. Thank you, Sam."

"No problem. I have to go home first and walk Siggy. If you get there before me, wait at the pretzel stand next to the clothing store."

"Mmm. Those pretzels are the best. I'll get us a snack."

Sam ended the call, taking one more look up toward Jennifer's apartment. Sam keenly remembered watching the life drain from his first love's eyes. They'd been seventeen, accosted while changing a tire on prom night. Every time he visited the family of a homicide victim, every time he spoke with parents grieving because their runaway teen had been found dead, he remembered the grief and the pain.

He knew how Jennifer felt. So did Kit.

It was why he and Kit had chosen their careers. Maybe that was also what made them both so good at what they did. He wanted to think so. That way, at least, there was purpose in their grief.

University City, San Diego, California
Sunday, January 8, 4:00 p.m.

Kit hated the mall. Hated it with the fiery passion of a thousand suns. But she'd suck it up for the sake of Shelley and her mother. She didn't know if Shelley's friend had been informed of her murder.

Kit hated the thought of doing a notification at the mall.

But she'd arrived before Sam and now had two giant pretzels filled with carbs and buttery goodness. She took a bite from hers as she scanned the store through the glass.

She had Julie Sparks's driver's license photo. The woman was nineteen, five feet two, and had light brown hair and big gray eyes. And . . . there she was, straightening the clothing on a display table.

She hadn't been crying. Didn't look sad.

She probably didn't know yet. *This is going to suck.*

"Kit?"

She turned at the familiar voice, a smile curving her lips unbidden. Sam was his nerdy, Clark Kent self. So damn earnest. Just like always.

It was nice that he didn't seem to change.

And that that fact made her stomach flutter with butterflies scared her silly.

"For you." She shoved the pretzel into his hands. "They're good."

"They are. Thank you." He bit off a huge bite. "Was hungry."

"Me too. Julie's working today. About a third of the way back, standing at the table with the neon-green sweaters."

"This store always gives me a headache. The colors are like a bad acid trip." He glanced at her, his eyes going wide. "Not that I'd know what an acid trip is like."

She laughed. "I believe you. For the record, neither do I. But let's agree to never ask Connor, because I think he was wilder in his youth than we were."

"I was boring. Just like now."

Her heart softened. "Steady."

He shrugged. "Same as boring."

"Not even close." She finished her pretzel and threw the wrapper away. "Ready?"

He shoved the last of his in his mouth. "Um-hm."

She laughed again, then sobered. "She doesn't know, I don't think."

Sam sighed. "I agree. I'll be quiet until you need me."

That she was positive she'd need him scared her, too.

Kit didn't like needing people. Needing people left you open.

But Pop was always telling her to open up. Maybe this was what he meant. It shouldn't be so damn terrifying, though.

Squaring her shoulders, she cleared her mind and entered the store, wincing at the volume of the music. "Should have worn earplugs," she muttered to Sam.

"I brought some," he muttered back.

She looked over at him. "You did not."

One corner of his mouth lifted. "Did so." He pulled a packet of disposable earplugs out of his pocket.

Kit had to clear her throat and think about death so she wouldn't laugh. *Julie doesn't know. Have some respect.*

The young woman in question looked up at that moment, her eyes going wide. "Can I help you?"

"Are you Julie Sparks?" Kit asked.

Julie nodded warily. "Why?"

"I'm Detective McKittrick with SDPD. This is my colleague, Dr. Reeves. Can we talk to you for a moment?"

She seemed to deflate. "Let me talk to my manager. Wait here."

"She knows something," Sam said quietly as they watched her walk to the back of the store.

"Yep. Feels like Carla Norton this morning. Like she was expecting bad news. Did you find any news on Carla's sons?"

"No, but the teens are spreading the word. It's only been a month. It might end up okay." Sam was optimistic that way.

Julie returned, her feet dragging. "She says we can use the storeroom, but I can only have fifteen minutes."

Kit followed her, Sam at her side.

Which somehow felt . . . right.

Only because he's good at his job. He'll make Julie feel better.

You are such a Lying McLiarface who lies.

Julie closed the storeroom door, the music immediately quieting.

Sam huffed a relieved breath. "Oh. Thank you. That's so loud."

Julie looked grim. "What's happened?"

Kit drew a breath. "I'm so sorry, Miss Sparks. Shelley Porter is dead."

"What?" Tears filled Julie's eyes. "No. She OD'd?"

"No," Kit said quietly. "She was murdered, probably Tuesday night."

Julie sagged, stumbling backward into the wall. Sam was at her side in a blink, helping her to a chair.

"Who did it? Who killed her?" She looked up, her eyes fierce through the tears. "Was it Ace?"

"We don't know," Kit said. "We were hoping you could give us information that would help us in our investigation."

Julie wiped her eyes with the back of her hand. "I don't know what you want to know."

Sam looked at Kit, wordlessly asking if he could take over. Kit gave him a nod.

"Julie," he said, "did you know if she was using since she got out of rehab?"

Julie nodded sadly. "I hated the drugs and what they turned her into. I tried to keep my distance because I didn't want to get dragged into her drama, but she's been my best friend since kindergarten. She asked to meet me here at the mall after my shift. That was the day she got out of rehab, so I did. She was high that night. One freaking day out of rehab and she was flying."

Sam sighed quietly. "Do you know where Shelley got the money for her drugs?"

Julie sighed. "She stole it from her mom and her aunt. Even from me. This was before rehab. That day after she got out of rehab, when I saw her high, I made her tell me where she'd gotten the drugs. She just laughed and said Jen had bought them for her. I knew that meant she'd stolen again. That was the last time I saw her. We talked on the phone a few times and texted after that, but I wouldn't see her in person."

Kit was disappointed. She'd hoped Julie would have more recent information. "Can we see your texts?"

"Yes, but she never admitted anything to me over text. She kept any mention of drugs off my phone because she knew I didn't approve. You might have better luck with the other people she was texting, because she was *always* texting someone. Did you find her phone?"

"We didn't," Kit said. Her killer had likely taken it.

"Did she keep her texts in the cloud?" Sam asked.

Whoa, Sam. Kit was more than impressed. *Good question.*

Julie nodded. "I think so. The night we met here at the mall, she'd just gotten a brand-new phone. I have no idea how she paid for it, but I went with her to the phone store—it's at the other end of the mall. I remember her telling them that transferring her stuff from the old phone to the new one would be quick, because she'd just backed up to the cloud."

Kit held her breath. "You wouldn't happen to know her cloud username and password, would you?"

Julie nodded, but reluctantly. "I don't know if I should tell you."

"It can't hurt her now," Sam said, so very gently. "It can only help us find her killer."

Julie swallowed audibly, new tears filling her eyes. "She never changed it in all the years we've had email accounts. Her user ID was her email." She spelled it out for them and gave them Shelley's password. "I hope I did the right thing in telling you."

"You did," Kit assured her, then realized she hadn't delivered all the bad news. "I'm sorry, but you should know that Shelley's mother was killed, too."

Julie closed her eyes. "Goddammit. Her mom was always nice to me." When she opened her eyes, they were full of misery. "Carol called me the day after I saw Shelley here at the mall. Begged me to help her. She knew Shell was using again. Ace dragged her back into it."

Kit wondered what else Ace had done. They'd have to find him. "Do you know his real name? It's not Ace Diamond."

Julie rolled her eyes. "Of course it isn't. The guy is as stupid as they come. Never was good for Shell. His name is Calvin Livingstone. Works at a butcher shop. He was her supplier. I'm sure of it."

"We'll find him," Kit said. "Thank you. Can I see your texts?"

Julie opened her phone and handed it over. "Go ahead."

Kit scrolled through the recent texts, noting the last one. "She texted you on Tuesday afternoon. Wanted you to go clubbing with her. You said you couldn't afford it."

"I said that because I didn't want to go. Mostly because she was using, but I didn't want to get into a fight with her, so I told her it was because of money."

Kit glanced at Sam. "Shelley tells Julie that she was coming into some cash and wanted to treat her."

"That cash is what got her killed, isn't it?" Julie asked sadly.

Almost certainly, Kit thought. "We don't know," she said, giving Julie back her phone. "But we'll find out."

Sam pressed a business card into her hand. "My boss is a good therapist. Call if you need someone to talk to. I can't talk to you because I'm working this case, but Dr. Carlisle will."

"I'll think about it. I've got to get back on the floor."

"Thank you," Kit said. "We'll be in touch if we have more questions."

"I hate doing that," Sam said when they were out of the store and could finally hear themselves think again. "How do you manage it?"

"I keep Snickers bars in my desk drawer," Kit said. "Sometimes chocolate is the only thing that soothes the sting."

"Where are you going next?" Sam asked.

Kit wished she had time to buy him dinner, but she didn't. "I have to get back to the precinct. Connor and I still have a ton of interviews to do and I need to get this login information to the computer guys. Are . . . are you gonna be okay?"

Sam nodded. "Yeah. I think I'll stop by Shady Oaks. I haven't seen Georgia and Eloise in a week. I'm overdue."

Kit smiled up at him. The elderly ladies at the retirement center were two of her favorite people. "Give them my best. Tell Georgia I still want to be her when I grow up."

The old lady was grumpy as hell, but wicked smart. And she adored Sam.

Sam chuckled. "She'll love that. Call me if you need me again."

"I will. Be safe, Sam."

"You too."

She watched him walk away, her stomach going all fluttery again. He was a very handsome man to begin with, with his dark hair and green eyes. And his Clark Kent glasses. But he looked equally good from behind.

Which was objectifying him, but somehow Kit didn't think he'd mind.

San Diego PD, San Diego, California
Sunday, January 8, 6:00 p.m.

"I heard you pulled the Munro case." Detective Bruce Goddard folded his tall frame into one of the chairs in the conference room that Kit's team had commandeered. "Can't say I'm jealous."

"We aren't happy about it," Connor said glumly.

"Same," Kevin Marshall grumbled, and his partner Alf Ashton grunted his agreement. Marshall and Ashton were the two detectives whom Navarro had assigned to run down leads on the Munro murder. And now the murders of Shelley and her mother Carol.

No one wanted this case, it seemed. Kit certainly didn't.

She sighed. "We have a million suspects and we haven't talked to any of them but the wife. We've spent all day tracking the trailer the killer used to get Munro and his Ferrari—"

"And his Rolex," Connor inserted.

Kit nodded. "And his Rolex out of the gated community."

"Well, we'll keep an eye out for chatter on the Ferrari and the Rolex," Goddard said, his Southern accent seeming thicker than normal, "but I wouldn't hold out a whole lotta hope. It's not a specialty collection, like coins and paintings. But we'll put out feelers at pawn shops and chop shops. Rolexes show up at pawn shops all the time. The Ferrari will probably be repainted and sold as-is."

"We were wondering if the killer might not just keep them," Connor said.

Goddard made a thoughtful face. "As souvenirs? Maybe. There was a lot of rage in that crime. Someone had a powerful need for revenge."

"Or someones," Kit said reluctantly. "The ME says it looks like a mob hit. Like, not the mafia, but a group of people."

"Lucky, lucky you," Goddard drawled. "We can put out feelers for the trailer, too. That's a loose end."

"It won't still be wrapped," Connor said. "That was a temporary way to hide it. Easy enough to remove it himself."

"Or herself," Kit murmured. "The mutilation of his genitalia may indicate a female doer. But Munro was a big man. Would be harder for a woman to drag him under that boulder in a windstorm."

"Unless she had a wheelbarrow," Goddard said.

"It's possible. Any tracks in the sand were long gone when Sam and I found his body. Or, more correctly, when our dogs found the body."

Goddard grinned. "So you and Sam finally had your date."

Kit frowned. Did everyone know about their date? "Kind of."

"Was it nice?" Goddard asked slyly. He was a shit-stirrer for sure. He'd asked Kit out, but Kit thought that was only because he'd wanted to nudge Sam into doing so himself.

Which made Kit feel protective of Sam. Another feeling she wasn't used to yet.

"It was very nice until we found a dead body," Kit said dryly. "Next topic, please."

Connor smirked, then sobered. "Were you able to get into Shelley Porter's cloud account?"

Kit nodded and brought Goddard, Marshall, and Ashton up to speed on their newest victims. "Jeff in IT got into her account. Shelley exchanged several texts with what turned out to be a burner phone. At this point it looks like she thought she was dealing with David Norton. The customer said that he was cash-strapped and that he'd give her the money for the wrap job in cash if he could pay in installments. Offered her sixty percent of the total for starters, which came out to about four grand. That had to have been a lot of money for an addict like Shelley making minimum wage at her aunt's auto body shop."

Goddard whistled. "That's a lot of money for most people."

"True enough," Kit agreed, not looking at Connor. She suspected that wasn't a lot of money for him, but she really didn't want to know for sure. "According to her texts with her boyfriend Ace, Shelley planned to leave town with the cash. She asked Ace to run away with her, but Ace told her no, that the money she'd be getting wouldn't last them a month on the road. Which surprised me, to be honest. From what I'd heard, he's a thug and would have snatched that money in a heartbeat. But in the texts, he tried to get her to stay."

"How did her killer get her cell phone number?" Marshall asked.

Kit sighed. "The body shop's call log shows that the burner number called their main line, and I assume he talked to Shelley. He might have gotten her number then. If he asked about paying on the side, she would have been happy to give him her cell so that her aunt didn't get suspicious. The first text from the burner number said, 'Hey, it's me. We talked on the phone about my wrap yesterday.'"

"Smooth," Goddard said. "Gave no names, so nothing to trip

himself up later. Does the body shop record their calls 'for quality assurance'?" He used air quotes.

"No," Kit said. "He must have known when Shelley would be there alone, and he had to have known she was the weakest link. We just need to figure out how."

"Security footage?" Goddard asked.

Marshall shook his head. "Ashton and I went to the body shop with CSU. The security cameras were spray-painted over, just like at Munro's house. So we got nothing there."

"Have you talked to this Ace person yet?" Ashton asked.

Kit shook her head. "He's our next stop. His real name is Calvin Livingstone."

"I'd call myself Ace, too," Goddard muttered. He rose, grimacing in pain. "I'll get right on trackin' the stolen goods. If you find out Munro's missing anything else, let me know."

"Will do," Connor said. "Why are you limping like that? You get hurt on the job?"

"I wish," Goddard said, disgruntled. "I went home to Louisiana for the holidays and my brother Liam tackled me in a game of football on New Year's Day. We both played ball for LSU back in the day, but he's kept his skills a little better honed than I have. Thought he'd busted my ACL at first, but it's just a knee sprain. He felt bad. Which I milked, of course."

Kit's lips twitched. "Of course. What did you get out of it?"

"Shrimp 'n' grits. Liam's a damn fine cook. He threw in some homemade pie in exchange for me not telling Mom." Goddard gave them a wave. "Later, guys. Call if you need me."

They watched Goddard limp away, all of them wincing along with him. Knee injuries were a bitch.

"I always want to hate that guy," Marshall said glumly. "He's got that Southern charm thing going on, and the women fall all over him. But he's too damn nice to hate."

Kit had to chuckle because she was pretty sure Sam felt the same way. "So, what have you found about this list of suspects?" She gestured to the whiteboard.

"All of them hated Munro's guts," Marshall said. "None of them have criminal records, and we're still working on the subpoena for his widow's financials. It's going to take a while, because her money is all tied up in a trust and her lawyer isn't cooperative."

"Wilhelmina said she'd stay until Munro is 'in the ground,'" Kit said. "So she's not going back east for at least a few days. Batra hasn't released the body yet, and I can ask her to delay as long as she can."

Ashton nodded. "Thanks. We started on the senders of the threatening emails he kept. The most threatening senders all have alibis for Wednesday night."

"We also got a list of contributors to his campaign," Marshall added. "We wondered if any of the contributions were actually payments for Munro getting charges dropped against people accused of crimes. Connor told us about what Munro tried to do to Sam."

"What an asshole," Ashton said. "Munro. Not Sam."

Kit huffed a laugh. "I knew what you meant." Nobody called Sam Reeves an asshole—it simply wasn't possible. "Were any of the contributions suspicious?"

"Not yet," Marshall said. "But there were some big hitters on that list. Lots of property developers and boards of directors of local charities. Makes me wonder what he promised them in exchange for their contributions." He slid a folder across the table to Kit. "These are the contributors in order of contributions. Deepest pockets at the top."

Kit scanned the list. Marshall was right. There were several familiar names on the list. In addition to developers and charity organizers, there were some of the city's wealthiest private citizens. "Have any of them received special consideration from the council in the last two years? Like, a building permit when it looked like they'd be refused? Or funding, like with New Horizons?"

"Not that we've found," Ashton said, "but we've barely started looking."

Kit set the list aside. "Munro had a lot of supporters. Was he looking to run for higher office?"

"Good question," Connor said. He added it to the list on the whiteboard. "The trailer with the landscaper's wrap is our most direct lead so far, so I say we keep going with that."

"Agreed." Kit checked the time. "I think we find Ace Diamond, a.k.a. Calvin Livingstone, then if it's not too late, pay Wilhelmina another visit to see if anything else is missing."

"Are you sure she'd tell you?" Marshall asked.

"I don't know," she admitted. "I still don't know that I trust her completely."

"Same," Connor said. "She and Rafferty tried really hard to seem transparent. They very well might be, but if I were in her shoes, I'd sure be tempted to hire someone to do away with my shitstain of a husband."

"He cheated on her, stole from her, and hit her," Kit explained to Marshall and Ashton. "She *said* that she was planning to file for divorce, but ending him with a hit man might have seemed like a more favorable alternative. For now, we'll focus on Ace. Hopefully he knows more about whatever transpired between Shelley and her killer. According to his record, he's got a recent conviction for drug possession and is currently on parole, so we may be able to leverage that to get him to talk if he clams up. I pulled his most recent address from his driver's license. If we can't find him there tonight, we'll try the butcher shop where he works tomorrow."

"Knives and butcher shops kind of go together," Ashton observed.

"Definitely true." Kit gathered her things. "He'd surely know how to make the fatal wounds that were done to Munro, and he's big enough to have dragged him to that boulder in Anza-Borrego. Do we still have the department car signed out, Connor?"

"We do. My turn to drive."

Kit smirked. "He's still annoyed that he had to sit in the back seat this morning," she told the others. "He rock-paper-scissored with Sam and lost, then whined about it for the rest of the morning."

"I'm too tall to get squished in the back," Connor grumbled. "Let's go. Happy paperwork, guys."

Ashton flipped Connor the bird as they left the conference room.

"Not the way to make friends and influence people," Kit said quietly.

Connor laughed. "Ashton was one of my instructors in the academy. It's my job to push his buttons now."

"Just don't make him so mad that he complains to Navarro, or we could be doing the paperwork ourselves next."

That knocked the grin off Connor's face. "Good point."

CHAPTER FIVE

Ace Diamond, a.k.a. Calvin Livingstone, was drunk off his ass.

He staggered back into his living room after opening his front door to Kit and Connor, and Kit had to clear her throat to keep from coughing at the smell of booze oozing from the man's pores.

"Maybe we should come back," Connor muttered. "This place reeks."

"Maybe he'll be more talkative," Kit muttered back.

"I can hear you," Ace said, grunting as he walked into a wall. "I'm drunk, not deaf."

"Why are you drunk, Mr. Livingstone?" Kit asked, venturing farther into the apartment that wasn't as trashy as she'd thought it would be. In fact, other than the empty bourbon bottle on the coffee table—and the six-pack of empty beer cans stacked in a pyramid beside it—the place was downright tidy.

Ace glared at her blearily. "Don't call me Livingstone. Name's Diamond. Ace Diamond."

"Okay, Mr. Diamond. Why are you drunk?"

He huffed. "Same reason you're here. Shelley. I saw it on the news."

Kit made a sympathetic noise. "We're sorry for your loss."

"Fuck off," he said with another grunt, managing to make it to the sofa, where he collapsed. "I don't know who killed her. I only know that I didn't."

Kit walked around the sofa so that she stared down at Ace. "She tried to get you to leave town with her."

Ace's head came up. "How do you know that?"

"We were able to access her cloud account," Kit said truthfully.

"How?" Then Ace blew out a breath that Kit could smell from where she stood. So much booze. "Julie," he muttered.

"Would you have told us?"

"Probably not. Shelley shouldn't have taken the money from that guy. I told her it was fishy." He opened one eye. "You didn't find any cash on her, did you?"

"Why do you want to know?" Connor asked from across the room. He was wandering around, seeing what Ace had left out in plain sight.

"Don't touch my stuff," Ace slurred. "I know my rights."

"Just staying upwind from your booze-a-thon," Connor said. "Why do you want to know about the cash? Did you have plans for it?"

"No! It's because I figure you didn't find any. That the bastard who killed her didn't plan to pay her at all. She died for nothing." The final words rushed out of his mouth on a ragged sob.

"What was she using?" Kit asked gently, playing good cop to Connor's bad cop.

"H."

Kit wanted to sigh. Heroin was a hard habit to break. "Julie said you were her supplier."

Ace opened his mouth, then closed it. A moment of silence passed while Kit waited him out. "I never sold to her. I gave it to her at first, but I stopped because I could see she was hooked. That's why she started stealing from her mom and her aunt, even before we both went into rehab. I tried to get her to stop."

"I saw that in your texts. You told her that money from the trailer wouldn't last her for a month."

Ace sighed. "It's the truth. She lived with her mom. She had no idea how much it costs to live on your own. Everyone thought I was a bad influence on her. They think I got Shell hooked, but it was the other way around. Shell got me hooked so that I'd score for her. I have a job. I make decent money, so she got me to buy it for her. When I stopped, she got mad. Said she'd find someone else to buy for her. She said she'd dump me if I didn't start buying for her again."

"Did that make you angry?" Kit asked, keeping her tone mild.

"Of course it did. But not so much that I'd ever hurt her. Look, I know that I look mean. I got tats. I swing a cleaver for a living, but I'm not . . . like that. I didn't hurt her. I'd never have hurt her." He swallowed hard. "Who killed her?"

"We're hoping you can help us find out," Kit said.

"What do you want to know?"

"Did she tell you who she was meeting Tuesday night?"

"No. She just said it was a customer who asked if he could get a discount if he paid her in cash. She was going to take the four Gs and run. She was fed up with her mom's rules, her aunt's rules. She wanted out." He sat up abruptly and groaned, holding his head. "Wait. Wait a minute."

Kit took a step back just in case the alcohol he'd consumed made a reappearance.

"Not gonna puke," he muttered. "Fuck, my head hurts."

"You drank a lot of booze," Kit said, hoping she sounded both sympathetic and judgmental at the same time. "You're lucky you're not kneeling in front of the toilet right now."

"Nah. Drank the beer first. Got a buzz. Beer on whiskey, mighty risky." He laughed, but it was more like a sob. "Whiskey on beer, never fear."

"Are you going to tell me something?"

Ace half snarled. "Gimme a minute. Brain's not . . . braining." He took a few deep breaths, then gasped softly. "Right. There's a camera. At her aunt's body shop."

That had been spray-painted over, just like the camera at Munro's house. "Not usable footage."

"Not the one that nerd Bran installed. The one *I* installed."

Kit hoped she hid her surprise. "Why did you install a camera at Jennifer's Body Shop?"

"Shell said that Bran had come on to her. That he groped her the day after she got out of rehab, when she went back to work. I was so fucking pissed at that nerdy piece of shit. But Shell lied a lot. I wanted to be sure before I punched his lights out."

"You installed a camera to check on Bran?"

"And Shell. I wanted to be sure she was okay. Bran never touched her, not that I saw. But Shell never knew about that camera."

"Where is the camera?"

"In the parking lot."

Yes. "You got the feed for those cameras?"

"On my laptop. It's in the bedroom." He lurched to his feet, weaving dangerously. "Fuck."

"Do you need me to walk you back there?"

"No. I know my rights. You need a warrant for that."

"We'll wait here," Kit promised. "Just don't fall and knock yourself unconscious. I need that feed."

Ace seemed to think that was hilarious. He laughed like a loon. "I might like you, except you're a damn cop."

"My heart is broken," she said sarcastically.

He just laughed some more.

Kit turned to Connor when Ace had closed his bedroom door. "Well?"

"He's either getting his laptop or a gun," Connor said dryly.

"His background check didn't turn up any registered guns," Kit said, moving her hand to her own service weapon—just in case.

"I can fucking hear you!" Ace shouted. "Still not deaf! Don't own a damn gun!" He reappeared, his laptop in his hand.

He plopped on the sofa again, squinting at the laptop screen. "Fuck, I'm wasted."

"You really are," Kit agreed. Gingerly, she sat next to him on the sofa.

Connor approached, his eyes never leaving Ace's hands. He still didn't trust the young man. Which was fine. Kit didn't completely trust him, either.

But if he had truly captured Shelley's killer on video, unaware? That was almost too good to be true.

San Diego PD, San Diego, California
Sunday, January 8, 8:15 p.m.

"Well, shit," Navarro said when Kit and Connor had finished playing the recording taken by Ace's cameras. They'd all gone to Sergeant Ryland's lab, where he had computers that he could safely use with an external drive of questionable origin.

The external hard drive belonged to Ace Diamond. He'd refused to give up his laptop, telling them to get a warrant.

Navarro pinched the bridge of his nose with a tired sigh. "Shelley Porter never had a chance. Rewind it and play it again."

Kit complied. The video was grainy and the audio wasn't amazing, but it was good enough to see—and hear—what had happened.

A Ford F-250 truck pulled into the parking lot of Jennifer's Body Shop at seven thirty on Tuesday night. It idled for a minute, the driver in the very edge of the frame. He wore a hoodie, obscuring his face.

"We put out a BOLO on the license plates of the truck," Connor said. "They were stolen last week. We'll get security footage from the cops who took the report from the owner of the plates, but I'm betting we see a guy in a hoodie again."

Said guy in the hoodie disappeared from the video frame for a moment, like he was reaching for something, then got out of the truck. He now wore the Halloween hockey mask he'd worn when he'd entered Munro's home.

"He's consistent," Navarro commented.

Because he'd also taken a can of spray paint and thoroughly covered the camera pointing toward the garage's extra-large door. It wasn't quite big enough for a semi-truck trailer, but big enough for the trailer that had driven in and out of Munro's neighborhood.

Shelley had opened the garage's bay door, taken one look at the man, and opened her mouth to scream. But he was ready for her, a gun glinting in the overhead lights.

He shoved the gun into her side. *"Give me the keys to the garage,"* he said, his voice muffled behind the mask.

Shelley dropped a set of keys into the man's hand. *"Don't hurt me. Just take the trailer and go."*

"You know too much. Sorry."

He didn't sound sorry at all.

Shelley's chin came up. *"My mom knows I was meeting you. If I don't come home, she'll call the cops."*

"That is a dilemma," the man said, his sarcasm thick. *"I guess Mama has to go, too."*

The man grabbed the piece of duct tape he'd stuck to the leg of his dark pants. Not jeans, but slacks. He pressed the tape to Shelley's mouth, then dragged the young woman to his truck, where he made quick work of restraining her wrists and ankles with zip ties.

He tossed her into the back seat of his truck, then stepped back, looking both ways to ensure he hadn't been seen. One of his hoodie sleeves had ridden up as he'd dispatched Shelley, and he tugged at the cuff of his long-sleeved shirt before pulling the sleeve of his hoodie past the cuff.

All of this was captured by Ace's camera but hidden from street view by the Ford truck. Shelley's muffled cries could be heard, but she couldn't be seen.

She wouldn't be seen again until Kit, Connor, and Sam discovered her body five days later.

The man closed the garage door with the trailer still inside, then drove away at seven thirty-five p.m., only to return forty-five minutes later.

"Time of Shelley and her mother's death was sometime between seven thirty-five and eight twenty," Connor murmured.

The man used the keys he'd taken from Shelley to open the garage door. He hooked the finished trailer to the hitch of his truck and drove it out of the garage before closing the garage door. And then he drove away.

"We requested street cam footage around Jennifer's Body Shop," Detective Marshall said. "It was one of the first things we did when we checked out the scene. We hoped he'd stop somewhere and get out so that we could get another look at his face, but he simply disappeared. It's like he knew where the cams were and took back roads, because we lost him. Didn't pick him up again until he drove into Munro's community early Wednesday morning."

"He has a working knowledge of the city," Navarro murmured. "And of its street cams."

Kit had thought of that. It was definitely something they could use to narrow their search.

"We can ask the public to come forward if anyone saw the trailer," Detective Ashton said, "but we'd be showing our hand."

"I want to know where he stayed Tuesday night," Navarro said. "That might be where he took Munro to do all the things he did. All the torture."

"And," Kit said, "if there was more than one person involved in the little stab fest, we might be able to identify them if we know where they went to do their little *Orient Express*. But Ashton's right. We'll show our hand. Your call, boss."

"We've already planned a press conference for tomorrow at ten a.m.," Navarro said. "We could make the announcement then. Are we sure that David Norton didn't have anything to do with this?"

Kit shook her head. "We aren't sure of anything except that Munro, Shelley, and her mother are dead, all were killed the same exact way, and that we have this hockey-mask guy on video twice—here and at Munro's."

"How did the boyfriend react to seeing this recording?" Navarro asked.

"He threw up," Connor said. "Barely made it to the toilet. It was not pleasant. I preferred the stink of stale booze to puke."

"I think he cared for her," Kit said. "I believed his story."

Navarro sighed. "What next?"

"We try to find out where the trailer spent Tuesday night," Kit said. "And we start investigating all our suspects. I think we start with William Weaver, the guy whose reputation Munro destroyed during the last election. Accused Weaver of pedophilia, which led to him losing his marriage, his family, his job, and his home. Of everyone on the list, he's got the most personal reason for revenge."

"And Ronald Tasker, the guy who's serving time now for chopping up his wife," Connor added.

Navarro nodded. "Tasker's the guy Munro wanted Sam to evaluate as being mentally unfit for trial."

"That's him," Connor said. "He couldn't have been the killer because he's behind bars, but he could have paid someone to do it."

"We'll visit William Weaver tonight," Kit said. "Then go to the prison tomorrow for Tasker. I also want to revisit Wilhelmina, see if her story's changed at all."

"It won't," Connor said confidently. "She had it down pat before we even got there. True or false, she'll stick with it."

Kit shrugged. "You're probably right. I'm kind of hoping to provoke Rafferty into spilling some tea. He seems to have a trigger temper."

"Can I be bad cop again?" Connor asked, looking so eager that Kit laughed.

"Knock yourself out," she said. "But I can be bad cop even when I'm being sweet."

Connor exaggerated a shudder. "You make grown men fear you."

"Damn straight."

Navarro just shook his head. "I have a raging headache, so I'm going home. Call me if you need me."

"Will do," Kit assured him. "We started at seven this morning with Sam, so we'll clock out after we speak to William Weaver."

Navarro lifted a brow. "Night shift sergeant said you were here at four a.m."

"I couldn't sleep. My brain was racing, so I came in. But I'll go home and sleep soon." She'd go to Mom and Pop's. It was Sunday and she'd missed family dinner, but her mother would have made her a plate.

She wondered what Sam was doing for dinner. He shouldn't be alone tonight, not after discovering three bodies in less than two days. Then she remembered he'd gone to see Georgia and Eloise. An evening at the retirement center always seemed to lift his spirits.

And that she was worried about how he was doing after such an emotional day? She'd freak out tonight when everyone else was asleep.

Kearny Mesa, San Diego, California
Sunday, January 8, 9:30 p.m.

William Weaver refused to let them into his apartment, a tiny little place in a not-so-great part of town. Considering he'd once owned a home in La Jolla and had been a respected professor, his social status had plummeted significantly.

Of all the people on the suspect list, Weaver had the biggest reason to want Munro dead. At least that they knew of so far.

"We can talk here," he said, leading them to a small picnic area outside his apartment building.

Though it wasn't a cold night, it was chillier than Kit liked. But at least Weaver hadn't completely shut the door in their faces.

"I've been expecting you," he said as they sat at a picnic table.

"Why?" Connor asked.

Weaver snorted. "Right. I've got to be at the top of your suspect list, considering I said in front of cameras that Munro would be sorry for what he'd done to me."

He'd given a press conference when he'd been formally cleared by the police of all child molestation charges three years ago, but not many reporters had shown up. The press conference hadn't been televised at all, and any print or online articles had been nearly impossible to find if one hadn't been expressly searching for them.

Which no one really had been. It was a sad fact of life that the media would splash a scandal on page one of the news and get it trending on social media, but a retraction was generally buried behind the obituaries.

"It might not have been your wisest move," Kit said.

Weaver shrugged. "I have literally nothing to lose at this point, Detective. My wife believed the lies. She took my children away. We have joint custody now, but I can see the doubt in my kids' eyes when it's my weekend. They come into my apartment, go straight to the room they have to share because a one-bedroom is all I can afford now, and I don't see them until their mother picks them up. When they do look at me, I see fear in their eyes and it guts me. Every single time. My wife has apologized for doubting me, but the damage has been done. I could never trust her to believe in me again." He exhaled wearily. "I'm suing the university for wrongful termination, but that's going to drag through the courts for years. No one will hire me in my chosen field. You know how I earn a living now, Detectives? Night shift at a convenience store. There is literally nowhere I can go, no job I can apply for, where the stink of Munro's false accusation doesn't follow me. Yes, I was cleared. But no one really believes it. Not enough to hire me."

"I'm sorry," Kit murmured. Because she was. She remembered the accusation and had wished the man to perdition for hurting children. Until she'd learned the charges had been dropped against him.

She'd questioned the move by the prosecutor's office at the time. It was far easier to believe the worst about someone than to believe they'd been purposely vilified.

Weaver sighed. "Thank you. Look, I'm glad the man's dead. I'm not going to lie about that. I hope he suffered. A lot. But I didn't kill him. I've led a boring life since my world fell apart. I go to work, come home, watch any old movies I can find for free on a laptop I bought used because the police destroyed the one they confiscated from me when they arrested me."

Kit winced. She'd read that in his file, too. The department owed this man some form of restitution, but she doubted he'd ever get it.

"Where were you on Tuesday evening, sir?" she asked. "Between seven and nine?"

A sad smile ghosted over his lips, leaving his eyes haunted. "One of my sons plays the violin and had a recital Tuesday night from seven to nine. The theme was New Year's Possibilities." His laugh was bitter. "I sat in the back. Left at eight forty-five. My son never knew I was there. But I couldn't miss it. I take whatever scraps I can get."

Bitter was nowhere close to what this man was feeling.

Kit couldn't say that she blamed him. "Did anyone see you there?"

"Yes, a few. One of the other parents saw me. Gave me a dirty look. Picked up his toddler and moved to another seat." He hesitated. "My ex-wife saw me, too. I'd hope that she'd tell the truth and confirm my alibi, but I don't know if she will."

"We'll ask her anyway," Kit said. "What about the music teacher?"

Weaver shrugged. "Her husband saw me. Wouldn't meet my eyes, but he knew I was there. When the last kid started to play, he leaned over my shoulder and asked if I'd leave. So that I didn't make a scene."

"Did you?" Connor asked.

"Of course. This was my son's evening. Not mine." He looked away, but not before Kit saw a tear streak down his cheek. "Nothing of his will ever be mine to share again." He cleared his throat, still looking away. "Did Munro suffer?"

Kit hesitated, then decided to tell the truth. "Yes."

"Good," he said on a hiss. "He's in hell now, I'm sure."

That's probably true.

Weaver's recital alibi covered the time of the murder of Shelley and her mother, but not the time of Munro's abduction.

"What about Wednesday, all day?" she asked. "Where were you then?"

"Wednesday I pulled a double because the day shift cashier got the flu. I was there from three o'clock on Wednesday afternoon until seven Thursday morning."

Both of his alibis would be easily confirmed. That took care of the time that Munro had been accosted in his home and he and his car removed in the landscaping trailer. Kit had to admit to being relieved on Weaver's behalf.

"Do you have any idea of who else we should be looking at, sir?"

"I think you need to follow the money," Weaver said. "Everyone knew that Brooks Munro was a kept man. But Wilhelmina had him on a short leash. He got an allowance—enough for living expenses and the occasional splurge, but nothing close to what he'd have needed for his lifestyle. He drove a Ferrari, for God's sake. Everyone assumed Wil bought it for him."

Kit studied him. "But you don't assume that?"

"No."

"Where do you think the money came from?" Connor pressed.

Weaver was quiet for a long moment. "I heard that he was taking bribes from developers," he said, still not looking at them. "But I'm sure you've heard those rumors, too."

Kit nodded. "We have. But you know something definitive." The man's body language screamed that he had details that he desperately wanted to pass on but for some reason was not doing so. When he remained silent, she asked, "How did you know he received an allowance?"

Weaver swallowed. "During the election I was suspicious of him. I . . ." He closed his eyes. "I hired a PI to gather whatever dirt he could find."

Kit wasn't too surprised. Politics was a nasty business. She was more surprised that Weaver hadn't used whatever he'd found to fight back when Munro circulated the accusations of child molestation. "What dirt did he find?"

"That he received an allowance of five grand a month. He paid for the Ferrari in cash. Stacks of it. One of his household staff allegedly said that he kept piles of cash in his safe. That's how he paid them—*allegedly*—so there was no paper trail."

"You keep saying 'allegedly,'" Connor noted.

"Because we didn't have proof," Weaver snapped. "If I'd had actual proof, I would have used it. And I did try, before you ask. I told the cops all of this, that I was being smeared, but Munro had friends in high places. I was ignored. My attorney advised me to stop publicly arguing and let him handle the case, so I did. Because by then, I was seriously afraid I'd go to prison. My marriage had already fallen apart and I'd been fired. All my savings either went to my wife in the divorce or to the attorney who did actually manage to keep me out of jail. I couldn't pay the PI at that point so he walked away." He exhaled. "I'm trying to move on."

"Which will be easier with Munro dead," Kit said.

"Yes."

It was said with simple certainty.

"How do you think Munro was supplementing his council income?" Connor asked. "Taking bribes from developers had to have been lucrative on some level, but was it enough to buy a Ferrari with cash?"

"I don't know, and that's the honest truth. But I do know he paid a lot of his bills with cash or money orders. I'd be surprised if you find much of a credit card trail."

"Did your PI manage to trace the source of this cash Munro was using?" Kit asked.

"I don't know. But by the time we got that far, I'd missed a few payments and he said he was deleting everything he'd gathered." Weaver scowled. "Do I think he really did that? No. But I was too busy defending myself by that point. I told my attorney that I'd hired a PI and he tried to get the information the man had gathered, but he was unsuccessful as well. And you can't talk to the PI. He's dead. Was shot while on a stakeout six months ago. I was finally ready to approach him again. I had a little money saved, enough to hopefully buy what he'd gathered, but before we could meet, he was killed. You should have the report in your department files."

"His name?" Connor asked, poised to write it down.

"Jacob Crocker."

They'd definitely be looking into him. "Who knew you were ready to meet with him?" Kit asked.

Weaver's smile was wry, like he'd already thought of the

possibility that Crocker had been killed because of their planned meeting. "My lawyer and Crocker. I trust my lawyer. I don't know if Crocker told anyone."

"How did you choose him?" Kit asked.

"Found him online. His rates were reasonable. I didn't tell anyone else. Once my life started to unravel, I would have used anything I could find against Munro. I didn't care how the information had been obtained. But by then it was too late."

"If Munro used money orders, there will be a paper trail," Kit said thoughtfully.

"He didn't buy them himself. His assistant did."

Kit tilted her head. "The same one he has now? Veronica Fitzgerald?"

"Yes. She's been with him for at least fifteen years. Long before he was married to Wilhelmina."

That was consistent with what Wilhelmina had shared. They hadn't talked to Veronica yet, having spent so much time tracking the landscaping trailer. They'd stop by city hall first thing in the morning, before they drove out to the prison to see Ronald Tasker.

"What do you think of Miss Fitzgerald?" Connor asked.

"She's fierce. Guarded Munro's privacy zealously."

"Anything between them?" Connor asked.

"I don't think so. She's got to be sixty."

"Munro's wife is sixty-one," Kit commented.

Weaver blinked. "I guess she is. Maybe he likes them older."

"Mr. Weaver, do you have anything more to tell us?" she asked.

"No, Detective. That's all."

She gave Weaver one of her business cards and Connor did the same. "Call us if you think of anything, no matter how small," she said.

She and Connor thanked him for his time and didn't speak

another word until they'd buckled their seat belts in the department car.

"We need to talk to Munro's admin ASAP," Kit said. "Especially if they were seeing each other outside of work."

"I don't know anything," Connor said as he drove away from the parking lot, "but I called my mom again before we left for Weaver's, and she said that Munro brought Veronica with him to a few country club events."

"Should we put your mom on the payroll?" Kit asked dryly.

"She would absolutely love that," Connor said fondly. "She's already told me that I can ask her for any information I need when it comes to 'that horrid man.'" He pitched his voice high in a poor imitation of his mother.

Kit had met the woman a few times and she was lovely, her voice melodious. A different kind of mom than Betsy McKittrick for sure. Susan Robinson had a cook and a maid, and Kit didn't think she'd ever gotten on her hands and knees to scrub a floor. But she clearly loved her family and would do anything for them. In that sense—the most important sense—she and Betsy were the same.

"We might need to pick her brain. That Munro brought his admin to country club functions is interesting. Munro's only been on the city council for seven years. Both Weaver and Wilhelmina said that Munro and Veronica Fitzgerald had worked together for fifteen years."

Back then, Munro had been in real estate development. Made some money, but nothing like he gained when he married Wilhelmina.

"I don't know. I'm sure we can verify that, though."

"Tomorrow," Kit decided. "My brain is tired."

"Thank God," Connor yawned. "How are you not falling asleep?"

"I will when I get home. That I guarantee."

"Where are you going?" Connor asked. "To the boat or McKittrick House?"

"McKittrick House. Snickerdoodle is there, probably being spoiled rotten by Rita, Emma, and Tiffany." Emma and Tiffany were the teenage girls her parents had begun fostering just before Thanksgiving. The girls hadn't trusted any of them right away. But Sam and her parents had quickly won them over. They were good kids, all of them. Kit was relieved they were all safe.

"Last week the three of them made dinner," she went on. "Gave Mom 'the night off.' The kitchen was a disaster, but they cleaned it up without complaining. Mom felt like a queen."

It made Kit feel guilty that she'd never offered to cook dinner for the family. Then again, she loved them too much to poison them with her awful cooking.

"She should," Connor said softly. "Harlan and Betsy change lives. Look, if you want to close your eyes, I'll wake you up when we get to your car."

She must have looked as tired as she felt. "Maybe I will. Just for a minute."

CHAPTER SIX

More pie, Sam?"

Betsy McKittrick didn't wait for his answer. A plate with a second generous slice of apple pie appeared before him, along with a pat on his shoulder.

After leaving Kit at the mall, he'd arrived at the Shady Oaks Retirement Village only to find Miss Georgia and Miss Eloise all dolled up and waiting to be picked up by Harlan McKittrick, having been invited for family Sunday dinner. The ladies had insisted he come along and he'd been unable to say no.

He hadn't really wanted to say no.

There was something so welcoming about McKittrick House. Entering the house was like being enveloped in the warmest of hugs.

And a fine evening it had been, too. Georgia and Eloise always blossomed around the McKittrick table. It had been only two months since they'd lost two of their dear friends at Shady Oaks, and getting out really improved their mood.

"You must give me the recipe for this pie," Eloise said.

Georgia sniffed. "Like you'd bake a pie."

Eloise gasped, affronted. "I'm an excellent baker."

Georgia shot her a pointed look. "Have you ever baked any-thing other than pot brownies?"

Eloise giggled, fluffing her blue hair. "Nope."

Suppressing a groan, Sam glanced at Betsy, whose lips were twitching. "I'm sorry," he murmured. "They tend to forget where they are sometimes."

Betsy patted his hand. "It's fine, Sam. We've had far worse said at this table."

Georgia harrumphed. "We do *not* forget where we are. At least I don't." She had the good grace to look embarrassed, though. "But I shouldn't have said that in front of children."

Tiffany scowled. "We're not children."

"We're fifteen," Emma added. "And Rita's fourteen."

Rita leaned forward. "Tell me more, Miss Eloise. Do you have a recipe?"

Eloise opened her mouth, then shut it with a snap, as if just realizing there were three impressionable teenagers hanging on her every word.

Rita laughed, the merry sound making Sam smile. The girl had been through so much, but she'd also blossomed since coming to live with the McKittricks.

Harlan just shook his head, sipping at his coffee. "Never a dull moment." Then he stiffened, checking his phone. "The entry alarm just buzzed. There's a car coming up the driveway."

Harlan and Betsy had added security features, including brand-new cameras, to give Rita piece of mind. She was nervous about the upcoming trial of her mother's murderer, which Sam completely understood. The man was a vile monster with far more money than morals, and Rita had been the one to accuse him. That he'd sexually assaulted her as well—and that he remained unaccused of that crime—was more of an issue, Sam thought.

"Hmm." Harlan pushed to his feet, a frown on his face. "I don't recognize the car. Who could be dropping by at this time of night?"

Rita had gone pale, so Sam squeezed her shoulder. "I'm sure it's nothing for you to be worried about. We'll just check it out."

"Don't get hurt," Rita whispered. "Not on my account."

"You're worth protecting, Rita," Sam said, wishing Drummond an eternity in hell. "But we won't get hurt."

Betsy put her arm around the girl's shoulders. "Go on, Sam. We'll start cleaning up the kitchen while you and Harlan check."

"And I heard you three took a trip to the animal shelter today," Eloise added in her chirpiest voice. "Did you find a dog?"

Sam left the girls to explain that, yes, they had found a dog and that they'd be picking him up in a few days, as he was being neutered on Tuesday. The dog had been Kit's doing, according to Harlan.

Harlan would do just about anything for his girls. Including standing in his driveway with a shotgun cradled in his arms.

Sam lifted his brows at the shotgun. "Prepared much?"

"Drummond's made a cloaked threat against Rita. Nothing that could get him in any trouble, but enough that I told Joel right away. Sent her a letter saying that he hoped she enjoyed the play she and the other girls were doing at school. Just to let us know he's watching her. Joel says he can't trace the letter to Drummond. I want to kill the bastard myself."

Sam understood that. That Drummond had gotten out on bail had infuriated him nine months ago. He was free as a bird until his trial. "Does Rita know?"

"Yeah. She read the letter first and immediately brought it to me, nearly hysterical with fear. I ordered the cameras that same day. One of my kids owns a security company. He installed an alarm system the next day and set up the cameras this morning."

Harlan and Betsy had been fostering for so many years that their "kids" had grown up and now worked all over the city. They had a chef, the captain of a fishing boat, a Subaru salesman—which was why all of them, including Kit, drove Subarus—and, of course, a decorated homicide detective. That a security expert was part of their sprawling family came as no surprise.

"You can go inside," Harlan added. "I'll wait."

The car was winding up the long driveway. "I'm not leaving you out here alone, Harlan. Wait a minute . . ." Sam squinted at the approaching sedan. "I think that's the SDPD car Connor checked out this morning."

Harlan tensed. "Why is Connor here this time of night?"

Kit. It had to have something to do with Kit. *She's okay,* Sam told his suddenly racing heart.

Facing down a potential threat to Rita hadn't scared him. But that something had happened to Kit? That terrified him.

"I'm sure she's fine," Sam murmured, more to convince himself than Harlan.

"She can take care of herself," Harlan said, but he sounded as unsure as Sam had.

Sure enough, when the car stopped, Connor Robinson got out, a finger pressed to his lips.

"She fell asleep when I was driving back to the precinct," he whispered. "She was heading back here tonight, so I just brought her."

"She was in the office early this morning," Sam said quietly. "I got there at seven and she'd already been there for hours."

Harlan sighed. "It's coming up on the anniversary. She always works too many hours in the months leading up to April."

The anniversary of Wren's murder. That went without saying for anyone who knew Kit.

"I know," Connor said, then pointed to the shotgun. "What's with that?"

"Threats to Rita," Harlan said.

Sam left the two of them to discuss Rita's safety, going around to the passenger side of the department sedan. He opened the door and crouched so that he looked up at Kit. She was sound asleep, her face softer than usual. The frown lines were smoothed over and Sam wished he could make it so that those lines would never reappear. But they were as much a part of Kit as her sharp wit and tender heart.

She looked so peaceful that he hated to wake her, but she couldn't stay out here all night.

"Kit?" He gently jostled her shoulder. "Time to wake up."

He thought she'd jolt awake, disoriented or irritated. Instead, her eyes slowly opened and she smiled at him.

His heart was in free fall. She'd never smiled at him like that before.

Then her eyes widened and she sat up so fast that the seat belt engaged and she was thrown back into the seat. "What?"

Sam chuckled. "Let me help." He reached over her and popped the seat belt latch. "You fell asleep. Connor brought you home."

She drew a breath, the frown returning, and suddenly she was his Kit again, prickly and a little bit dangerous. And what did that say about him that he liked prickly and dangerous?

"That little shit," she muttered. "He made it so that someone will have to drive me in tomorrow morning and he knows I won't make Pop take me in as early as I'd go in myself."

Sam laughed. "I think you're rubbing off on Connor. He's gotten sneaky."

Kit's eyes narrowed but then she laughed, too. "I guess I'm a good teacher. What're you doing here?"

But it wasn't said with any ire. Just mild curiosity.

"Your folks had invited Georgia and Eloise for dinner. I was dragged in their wake."

"What was for dinner?"

He held out his hand. "Come and find out. I bet your mom has already made you a plate."

"Sucker bet." She took his hand and let him pull her to her feet. "I guess I was more tired than I thought." She took one look at the shotgun in Harlan's hand and her eyes widened once more. "Why does Pop have a gun?"

"Christopher Drummond's threats against Rita. We didn't recognize the car."

Kit scowled. "That motherfucker. Thinks he can scare a little girl out of testifying against him in court. I want to smash his face in."

"I want to help you."

She closed her eyes on an exhale and when she opened them up, she was calm and collected once again. "Hey, Connor."

Connor stopped talking to Harlan and slowly turned to face her, the sudden fear on his face a thing of beauty.

Sam waited for Kit to flay Connor alive with her sharp tongue, but instead she smiled sweetly.

Connor took a step back. "You were tired."

"Oh, I know. And I'll be sure to repay your kindness someday."

Connor frowned. "I don't know if that's thanks or a threat."

Harlan's laugh boomed in the night. "The second one, son. Definitely the second one."

"That's what I thought," Connor said with a sigh. "Just . . . leave me pretty, okay? CeCe likes my face."

Kit chuckled. "Okay. Go home, Connor. I'll see you in the office tomorrow. Eight sharp. I'll catch a ride in with Pop." She linked her arm through Harlan's and gestured for Sam to follow them into the house. "Is the shotgun loaded?"

"Yep. Never know when I'll have to shoot a snake."

Kit sighed. "Don't shoot unless your life's in danger, okay? There are some things I can't clean up."

"Understood." Harlan dropped a kiss on Kit's head.

She leaned into him. "Go on in. I need to talk to Sam about some interviews."

Harlan's chuckle was a little wicked. "Is that what the kids are calling it now?"

"Pop! I'm serious. Jeez." Flustered, Kit shooed her father into the house. "Sorry about that," she said to Sam.

"I'm not," he answered, and he could see her blush in the porch lights.

She looked so young and carefree when she blushed. He resolved to make it happen as often as he could.

"Are you busy tomorrow morning?" she asked.

Sam checked his phone calendar. "I have a morning appointment with a client, but it's early. I'll be done by eight thirty. My next appointment isn't until one in the afternoon. Why?"

"We're doing two interviews tomorrow that I'd like your help with. One is Munro's admin. She's worked for him for fifteen years and we suspect that there's more to their relationship than just boss/admin."

"If they were romantically involved, she might be willing to do a lot to shield his crimes," Sam said thoughtfully.

"Exactly. I'd like you to observe. We'll test her grief, try to get under her defenses. I want your take on the veracity of what she gives us."

"Done. What's the second interview?"

"Ronald Tasker at the prison."

Sam hated prison visits. He especially hated the thought of visiting Ronald Tasker. But of course he'd go. "You think he'll talk to you?"

"I don't know. From what I've read about him, he doesn't respect women. Again, I'm hoping to get under his defenses. He knows something about Munro. Even if it's only how Munro makes these under-the-table deals, that would be helpful. We talked to William Weaver tonight. I think he knows more than he's saying, but he got the information in a less than legal way. He's determined to stick to the straight and narrow now since he had such a *pleasant* experience with SDPD last time."

The sarcasm rang heavy in her voice, surprising Sam. "You believe Weaver's innocent?"

"I don't know. But if he is, his life's been ruined for no reason other than Munro's lust for power."

"Such a small fiefdom, too," Sam said. "It's not like Munro was a U.S. senator. He was a city councilman, for God's sake."

"But he was apparently making a buttload of cash somewhere, and that's something he didn't want to give up. I'm hoping Munro's admin can shed some light on where the cash was coming from. Can we pick you up at eight forty-five? Does that give you enough time after your client?"

"I'll be ready. Now, let's go inside so you can eat your dinner and I can stop Miss Eloise from giving Rita her pot brownie recipe."

Tall, blond, and willowy, Munro's office admin looked an awful lot like Wilhelmina Munro, Kit thought as she, Connor, and Sam filed into the woman's office.

Veronica Fitzgerald's eyes were red-rimmed and swollen. Either she had the world's worst allergies or she'd been crying for a long time. She'd tried to cover up the damage with elegantly applied makeup but had been largely unsuccessful.

Veronica sat at her desk and rested her folded hands on its surface. "How can I help you today?"

She'd flinched when she'd been introduced to Sam. It appeared that the woman remembered that Sam had visited Munro, even though the meeting had taken place at Munro's house. And, from her reaction, she might just fear what Sam had said about the meeting.

Good. Kit wanted Veronica off her stride.

Kit smiled. "We have a few questions about Mr. Munro's business associates."

Veronica lifted one heavily tweezed brow. "He's a city councilman, Detective. He interfaces with many businesses around the city. To which associates do you refer?"

"He *was* a city councilman," Kit said, playing bad cop to the hilt.

It worked. Veronica flinched again.

"No need to be cruel, Detective," she murmured.

"I'm sorry for your loss," Kit said, and on some level she was. Veronica Fitzgerald had clearly cared for Munro.

Veronica glared. "Get to the point of this visit."

"I told you. We're here to ask about your former boss's business associates." Kit took out her phone and opened the

Notes app. "City council wasn't Munro's only job. He spent too much money for that."

Veronica's eyes hardened. "He had a rich wife."

Ooh. Ouch. Veronica did not like the rich wife at all.

"She had him on an allowance," Connor said with a faux-awkward smile. "I can't imagine he liked that too much."

Veronica turned her glare on Connor. "I wouldn't know."

Oh, I think you do. Kit made a point of scrolling through her notes. "You two were . . . *together* for fifteen years. Is that correct?"

Veronica's eyes flashed in anger. "He was my employer, yes."

"And you followed him to the city council from his earlier business endeavor," Kit pressed.

"I did."

"So you know his business associates from at least the past fifteen years."

Veronica smiled coldly. "From *before* his tenure on the council, yes."

"May we have a list of those associates?" Kit asked.

Veronica blinked. "You want his old client list?"

"I do," Kit said evenly. "He was going to be out of office in a year due to term limits. Surely, he had to be planning for what came next. Especially as his rich wife was going to divorce him."

Veronica's eyes flashed again, but this time in what appeared to be pain. "I think it would have been far easier for her to kill him, don't you agree, Detective?"

"I don't know," Kit said honestly. "Do you think she killed him?"

"She had motive," Veronica said bitterly. "She certainly had the means."

Kit stared the woman in the eye. "She has an alibi."

"She could have hired someone to do it."

"We're keeping all avenues of investigation open," Kit said. "Which is why we are asking for his business associates."

"No one else hated him," Veronica said, her expression daring Kit to disagree.

"Oh," Connor said softly, "I think a great many people hated him. He got all kinds of hate mail. As his admin, I'm sure you knew this."

"Many of his constituents had complaints, but he was a stellar councilman. He worked tirelessly for his district."

"Maybe you could give us your copies of the constituent complaints?" Connor asked, even though they'd already taken Munro's file of complaints from his home office on Saturday night. "It would help us find out who killed him."

"Absolutely." She pulled a key from her pocket and rose to open a five-drawer filing cabinet in the corner of the office. She withdrew a large file folder and quickly relocked the drawer. "Here you are, Detective."

"And now the list of business associates," Kit said with a note of impatience.

Veronica sat at her desk, glaring at Kit once again. "I told you that there are no business associates."

"What were his plans for next year?" Kit asked. "After his term was over?"

Veronica swallowed. "He was going to see the world."

That was an unexpected reply and one that seemed to cause Veronica pain.

Kit tilted her head. "With you?"

"No. We weren't . . . it wasn't like that."

"That's not what I heard," Kit said. "I heard that you were his date to many country club events. That you danced cheek to cheek. Very cozy."

Veronica's cheeks darkened. "Those people are gossips. Yes, I attended because his wife couldn't be bothered to. We went as friends. Nothing more."

Kit wondered if Veronica really believed that Wilhelmina couldn't be bothered, or if that was the line that Munro had fed her.

"Well, that's good," Kit said, waiting until Veronica relaxed a fraction. "Because the country club set said you were far too trashy a date. That you couldn't hope to match his social status."

Veronica's jaw tightened. "I don't care what the gossips say."

"Well, that's good," Kit said again. "Because they say that Munro was about to be thrown out. Nonrenewed, I think the term was. Connor?"

"Nonrenewed is fine," he said mildly.

Veronica's chest rose and fell more quickly. "Not true. As long as he paid them money, they were fine with him."

"There are rules of conduct," Connor said with a shrug. "Munro didn't follow them. Rumor has it that he was going to be asked to leave quietly. And if he didn't, they'd revoke his membership and instruct security to make sure he didn't return."

Veronica's eyes narrowed. "You're lying."

Of course they were. But the woman believed them. Kit could see it in her expression.

Kit shrugged. "Just telling it to you like it was told to us. Munro was not well liked anywhere. His constituents hated him, his social set barely tolerated him, and his rich wife was going to divorce him. And you still haven't answered how he was able to afford his lifestyle on the small allowance his wife paid him."

"I wasn't involved in any of Mr. Munro's outside endeavors," Veronica snapped. "If he had plans for after his council term was ended, I didn't know about them."

Sam spoke up quietly. "I thought you said he was going to see the world." He paused, his voice so kind. "It was going to be with you, wasn't it?"

Veronica's eyes filled with tears. "I have work to do. Please leave."

Kit gestured back to the chair when Sam started to rise. "We'll leave when the interview is finished, Dr. Reeves." He stilled. The command left her feeling . . . unsettled inside. She didn't dislike playing bad cop, but she didn't want Sam to witness it. "Miss Fitzgerald, you were his closest colleague for fifteen years. I think you were romantically involved. I'd think you'd want us to find out who stabbed him twenty-five times, chopped off his fingers and toes, and left his body in the desert to be eaten by animals."

Veronica had paled. "What?" she whispered.

Kit had her now. "Yes. He was tortured, his body mutilated. Someone had to have hated him a great deal to inflict so much damage. And pain, ma'am. He was alive for most of it, if not all of it. I'd think that you—as his trusted colleague and likely romantic partner—would want us to find those responsible and put them in prison for the rest of their lives."

Tears leaked from Veronica's eyes, streaking her makeup. "*Those* responsible? *Their* lives?"

"Our medical examiner has theorized that he was stabbed by multiple hands. If you know anything, this is the time to tell us." Kit softened her tone, just a fraction, hoping to set the hook. "We need your help."

Veronica shook her head, the movement jerky. "I don't know anything. Please leave."

Kit stood. "We'll be back. You know something and we *will* find out what that is."

With a shaking hand, Veronica wrote a single name on a notepad and ripped the paper free. "My attorney. All further communications should go through him."

Kit took the paper and nodded. "As you wish. Gentlemen? We'll see ourselves out."

Kit left the woman's office, followed by Connor and Sam. Kit didn't look at Sam. Didn't want to see the censure in his eyes. The disappointment. Because he was good and kind.

And I am not.

Veronica closed the door sharply, quieter than a slam but the sentiment was the same.

When Sam and Connor started for the stairs, Kit held up a hand, beckoning them to return. Holding a finger to her lips, she cocked her head toward the door.

From within Veronica's office came the sounds of retching and a single, brutal sob that was immediately silenced.

A minute followed, an entire minute. Kit was counting in her head. And then, Veronica's voice, urgent and thick with tears.

"The cops were just here. They know."

A pause.

"I don't know what they know, but it's *something.*" Another pause. "No, I haven't found it yet, and I've searched. They've sealed his office up—both here and at his house. I can't look for it in either place. We need to get out of here. Today." Another pause, shorter this time. "I'll make the arrangements. Just be ready."

Kit met Connor's eyes. He looked satisfied, like he'd expected something like this. She still couldn't bring herself to look at Sam.

More silence followed, and when it became clear that Veronica's conversation was over, Kit led them to the stairs and out the front door, dialing Navarro as she walked.

"We need eyes on city hall ASAP," she told her boss. "I'll

bring you up to speed when we're in a secure location, but get someone over here as soon as humanly possible. We'll wait in our car until they arrive. I'll call you back in a few minutes." She ended the call with Navarro, then glanced at Connor. "Would you mind bringing the car up to the front? I need to see if there's a back entrance she can slip through."

Connor saluted with a grin. "C'mon, Sammy. You can ride shotgun. Let Kit get the back seat this time."

From the corner of her eye, she saw Sam give her a careful look before silently following Connor to the car.

She'd been a bitch to Veronica Fitzgerald, but that was required from time to time. More often than Kit would like to admit. Normally she didn't give interviews like this one a second thought, but . . . dammit. She hated that Sam had seen that ugly part of her. She hated even more that she cared so much.

Shaking off the feeling of disquiet, she went back inside and found the uniformed guard. He'd been watching them outside and didn't seem surprised to see her again.

"Back so soon, Detective?"

His name tag said **D. MACEK**. He was an older man, about the same age as her father.

She offered him a small smile. "Can you tell me how many exits this building has?"

"More than you and the other two can watch by yourselves," he said, his tone indicating that he knew why she was asking or at least wasn't surprised by the question. "Everyone is supposed to file through here on their way in and out, but there are emergency exits, of course."

"Of course." Kit found she'd shoved her hand in her pants pocket, her thumb rubbing the cat-bird carving that Harlan had given her nearly a year ago. "You don't seem surprised that I'd ask."

"Because I'm not. I figured you'd be in to talk to Fitzgerald at some point today. I hear the rumors, Detective. A lot of people liked Munro. He could be very likable and a lot of the women admired him. But I think that Munro was rotten to the core and that admin of his was up to her eyeballs in it with him."

"Are you a retired cop?" Because he sure sounded like one.

"Twenty-five years on the force. Got this job because retirement was a lot more boring than I'd expected."

"What can you tell me about Munro and Fitzgerald, sir?"

"Nothing concrete. You know that he drove a Ferrari—the one that's missing. That was in the newspaper. But she also drives a fancy car, and the other admins talk about the trips she takes to the Caymans several times a year. She also gets deliveries from a lot of upscale stores. She lives well. Which, y'know, isn't a crime, but . . ." He shrugged.

The mention of the Caymans was interesting. That was a long way to fly when there were beach destinations so much closer to San Diego. Money laundering was Kit's first thought. Lots of offshore banking happened in that part of the world. "When was her most recent trip to the Caymans?"

He frowned. "I'm thinking it was in October. I overheard two of the other admins complaining about her getting special treatment, what with all the vacation time she takes. It's more than the others get—and they compare notes. One of the women said that Fitzgerald made some noise about a friend having a time-share there that they had to use or lose. Which, y'know, could be true, but . . ." Another shrug.

"Do you remember which admins were talking about her?"

He snorted a quiet laugh. "All of them. They say she's self-important and a real bitch. Some of them are jealous that she works for Munro because they wish they did, but others have been shredded by her sharp tongue. I don't one hundred percent remember who made the comment about her vacation, but if I do, I'll tell you."

"Thank you, sir. Have you had any media in here today?" She was specifically thinking of Tamsin Kavanaugh, the reporter who'd been having an affair with Munro.

Macek rolled his eyes. "They were all over the place at the end of last week when he went missing. I thought they'd be back in force today, since his body was found on Saturday, but so far they've only been hanging around outside. Doing reports with the building in the background. Sound bites, that kind of thing."

"Do you remember any media visiting here in the past? Asking to see Councilmember Munro?"

"Oh." He scowled. "You're asking about Tamsin Kavanaugh."

Kit had to fight back a smile at his aggrieved expression. It appeared that Mr. Macek shared her dislike for that woman. "She visited?"

He gave her an impatient look. "I think you know about that already. The two were going at it hot and heavy a few years ago. Afternoon delight in his office and all that. The staff all over the building knew. That woman would leave here with a smirk."

"You didn't approve?"

"He was married. And Kavanaugh's . . . well, she's just awful. I'm not sure what Fitzgerald thought about it, although that was heartily discussed, let me tell you. Admins, council staff, even guys in the mail room. Everyone had an opinion. It couldn't have made Fitzgerald too happy, having to share him."

"So Fitzgerald and Munro were involved?"

"Of course. Everyone knew about that, too. Fitzgerald is this ice queen. Holds herself like she owns the earth. Never threw herself at Munro like the Kavanaugh woman, but they were totally doing it."

"Did you see them in the act or is that your opinion?"

"My opinion based on twenty-five years as a cop."

"It does seem . . . convenient that she followed him here from their old job."

"Exactly. They both seemed to be living a good life. Fitzgerald looked like ground hamburger this morning, she'd been crying so hard. I was surprised to see her here, honestly. I thought she would have taken the day off. I didn't think she'd let us see her that torn up."

Kit thought that Veronica Fitzgerald had probably come in to search Munro's office for whatever it was that she'd been unable to find. "Can you call me if you think of anything else, even if it's not concrete?"

"Absolutely. And for now, I can have my guys watch the monitors. If anyone leaves through any door other than that one"—he pointed at the front door—"we'll let you know."

"Thank you, Mr. Macek."

"You're welcome, Detective McKittrick."

Connor had the car waiting at the curb, so she jogged over and slid into the empty back seat. She couldn't avoid looking at Sam any longer. He was in the front passenger seat, twisted so that his gaze was locked on her face.

She readied herself for the disappointment. But there was none in the green eyes behind his Clark Kent glasses. They were clear and filled with respect.

Kit exhaled. "You okay, Sam?"

"I was going to ask you the same question. You had to be hard on her in there. Can't have been easy."

So he understood. She was nearly dizzy with the flood of relief. "Not my warm and fuzzy side."

"Your awesome side," Connor corrected. "Now, all awesomeness a*side*—get it?—we owe the boss a call back."

Sam listened quietly as Kit and Connor brought Navarro up to speed with what they'd learned from Veronica Fitzgerald and the security guard.

None of what they were saying surprised Sam at all. He'd known Veronica was a snake from the moment he'd first interacted with her, back when he was trying to schedule a meeting with Munro about the New Horizons funding. The woman oozed arrogant malice.

No, what had surprised Sam was Kit's reluctance to meet his eyes as they'd left Veronica's office. She'd consciously avoided him. And when she did look at him, her eyes had been filled with something close to fear. And shame.

She'd thought he'd disapprove of her tactics with Veronica Fitzgerald. That he'd thought her too rough on a clearly grieving woman. The opposite was true. He'd known what kind of woman Veronica was and Kit put exactly the right kind of pressure on her.

They'd waited outside city hall until several unmarked cars had arrived. Leaving them to guard the exits—and to follow Veronica when she inevitably made her escape—Connor had begun their drive to the prison where Ronald Tasker was serving life without parole for murdering his wife.

Sam was wary about meeting the man face-to-face. He had, after all, been the reason Tasker had stood trial.

Well, that wasn't true. Tasker had stood trial because there had been enough evidence for the prosecutor to charge him. But had Sam caved to Munro's demands, Tasker could have gone for an insanity plea. Still not pleasant, but not nearly as bad as a murder charge.

Sam wasn't looking forward to this interview.

He pushed the concerns away and turned around in his seat to study Kit, who was bringing the call with Navarro to a close.

"If you can get us a search warrant for Fitzgerald's office and home, that would be great," Kit was saying. "The evidence is light, but it's worth a try."

"The three of you heard her say she'd searched for something that belonged to Munro," Navarro said, "and that she and her caller had to get out. I think it's at least enough for a search warrant for her suitcases if she tries to run. I'll let you know when I have it. With all the focus on this case, I think I can push it through quickly if I get the right judge."

"Thank you, sir. We'll continue with our plan for the day. We're a few minutes from the prison."

"Tasker's something of a loose cannon," Navarro cautioned. "I'm not pinning great hopes on what he'll give you."

"We at least have to talk to him." She ended the call and sighed. "He's right, you know. Tasker isn't going to tell us anything."

"It's not like we can even offer him anything," Connor grumbled. "Guy's serving life without parole."

"There's always something they want," Sam said quietly. He hoped. "Can we talk about Veronica Fitzgerald before we see Tasker?"

Kit's gaze twitched away, then slowly returned. Sam could almost feel the effort it took her to meet his eyes. The fear was gone, but the shame was still there and that could not stand.

"What about her?" she asked.

"You asked me to be a part of this for my opinion, but you never asked me what I thought about her."

Connor glanced at him briefly before returning his eyes to the road. "What did you think?"

Kit drew a breath. "Yes. What did you think of Veronica Fitzgerald?"

"She's a snake. I think you could have been rougher with her."

Kit's mouth dropped open. "What?"

He almost laughed but didn't dare. Kit seemed too fragile at the moment. "You were rough on her, giving her the list of Munro's injuries like you did, but I think you could have gone further. You never mentioned the damage done to his genitalia."

As if on cue, Connor winced. "Fuck," he muttered.

"Yeah, well, not my favorite topic, either," Sam admitted, "but it's a reality of this case. Seeing as how they were almost definitely involved—sexually if not also romantically—I think that could have enraged her into saying something. I mean, they were together for fifteen years."

Kit's mouth was working but no sound emerged.

Connor smirked, looking at his partner in the rearview mirror. "You broke her, Sammy."

"I doubt that. It would take a lot more to break Kit McKittrick." He sighed. "Did you think I couldn't take seeing you play bad cop?"

"No," she finally said. "I knew you could take it. We did it to you, after all."

They had. When he'd been suspected of murder nine months before. He'd had the same reaction as Veronica Fitzgerald after his interview. He'd barely made it to the bathroom before he'd thrown up everything he'd eaten that day.

"True enough. I knew about Veronica before we walked into her office. She gave me the runaround when I was trying to make an appointment with him over the summer, when New Horizons's funding was up for a vote."

Kit's eyes were suddenly sharp. "What did she say to you?"

Good. Kit was back. "Said he was a busy man, that he didn't have time for such matters. Said that I might be able to get on his calendar . . ." He trailed off, the details of the conversation coming back in a rush. "Well, shit. She was shaking me down."

Kit leaned forward as much as her seat belt would allow. "What do you mean?"

"She said I could get on his calendar several weeks from my call, but that would have been too late. I told her that, and she said that campaign donors could 'sometimes be worked in.'" He used air quotes. "She was trying to shake me down for a campaign contribution. At the time I didn't think anything of it other than she seemed sleazy, but I wonder how many people had to pay to see Munro."

Kit frowned. "Why would she be able to ask for a donation to begin with? He's not running again. He's not allowed. Term limits."

Connor held up a finger. "What if he had higher aspirations? State senate or even higher than that? Remember that list of campaign donors that Marshall and Ashton found in his files? A number of those donations were recent, like within the past few months."

"Let's check that out, then." Kit typed it into her Notes app. "I almost wish you'd paid her, Sam, so we could know what she would have done with it. If it was a simple shakedown and not a contribution, there would have been no paper trail."

"We can search his calendar," Connor said. "Check the people he did meet with before he disappeared, find out if any of them paid to play."

"What a dirtbag," Sam muttered.

Kit met his eyes, one side of her mouth lifted in an almost-smile. "Yeah, well, we knew that already."

Everything was now back to normal. The reticence was gone,

along with the shame. Sam was relieved, but he still wanted to talk to her about what had happened in Veronica's office.

But not with Connor around. This was private. He'd wait until they were alone.

She was tapping on her phone again, her brows furrowed. "San Diego has limits to how much city council members can accept from any one individual. It's not much. Munro would have needed over three hundred donors giving the max to buy that Ferrari."

"And, again," Sam said, "there would be a money trail. Candidates aren't allowed to use campaign funds for personal expenses like that."

Kit pursed her lips. "Or there were other 'donations' that were never recorded. Simple shakedowns. I wonder what Fitzgerald was doing on all those trips to the Caymans?"

"Offshore banking," Sam said with a sigh. "Why is it always a secret bank account?"

"So they can buy Ferraris," Kit said lightly. "Everyone would have just thought it was a gift from his rich wife. Only Wilhelmina would know differently."

"*Was* the car a gift from Wilhelmina?" Sam asked as Connor pulled up to the guard shack at the prison.

Connor showed his ID and they passed through. There would be a more rigorous identification process inside the prison walls. Sam really hated going to the prison. He'd been here several times over the years, meeting with clients, but every time it gave him the creeps. He knew that he was helping people and that the work was worthwhile, but the sound of those slamming doors never failed to shake him up.

Connor shook his head. "Her caretaker—Rafferty—told us that Munro had bought the car himself."

"Maybe Rafferty didn't know," Kit said thoughtfully. "Maybe Wilhelmina didn't tell him. He would not have approved."

"Good point," Connor said. "We need to pay another visit to Mrs. Munro and ask her questions with Rafferty outside the room." He found a parking place and turned off the engine. "Let's get this visit over with. I hate this place."

"So do I," Sam muttered, then turned to Connor. "Can you give us a minute? We can meet you in the lobby."

Connor's brows lifted but, to his credit, he asked no questions. "Sure thing." He handed Sam the car keys. "Lock up. Not a great neighborhood."

With a chuckle at his own joke, Connor was out of the car and headed for the prison's front entrance.

Sam drew a breath and met Kit's eyes. "Why did you think I'd be upset about your interview with Veronica Fitzgerald?"

Kit sighed. "I . . . I guess I didn't want you to think I was . . ." She shrugged. "Mean. I guess there are good reasons not to date coworkers."

Sam felt a frisson of fear dance down his spine. "We're not coworkers. We're . . . colleagues."

Kit huffed. "Po-tay-to, po-tah-to."

"No." Sam shook his head because the thought of not working with her was overshadowed by the thought of having to walk away from dating her. "I'm a consultant. And I know what you do. I know how you have to do it. And today I think you held back because of me. All that I'm saying is you don't have to hold back. Do your job. I won't think less of you."

"You don't know that."

"Kit. You *arrested* me. Your old partner threatened to *shoot* my *dog*."

"Baz wouldn't have done that."

"*I* didn't know that at the time." Sam shook off the memory, not one of his better ones. As meet-cutes went, his and Kit's had been severely lacking any cuteness whatsoever. "What I'm saying is, when the dust settled, I understood. I didn't like it because it was happening to me, but I still understood. I know you. You might think that you're mysterious, but I at least know enough to be certain that you'd have shown compassion for her grief this morning if Fitzgerald weren't hip-deep in Munro's crap."

"The security guard said she was eyeball-deep."

She was deflecting and he needed her to listen. "*Kit.* You did your job. And if I had a problem—which I did not—I would have told you. But nicely and not in front of the witness. Or suspect, whichever she is. You have to trust me, Kit."

She drew a deep breath and slowly let it out. "That's hard for me."

"I know," he said quietly. "But I'm worth it."

That earned him a full, brilliant smile. "I know. I'll try very hard."

"Good." It was his turn to draw a breath. "Now, let's go visit the guy I helped put behind bars because I wouldn't say he was batshit crazy."

Kit flinched. "Oh my God. I didn't think . . . Sam, why didn't you say you didn't want to see him?"

That irritated him. "Because *it's my job*, Kit. Just like Fitzgerald was yours. I trust you, personally and professionally. If you can't trust me with your heart, at least trust that I know what I'm doing *in my job.*"

She flinched again. "I did that, didn't I? Distrusted you."

He grimaced. "Kind of. Yes."

"I apologize," she said sincerely. "I didn't think of that. I . . . I'm protective over you."

"And I like that. To a point. I'm good at my job, Kit. Let me do it."

"Okay. And, just so you know, I'm not giving this asshole any concessions. No offers of time off. No offers to transfer to a better prison."

"I didn't expect anything else."

CHAPTER SEVEN

Kit had seen photos of Ronald Tasker both before and after his arrest. But she hadn't seen any photos of him since he'd begun serving his sentence.

He looked like an entirely different person.

She'd known he was bald, of course. His toupee had been removed for the booking photo, but in all the other photos—including those of him during his trial—he'd been wearing the hairpiece.

Not so today. He sat before them, small, pale, bald, and yet still defiant. He smirked at Kit, apparently noting the surprise that she thought she'd hidden. "I could still make you scream with pleasure, honey."

Connor stiffened, but Sam showed no reaction.

He really was good at his job.

She didn't respond to Tasker's bait. "Do you know why we're here, Mr. Tasker?"

"I have a decent idea. I saw the news. Munro bit it." He looked delighted.

"You don't seem upset by this," Connor said evenly.

"I'm not. He's a weasel. *Was* a weasel." He snorted a laugh, then turned to Sam. "I'm surprised you had the balls to visit me here."

"Why?" Sam asked mildly.

Tasker blinked once. "You're the shrink, right? The one I paid to declare me unfit for trial?"

"I'm a psychologist, yes. I took no payment for any such thing."

He was calmer than if he'd been denying having ordered pickles on his burger.

Tasker studied Sam. "You took no money? At all? Was it offered?"

"No money was offered and I never asked for any. Munro expected a little quid pro quo that I was unwilling to even consider."

"Huh. So you said no. Munro never told me that. Just said that he paid you and you took the money and reported him."

Sam only smiled. "In that case, I'm surprised I'm still breathing."

Tasker cackled. "Thank you, son. That makes me feel better, believe it or not."

"Oh, I can believe it," Sam said. "Why didn't you have me bumped off?"

"Thought about it. But Munro lied like he breathed. My associates said they'd off you for free, but I told them not to. Just in case Munro was lying."

"Spoiler alert," Sam said. "He was lying."

Tasker cackled some more. "Well, that flies. I figured if you'd taken the money, you wouldn't have reported him. And if you had reported him and had the money as proof, Munro would be in here with me. He never thought people were as smart as he was. What an idiot."

"So my life is saved," Sam said dryly. "Thank you."

Tasker laughed until tears gathered in his eyes. "I like you. I'm glad I didn't kill you, too." He lifted a brow. "Not that I killed anyone else. Like my lying, whoring wife."

"Oh no," Sam said, still dry as dust. "If you knew Munro was lying to you, why didn't you kill him?"

Tasker stilled. "How do you know I didn't?"

"Because you're in here."

"Could have ordered it at any time," Tasker boasted. "But I didn't."

"Why not?" Kit asked.

Tasker cocked his head again, studying Kit this time. "What's it worth for me to tell you?"

"Your self-respect?" she asked sweetly.

He just huffed a chuckle. "You're cute, honey. You look like the girl next door, but I bet you're dynamite in the sack."

Connor drew a breath, but Sam shook his head, making Connor settle back into his chair with a scowl.

"What do you want?" Sam asked.

Kit barely swallowed her bark of outrage. They'd agreed not to offer any concessions. But . . . Sam had asked her to trust him.

Connor wasn't as controlled. He swiveled toward Sam. "No way."

Sam only shrugged, as if he hadn't a care in the world. "Didn't say he'd get it, but it's good to know where we're starting from. What do you want, Mr. Tasker?"

Tasker eyed them all cagily. "Time off for good behavior."

"Can't do that," Sam said, still calm. "Next?"

Tasker scowled like a child denied a treat. "Conjugal visits."

Sam shrugged. "Should have thought of that before you chopped your wife into pieces."

Tasker started to laugh again. "Oh, you're something else. I guess you're one of those assholes with ethics."

Sam smiled. "Guilty as charged. What do you really want, Mr. Tasker? Seriously?"

"I want all of those things."

Steadily, Sam met the man's gaze. "What do you want that we can actually provide? You're still wealthy. Someone on the outside must be sending you money through the prison's JPay system. You have funds to get what you want from the commissary, within reason, of course. What else can we offer other than time off or similar compensation? Because you have to know that those things won't happen."

Tasker grew thoughtful. "I don't know."

Kit opened her mouth to get the conversation back on topic, but Sam stayed her with another shake of his head.

"You collected comic books," Sam said.

Kit stared at Sam in surprise.

Tasker smiled, a genuine smile of pleasure. "I did. I miss my comics. Can't get the ones I like in the commissary, and the ones in the library are ripped up."

"How about five new comic books, whichever are the top sellers at the comic book store?" Sam asked.

"Ten."

"Seven," Sam countered. "And no collectibles. Whatever is hot off the press."

Tasker nodded once. "Okay. I'll tell you what I know about Munro." He glanced sharply at Kit. "*He* treats me like a person."

But Tasker wasn't a person, Kit thought. At least not a good one. He'd murdered his wife and chopped her into pieces. But she was going to trust Sam. He'd been handling Tasker perfectly thus far.

"Understood," she said. "Dr. Reeves?"

Sam folded his hands on the table, and it was then that Kit knew how very nervous he was. That, she'd learned, was one of his tells.

Her respect for Sam Reeves shot to the moon. He was terrified and no one would ever have known.

"Why didn't you have Munro killed?" Sam asked.

Tasker was quiet for a long moment. Then he shrugged. "He has a kind of dead man's switch, if you will," Tasker said. "A list of all the bad things a person has done. If he's killed, it will be made public."

But nothing had been made public. Not yet.

Kit remembered Veronica's voice as she'd made that call after they'd left her office. *I haven't found it yet, and I've searched.*

Was that what she'd been looking for? Munro's dead man's switch? And why had she been searching for it? Was she the one who was supposed to publish it? Or did she want to destroy it because her name was included on the list? Kit didn't know. Yet.

"All the bad things a 'person' has done?" Sam asked. "Or you?"

Tasker only shrugged.

"But you're already in prison," Sam said. "What could be on the list that is worse than what you were charged with?"

Tasker shook his head. "Nothing."

Lie, Kit thought. That was a big, fat lie. But she wondered the same thing that Sam had asked. What could be worse than the time he was serving in prison?

"I don't think that's entirely true," she said softly.

Tasker's head whipped around to glare at her. "Are you calling me a liar, Detective?"

Kit wouldn't deny it. "I'm just saying that if you didn't fear the list, Munro would have been killed sooner. It's only logical."

"Who else is on the list, Mr. Tasker?" Sam asked, redirecting Tasker's attention back to him.

Tasker grinned, an unholy sight. "That would require a lot more than comic books, Dr. Reeves. Movers and shakers, for sure. You'd be astounded."

"I probably wouldn't," Sam said. "I've learned that everyone has secrets."

"Maybe, maybe not. But I'm telling you that if you find that list, you'll find out who killed him. And it wasn't me."

"Are you suggesting that Mr. Munro was blackmailing the people on this list?" Kit asked, already knowing the answer. Now Munro's Ferrari made more sense.

"Ding, ding, ding," Tasker sang. "The pretty lady wins the prize."

"Who helped him uncover all the secrets?" Connor asked. "Or did he manage it by himself?"

Tasker gave Connor a *duh* stare. "Who do you *think*, Detective?"

"His admin," Connor said grimly. "Veronica Fitzgerald."

"Ding. Ding," Tasker deadpanned.

"She's the brains," Kit guessed but made it sound like she knew.

Tasker touched his nose.

So Veronica was unlikely to be on the list herself, Kit thought. She might be the person Munro had chosen to make the list public after his death.

Kit nodded slowly, mentally reviewing Tasker's testimony in

court. How his wife had learned that he'd been keeping two sets of books and had threatened to turn him in. How, with him in prison, she'd be able to control his money. And then, when he'd been so full of rage, a folder of photos had miraculously appeared in his mailbox—a folder that contained photos of his wife having sex with another man. He'd gotten mad, he'd testified. Like any man would.

He'd also chopped her into little pieces. Kit supposed he'd been *really* mad.

"Which is the real reason you're telling us this," she murmured. "Because Veronica Fitzgerald's the brains of their operation. Were you late with your payment to Munro? Is that why he told your wife about your illegal business deals? Is that why he sent you the photos of your wife and her lover? He wanted to show you what you stood to lose if you didn't pay him?"

Tasker gave her an up-and-down leer. "I didn't give you enough credit. You have a brain to go with that body of yours."

Once again, Kit ignored the sexual barb. "Munro's dead, but you also want Miss Fitzgerald to pay. They destroyed your marriage, your business, and took your freedom." Tasker had done all that himself, Kit knew, but Sam wasn't the only one who could play along. "So you're willing to spill the tea for us. You're not going to squeal on the others on that list, because you don't know who they are. But now we know what to look for, so your job is pretty much done. And when we do find the list, it can't keep you in prison any longer than you're already facing, but at least you will have had your revenge."

Tasker only smiled and said nothing. It appeared he was done sharing.

Sam had been quiet through this exchange. When he spoke, it was gently. "It's personal for you, then. Whatever's on that list is something you don't want a person who you respect to find out. You might not get any more prison time, but someone you care about will no longer love you."

Tasker's eyes widened with shock. "How—" He shook his head hard and pushed away from the table, jangling the chain that attached his handcuffs to his ankle shackles. "I'm done. I expect those comic books, Dr. Reeves."

"I keep my word, Mr. Tasker."

He nodded once. "I'm counting on it. You've got ethics and I don't know many people who do. You can relax. I won't be coming after you. Even if I never get the comics."

Sam shook his head. "I said that I keep my word. I will send them, but they'll have to go through one of the approved package vendors. It might take a few weeks."

Tasker looked over his shoulder to the guard standing by the door. "Take me back to my cell."

Kit, Connor, and Sam remained seated as the guard led Tasker through the door of the interview room. Tasker looked back at the last moment.

"She's my daughter. I did some things I'm not proud of and I don't want her to know. None of that was illegal. But I still don't want her to know. But it doesn't really matter because she disowned me after I ki—" He drew a breath. "After I was convicted of killing her mother. So if you find the list, go ahead and tell her. She hates me anyway."

Shoulders slumped, he shuffled away, leaving the three of them to sit in stunned silence.

Finally, Connor cleared his throat. "I think I just attended a master class. Sam, you are the man. How did you know about the comic books?"

"I researched him," Sam said simply.

"So did we," Connor said.

"We were looking at his priors, work history, and business associations. Sam was looking at *him*. Like he was a person." Kit needed to remember that in the future. She'd let the magnitude of the man's crime blind her to the vulnerability most humans had on some level. But Sam had *seen* him. "I think we're ready to go."

Sam's laugh was shaky. "I know I am. I need a drink."

Connor stared at him. "You're freaked out *now*? It's over, dude."

"He was freaked out before we walked through the front entrance," Kit said quietly. "But he's right, Sam. That was a master class." Hoping to comfort him, she ran her hand down Sam's arm, feeling him tremble. "Come on. We'll call Navarro from the car and see if Tasker's info can be added to the search warrant. And then we'll get lunch. And maybe a margarita for you."

Sam stood, then straightened his back. "That sounds like the best idea I've heard in forever."

Scripps Ranch, San Diego, California
Monday, January 9, 1:30 p.m.

"It was good to see the old ladies again," Connor said as he and Kit left the Shady Oaks Retirement Village.

Kit waved fondly at the two elderly women who stood on either side of a slightly tipsy Sam Reeves. Kit hadn't wanted to leave him alone at home after his margarita lunch and knew Miss Georgia and Miss Eloise would take good care of him.

Sam had earned those two drinks and then some. Kit was only mildly surprised that it had taken only two rather weak margaritas to make the psychologist wobbly. Sam didn't drink much.

It was one of the things she liked about him.

"Don't let them hear you call them old," Kit warned. Because Georgia and Eloise were still forces of nature despite being octo-genarians.

Connor shuddered. "Not on your life."

Kit slid into the passenger seat. Neither she nor Connor was tipsy, having refrained from any alcohol at lunch. They were still on duty, after all. But Kit would have stayed sober anyway. Sam was far more shaken than he'd let Connor see, and she'd needed to take care of him.

It was a new feeling, this protectiveness. She felt it for her parents, for her sisters and brothers, but she'd never felt this way for anyone else.

It scared her to death.

Because what if Tasker changed his mind? What if he did send hired thugs to hurt Sam? Or worse?

He could do the same to you.

Which was true, she allowed. *But I can take care of myself.*

So can Sam.

He'd proven that many times.

But she still worried. The only thing to take her mind off the worry was work. "So we have a dead-man's-switch list out there somewhere. I wonder who Munro was blackmailing."

"Movers and shakers, according to Tasker," Connor said, pulling out of the Shady Oaks parking lot. "That could include a lot of people who'd never be on our radar."

"Because they all keep it secret. Presumably no one knows who else is on the list," Kit mused.

"Telling would trip them up, too. It's a pretty ingenious way of keeping his victims in check."

"Somebody objected. Or multiple somebodies, if Alicia is right about multiple hands stabbing him."

Connor sighed. "It might not have been anyone on that list. It still could have been angry constituents or a jealous husband. Or even a local developer who didn't get a contract."

"But blackmail makes a lot of sense. Especially since Veronica is looking for something she hasn't been able to find."

Connor's mouth bent down thoughtfully. "I wonder if she was the mechanism for the list getting out. Someone or something had to be triggered by news of Munro's death. That's the whole point of a dead man's switch."

"I wondered the same thing while we were talking to Tasker. I hope Marshall and Ashton have made some progress searching the files we took from Munro's home office. Maybe the list is in those papers. If it were me, I'd have kept the list close at hand."

"There wasn't anything on his home computer," Connor said. "Nothing that screamed 'I'm a list of scumbags who're paying for Munro's Ferrari.'"

Kit chuckled at the image. "That would be too easy."

"I personally wouldn't have kept it close at hand. I would have put it in a safe-deposit box and would have given both a key and written permission to access the box to the person charged with making sure the list was shared. My lawyer would have had the key."

"Munro didn't have a safe-deposit box at his bank."

"Not the bank he openly used." Connor merged onto the freeway. "Veronica's trips to the Caymans could mean an offshore account there."

"Wouldn't be the first person to hide ill-gotten gains."

"Nope. Who is Munro's attorney?"

Kit was annoyed at herself for not having already talked to Munro's lawyer. "It might be the same attorney whose name

Veronica gave us when she threw us out of her office." She pulled the folded piece of paper from her pocket. "Lucas King."

"I've heard of him," Connor said. "He does estate planning for the newly rich and the 'middle-class millionaires.'"

"Middle-class millionaires? That's a thing?"

"Yep. People who slowly built their wealth or got it through selling real estate they bought fifty years ago. They're a few steps below the mega-wealthy. Some of my parents' friends have mentioned that lawyer. He doesn't typically handle defense cases, but Veronica might not have thought she'd need one. She seems arrogant enough."

Using her phone, Kit paged through the notes that Marshall and Ashton had uploaded to the department server and gaped when she got to the page that listed Munro's attorney of record. "Oh my God. You're not going to believe who's Munro's attorney. It's Laura Letterman."

Connor did a double take, glancing at her before returning his gaze to the road. "Sam's ex?"

"One and the same." Kit leaned back into the headrest. "Sam's gonna freak out."

"Not like he did today, though, right? She's not a danger to him."

"Laura still cares about him in her own way. She worked hard to represent him when we thought he was a suspect nine months ago. So a totally different kind of freak-out than talking to Tasker today."

"Still can't get over how cool he was," Connor muttered. "I thought the man wore his feelings on his face. Now I have to wonder."

"He usually does," Kit said, still staring at Laura Letterman's name. "But his job requires him to compartmentalize when he has to. That's what we saw today. I wonder if we should pay Miss Letterman a visit."

"She won't tell us anything about Munro. Privilege and all that shit."

Kit lifted a brow. "Well, she doesn't represent Veronica, does she?"

Connor grinned. "Damn good point. What's her address? She'll be in her office unless she's in court. Either way, we should find her."

Kit was googling Laura's address when her phone buzzed with an incoming call. "It's Navarro," she told Connor, then hit accept. "What's up, boss?"

"Veronica Fitzgerald left city hall ten minutes ago and appears to be on her way to her apartment." He gave them the address, an expensive building downtown. "Bring her in."

"On it." Kit punched the address into their GPS and Connor upped his speed. "I'm assuming we don't have enough for an arrest warrant?"

"Not yet," Navarro said ruefully. "The word of a convicted murderer who cut his wife into pieces isn't enough, unfortunately. But I did get you a search warrant, freshly signed by the judge. It's only for her bags, including her purse. She should have some luggage if she's running away like we're assuming. If she has anything in her bags that's remotely suspicious, arrest her and bring her in. I'll send a uniform over with a signed copy of the warrant, just in case she resists the search."

"I hope she resists," Kit said. "I'd like to slap some cuffs on her. She's a snake." *Trying to shake Sam down like that.*

"Hiss," Connor muttered in agreement.

"Understood. Keep it classy, though. I don't want her slithering away."

"Of course," Kit said. "We'll call you when we have her. We're about seven minutes out. If she tries to leave before we get there, have the uniforms on watch keep her there."

Kit ended the call and fixed the flashing blue light to the top of the car. "Step on it."

Connor complied with glee because driving fast and furious was one of his favorite things. Kit fought the urge to close her eyes as he dodged traffic, breathing her relief when they finally slowed to a stop in front of Veronica's building.

"Four and a half minutes," Connor crowed. "I love this job."

"I need one of Sam's margaritas," Kit muttered, releasing the grab handle and shaking out her stiff fingers. "Let's bring her in."

They found the uniforms who'd followed her waiting for them. "She went up just a few minutes ago," one of them said. "Her apartment is on the tenth floor and faces the water."

Away from them, then. That was good. She wouldn't be able to see them gathered and talking.

"How many exits?" Connor asked.

"Two," the second uniform replied. "This one and the emergency exit in back. Two more cops are guarding that door."

Connor gave the men a nod. "Thank you."

Kit echoed her thanks as she and Connor walked to the elevator. "This could be messy if she won't comply," she said when the doors closed and the elevator started its ascent.

"You wearing a vest?" Connor asked.

"Yep. You?"

"Yeah," he muttered. "CeCe made me promise to always wear one."

"CeCe cares about you. Veronica doesn't own a registered gun, but that doesn't mean she won't have one. If Tasker is right, she's every bit as dangerous as Munro was."

When the elevator doors opened, they immediately heard Veronica's voice through her door. It was muted, but shrill and panicked enough that it carried.

"I don't care. You meet me at the field. Twenty minutes," she said. "I've spent hours making all the arrangements. All you have to do is bring your passport and fly the damn plane."

Kit texted Navarro. *She's talking about taking a small plane out of the country. Told the pilot to meet her at the field in 20 min. She hasn't been in her apt long. Can't have packed much.*

Traveling lite makes sense when u r fleeing came the reply. *Bring her in in cuffs if you have to. Contact me when it's done. Has the warrant arrived?*

As if on cue, the other elevator's door slid open and a uniformed officer stepped out, a short stack of papers in his hand. Kit pressed her finger to her lips, then pointed at the door. Understanding, the officer silently gave her three copies of the search warrant.

"Is your body cam on?" she asked in a barely audible whisper, and he nodded. *Please stay here,* she mouthed.

Just got the warrant, Kit texted to Navarro. *Thx boss.*

Kit looked at Connor. *Now we wait,* she mouthed.

They didn't have to wait long. The door to Veronica's apartment opened and she stumbled back with a gasp, her eyes widening at the sight of Kit and Connor. She had a large shoulder bag and a backpack.

"What is the meaning of this?" Veronica demanded.

Kit held up a copy of the warrant. "We have a warrant to search your bags."

Veronica's mouth dropped open in shock. She took another step back, almost into her apartment. "No! These are my private bags. You have no right."

Kit snatched the shoulder bag and yanked, causing the woman to stumble forward. Connor took the backpack.

Veronica's chin lifted. "I know my rights. I demand to read the warrant."

Kit gave her a copy and, pulling on disposable gloves,

proceeded to search her bag. "Who is the pilot?" she asked conversationally.

Veronica's lips tightened and she said nothing.

Kit wasn't surprised. The woman did know her rights, after all. Kit found two cell phones and held the more generic-looking one up to Veronica's face before she could shut her eyes.

"You can't do that!" Veronica shouted. "I'm calling my attorney."

"Go ahead," Connor said. "You'll get one phone call. Probably not on your cell phone, though. Depends on what we find."

"She called an Uber," Kit said, swiping through the open apps on the phone, which was probably a burner. The other phone's case was decorated with glittering green shamrocks—probably her personal cell. Kit would look through it in a few minutes. "And she made reservations at a hotel in Mexico City for tonight." Proceeding with her search, Kit pulled out an unregistered handgun. "Oh *my*. This is not good, Veronica."

Connor set the large backpack on the floor in full view of the officer's body cam. Crouching beside it, he unzipped the first compartment. "Underwear and a change of clothes," he said for the camera. "One bottle of thyroid medication." He unzipped the larger compartment. "Oh *my*," he said, echoing Kit. "What have we here?"

He pulled a stack of money from the backpack. "There's quite a bit here. These are all fifties. If the rest of them are as well, I'm estimating she's got at least a hundred grand in this backpack. Maybe more."

"Veronica," Kit chided. "Where did that money come from?"

Veronica glared at her and said nothing.

Kit pulled a passport from the handbag. "And the pièce de résistance. A passport in the name of Viola Feinstein but with your photo. At least you wouldn't have to throw away your monogrammed items." She pulled her handcuffs from her jacket pocket and slapped them on Veronica's wrists with relish. *That's for trying to shake down Sam, you bitch.* "Veronica Fitzgerald, you're under arrest for extortion. The passport fraud is a federal offense, so we'll leave that up to them."

Veronica tried to yank out of Kit's hold, but Kit tightened her grip. "I'm innocent."

"Then you can explain where all this cash came from," Connor said. "Let's go."

Still gripping Veronica's arm, Kit dragged her into the elevator. "Officer, if you could stay with us until we get her in our car, I'd appreciate it." She wanted every second of this arrest recorded.

San Diego PD, San Diego, California
Monday, January 9, 4:00 p.m.

"That was good work," Navarro said as he settled into a chair in the observation room, Kit and Connor on either side of him. "If we hadn't had eyes on Fitzgerald, we'd have lost her and she'd be God knows where by now."

Veronica Fitzgerald sat at the interview table on the other side of the glass. They were waiting for her attorney to arrive before they began the interview, because Veronica had immediately lawyered up.

"On her way to Mexico City," Kit said. "I don't know where she'd have gone after that."

"Marshall and Ashton picked up the pilot," Connor went on. "They're on their way in with him. We were able to triangulate Veronica's last call with the towers. Steven Neal was waiting for Veronica at a small airfield near the prison we were at this morning, ironically enough. He'd filed a flight plan and was still waiting for clearance."

"She probably intended to bribe someone in customs with some of that money," Navarro said. "She had plenty of it. The money, the gun, and the fake passport were the final nails in her coffin." He looked around the small room. "I thought Sam would be here."

Kit winced a little. "He took the afternoon off."

"He was freaked out about talking to Ronald Tasker," Connor said. "Had a few drinks afterward. But you never would have known he was nervous at all. The man was as cool as a cucumber."

"Comic books," Navarro said, shaking his head. "I never would have thought of that."

Kit smiled, proud of Sam. "Neither would I. I'm glad Sam did. So who's going to be the bad cop in there with her?"

"You should," Connor said. "You already established that role this morning."

"I brought Munro's autopsy photos this time," Kit said. "Sam thought I could have been harder on her this morning, so this time I thought I'd show her what was done to her lover."

"Do we know for sure that they were lovers?" Navarro asked.

Kit shook her head. "Not confirmed yet, but the camera feed from her apartment building shows Munro entering Tuesday evening wearing one suit, then leaving at eight thirty the next morning in a different suit."

"He spent the night," Navarro said.

"Which Fitzgerald can claim was platonic or that he spent the night with someone else in the building. CSU is in her apartment now. They'll take DNA samples from her sheets. If he was in her bed, hopefully we'll find evidence. This does answer one of my earlier questions, though—about why the killer drove the trailer to Munro's house so early in the morning. I think he was hoping to catch Munro coming out of his house, but he was sleeping with Fitzgerald. So he had to wait until Munro came home."

But that was still a very long time for the killer to sit idly, waiting. Her gut told her that there was something she was missing.

"That sounds right." Then Navarro grimaced. "What was it about Munro that had the women lining up to sleep with him? Veronica, the widow, and the reporter."

"Tamsin Kavanaugh," Kit growled. "I can't wait to talk to her."

Navarro chuckled. "Maybe you should let Connor take that interview."

"She makes me growl too, boss. Woman's slimy." Then Connor sat up straight, staring at the glass. "What the fuck?"

Kit's gaze went to the glass and she stared as well. "What the fuck?" she whispered. "That is not the attorney she told us to call this morning."

Laura Letterman had entered the interview room.

"You said she was Munro's attorney," Navarro said. "Smart move on Veronica's part. Now you can't ask Letterman anything about either of them."

"Bitch," Kit muttered.

"The accused or the lawyer?" Navarro asked.

Kit scowled. "Both?" Veronica had tried to shake Sam down, but Laura had cheated on him.

"Maybe let Connor take this interview," Navarro said carefully. "Just because you've gone up against Letterman before and she knows your style. Connor will be an unknown entity."

Kit sighed. "I hate that you're right."

The door opened and closed before another voice muttered, "What the fuck?"

Joel Haley was staring through the glass much as Kit and Connor had. "*She's* Fitzgerald's attorney?"

Kit sighed. "We were surprised, too. Have a seat, Joel."

"I'm glad that Sam was too intoxicated to be here," Joel said as he took the seat next to Kit.

Me too. "Better get started, Connor. We still have a million interviews to do."

"What are you hoping to get out of Fitzgerald today?" Joel asked.

"Probably nothing," Connor admitted. "She seems too smart to mouth off. But I'm hoping the autopsy photos will loosen her tongue. Plus, I'll say that we know they were sleeping together, that the DNA found in her apartment came back positive. It hasn't yet, I'm just hoping to get a reaction. We think she's been searching for Munro's dead man's switch."

Navarro had called Joel with the update after they'd left the prison that morning. It had helped secure the warrant for Veronica's bags.

"That makes a lot of sense," Joel said. "Especially if Munro's wife wasn't financing his lifestyle. Have we come any closer to tracking the trailer that hauled Munro's Ferrari away?"

Connor shook his head. "Unfortunately, no. The driver must have removed the wrap from the trailer shortly after leaving Munro's neighborhood. He may have even changed the truck he was using to haul it. There are a number of trailers in the local street cams, but none are being pulled by the Ford we saw in Ace Diamond's camera feed. We've effectively lost the trail."

"Marshall and Ashton went out to interview the guard at the neighborhood entrance," Navarro went on. "It was our second attempt. The guard wasn't home, so we can't get his description of the trailer's driver. They'll try again later."

Kit frowned. "Shelley was a loose end, and now she and her

mom are dead. How do we know this guy hasn't killed Munro's gate guard?"

"We don't," Navarro said grimly. "We've put out a BOLO on him as a person of interest and Marshall and Ashton are following up with his friends and family, trying to find him."

"I don't think we're going to get the killer's description out of him," Connor said.

Kit didn't think so, either. *Dammit.*

They were all quiet for a long moment, and then Joel broke the silence.

"What are the next steps after talking to Fitzgerald?" Joel asked. "Assuming you don't get anything out of her, I mean."

"We're going to cycle back to Mrs. Munro," Kit said. "We have a number of unanswered questions about Munro's finances. We know he was spending a lot of money, but other than the Ferrari, we don't know the other big-ticket items he was spending it on. We have tons of data to wade through, although Marshall and Ashton are handling a lot of that. We have Alicia Batra's theory that it was more than one person, so that could either be people he was blackmailing or people he'd screwed over in business or politics."

"So you really don't know," Joel said.

Kit shook her head. "We really don't. We need to follow up on the credible threats he received and get alibis for those suspects so we can at least cross them off the list."

"We know that Wilhelmina knew Munro was dirty, but couldn't find the proof," Connor said.

"Or that's what she claimed," Kit murmured. "We know that Munro's killer also killed Shelley Porter and her mother Carol, but no one saw anyone go into the house that night. We need to recanvass the neighborhood and ask again. Someone had to have seen something."

Connor sighed. "The only person I really believe right now is the tattooed thug whose real name is not Ace Diamond. He said that Shelley got him hooked." He cocked his head. "But her killer knew that four grand would be a surefire bait to bribe her that night. He might have assumed that she'd simply want the money or he could have known she was an addict who'd take that money in a heartbeat. Who else knew that Shelley Porter was an addict?"

"There you go," Joel said. "That's a fresh thread to pull."

"We will pull it," Kit said, then turned to the glass when Laura Letterman knocked. "I think you're up, Connor."

"Lucky me."

"See if you can get Veronica to tell you who she was talking to in her office," she said. "I don't think it was the pilot. The numbers in her call log were different."

"Easy peasy," Connor said sarcastically. He took the folder with the autopsy photos and headed into the interview room.

CHAPTER EIGHT

Connor walked into the interview room, a friendly smile on his face. "Miss Fitzgerald, so nice to see you again."

Veronica sneered at him and said nothing.

"You don't have any reason to keep my client here," Laura said boldly.

Connor chuckled. "I'd say we have two hundred thousand, four hundred and fifty reasons to keep her here. Plus the fake passport, of course. The Feds will handle that one, but they're letting us have our go first. Isn't that nice? We all just get along."

Laura didn't smile. "I've advised my client not to say anything."

"I'm sure you have. I just wanted to clear the air with her. Hopefully get a few things straight." He set the folder on the table. "So. You drive a Chevy Stingray. Hot car, by the way. I wish I had one. But on a cop's salary, I can't afford it."

Veronica snorted. "Your rich parents would buy you one."

"Veronica," Laura said quietly.

Veronica rolled her eyes. "I know his parents from the country club. All they can talk about is their important son who's an important detective. I am not impressed."

Connor grinned. "I am. I didn't know they bragged about me. Now, I must commend you on your frugality. Munro bought himself a quarter-mil Ferrari, but you bought a much less expensive car. Seventy-five thousand retail. Still, how does an admin assistant to a city councilmember afford a car like that?"

"It was a gift," Veronica said stiffly. "And I can prove that."

"From Munro?"

Laura sighed. "Don't answer that, Veronica. I'm serious."

"Hell of an admin appreciation day gift," Connor commented. "We tallied your rent, the car, and did a cursory check on your credit cards. You spend a lot more than you make. And you have no debt. You paid your bills and Munro's with money orders. That was real nice of you, ma'am. Getting money orders for him when you bought yours. Or maybe the money was coming out of the same pot?"

Veronica looked away, her lips pursed.

"Okay. You've made ten trips to the Caymans in the last four years under your Viola Feinstein passport. Any reason?"

"Vacation," she said, lifting her chin.

"You must really love it there. I'm wondering if we'll find that you've also opened accounts in Cayman banks under the Viola alias. Or if you have a third passport we just haven't found yet."

"You're fishing, Detective," Laura said.

"Of course I am," Connor said, still pleasant. "I wonder if Steven Neal—he's the pilot we just picked up, Miss Letterman— will tell us about some of Veronica's trips."

Veronica's eyes flashed anger. "He didn't fly me there."

Connor smiled. "Will he back you up? You're going down for felony passport fraud and, if you can't explain where all that money came from, extortion as well. He's just in trouble for being your pilot at this point. He claims that he wasn't the person you called this morning when you said 'They know,' and 'We have to get out of here.'"

Her eyes widened and she opened her mouth, then shut it when Laura hissed her name.

"Yeah," Connor said, "we were listening. I wish you hadn't thrown up, though. I'm a sympathetic puker."

"He's not," Kit said in the observation room. "I think Sam is, though."

"He totally is," Joel agreed.

On the other side of the glass, Veronica glared at Connor.

Laura sighed. "Are you going somewhere with this, Detective?"

"Of course." He turned to Veronica. "We'll check into the flights you took with your Viola passport. I'm thinking you did the trip in two legs—San Diego to Mexico City and then to Grand Cayman. We'll find the flight records. Steven Neal doesn't strike me as the kind of guy who'd stay quiet to save you."

"Did Connor meet the pilot?" Navarro asked.

"Nope," Kit said. "He's really improving his interview technique. Veronica bought that line."

"If he knew anything about what you were doing," Connor continued, "and I suspect he did because you were bullying him into flying you today—then we'll offer him a deal to tell us everything he knows about you. We're especially interested in your partner. The one who wasn't gutted like a pig."

He said that like he was discussing a sunny day.

Veronica flinched and held herself very still as Connor changed the subject from Munro's body back to her flights.

"They were generally long weekends, your trips to Grand Cayman. That's a hell of a long flight for a short visit."

"So?" Veronica asked belligerently.

"So, we plan to start with the supposition that you boarded each of those flights with a backpack full of cash, like you had today. And that you deposited it, then turned around and came back. We're also assuming that Munro didn't keep the cash. You did. You bore the entire responsibility should you have been caught. He doesn't seem very nice to me."

"He didn't have to be nice," she said with rigid dignity. "He was my employer."

"And your lover," Connor said in a tone just short of singsong.

Veronica maintained her composure, but it was a close thing. If Connor played her right, he could break her walls down.

"You can't prove that," Veronica said.

"Ah, but we can. Right after we hauled you into booking, we had CSU go over your apartment with a fine-toothed comb. Tested the hell out of those sheets. Hell of a thing, rapid DNA testing. Cuts the wait time down to two hours. Results are in, and guess whose DNA we found?"

Veronica's face slowly grew a waxy shade of green. But, to her credit, she said nothing.

"Oh, come on," Connor coaxed. "Not even a guess? Well, I suppose you already know. You were having . . . carnal relations with him. Good old Brooks Munro. Does your other partner know about the two of you? I think you two were the brains of the operation, not Munro. If his killer figures that out . . . well, I wouldn't want to be either of you."

Veronica drew a breath and let it out. She opened her mouth, but no words emerged.

There was a tension in the interview room that Kit could feel on the other side of the glass. She realized she'd leaned forward—as had Navarro and Joel.

"Who's the PI, Veronica?" Connor asked.

Veronica flinched, her eyes registering shock.

"Very nice, Connor," Kit murmured. "Very nice indeed."

"Did you know there was a PI?" Joel asked.

"No," Kit said. "It makes sense, though. If Brooks Munro had a list of secrets, someone had to have dug them up. I can't see random people confiding in Munro."

Navarro sat back with a grim smile. "Get the PI's name, Robinson."

That, Kit thought, might be asking too much. "We might be able to find his name on her phone. Having confirmation that she was working with a PI is good, though."

"I mean," Connor was saying casually, "everyone knows that Munro wasn't the type to pry secrets out of powerful people. Movers and shakers, our source said. But Munro was a sleazy man. I'm surprised anyone stuck with him for more than a few weeks. You were his lover for fifteen years." He said it like he was truly impressed. "Everyone in city hall knows you two were going at it like rabbits, by the way, so nobody will be surprised. What does surprise me is that you'd let the person who did *this* to the man you've slept with for fifteen years go free."

He opened the folder and spread the photos across the table. Veronica gagged, but nothing came up.

"Really, Detective," Laura snapped, turning the photos over.

"Stop," Connor commanded, his tone suddenly hostile and aggressive. "*Look* at these, Veronica. Look at what they *did* to him. They stabbed him *twenty-five* times. They cut off his fingers and toes. And they mauled the hell out of his dick." Connor rose from his chair, leaning across the table to dangle the photo of

Munro's mutilated genitalia in front of Veronica's face. "*I. Said. Look.*"

Veronica looked, her eyes frozen on the photo as what color was left in her face drained away. She then curled into herself on a ragged sob.

If Kit didn't dislike her so much, she might feel sorry for her.

"Don't you want to know who did this?" Connor demanded. Laura urgently called her client's name, but Connor shouted over her. "He felt every one of these brutalities, Veronica. Every single one. They *hurt* him. The man you loved was *tortured*. Over and over and over again. Don't you want whoever hurt him to pay?"

"Yes," Veronica cried on a strangled gasp. "I want *them* to pay. But I don't know who *they* are."

"You know who's on the list," Connor countered coldly, his pleasant facade no more.

Veronica shook her head. "I don't. I managed the money. That's all."

Laura sighed. "We'll want to talk a deal with the prosecutor."

Connor sank into his seat. He slid the photos back in the folder. "That's not up to me. Where did you think he'd put the list, Veronica?"

"It was supposed to be in his house. In his study. I looked in his study, but it wasn't there. Then *she* came home and I couldn't look anymore. I searched the office at city hall, but it wasn't there either, and then it got sealed off by you people and I couldn't look anymore."

"She" would be Wilhelmina, Kit thought. She wondered if Wilhelmina suspected that Munro's home office had been searched. It didn't seem like it had been searched when Kit and Connor had been there on Saturday night. Not a paper was out of place.

Either Veronica was a neatnik or Wilhelmina—or someone else—had altered the scene. They'd had CSU go over every inch of that study and hadn't found any prints that didn't belong to Munro himself. They'd search again, but Kit didn't think they'd find the list. It was likely that whoever had tortured Munro had gleaned the location of the list and had taken it for themselves.

But why? How did they plan to use the information? How did they even know the list existed to begin with?

Connor's voice had settled back to calm, but there was no more pleasantry. "Are we looking for an electronic file or a piece of paper?"

"A notebook," Veronica said. "In a three-ring binder. It wasn't online. Brooks didn't trust that he wouldn't be hacked. I never saw the contents. The PI never saw the payments. I never even knew the PI's name."

Connor regarded her in silence for a moment before asking, "Was it Jacob Crocker?"

Veronica's shock was apparent. "No."

"Who's Crocker?" Joel asked.

"PI to William Weaver," Kit said, "the guy whose life Munro ruined over a council seat. Crocker's dead. Shot while on a stakeout for another client, according to Weaver. We wondered if Munro had anything to do with that because Weaver was about to hire Crocker again. I guess we have the answer to that question. Veronica knows exactly who Jacob Crocker was."

"Okay," Connor was saying evenly. "So you never saw the names. Clearly Brooks knew who they were, as did the PI since he was the one who dug up the dirt to begin with. What was your role?"

"I handled the payments and kept the money straight. Told Brooks who wasn't paying on time. I don't know what he did with that information."

"That's a lie," Kit said. "Or at least Ronald Tasker thought so. He thought Munro and Fitzgerald sent him the compromising photos of his wife as retaliation for nonpayment. They wanted Tasker to blow up, goading her to report his illegal dealings to the police. Which Tasker's wife knew about because Munro and Fitzgerald told her about them. At least that was Tasker's take."

"He blew up all right," Navarro muttered.

"I don't know if they expected Tasker to murder his wife *and* chop her into pieces," Kit said dryly.

"Hush," Joel said, because Veronica was still talking.

"Each of us had a piece of the pie," she said, "so none of us could betray the others and steal it all."

"No trust among thieves," Connor murmured. "How long had this been going on?"

"Eight years. Before Brooks was first elected to the city council."

"Why was it so important for Munro to be on the council?" Connor asked. "It's just the city council."

Veronica sighed wearily. "To you, maybe. You grew up with a silver spoon in your mouth. Brooks and I didn't. He wanted to be a U.S. senator. To have respect."

"So he stole to get it."

The woman lifted a shoulder. "Not like he was the first to do that."

Connor frowned. "That doesn't make it right. How much money are we talking about?"

"It varied."

"*Guess*," Connor snapped.

"I would go to the Caymans when I had a half mil saved up."

"So ten trips means five million dollars. Not as much as I thought, especially not split three ways."

"Split into quarters," she said, looking twenty years older than she had that morning. "I don't know where the others put their money."

"That's more like it," Connor said. "You said quarters. Is there a fourth partner or did you all take a different percentage?"

Veronica slowly shook her head. "No fourth partner. Brooks got half. The PI and I each got a quarter."

"Didn't that make you angry?"

"Only a little. Brooks was taking the risks. The PI and I were faceless. The targets knew only that Brooks held their secrets. So he got a bigger percentage of the take."

"If you kept track of the money and never met the PI, how did he get his cut?"

"Brooks gave it to him. I'd prepare the accounting statement and give Brooks seventy-five percent of the take—his and the PI's share. I only knew the targets by a number. Brooks knew the numbers and the names. The PI only knew the names."

"So you'd put a million and a half dollars in a suitcase and hand it to Munro?"

She frowned. "Where did you get—? Oh. I said I'd save up a half mil before going to the Caymans. That took me several months to save up. I paid out the funds every month to Brooks, who then paid the PI. Like I said, I don't know where they hid theirs."

"How did your blackmail victims pay you?" Connor was asking.

"Cash. Nonsequential fifties. Left in a storage locker."

"Where was the storage locker?" Connor asked.

"Only Brooks and I had a key, but it was too risky for Brooks to check. That was my job."

"He trusted you one helluva lot."

"He did."

"Why?"

"We were lovers," she said bitterly. "As you said."

"Had to have been more than that. Where was the storage locker?"

"It changed locations, month to month," Veronica said. "That was Brooks's idea. He didn't want our targets to be able to go to the cops. Most of them could afford the money we charged. They were all too rich for their own good. Needed to be taken down a peg or two."

"How do you know they were rich enough to afford your blackmail?"

"Brooks said so. I believed him. He never lied to me."

"You mentioned that neither of you grew up with a silver spoon. Does that mean you knew him growing up?"

She closed her eyes, then nodded. "Yes."

"Where?"

Veronica shook her head, for some reason unwilling to share that information.

"Who do you think killed him? Was it over the blackmail list? Or do you think it was his constituents?"

"I don't know," Veronica said. "And that's the truth."

"That's a lie," Kit said quietly. "She's got to know it was the blackmail list. They tortured him for the location. Unless she did find it, hid it, and is lying to all of us, including the PI. That's a distinct possibility."

"It is," Navarro said. "But you'll get to the bottom of it. You two make a hell of an investigative team. Add in Sam Reeves, and you're unstoppable."

Kit just hoped that was true.

Connor's shoulders sagged, his exhaustion starting to show. These kinds of interviews were as hard on the cop as they were on the suspect. Well, in different ways. Connor got to go home at the end of the ordeal. Veronica would go to a cell.

"Anything else?" he asked.

Veronica shot him an icy glare. "Isn't this enough?"

Laura's sigh sounded defeated. "More than enough. My

client wishes to go to her cell now. I'll see you at the arraignment, Veronica. Please don't say any more."

"There's no more to say," she muttered mournfully.

"Another lie," Kit murmured. "She knows so much more."

"Yep," Navarro agreed. "We'll keep working on her."

Connor got up and was at the door when Veronica spoke again. "Detective, have you found his car? The Ferrari?"

"No. Why?"

"I left a bracelet in the glove box. It was my mother's. Nothing expensive. Just . . . sentimental value. I'd like to get it back."

"If we find it, I'll check." Connor left the interview room and joined them in observation. "Fucking hell," he muttered, dropping into a chair.

"Nicely done," Kit said.

Joel squeezed Connor's shoulder. "What she said."

Connor closed his eyes. "I need a nap."

Kit had to smile. He sounded three years old. "Go crash. I'll do a summary and pull together our next steps."

San Diego PD, San Diego, California
Monday, January 9, 8:15 p.m.

"Hey."

Kit turned from the whiteboard at the sheepish voice, smiling when she saw Sam standing in the doorway to the SDPD conference room. "Hey, yourself. Did you get some sleep?"

"I did. Then I got fed. You have a visitor. Is it okay to let her in?"

A familiar voice came from behind him. "It means put all the gory photos away," Akiko said. "I've got your dinner."

Kit gathered the autopsy photos and any crime scene details

that her sister shouldn't see. "All the gory photos are put away. Please, let her in. I'm starving."

Akiko ducked under Sam's arm, a covered glass baking dish in her hand. "I got a great haul today. White sea bass and lingcod. Mom and I cooked them up and we had a feast at the house." She arched a brow. "I texted."

Kit sighed. "I'm sorry. I got distracted and forgot to reply. But it smells really good."

Akiko had come to McKittrick House shortly after Wren's murder. She and Kit had become friends first, then sisters. Out of all the kids fostered by Harlan and Betsy, Kit was closest to Akiko, who operated a fishing charter. The family benefited when she had a good day on the water.

"How did you and Sam come up together?" Kit asked, digging into the meal.

Sam sat at the conference table, rubbing the back of his neck awkwardly. "Your folks invited Georgia and Eloise for fish and I was with them."

"He was still tipsy," Akiko stage-whispered, then laughed when Sam shot her a dirty look. "Well, you were. I picked them up on my way from the harbor. Stopped by to get your mail too, since you haven't slept on the boat in a while."

Kit stopped chewing to consider that. It had been days since she'd slept in her own bed. Going home to McKittrick House was so much nicer.

"So I had dinner with them and Betsy made me drink a gallon of coffee," Sam said. "But the dinner was amazing, so it was worth it in the end. Akiko brought me back here because I left my car in the lot this morning. Where's Connor?"

"He took a break to have dinner with CeCe and her parents. He'll be back soon, and he'll definitely want some of this fish.

They're vegetarians. He doesn't want to be rude, so he eats a meal there, then goes somewhere for meat."

While Kit explained, she was watching her sister. There was something wrong. Kit was almost certain of it. Akiko had yet to meet her eyes. But she'd ask later. Kit trusted Sam, but Akiko might want to keep whatever was wrong private.

"Vegetarian is an extremely healthy lifestyle," Akiko said. "But I get his point." She stood up and headed for the door. "Enjoy the food. Mom says to bring the dish the next time you come home. She says that will probably be tonight."

Kit's mother was not wrong. But Kit did have to go back to her boat soon. It technically wasn't her boat. She rented it from one of her older foster brothers who was in the navy, stationed too far away to use it.

She really didn't spend much time on the boat anymore, now that she thought about it. "I'll walk you out. Sam, can you stay? I need to bring you up to speed."

"Of course," he said in a way that made Kit wonder if he'd seen Akiko's preoccupation, too.

Kit waited until she and Akiko were at the double doors leading out of the homicide division. "What's wrong?"

Akiko shook her head. "It's tough having you for a sister. I can't hide anything."

"Akiko . . ."

Her sister sighed. "I got a call a few days ago from someone I didn't know. She wants to meet me. She claims to have known my mother."

Kit blinked, too stunned for a moment to speak. "Your mother?"

Akiko had no memory of her mother. She'd been left outside a firehouse as an infant and had been immediately sucked into the foster care system.

Akiko nodded. "I don't know what to tell her."

"How did she know your mother?"

"I don't know. She said she'd tell me when we met. I told her I'd think about it and call her back. I don't know what to do."

Alarm bells were clanging in Kit's head. "Give me the number the woman called from. I'll check it out. And if you decide to go, I'll go with you."

Akiko closed her eyes in relief. "I hoped you'd say that."

"Like there was any doubt." She could see that her sister needed a hug. She opened her arms. "Come on."

Akiko looked surprised, and then her eyes grew glassy with tears. She moved into Kit's embrace and held on tight. "Thank you. I needed this."

Kit wrapped her arms around her slender sister. "I could tell. Promise me you'll wait until I can go with you. As soon as this case is over. Promise me."

"I promise." Akiko pulled away. "You can tell Sam if you want. I know he was wondering, too."

"If he asks, then fine. But I won't volunteer your personal information."

"I trust you. I always have."

Kit felt her own eyes sting. "And I you. Be careful. Do you have any charters booked?"

"Yes, but they're all parties I've booked before and Paolo will be with me."

Kit knew Akiko's first mate, and the man was more than able to defend them. Akiko could take care of herself in a pinch, but Kit was always comforted when Paolo went out on the charters. Akiko took her clients far off the coast, where the fish were big. Too far to get help if she needed it. Paolo was a lifesaver.

"Good." Kit remained calm for her sister's sake, but her gut was screaming that something was wrong with this setup.

"Don't fret. We'll get to the bottom of this. Did she give you your mother's name?"

Another shake of her sister's head. "Said she'd tell me everything when we met."

"I don't like mysterious people," Kit grumbled. "Just . . . be careful." She waited until Akiko had passed through the doors before returning to the conference room, where Sam was studying her whiteboard.

"You've added some names," he said.

"Yep. Today was an eye-opener for sure."

He glanced at her as she sat beside him. "I know about Connor's interview with Veronica Fitzgerald and that Laura Letterman is her defense attorney. Joel called to let me know. After he gave me shit about getting trashed on two margaritas."

Sam's cheeks had pinked up, and Kit thought it was cute. Not that she'd say so. Sam seemed embarrassed enough.

"Don't feel bad. After that interview, Connor took a nap like a baby."

"While you worked." He looked meaningfully at the board.

"Well, yeah. He's done the same for me when I've been too tired to function. He woke up and we interviewed the pilot. He knew Veronica was transporting cash. He'd searched her backpack once when she'd fallen asleep on one of the flights to the Caymans. Said he wanted to make sure she didn't have any guns. He could overlook the cash, but not guns. She wasn't armed, so he let it slide."

"She had a gun today when you picked her up."

"That was in her handbag, not the backpack. He said he would have searched her handbag too, but she was clutching it to her even in her sleep. The money she paid him for each flight was too good for him to make waves. So he kept his mouth shut and did what she asked."

"Did he know anything about the other guy? The PI whose name Veronica claims not to know?"

"No. The pilot said that he only flew her."

"Not very economical on Veronica's part," Sam observed. "There were other ways to hide cash much closer to home."

Kit smiled. "I thought of that as we were talking to the pilot. Turns out she'd bought a town house in George Town in the Caymans. Paid cash. The title is under her Viola Feinstein alias."

"The bad guys always seem to go for houses on the beach."

Kit shrugged. "Not everyone enjoys the desert."

"True." He pointed to the whiteboard. "What's next?"

Kit brought him up to speed, including her plans to reinterview Wilhelmina Munro and to find out who might have known of—and taken advantage of—Shelley Porter's addiction.

"I can find out where she went to rehab," Sam offered. "There could be a connection there. If they knew she was an addict and still using, they'd know she'd grab the cash bait."

Kit wrote that on the whiteboard as a next step. "We're also taking another look at the murder of Jacob Crocker, William Weaver's PI. No one was arrested for his murder. There may have been some physical evidence that can help us. As luck would have it, that was Marshall and Ashton's case. They were upset that they couldn't solve it, so they've taken point."

Sam smiled at her. "Look at you, delegating like a pro."

She lifted her brows. "I *am* a pro."

"Not at delegating."

She sighed. "Fair point. I'm learning."

"I have something else for you. I got another call tonight while Akiko was driving me here. Carla Norton, the landscaper's wife. She'd called Jennifer Porter to offer her condolences on the loss of her sister and niece. Jennifer asked her how someone could have known that she did the wraps for Norton Landscaping."

"I just assumed the killer had seen it on Jennifer's website. Norton's wraps are in their photo gallery."

"Well, the killer would have had to check the website for every auto body shop in the area. Possible, but time-consuming. Carla asked their staff if anyone had requested a recommendation for detailing trailers. One of her landscapers said he was approached by a 'dude with a neckbeard and sunglasses' who asked who'd done the wrap. Her employee told him."

Kit made a face. "A neckbeard and sunglasses means the employee didn't get a good look at his face. Great disguise unless he actually has a neckbeard. When was this?"

"At least two months ago, according to Carla Norton. She said her employee was working on a lawn at the time and didn't think anything of someone asking about the wrap."

"Why would he? And two months ago? That means Munro's killer has been planning this for a while."

"Not terribly surprising. Getting the wrap done—and coordinating a potential mob to help him kill Munro—that would take some time."

She grimaced, still hating the multiple-hands theory. But she had to consider it, of course. It was just . . .

Someone would have spilled that secret, either before the deed or in the days after. There was still time. Someone might come forward. But Kit's gut told her not to hold her breath waiting.

Her gut also told her that Sam had more to say. "You look like you're busting to share."

He grinned. "I am. Neckbeard was driving a tan Chevy Suburban, a model somewhere between 2015 and 2018. Carla's employee didn't get the plates, but it could be a lead."

Kit sat up straighter. "Not the Ford truck he drove when he picked up the trailer?"

"Nope. Maybe you can look at the street cams again. A tan

Chevy Suburban dragging a trailer with no wrap, assuming he cut the wrap off after abducting Munro and stealing the Ferrari."

Kit smiled at him, feeling a zing of excitement at the new direction. "Now, *that* we can do." She wrote it on the board. "We don't know where he took Munro between Wednesday night when he grabbed him and when he dumped him in Anza-Borrego. We don't know where the torture took place."

"If it were me, I would have just done it in the trailer. Backed the Ferrari out and . . . well, do what he did. Then I would have abandoned the trailer. If someone found it, so what? It couldn't be linked to me."

"I'm not sure if I'm impressed or scared that you're putting yourself in a killer's mind."

"Part of my job," he said lightly, but she could hear his irritation.

"Sorry. I did it again. I know you deal with killers. It's just that you're so damn . . . *nice*."

"So are you."

"Not really. Not nearly as nice as you."

"*That* could be true." He said it with a smile that told her she was forgiven. Again. "Carla Norton gave me the name of the landscaper who talked to the man. Said he'd be happy to talk to you. I emailed the guy's contact info to you."

Kit checked her phone and, sure enough, there was the email from Sam. "We'll try to talk to him tomorrow. Wanna come with?"

"Can't, sorry. Have sessions most of tomorrow and I'm on duty at New Horizons starting at four."

"Pesky day job."

He shrugged. "Pays the bills. SDPD doesn't pay enough to cover my rent."

"Certainly not enough to put you in the crosshairs of someone like Ronald Tasker. Promise me that you'll be careful. I don't trust that man."

"Neither do I. But if he meant me harm, I'd already be dead."

Kit shuddered. "Don't say that."

"Doesn't make it any more likely to happen, Kit."

"I know." She pointed to her head. "Here. But here . . ." She tapped her chest. "Gives me the wiggins."

"That's something, I guess."

"That's a lot," she said quietly. "Be careful, Sam. Promise me."

He met her eyes, his sober. "I promise. If you promise the same."

She nodded once and held out her pinkie.

He chuckled and pinkie-swore with her. "Feel better now?" he asked.

"Not really. I'd feel better if you went into a bunker and never came out, but I feel that way about everyone I care about." She sucked in a breath, realizing what she'd said as soon as the words had come out of her mouth. The words, and the sentiment behind them, hovered between them.

Sam just regarded her evenly from behind his Clark Kent glasses. "Gonna take it back?"

"No," she said firmly. "No take-backs."

His gaze grew heated as it dropped to her mouth, but he quickly turned his focus to the whiteboard. "Anything else?"

She was disappointed. He'd considered kissing her and he hadn't. They were at work, though. *Maybe later.*

"The Ferrari," she said. "That's been bugging me. Goddard hasn't found a trace of it online and none of the car dealers have seen it. Munro's killer could be taking it far away to sell and could even be keeping it as a souvenir, like you said. But why? Why take the car at all? It complicates everything. I might have thought that it was a last-minute decision, that maybe there was evidence in or on the car that could connect to the killer, but he was planning this *two months* ago." That he'd asked one of Norton's employees about the wrap so long ago was important new information and had shifted her perspective. "So why go to all the trouble of stealing the car?"

"If I were that filled with rage at Munro, enough to be able to do those things that were done to him—either by myself or as part of a group—and if I'd been a *victim* of Munro's blackmailing..."

She sat up straighter. "I'd see that Ferrari as *mine. My* money bought it. My money that Munro *stole.* I'd want something back for the money he took."

"Bingo."

"Huh." She tilted her head, considering it. "So he might not ever sell it or even drive it. Just having it might be enough."

"Like the people who buy stolen paintings and hide them in a vault. They know they have it and no one else can enjoy it and that's part of the appeal."

"So there's a good chance his killer still has the car."

"I'd say there's a very good chance."

"And when we find the killer, we'll find the car and that will be enough to put him away right there."

"Assuming there was just one killer."

Kit made a face. "Dammit."

"Why are you so against multiple killers? It worked for Agatha Christie."

Kit laughed. "Yeah, well, I'm no Poirot."

"You're better."

Her cheeks heated. "Aw, shucks." She pointed to the whiteboard, uncomfortable with his compliment. "What about the mysterious PI?"

He settled in the chair. "I've been thinking about that, too. To be making the kind of money Munro was pulling in—sounds like about ten million over the last eight years?"

"Give or take. Veronica made five million and Munro kept twice that."

"Joel said that Munro and Veronica grew up together. She was ten years older than he was."

"True. They wouldn't have been in the same school. We need to find out how they met."

Sam hesitated, then shrugged. "It might be a long shot, but try the foster care system."

Kit flinched. "What?"

"The bonds you've forged with your brothers and sisters are through shared pain. Sounds like Veronica and Munro shared the same strong bond. Strong enough for him to trust her with millions of dollars. She held all the cash. She *could* have stolen from him."

"Maybe she did."

"Do you think so?"

"I don't know. I'll dig into Munro's background. He never mentioned anything about growing up in foster care or even growing up poor."

"He wanted to be respected. He wanted to be upper crust. Having a poor childhood would have barred him from some circles."

"Sad but true," Kit murmured. "But that is an excellent point." She frowned, rewinding their conversation. Then she got it. "You think the PI was one of Munro's childhood friends, too."

"Maybe. It's a theory, at least. It would have taken a lot of trust—on both Munro's part and the PI's—to agree to a scheme like this. Especially with the arrangement Veronica claimed they had. That not one of them had all the information."

"Except Brooks Munro."

"He had the information, but he let Veronica handle the money."

"True." Kit's mind was reeling. "We need to have dinner more often. You've given me several more threads to pull."

Sam smiled. "Happy to be of service. But to be technical, we didn't have dinner together."

Kit nodded once. "We need to rectify that situation."

He held her gaze, his green eyes steady. "We do."

"After this case is solved."

"Or Saturday night, whichever comes first." He held up his hand when she opened her mouth to argue. "Connor is having dinner with CeCe. He makes the time. You can, too."

Her argument fizzled. "You're right again. Saturday night. Where will we go?"

"I'll let you know."

And that she wasn't nervous about it? Or annoyed at losing an entire night of investigating?

That should scare the hell out of me.

But it didn't. Because it was Sam. And she trusted him.

CHAPTER NINE

Thank you so very much," Kit said into the speakerphone. She looked at Connor, who crossed his fingers. "We really appreciate you calling us back."

"It's no problem, Detective." Mary Cowen was the office manager for foster care in Tulsa, Oklahoma. "I'm happy to help. What do you need?"

"Well, we're looking for the records of a Viola Feinstein. She's sixty-one now, so she would have aged out of the system forty-three years ago."

It was just a hunch, but Kit had hope. Taking Sam's theory to heart, she'd searched for—and found—the birth certificate associated with Veronica's fake passport. Viola Feinstein, a.k.a. Veronica Fitzgerald, had been born sixty-one years ago in a suburb of Tulsa.

There had been no record of a legal name change, but Kit thought that Veronica was smart enough to figure out how to change her identity. It had been much easier to do forty-three years ago.

Of course, Veronica could have found Viola Feinstein's name on a tombstone and gotten her birth certificate and social security number, but it made more sense that she'd have kept the ones originally issued to her.

At least Kit hoped she had.

"Give me just a moment. Those are old records, but we've done some digitization over the years." There was the sound of clacking keyboard keys and then a satisfied hum. "Yes, here she is. Viola Feinstein entered the foster system at the age of five. She was never adopted. She aged out at eighteen. We don't keep track of them after that. I wish we did."

"I wish you did, too," Kit said, "but this information is valuable. Would it be possible to get a copy of her full file?"

"Oh. Well, most of those records remain confidential. What exactly are you looking for?"

"She's a suspect in a case we're working, ma'am," Connor said. "We're trying to trace her background, including family and childhood friends."

"You're going to need to file for an exception or get a warrant," Mary said. "I'm sorry. I'd like to help you, but there are some things I simply can't share."

She wasn't rude or unpleasant, just bound by the rules of her office and Kit could respect that. "We understand. Thank you for your help." Kit ended the call. "What now?"

"Well," Connor said, "now we know where Veronica started out. Part of me wanted to ask if she'd ever applied to be a guardian herself. Like maybe she'd met Munro while they were in the system together, and she wanted to take care of him. But that they later became lovers is just too icky."

Kit grimaced. "That is icky. But a possibility. If we can't find anything else, we'll circle back. But . . . yeah. Icky."

"If we knew what Brooks Munro's birth name was, we could dig a lot deeper. But I'm wondering when they met—in foster care or later? What if it was before they arrived in San Diego? The fifteen years she worked for him was only here."

Kit had another hunch and brought up the background search site. "Marriage certificates. Viola Feinstein." She waited and then grinned once she'd sorted the results. "Got it. Viola Feinstein married Monroe Brookman in . . . oh."

Connor rolled his chair closer to see her screen, then winced. "Oh. That's . . ."

"They married thirty-three years ago," Kit said. "She would have been twenty-eight. He would have been eighteen."

Connor's wince became a grimace. "It could be worse. He could have been thirteen or fourteen."

"They weren't together for fifteen years. They were together for more than *thirty* years. I'm shocked she kept her composure when we interviewed her yesterday morning."

"Explains the tears, though," Connor said. "I'm surprised she allowed Munro to marry Wilhelmina. I guess we can add bigamy to Munro's sins."

"Little late now. Plus, I think we'll find that's the least of his sins. He either killed William Weaver's PI or had him killed."

"I guess that would be the worst—so far. But blackmail's pretty damn bad, too. What do we know about Monroe Brookman?"

Kit typed Munro's real name into the search engine. "Also born in Tulsa."

"How did they meet?"

"That's going to take a little more digging."

"Then when did they start their life of crime?" Connor asked. "I don't think they suddenly became Bonnie and Clyde when they arrived in San Diego."

"I agree. Let's do a deeper dive for criminal records."

Connor rose. "I'm getting some coffee. Want some?"

"Yes, please." Kit hunched over her keyboard, intent on discovering all the details of Viola Feinstein's and Monroe Brookman's pasts.

By the time Connor came back with coffee—from the coffee shop next door and not the sludge in the bullpen—she had a decent start.

"I was standing in line, thinking about this," Connor said as he put Kit's coffee in front of her. "I kept thinking that if they had a criminal past, wouldn't that have shown up in background checks when Munro ran for city council, so I called one of my contacts at city hall. They don't do full police checks on the candidates. And we didn't run fingerprints on Munro after he died because all his fingers were gone. The ME used dental records for the ID."

Kit inhaled the aroma of the dark roast, with cream and sugar the way she liked it. "Thank you. Yeah, I thought the same thing but haven't made the call yet because I hit pay dirt. I called Mary Cowen back and she confirmed that Monroe Brookman was also in the foster system."

"So Sam was right."

"He was. Cowen couldn't help me discover how their paths intersected, so I did criminal background checks. Bonnie and Clyde, a.k.a. Viola and Monroe, started their lives of crime about two years after their wedding. Or at least that was the first time they got caught. He did some time in a county jail for theft. She was picked up a few years later for grand theft. She stole a gold bracelet."

"I wonder if it was the one she left in the Ferrari."

"Maybe. I doubt that anything her mother gave her would have lasted thirteen years in the foster system and time in and out of jail. I could be wrong, but . . ." Kit shrugged. "They went on to do more crimes over the next ten years. Then they just up and disappeared twenty years ago. The last thing on Monroe Brookman's record is jumping bail on an arrest for swindling."

"And they became Veronica Fitzgerald and Brooks Munro. They must have paid someone a lot of cash for their new identities. No one has even questioned them up until now."

"That we're aware of," Kit said. "If they're involved in the murder of Weaver's PI, who knows what else they've done to protect themselves? And maybe that's what Weaver's PI found out."

"Maybe." Connor frowned at the whiteboard. "Still, nobody noticed when he ran for city council? His face was all over the TV and the internet."

"He was a small-time crook in another state. Maybe no one was looking for him." Kit brought up one of Monroe Brookman's mug shots. "Plus, he's changed a lot. Had some work done."

"You're right. He's changed enough that facial recognition software wouldn't have picked him out. What about the PI?" Connor asked. "Munro's PI, I mean, not Weaver's dead PI. Are there any criminal cohorts that Munro could have been pals with back then?"

"I don't know. Let's place a few calls to the law enforcement agencies who arrested them over the years. We could get lucky and find out that someone got arrested along with them."

"Veronica would have known the PI's name, then."

"Yeah. I didn't think she was telling the truth about that," Kit said.

"Neither did I. But something else is puzzling me. The house in the Caymans."

Kit set her laptop aside. "I'm listening."

"She's crazy in love with Brooks Munro, they're tearing up the sheets and have a love for the ages."

Kit huffed. "I didn't need the tearing-up-the-sheets mental image, so thanks for that."

"You're welcome. Why would she buy a house in the Caymans with her share of the take if Munro was always here?"

"He couldn't have expected to stay married to Wilhelmina forever," Kit reasoned. "Maybe he planned to join Veronica in paradise after the inevitable divorce."

Connor raised a brow. "*Or* what if Veronica was doing the PI on the side because Munro was married and that pissed her off? Maybe the PI planned to join her in paradise. She did tell him that they had to get away. It sounded like she meant together."

"Huh. I never even considered that."

"It might not be true. But I didn't believe she didn't know the guy's name."

"The pilot said he flew her alone," Kit said.

"What if the pilot lied? She was paying him for his discretion."

"Maybe," Kit allowed. "Or he could be afraid the PI would come after him."

"More likely," Connor agreed.

"Do we *know* that Brooks Munro never traveled with her?"

Connor shook his head. "No, we don't, but we only checked his current alias. Let's find out if Monroe Brookman's passport has been to the Caymans."

Kit made a call to one of her contacts at the State Department, just as she'd done for Veronica's passport the day before. "Hey, Richard. It's Kit McKittrick again."

"Another passport search?"

"Yep. Can you look up Monroe Brookman? He's fifty-one years old, if that helps narrow it down."

"Give me a minute." A moment later he was back. "No record of Monroe Brookman having a passport."

Kit thanked him and ended the call. "That was a bust."

"For now, let's focus on the PI," Connor said. "If we find him, we'll know who they were blackmailing."

"True. We can come at the PI from the past and present. If the PI did accompany Veronica to the Caymans, the pilot might be able to give us a current name. If we're lucky, we might be able to ID him from Munro's past arrest records, if he was someone Munro knew from the past. Let's get numbers for all the jurisdictions where Munro and Veronica were arrested back in the day, and then we can make calls." She sat back in the chair and studied Connor. "Did you believe Veronica didn't know the names on the list?"

"Mostly, yes. Only because she doesn't have much to lose at this point. She's admitted to blackmail, she was caught with the ill-gotten gains thereof, and she'll go down for passport fraud."

"Will she, though? It was her real identity."

"Good point. One I'm sure her lawyer will pounce on once Veronica comes clean about it. But we did find more than two hundred grand of unreported income on her person, and she has official state documents in a fake name, like her driver's license, so she'll be in trouble with someone. In any case, I think that she would have spilled the tea on the blackmail list had she known their names. She was in an intense mental place."

"She was. You helped to get her to that point. Nicely done, by the way."

"Thank you." He cut a small bow. "But what if we hit a brick wall in our search for the PI?"

"Then we go back to the trailer—our most concrete tie to Munro's killer. We look for a tan Chevy Suburban towing a trailer."

Connor nodded. "I'd say ask Marshall and Ashton to view the street cams, but they're off looking into Jacob Crocker's murder."

"I already asked Navarro to put one of the analysts on it and he assigned someone, so that's being covered. New question: how do you think Munro found out that William Weaver was about to rehire Jacob Crocker as his PI? Was that what triggered Munro to have him killed?"

"Maybe Munro didn't find out. Maybe Crocker didn't get rid of the information he found out about Munro. Maybe he tried to blackmail Munro and got himself killed."

"All possibilities. For now, let's focus on finding Munro's PI. He has the information we need."

"For all we know, he's fled to the Caymans. If I was Munro's partner and I found out what had happened to him, I'd be on the first plane out. We should check Veronica's house in the Caymans." He raised his hand. "I'll go."

Kit laughed. "It's a good idea, but I think we can ask for local law enforcement assistance on that."

"Fine," Connor groused. "You're no fun. Give me a list of people to call about Viola and Monroe's past life of crime. We could be on our way to the Caymans, but noooo."

"Pretty sure you'll live. Let's start by calling prison wardens. I want to know who Munro's best friends were along the way."

"Sam." A woman sitting at one of the coffee shop's tables waved to him.

With a smile, he joined her at the table. "Maggie. It's been too long."

Maggie Doyle managed one of the drug rehab facilities in San Diego. Shelley had completed her thirty-day stint in Maggie's clinic, under the care of one of her rehab counselors. But Maggie, a recovering addict herself, was a hands-on manager and interacted with the clients and their families as needed.

"It has. I'd love to spend all afternoon catching up with you, but I don't have much time."

"Neither do I. This is my lunch break." Sam asked a server for his coffee in a to-go cup, then studied Maggie, who was sipping her coffee.

"So," Maggie said. "You asked about Shelley Porter when you called this morning. What do you need to know that couldn't have been handled with an email?"

"She was murdered last week."

Maggie gasped. "*What?* How? By whom? Although I guess that's what you're trying to find out."

"It is. Someone lured her out with the promise of ready cash."

"Done deal for Shelley," Maggie murmured sadly. "I didn't have high hopes for her when she left after her thirty days."

Sam leaned in, aware that Maggie was unlikely to be able to share everything he wanted to know, what with HIPAA laws and all. "Why not? And I'll also tell you that her mother's body was found alongside hers."

Maggie's shoulders sagged. "I liked her mom. She wanted

Shelley to be sober so badly. Unfortunately, Shelley didn't want to be sober. She liked using. I think she was just biding her time until she could go home and use again. She didn't like using alone, though, so she was always trying to drag people into her circle."

"We think that someone knew her vulnerability and used the promise of several thousand dollars in cash to get her to break the rules of her workplace, to deliver some finished merchandise her killer hadn't paid for."

"You want to know who knew she would be desperate for dough?"

"Yes. Am I looking for a needle in a haystack?"

"I think you're looking for a particular piece of hay in a hay-stack," Maggie said ruefully. "Shelley wanted to be tough, but underneath she was just another addict desperate for her next fix. Anyone with an eye could have seen it."

"Did she have any visitors while she was with you?"

"I thought you might ask me that." Maggie pulled a sheet of paper from her pocket. "I did *not* give this to you."

"Nope. Never saw it before. Never even saw *you* before."

Maggie chuckled. "You don't have to go that far."

Sam took the page and scanned its contents. "She got visits from her mom and her aunt Jennifer. Her friend Julie visited a few times."

"Nice girl. I really hoped that Shelley wouldn't drag Julie down with her."

"I don't think she did. Julie seemed very sober when we talked to her."

"You've been busy."

"Yeah." Sam pointed to an unfamiliar name. "Who's LeRoy Hawkins?"

She frowned. "He visited once. Said he was a minister with a local church's youth group. I know the youth minister at that church and his name isn't LeRoy. So I called the church, but they'd never heard of LeRoy. Unfortunately, by then the man had ended his visit with Shelley and was gone."

Sam went with a hunch. "Did he happen to have a neck-beard?"

Maggie's eyes widened. "He did, yes. Do you know him?"

"No, but I want to meet him," Sam said grimly.

"I see. Is it best if I don't ask more questions?"

"Probably, but I have a few more. How long do you keep the recordings from your security cams?"

"Three months. Do you need to see them?"

"I think my colleagues at SDPD will. Did you happen to see what LeRoy Hawkins was driving?"

"A motorcycle. Or at least he had a helmet under his arm. I remember wondering how he got the thing fastened under his chin with his thick beard. And I only remember that because the church youth minister he lied about working for asked for his description, so the helmet was in my mind."

Sam was disappointed. He'd hoped they could get the Sub-urban on video and check its plates. But at least they had the guy with the neckbeard. Kit would be able to work with that, he was sure.

"He only visited the one time?" Sam asked. "Midway through Shelley's stay?"

"That's what the logs show, and we're pretty diligent."

"I know you are," he said warmly. "Did Shelley seem happy to see him?"

"Not really. She didn't seem to know him."

"Anything else you can remember about Shelley?"

Maggie shook her head. "Just that she seemed so lost when she finally got clean. I think she'd been using for a long time." She checked the time. "I'm so sorry, Sam, but I have to get back."

"So do I. My next session starts in ten minutes."

"Will you get lunch?" she asked, her tone motherly.

"I have a sandwich in my desk drawer."

They rose together, Sam spying the server bringing him his coffee. "I'll get both of these," he said, giving the server enough cash for both his and Maggie's coffee, plus a generous tip.

The server beamed. "Thank you, Dr. Reeves. Have a nice day."

Maggie linked her hand through his arm as they left the coffee shop. "Come here often?"

"Too often. I need to kick the caffeine habit, but that's not going to happen today." They got outside and Sam gave her hand a squeeze. "Don't be a stranger, Maggie."

"Same, Sam. And enjoy your new job. I catch your name in the news every so often. You seem to be doing well."

Sam smiled. "I am."

Maggie began to walk away, backward so that she could still see him. "You're happy?"

"Yes, ma'am. Very happy."

"Good. You deserve some happy." She waved before heading to her car.

Sam took a sip of the coffee, hoping it would keep him going for the rest of the afternoon. He hadn't slept well last night. Thoughts of Kit had kept him awake.

She'd said she cared about him. Which he'd already known, but it was really nice to hear. But that she'd admitted it had scared her. Still, she hadn't taken it back and he'd almost kissed her.

He hadn't because he was hoping to leave her wanting more.

Too much of Sam and she'd be all one-and-done. She'd walk away before they'd even gotten started. So he'd left her hanging and—at the time—had been glad he had. She'd nearly pouted.

Later, lying alone in his bed, he'd wished that he'd kissed her.

But he'd have to be strong. Kit needed slow and steady, no matter how much it was killing him.

At least he could give her some new intel. They now knew how Shelley's killer found out she was an addict.

Navarro sat behind his desk, his chin resting on his steepled fingers as Kit and Connor brought him up to speed.

"So did you find who you were looking for?" Navarro asked. "Anyone who might have been the BFF of Brooks Munro, a.k.a. Monroe Brookman?"

"We might have," Kit said. "We were able to talk to the wardens or sheriffs of four of the jails where Munro did time over the years."

"All as Monroe Brookman?"

Connor nodded. "Theft mostly. A lot of swindling."

"And his BFF?" Navarro asked.

"Munro seemed to make friends wherever he went," Kit said, "but we've crossed most of the names off the list because they're either in prison or dead. We've got two possibilities. Two distinctly different people from a height standpoint, so we don't have one guy changing his name again. At least not before he came to San Diego. The first is Walter Grossman. He's over six feet tall and built like a tank. He's done time for forgery. The other is Darrin Carter. He's five-four and, from his photo, he looks like a light breeze would blow him away. We've got mug shots of both, and we're going to show them to the pilot who was going to fly Veronica out of here yesterday."

"He said he flew her alone," Navarro said.

Connor shrugged. "We're hoping he lied. We've run both men's names and their photos through the PI licenses in the state's database. None of them are a match, but he might not have a license in California. Maybe not anywhere. We're still hopeful the pilot can point us in the right direction."

Navarro crossed the fingers of both hands. "Good luck. I'll give the brass an update. You're making progress."

"Any news from the analyst who's checking street cams for the trailer?" Connor asked.

"Not yet. I'll let you know when he's got something."

Kit started to stand, then sat again when her cell phone began to buzz with an incoming call. "It's Sam," she told the others before hitting accept and putting the phone to her ear. "Hey. What's up?"

"A guy with a neckbeard visited Shelley Porter in rehab," Sam said.

Kit perked up. That information was almost as good as caffeine. "I'm putting you on speaker. I'm with Connor and Navarro."

"Hi," Sam said once they could hear him. "I was just telling Kit that a man with a neckbeard visited Shelley Porter in rehab. Gave his name as LeRoy Hawkins, but I'm pretty sure that was an alias."

"A guy with a neckbeard asked Norton Landscaping where they got their wraps done." Navarro exhaled. "I guess we know now how he knew that Shelley was susceptible to a bribe."

"The rehab manager I talked to said that Shelley was just biding her time until she could go home and use again, and that if anyone had an inclination to see, they would have known. Neckbeard Guy could have picked up on her desperation."

"How did he know she was in rehab?" Connor asked.

"I'm thinking it was her mother's Facebook page," Sam said

with a sigh. "Or her aunt Jennifer's. I just checked and they both asked for prayers for Shelley. They asked friends if they'd visit Shelley, maybe give her a reason to get sober for good. If the neckbeard guy had been watching Jennifer's social media, he would have seen that Shelley was in rehab."

"So that box is checked," Kit said sadly.

"One more thing," Sam said. "He wasn't driving a Suburban at that point. He had a motorcycle. Or at least he carried a helmet into the rehab center with him. Damn, I have to go. I have a session starting in three minutes."

"Bye, Sam," she, Connor, and Navarro chorused. "Thank you, Sam," Kit added.

"You're welcome. Talk to you all soon."

Kit ended the call, her mind already trying to place this new information. "One of the things that's bothered me is how long that trailer was in Munro's neighborhood on Wednesday. It arrived around six that morning. Monroe was with Veronica all night on Tuesday and, according to the guard shack logs, didn't go home afterward on Wednesday morning. He didn't get home from work that night until five or so. I kept wondering what the killer did all day while he waited."

"And?" Navarro prompted.

"And, if he had a motorcycle . . ." She let the thought trail off.

"He could have left for the day and returned later to take both the Ferrari and Munro," Connor finished. "We should check the guard shack's camera feed for a motorcycle."

"I'll have the analyst do that," Navarro said. "You focus on finding this PI. Speaking of whom, are either of Munro's old prison pals the same size as the guy with the neckbeard?"

Kit shook her head. "We thought of that. Neckbeard Guy is about five-ten with an average build, based on the video Ace Diamond gave us. Neither of Munro's former prison pals fit that description. We're hoping the pilot can give us more info. We're off to question him now. We'll keep you up to date, boss."

Connor groaned. "Not again."

Kit joined Connor at the observation room glass. Then sighed.

Sitting at the table in the interview room was Steven Neal, the pilot who'd flown Veronica to the Caymans multiple times. He was joined by his attorney.

Laura Letterman.

"Did she give out a two-for-one discount?" Kit asked.

Connor snorted softly. "BOGO get-out-of-jail-free cards. You or me?" He pulled a coin from his pocket. "Flip you for it."

Kit smiled, feeling a little feral. "Let's both go in. Shake Miss Letterman up a little."

"Cool. What's our strategy?"

Kit shrugged. "Show the pilot the mug shots of Munro's prison BFFs. Let's see how he reacts."

"I think we should have a better game plan than that. I pulled his financials."

"When did you do that?" Kit asked, wishing she'd done the same.

"I came in early this morning since I had to take off for dinner with CeCe's folks. Steven Neal owns his plane, but financially he's barely holding on by his fingernails. He's living month to month. He's behind on his taxes and his checking account balance is less than a hundred bucks."

"A private pilot who owns his own plane should be able to consistently pull in decent money."

"He actually does," Connor said. "His schedule is booked for the next four months, and his documented income stream is consistent and robust. Those are the customers who paid for their flights with a credit card or wire transfer. We know at least one customer—Veronica—paid in cash, so there might be even more money coming in that doesn't go through his business accounts. We can check any flight plans he submitted to see how many extras he flew. But he spent a *hell* of a lot of money at the racetrack over the summer. By September, he was charging thousands of dollars to his credit cards up at Del Mar."

The horse racing track had never held appeal for Kit. The animals were beautiful, but even the thought of gambling had always made her slightly ill.

"And that was just his credit cards," Connor went on. "Who knows what he's done with the cash payments and tips?"

"Huh." She went back to studying the pilot, who now sat with his head in his hands. "That means if he gets stuck in jail, he won't be able to fulfill his contracted jobs."

"Which means he'll be deep in debt in less than two weeks."

She looked up at Connor again. "You're right. Scaring him with jail time is a better way to go in. Anything else?"

"He was divorced two years ago and has shared custody of his two daughters. Child support is a hefty part of his monthly expenses. He'd be more than able to afford it if he hadn't spent so much at the racetrack."

"At least he pays child support," Kit muttered, because so many parents did not. "But that he does pay it means he cares about his kids and will want to see them grow up, not see them through plexiglass on prison visitation day. Nice work."

"Thank you. I felt bad leaving last night."

She smiled at him. "You shouldn't. It's balance, and you're doing well with that. Don't be like me."

Connor nudged her shoulder with his. "You're improving. Everyone says so. Come on. Let's find out if the pilot knows either of Munro's prison buddies. Bad cop or good cop?"

"You be bad cop. Letterman isn't going to believe your good cop again so soon. It's been months since I've tangled with her."

"Oh, I think she remembers you," Connor said slyly. "You got the one she let get away."

"She *drove* Sam away," Kit corrected with a huff. "Cheating on him."

Connor chuckled. "Down, girl."

Kit sighed. She needed to stow her personal issues with Laura Letterman. And Kit had "got" Sam?

She guessed that time would tell.

By the time they walked into the interview room, Kit was composed and ready for Laura Letterman. The woman wouldn't want her client to say a word, but she and Connor could make the man talk. Kit was certain of it.

Laura gave Kit and Connor a narrow-eyed glare. "I've told my client that you'll try to rattle him. He's not to say a word."

Steven Neal lifted his head. His eyes were bleary, as if he hadn't slept a wink. His skin was pale and his hands shook.

Kit wondered if gambling was the man's only vice. He looked like he was going through withdrawal.

"We really just want his help," Kit said, taking a seat across from the pilot, Connor sitting on her left. He set the folder holding the mug shots on the table.

"Uh-huh," Laura said, unconvinced. "What kind of help?"

"We're trying to identify two men who might have been connected to Mr. Munro," Kit said.

Laura shook her head. "He said that he didn't know Munro, nor did he fly him anywhere. Are we done?"

"No," Kit said sweetly. "Mr. Neal, do you know a man named

Walter Grossman?" He was the taller, more heavily built of the two ex-cons.

"I don't know that name." He seemed to have radically aged since the night before. Perspiration beaded on his forehead even though it wasn't hot in the room. His body was visibly shaking.

Definitely some kind of withdrawal going on.

"Mr. Neal, would you like a glass of water?" Kit asked, her concern true. If the man passed out, he'd be of no use to them.

"No," Steven said through gritted teeth. "Who's the other man you're looking for?"

"Darrin Carter," Connor said.

Once again, the pilot shook his head. "No."

Laura Letterman gathered her purse. "I think we're done, then. Always nice to see you, Detectives."

"Not so fast." Kit patted the table and the pilot looked back up. Without saying another word, Connor slid the photos of Walter Grossman and Darrin Carter across the table.

Laura glanced at the photos, trepidation clear in her expression. Kit guessed that the attorney had been expecting another gruesome autopsy photo like the one Connor had shown Veronica the day before. When she saw they were only mug shots, she relaxed.

Steven Neal, however, did not relax. His eyes widened, filling with fear as his gaze locked on to the photo of Walter Grossman. Then he closed his eyes as his shoulders sagged.

"You do recognize his face, then," Kit said in her kindest voice. "Who is he, Mr. Neal?"

"Do not say another word," Laura instructed.

Steven buried his face in his hands again. "I just wanted to fly," he muttered mournfully.

"You never intended to get caught up in Veronica Fitzgerald's shenanigans," Kit said, still kindly. It didn't matter what the man had intended. He'd knowingly transported a woman carrying large quantities of cash out of the country. But she'd be sweet. For now. "I get that. Where did you see the man in this photo?"

"Steven," Laura warned.

Connor leaned forward, elbows on the table, taking up more space than he needed. He looked bigger and tougher than he had moments before.

"We know you're teetering on financial ruin," Connor said coldly. "We know that between your gambling and child support, you don't have two pennies to rub together. I'm not even sure how you're managing to pay your attorney here, but that's your business."

That was a good point, and Kit made a mental note to find out who was paying Laura Letterman. She'd bet it was Veronica.

"Is there a question in there, Detective?" Laura asked, just as coldly.

"More a statement of fact, Miss Letterman," Connor said, his sneer rather remarkable. "We can keep Mr. Neal here for a long time while he waits for his trial. He can't afford to miss a single chartered flight, much less weeks of missed income. Maybe months. By the time he's released, he'll have nothing to return to. His business will have failed, his plane will have been impounded, and his wife will probably want to revoke his parental custody because he won't have been able to pay his child support."

Steven looked up then, panic in his eyes. "No."

"They're trying to scare you, Steven," Laura said calmly.

Steven swallowed. "It's working."

Kit smiled. "We can ask the prosecutor to make a deal. Maybe let you out on your own recognizance." Like *that* would ever happen. The man owned a plane, for God's sake. He could fly anywhere.

"You know that's not going to happen," Laura snapped. "He'd be a flight risk. They won't allow him to continue flying."

"Better to be out and working somewhere," Kit said cheerfully, "than to be in jail and lose what little custody he has of his kids. Flying a plane isn't the only job on the face of the earth. And he still owns the plane. If he cooperates, he could sell it and start over in a new career."

Laura just shook her head. "Does anyone ever believe you? That is the biggest sack of lies I've ever heard spewed."

The woman was trying to get a rise out of her. "I might lie when the need arises, Miss Letterman, but I'm telling the truth now, and you know it. If Mr. Neal cooperates, he can at least partially salvage his financial situation and hopefully retain custody of his children." She turned her gaze on the pilot. "You pay your child support on time. You fought for custody." Which she didn't know but felt comfortable guessing. "You must love your children, sir. I'm not going to tell you that you won't serve any jail time. That's not mine to promise, one way or another. That's the prosecutor's job. I will tell you that helping us identify the man in this photo will only help your chances of getting out of this with the least possible disruption to your life—or the lives of your daughters."

Steven had paled even further. "He'll kill me."

"Who?" Laura asked, suddenly concerned. "The man in this photo?"

Steven nodded, his swallow audible.

"Then it's best if you help us catch him, isn't it?" Kit asked, keeping the sarcasm out of her tone, even though she felt it in her mind. "If you don't, eventually you'll get out and you'll be looking over your shoulder forever."

Steven scrubbed his palms over his face. "Damned if I do tell you and damned if I don't."

"More damned if you don't," Connor snapped.

"He's right," Kit said. "Look, you flew Veronica Fitzgerald out of the country knowing she held a fake passport. You had to have known. You knew she was carrying a lot of cash. If she's found guilty of money laundering—which I'm certain she will be, considering she was carrying over two hundred thousand dollars in cash yesterday—then you could be charged as a co-conspirator. Altogether, you're talking about a potentially long time behind bars. We need this man's name." She tapped the mug shot. "Now."

"Or you might not see your kids again," Connor said quietly, but his voice was sterner than Kit had ever heard it. "Or, if you do, it'll be through a plexiglass window on visitation day. Is that how you want them to see you, Steven?"

Steven's jaw tightened, and his eyes filled with tears. "No," he whispered.

"There's also the issue of whatever drug has you in withdrawal right now," Kit went on. "We can try to get you some help. Your situation is still salvageable, Steven. Work with us here."

Steven closed his eyes, sending tears streaking down his cheeks. "Miss Letterman? What should I do?"

Kit felt a small morsel of sympathy. The man had no priors that they knew of. He really might have gotten in over his head. But she couldn't afford sympathy now.

Kit met Laura's gaze directly. "You know we're right. Tell him."

Laura looked away on a sigh. "I won't let him tell you anything until I have an agreement in writing from the DA."

Kit pushed away from the table. "Of course."

CHAPTER TEN

Sam looked up from his paperwork at the knock on the doorframe of the New Horizons office he shared with some of the other volunteers. "Sheila. What can I do for you?"

Sheila Sunley came into his office, two cups of coffee in hand. "I needed a pick-me-up, so I got you one, too."

The pint-sized dynamo was the director of New Horizons. Very few teenagers could resist her bubbly personality.

Sam accepted the coffee with a grateful smile. "I feel like I've read these pages ten times already and I still can't tell you what they say."

The stack of papers was part of a new state policy governing nonprofit therapy groups. It was written in legalese, which Sam could usually parse. But his mind was elsewhere today.

He had another date with Kit on Saturday night.

Sheila nodded at the pages in his hand. "I had the same problem. That's why I handed them over to you."

"Gee, thanks," he said dryly.

"You're welcome," she chirped. "I do have other news for you, and I guarantee that your 'thank you' will be far more sincere."

Sam sat up straighter. "Hit me."

She smiled at him. "The Norton boys, Davy and Danny."

Sam couldn't contain his grin. "You found them?"

"Yep. I sent out their photos to shelters across the state. I got one reply just now, from a shelter up in Ukiah."

"Ukiah? I've heard of it, but . . ." He searched the name on his phone and blinked. "That's over six hundred miles north of here. How the hell did they get way up there?"

"Hitchhiked, according to the shelter director."

"Makes sense, I guess. Ukiah's right off the 101. Are they still there?"

"They left this morning, but she thinks they'll be back this evening for dinner and a bed. I thought you might want to pass the news on to their mom."

"I'm nearly positive she'll get in her car right away," Sam said. "She could be there by morning, for sure. Will the boys go home with her?"

Sheila shrugged. "The woman I talked to said she got the feeling that the kids were tired of moving around. The director said she'd call if they came back."

"I'll call Mrs. Norton right away. Thank you, Sheila."

"You're more than welcome. Sometimes the kids' stories end well, Sam. We grab onto those and let them carry us through the stories that don't. I have to help the kitchen get ready for dinner. We've got a full house." Her cheeks dimpled. "We've even recruited some new volunteers to help serve."

Sam paused, his cell phone in his hand. "New volunteers? Who?"

"You'll see. Bye, Sam."

She took her coffee and left the office, humming under her breath.

Sam pushed his curiosity for the new volunteers aside and dialed Carla Norton. She answered on the first ring.

"Mrs. Norton, this is Dr. Reeves. I might have a location on your boys."

Her gasp ended in a choked sob. "Where? I'll go right now."

"They're up in Ukiah, at a homeless shelter. They were this morning, anyway. The director thinks they'll be back for dinner and a bed. I figured you would want to get up there ASAP."

"Absolutely. Thank you, Dr. Reeves. Thank you so very much."

"You're welcome. Drive safely." He ended the call and sighed in relief.

There were so many homeless kids wandering the country. Hopefully by tomorrow two of those kids would be on their way home. He only hoped that Mr. Norton would be able to mend the rift with his sons.

But that was their business now.

He'd readjusted his glasses so that he could once again try reading the new state rules when giggles met his ears. This time when he looked up, he saw three teenage girls gathered in his doorway.

"Here's trouble," he said with a smile.

Rita, Tiffany, and Emma giggled again and piled into his office. "Are you feeling better, Dr. Sam?" Rita asked. "I mean, my real name is Margarita, but I won't drink the things. Tequila is nasty."

His cheeks heated. That the kids had seen him under the influence had been embarrassing when he'd been tipsy. Now that he was sober, it was even worse. "How do you know what tequila tastes like?"

Rita rolled her eyes. "My last foster home before Mom and Pop McK had a fully stocked bar."

Sam's eyes widened. "Your foster parents gave you access to a fully stocked bar?"

"No," Rita said in a *duh* tone of voice. "But one of the kids could pick locks and stole a bottle one night."

Tiffany turned to study her friend. "Did the kid teach you to pick locks?"

"He did," Rita said. "I'll show you both later."

Sam pinched the bridge of his nose. "Just don't use your knowledge for evil, okay?"

"I won't," Rita promised. "The only thing Pop McK keeps locked up is his shotgun. I don't want to even touch it."

Both Tiffany and Emma shuddered in agreement.

"Are you the new volunteers Miss Sunley mentioned to me?"

Tiffany nodded. "We are. We wanted to earn community service credits for graduation. Rita figured we'd work here and give back."

Sam's chest warmed. He'd met Rita through the McKittricks as she'd just been placed with them when he'd met Kit back in the spring. Tiffany and Emma had been runaways Sam had discovered on a street corner downtown. That they were all planning for high school graduation made his heart happy.

"I think that's amazing. You girls make me so proud of you."

"Awwww," the three chorused in unison. "Thank you, Dr. Sam."

He laughed. "Go on now. Dinner isn't going to serve itself. Who brought you down here?"

"Pop," Rita said. "He's whittling in the common room. He

had a bunch of kids gathered around him to watch." She smiled slyly. "He's making something for you."

More warmth bloomed in Sam's chest. He'd already had one Harlan McKittrick carving—of Siggy. He couldn't wait to see what Harlan carved next.

But both Tiffany and Emma had turned to shush Rita. "That was supposed to be a secret," Emma hissed.

Rita looked crestfallen. "It was? I'm sorry, Dr. Sam."

Sam could only smile affectionately at the three of them. "I'm old, girls. I'll have forgotten about it before you're halfway to the kitchen."

"You're not that old," Tiffany said pragmatically. "Like, maybe forty?"

Sam winced. "Ouch. I'm only thirty-six. Go on before you decide I'm ready for retirement."

They left as they'd come in, giggling.

Sam hoped he'd hear them laugh for a very long time.

He'd settled in to read the new rules once again when his cell phone buzzed. Sighing, he checked the caller ID and was once again alert. "Maggie Doyle," he said once he'd hit ACCEPT. "How are you?"

The rehab director didn't waste time on pleasantries. "I've got the footage from our security cameras from the day LeRoy Hawkins visited Shelley Porter. Who should I send it to?"

"Kit McKittrick or Connor Robinson. They're the lead detectives. Did you get a clear view of his face?"

"Not clear. Now that I'm looking at the recording, I can see that his beard isn't real, but I didn't notice that when he came in that day. It's a thick beard, designed to make you notice it and not his face. I hope it helps."

"I hope it does, too," Sam said. "Thank you, Maggie."

"You're always welcome. Gotta run. Don't be a stranger."

With a sigh, he gave up on looking at the new rules and called Kit.

"Are you all right?" was her first question, before she even said hello.

"I'm fine. At New Horizons. Heads up, the director from Shelley's rehab, Maggie Doyle, is sending you security footage from when the neckbeard guy came to see Shelley."

"Excellent. It'll give us something to do while we wait for Joel and Laura to hammer out a plea agreement for the pilot."

Sam winced. "Laura?"

Kit sighed. "Sorry, Sam. Both Veronica Fitzgerald and Steven Neal, the pilot, have obtained legal counsel. Laura Letterman."

Sam pinched the bridge of his nose once again. "I bet Joel is having a fun time."

"Not so much. He hates her a lot more than you do."

Which was odd, really. Sam should hate Laura Letterman more than he did. She had cheated on him, after all—with Joel, a stranger at the time who hadn't known Laura had a fiancé. Not until Sam had walked in on the two of them in bed.

He grimaced, the mental picture still crisp.

But it had led to Joel and Sam becoming best friends, so there was that.

"I don't have to see her, do I?"

"Nope. Hopefully the pilot will give us the name of Munro's PI."

"You got a lead on the PI? Good job, Kit."

"Thank you," she said, which was a cause for celebration right there. Kit never simply said thank you without diminishing her own achievements. "We found a few of Munro's buddies from prison. The pilot recognized one of them, but Laura wouldn't let him give us the name the guy's currently using until Joel put his plea offer in writing. He was in court today, so he's just getting started on the plea deal. We're headed to see Wilhelmina Munro while we're waiting. We have news for her."

"What kind of news?"

"Munro and Fitzgerald were married thirty-three years ago. Wilhelmina's not Munro's legal wife."

"Oof. That's not going to be a fun conversation."

"No, I don't think it will be."

"Could they have gotten divorced before Munro married Wilhelmina?" Sam asked.

"There's no record of a divorce—and we've been searching. Anyway, thanks for the heads-up. See you later."

This time when the call ended, Sam put his phone away, grabbed the cooling coffee Sheila had brought him, and went to the kitchen to help with dinner. And if he happened to see what Harlan was carving, he wouldn't let on that he knew it was for him.

The state's new rules could wait another day.

San Diego, California
Tuesday, January 10, 4:15 p.m.

"I'd almost prefer a death notification," Connor muttered as he knocked on the front door of Wilhelmina Munro's rented condo.

"I don't imagine she's going to take the news well," Kit said.

They'd come to tell Wilhelmina Munro that she wasn't legally married since he'd already been married to Veronica Fitzgerald. This was not going to be fun.

At the same time, if Wilhelmina had had any part in Munro's murder, hopefully discovering that she wasn't legally bound to the man—and had never been—might make her upset enough to let something slip. Murder might have been cheaper than a divorce, but she was about to learn she hadn't needed to do either of those.

Connor was frowning at the door that no one was opening. "I can hear movement in there, so someone's home. Mrs. Munro?" he called, knocking again. "It's San Diego PD. We need to talk with you."

"Just a minute!" a voice called back from inside.

It was at least a minute. More like two minutes before the door opened, revealing a slightly sweaty and disheveled Wilhelmina Munro. "Can I help you?" she asked, dabbing at her brow with a tissue. "I was just working out."

"We need to talk to you, ma'am," Kit said. "May we come in?"

Wilhelmina sighed. "I guess so." She opened the door wider and Connor and Kit filed in. "Would you like to sit down?"

Kit sidestepped the yoga mat on the living-room floor. "Thank you. Where is Mr. Rafferty?"

"He went grocery shopping. Why? Should he be here?"

"Oh no. I was just curious." It was better that the man wasn't there. They might get different answers from Wilhelmina without Rafferty hanging on her every word. When they were all seated, Kit drew a breath. "We've learned new information about Mr. Munro."

Wilhelmina's brows lifted. "What did he do?"

At least the woman wouldn't be surprised that Munro had lied. "He wasn't born Brooks Munro," Connor began. "He was originally Monroe Brookman and he's served time in prison."

Wilhelmina's body stilled. "For what?"

"Mostly white-collar crime," Connor said. "He . . . well, he had a partner."

"Veronica Fitzgerald," Wilhelmina said flatly. "Those two

were thick as thieves." Her laugh was hollow. "I guess it's because they were thieves."

"Among other things," Connor said. "They were also married."

Wilhelmina's eyes widened. "They were *what*?"

"Married," Kit said. "They married thirty-three years ago. They still are married."

Wilhelmina paled. "He . . ." She cleared her throat. "He's a bigamist?"

"Yes, ma'am," Kit said. "We're sorry to have to tell you this."

Wilhelmina looked down, her hair falling forward to cover her face. Her shoulders began to shake and Kit wondered if they should have waited for Rafferty. Then Wilhelmina made a gasping sound and raised her head, and Kit realized that the woman hadn't been crying, after all.

She was laughing. "Oh my God. You're kidding me. Please say you're not kidding me."

"We're not," Kit said warily. "We thought you'd be upset."

"Oh, I am," Wilhelmina said, wiping her eyes. "I'm furious." Her laughter abruptly halted. "It's just that Raffie will feel so vindicated. He never liked Brooks. I knew something was going on between Brooks and Veronica, but I didn't think they were *married*. And for how long?"

"Thirty-three years," Connor said, watching Wilhelmina like one might a cornered wildcat.

"Wow." She sat back and dabbed at her eyes with the tissue she still held. "So what about the house? The one that I bought for him?"

Kit fought not to wince. "I'm not certain. Veronica might inherit, given she's his legal wife."

Wilhelmina's lovely features morphed into a scowl. "Over my dead body."

Kit winced again but said nothing because Wilhelmina had lurched to her feet and was pacing the room.

"That sonofabitch," Wilhelmina muttered. "That selfish, criminal sonofabitch."

That about summed up Brooks Munro, Kit thought. "It's best if you contact your attorney, ma'am. I'm sure they can unravel any financial complications Munro's deceit has caused you."

Wilhelmina hadn't stopped pacing. "Oh, I will. That sonofa-bitch."

"What are your plans?" Connor asked. "Will you be re-turning to Boston?"

"Yes." Wilhelmina stopped pacing to face them. "But not until this case is closed. I want to know who to thank for killing that no-good thief. Not only did he take my money—a lot of money—but he took five years of my life. I thought our marriage was legal. I dreaded divorcing him, but Veronica saved me from that anyway. Do I have to bury him?"

"No, ma'am," Kit said. "That's Veronica's responsibility."

"Well, at least there's that," she muttered.

Connor had relaxed, the difficult news now out of the way. "We were also wondering if you knew how Mr. Munro paid his employees."

"Cash. He paid all the household bills with cash or money orders. He wanted to minimize any financial transactions. He said it was so that no one could report to his constituents how much money we spent. How well we lived. It could make him look inaccessible to his public." She winced. "Plus, I don't think the housekeeper was documented, so he definitely paid her with cash. I stayed out of all those dealings. But there's a safe in his office, on the shelf behind his desk. I don't know the combi-nation, but I assume you can blow it open or whatever. Is there anything else?"

There had been a safe in Munro's home office, but it had been empty when CSU had gotten it open. So they still didn't know where Munro had hidden the profits from his blackmail scheme.

Kit pulled a copy of Walter Grossman's mug shot from her pocket. "Do you recognize this man? He may have been one of Munro's friends or colleagues."

Wilhelmina studied the photo. "He looks familiar, but I don't think I ever met him. Maybe I once saw him talking to Brooks a long time ago? I don't know his name. I'm sorry."

"No worries," Kit said. Hopefully Joel was getting the name the man had been using in San Diego, because there was no record of a Walter Grossman living in San Diego County. "We'll be going now if you don't have any questions for us."

Wilhelmina began walking to the door. "No questions. Please let me know when this case is solved. I'd like to close this chapter of my life and move on."

"Yes, ma'am." Kit paused as she passed the yoga mat. "You dropped something, ma'am."

A fifty-dollar bill peeked out from beneath the mat.

"Dammit," Wilhelmina muttered, grabbing the bill from the floor. "Rafferty dropped some of the money I gave him to buy groceries. I hope he realizes it before he gets to the cash register. If you see him on your way out, please tell him to come back. He didn't leave too long ago."

"We will," Connor said. "Have a good day, ma'am."

Kit and Connor said nothing until they were back in the department sedan. "She took it better than I would have," Kit said.

Connor huffed a laugh. "I thought she'd be throwing things."

"She still might. She just might not have done so while we were there."

"Then I hope the owners of that rental have good insurance. There were some expensive sculptures on the shelves. The one next to the front door was worth at least twenty-five thousand dollars. Maybe more."

"For a statue?" Kit should her head. *Rich people.* Then she frowned. "Wait. Is that normal? I mean, for luxury rentals to have expensive artwork?"

"Depends on who she rented it from." Hands on the steering wheel, Connor stared at the building, a thoughtful look on his face. "She lived in San Diego for years, so she might know the owner. If that's the case, I wouldn't be surprised. But if it's just an Airbnb? I'd say that's unusual. Let's find out who owns it."

Kit did a property search. "It's owned by Robert Jackson." She googled the man and nodded. "He owns the Cliff Hotel franchise here in the city. She's the heiress of the Cliff fortune. They probably know each other."

"I've heard his name. He's certainly rich enough to afford sculptures of that quality and if they knew each other from the hotel business, he'd trust her not to steal them. We should still check with him, though."

"I'll get his contact info and call him while you drive back to the precinct. Let's get going. I'm hoping we'll find that Joel has pried an alternate name for Walter Grossman out of the pilot."

Mira Mesa, San Diego, California
Tuesday, January 10, 6:30 p.m.

Walter Grossman, now known by his Wayne Walters alias, lived in a small bungalow-style home that was completely dark.

Standing on the curb, Connor studied the house with a frown. "His car's in the driveway. If he's home, he should have at least one light on."

"He could be waiting for us, especially after Veronica warned him that we 'knew something.' Let's do a walk around before we knock on the door."

"He might have cameras. He'll see us."

"Then I'll walk around, and you watch the front door. If he tries to leave, stop him."

"Thank you for your wise words of wisdom," Connor said sarcastically. "I say we call for backup."

He was right, especially since Grossman was Munro's muscle. "I'll still cover the back. I don't want him getting away. We won't attempt entry until backup arrives."

It had taken several hours for Joel Haley to get Wayne Walters's name from Steven Neal. The pilot had heeded his attorney's advice, waiting for the prosecutor to offer him a deal in writing.

Kit hoped they weren't too late. Veronica had warned the PI yesterday that they had to get away. Walter Grossman, a.k.a. Wayne Walters, might have already left town. Or the country.

Steven Neal also admitted to having flown Veronica and the PI to the Caymans together many times. He believed the two had been sexual partners but were more like friends with benefits than in a deep relationship.

Connor had become annoyingly smug about that, seeing as his hunch had been right. Veronica had been fooling around with the PI and had lied about knowing him to protect him from being captured by the police.

Kit quietly made her way around the man's house, looking for cameras. If they existed, they were well hidden.

When she got to his back door, she sighed. Drawing her weapon with one hand, she dialed Connor on her cell with the other. "The window in the back door has been broken. The door itself is ajar."

"Dammit," Connor hissed. "Don't do anything yet. Backup's only a minute away."

A minute and a half later, Connor had joined her at the rear of the house, his weapon drawn. Two uniformed officers followed him.

"There are two more at the front," Connor told her.

"Then let's do this." Kit nudged at the door with her toe, sending the door opening on a squeak of hinges.

"Police!" Kit called as she and Connor entered the home.

"Fuck," Connor muttered, because the place had been tossed.

The kitchen was a disaster area with piles of flour and sugar on the countertops. Broken crockery and glassware littered the floor. Every drawer and cabinet had been emptied.

Someone had even pulled the porcelain sink out and tossed it on the floor, where its pieces mixed with the shattered glass.

Carefully, Kit moved toward the living room, taking care not to disturb the scene. Connor followed close behind.

The living room was in a similar state, the sofa and chair cushions slashed, their filling covering the floor like snow. The flatscreen had been yanked from the wall and lay on the floor, also shattered.

Holes had been punched in the walls, the drywall pulled away, leaving the studs in plain view. Even the insulation had been removed.

With every step they took they found more debris.

The spare bedroom/home office was also a mess. Half of it anyway. One side of the room was a disaster area. Books had been pulled from the shelves, the ripped-out pages littering the floor.

But the other side of the office was pristine, except for a single wall where a painting had been removed and thrown on the floor. On top of the painting was a square panel of drywall about three feet square. The panel had been removed from the wall, revealing a wall safe. The safe was completely empty, its door left open.

"He found what he was looking for," Connor murmured.

Kit nodded once, then kept going—until she got to the bedroom, where a single lamp on the nightstand dimly burned. "Dammit," she hissed.

They were too late.

Walter Grossman lay on the floor next to his bed, his throat slit, killed in the same way that Munro, Shelley, and her mother had been.

They knew he'd been killed sometime after nine on Monday morning, when Veronica had called him in a panic, telling him that they had to get away.

The suitcase he'd clearly been packing had been dumped, its contents all over the floor and the inside lining slashed with a knife. The mattress had also been hacked apart, its stuffing strewn about.

"Shit," Connor said as he crouched next to the victim. "Six of his fingers are missing, two on the right hand and four on the left. And . . . there they are in a neat little pile." He pointed to the dresser where the killer had left Grossman's fingers stacked in a pyramid.

"More torture," Kit said grimly.

"The PI would have had the blackmail list. His killer wanted it, just like he wanted Munro's. If he has both, nobody else will know who's on it."

"I wonder if that means Veronica also knows who's on the list," Kit said thoughtfully. "If she was sleeping with the PI."

"Maybe." But he sounded doubtful. "If she does know, maybe showing her a crime scene photo of Grossman will loosen her tongue. I wonder if she would have been the next victim. Our arresting her could have saved her life."

"This means the killer knew who the PI was," Kit said. "I wonder how he knew."

Connor grimaced. "I bet Munro told him after losing a few fingers and toes."

"Then why wasn't Grossman already dead before Veronica called him yesterday morning?"

"Good question. Maybe he was out of town. Veronica will hopefully know."

Kit crouched on the other side of the body. The victim's hands were zip-tied in front of him, his legs tied at the ankles. "Grossman had a gun." She pointed to the end of the barrel, just visible under the dead man's hip. "I wonder if he got a chance to use it, and why his killer didn't take it."

"Maybe his killer didn't want the hassle of a gun that might be traceable."

"Makes sense. I wonder if Grossman killed Jacob Crocker, the PI who was working for William Weaver?"

"We can have the ballistics of this gun checked." Connor frowned. "I want to know how the killer got the jump on Grossman. If the killer really is the guy with the neckbeard, Grossman was a lot bigger. Grossman's profile from the prison says he was trained in martial arts. He should have been able to take out a guy with a knife or at least do some damage."

Kit flipped the switch on the wall, turning on the much brighter overhead light. "Maybe that's why." She pointed at Grossman's leg, where there was evidence of a gunshot.

The left thigh of his black cargo pants was darker than the rest of the fabric.

"He had a gun when he grabbed Shelley from the body shop. No surprise that he used it to incapacitate Grossman." Connor inspected the wound without touching the body. "Bullet's gone. The fabric around the wound is cut away and the skin's been hacked open."

"He's thorough. We've got to give him that. I'll call this in and get CSU and the ME out here ASAP."

San Diego PD, San Diego, California
Tuesday, January 10, 8:05 p.m.

"What is it *now*, Detectives?" Laura Letterman demanded as she took the chair next to a weary Veronica Fitzgerald.

Kit and Connor took their seats opposite the lawyer and her client. On the other side of the glass were Navarro, Joel Haley, and Sam.

At least Kit had been able to prepare Sam for seeing his ex. He hadn't been happy about it but had agreed to observe.

Kit wanted his opinion, especially as Veronica had lied about so many things.

"Walter Grossman—or Wayne Walters, as you might have known him—is dead," Kit said flatly.

Veronica flinched as if she'd been slapped. "No."

"Veronica," Laura warned. "We agreed. Say nothing."

"You knew him, Miss Fitzgerald," Connor said. "Your lawyer knows that we know that you've been traveling with him to the Caymans, because the pilot—her other client—told us so. Walter Grossman accompanied you on nearly every trip. You've been screwing him even though you claim to have loved Brooks Munro. We're tired of your lies, Miss Fitzgerald."

Laura glanced at her client, who'd closed her eyes and pursed her lips. "She's not talking to you."

"His throat was slit, Veronica," Kit said, her tone terse. "And six of his fingers were cut off. His house had been thoroughly searched. Except for his home office. Half was trashed, the other half had been left alone. Walter kept his blackmail binder in the office, didn't he?"

Veronica's head shake was barely noticeable.

"He didn't?" Kit asked.

"He can't be dead," Veronica whispered.

"We know it was him who you were talking to on Monday morning," Connor said. "When you said that you had to get away. We found a burner phone in his pocket and his call log showed a call from your burner."

Veronica lifted her chin. "How did you get into his cell phone?" she demanded. "He kept it locked. Even I don't know the password."

"We didn't," Kit said with a shrug. "We just lied." She nearly laughed at the outrage on Veronica's face. "Doesn't feel good to be lied to, does it?"

"Detective," Laura said in an irritated tone.

"Counselor," Kit returned in the same tone. "Your client has lied to us multiple times. If she can possibly, *for once*, tell the truth the first time we ask, we might be able to catch the person who killed both of her partners. Where was Walter Grossman when you called him from your office yesterday morning?"

Veronica leaned in to whisper in her attorney's ear.

Laura shrugged. "I don't think that can hurt you. Go ahead."

"He was in Vegas on a job."

"A job for whom?" Connor asked.

"For himself. He didn't just work for Brooks. He was a free-lance PI."

"He isn't licensed," Kit said.

"Didn't need to be. His clients preferred that he wasn't, actually."

"Did he own a gun?" Connor asked.

Veronica nodded. "He carried everywhere he went."

Kit studied the older woman. "Didn't Munro get angry that you and Grossman were doing the horizontal tango?"

Veronica shrugged. "Maybe. But he was married to *her*. I had needs. I knew he wasn't marrying for love, but he did marry her. Up until this past month, he was living with her. I told him when he first married her that I wouldn't be celibate while he was married."

"He slept in your condo the night before he died."

Sadness flickered in Veronica's eyes. "She was gone. Even when she lived with him, I only got the scraps. He could have divorced her. Could have been with me full time. He liked her money, though."

"How did he pick Wilhelmina?" Connor asked. "I assume he chose her for her money."

Veronica glanced at Laura, who shrugged. "Go ahead."

"He had Walter check out all the available rich women in town. Then Brooks signed up for her yoga class. He could be very persuasive when he wanted to be. He'd done his research, knew all the right things to say. She fell hard and fast."

"Made him sign a prenup, though," Kit said.

Veronica lifted one shoulder. "He expected that. He figured he'd take her for all he could get until she divorced him."

"Then move on to the next rich woman?" Kit asked.

"Maybe. Depended on how much he was able to get from her. He got the house as a wedding present, so that was helpful. He'd had his eye on that property for a long time before he'd even met her. He lived in the general area when he was first elected to the city council, but it was a small house. He wanted more." Her mouth curved bitterly. "*She* was his ticket to ride."

"But why?" Kit asked. "Why did he need to marry Wilhelmina? You said he started blackmailing people eight years ago. Why did he need her money?"

Veronica's lip curled in disgust. "He had money, but he wanted the respectability her name would give him. He wanted to be invited to all the parties. He wanted to be dignified. Plus, she gave him access to rich people that wouldn't have given him the time of day on his own. And rich people pay more blackmail."

"And the house?" Kit pressed. "If he wanted it so much, why didn't he just buy it himself?"

"He didn't want a record that he'd bought the house with cash, and on paper he wasn't worth that much before he married her. Her buying the house for him solved the paperwork issue."

"What about Tamsin Kavanaugh?" Connor asked. "The reporter. His wife said they were having an affair."

Veronica shrugged. "That was just a fling. We didn't have the kind of relationship you're thinking. I didn't mind his flings."

"You were married," Kit said dryly, noting Veronica's surprise before the woman evened out her expression. "Robbed the cradle there, didn't you?"

"Detective," Laura snapped. "Are you finished?"

"No," Kit said easily. "How did the whole scam start? Were you drinking with Munro and Walter Grossman one night and you all thought it sounded like a good idea?"

Veronica shot her an icy look. "No." She leaned over to whisper in Laura's ear again.

Laura shook her head. "You get a deal first, then you tell them that. Any other questions, Detectives?"

"Do you know a guy with a neckbeard?" Connor asked.

Veronica laughed, a shrill, hysterical sound. "No. Why?"

"We think he killed your husband and your lover," Connor told her. "He also killed a young woman and her mother. They were unfortunate loose ends. She was only nineteen."

"Sucks to be her, then," Veronica muttered. "I don't know anyone with a neckbeard."

"What about a tan Chevy Suburban?" Kit asked.

Again, Veronica shook her head. It had been worth a try.

Kit figured she'd try one more question. "Do you know who's on the blackmail list?"

Veronica met her eyes. "No. I truly don't. I have everything to gain by telling you, but I don't know. Can I go now?"

"In a minute." Kit turned to Laura. "I'll ask the prosecutor to contact you with a possible deal for the information about how the scam started. If we can figure out just one person on that list, we may be able to figure out who killed Brooks Munro. I really hope your client wants to help us."

"She will help you only if she can protect herself in the process," Laura said. "That's how it goes, Detective. Surely you're not so naive as to believe otherwise."

Kit just smiled, the barb missing its target. "I don't think anyone has ever called me naive, Counselor. It's kind of nice. Thank you."

Laura looked irritated once again. "Take my client back to her cell. Veronica, I'll see you tomorrow morning for your arraignment. Say nothing to anyone. I'm serious."

Veronica nodded, then turned back to Kit and Connor. "What will happen to Walter's body?"

Kit softened her voice. It benefited no one for her to be cruel to Veronica at this moment. It might even leave the woman with a favorable impression that could be useful later. "If no one claims his body within thirty days, he'll be cremated and his remains held for three years. At that time, he'll be buried in a mass grave with a service. It's nondenominational. I've been to a few. They aren't fancy, but they're respectful."

Veronica swallowed. "Same with Brooks?"

"Only if you can't claim his body," Kit said. "You, as his legal wife, are his next of kin. You'll be contacted so that you can make decisions."

"What about *her*?" Veronica said, trying for a sneer, but it fell flat when her voice cracked.

"Munro committed bigamy. She isn't his legal wife. You will have the final decision."

Veronica's face tightened in satisfaction. "Thank you, Detective."

Kit nodded once. "You're welcome. We are sorry for your losses, ma'am."

Veronica gave a curt nod and followed the uniformed officer from the room.

Kit was gathering her things when Laura spoke, her tone icy and bitter.

"It won't work, you know. You, being nice to her. You're just trying to get her to open up and talk to you. I should think you'd be ashamed of yourself, but you don't have shame and you don't have compassion. You only care about what you want."

Kit kept her voice soft, even though she was angry inside. Most of her anger was aimed at the defense attorney, but some of it was aimed at herself. At one time, Laura's words had been true and that stung.

But they didn't have to be true forever. People could change. *I can change.*

I have *changed for the better.* And at least some of that was due to knowing Sam Reeves.

"I can be nice and still hope she tells me what I want to know. Kindness isn't a zero-sum. You were . . . nicer the last time we worked on the same case." Then again, Kit hadn't been seeing Sam the last time she and Laura had crossed paths on a case. She'd chalk today's venom up to jealousy. "I hope we can have an amiable working relationship in the future. Have a good evening."

Connor followed her out and into the observation room.

Sam was smiling at her as she came in. "That was nice, Kit."

Tension fell away like shrugging out of a heavy coat. "Thank you. She wasn't necessarily wrong."

Sam shrugged. "Well, neither were you. Kindness isn't a zero-sum."

Navarro cleared his throat. "So now what?"

"I'll draft a deal," Joel said. "It's up to Veronica if she takes it. How much is the start of their scam worth to you?"

Connor scratched his head. "We don't know. If we can't get at least one person from the blackmail list, it's worth nothing."

"We're back to square one on the damn list," Kit said. "Sam, did you believe Veronica when she said she didn't know who was on the list?"

"I did, actually. Something that big would be valuable in negotiating a better deal. If she knew, Joel would already have heard from Laura."

"I agree," Joel said. "I'll talk to my boss about it. We'll come up with something. In the meantime, what's next?"

Kit looked at Navarro. "Have Marshall and Ashton had any luck finding the guard from Munro's neighborhood guard shack?"

Navarro shook his head. "The man wasn't from San Diego and his family hasn't heard from him in several years. Marshall and Ashton are still tracking down his friends. Guy was kind of a loner, it seems, but he was a reliable employee. He hasn't shown up for his shift all week."

"Not good," Joel said grimly. "I don't want to borrow misery, but we need to assume he's dead. Have we put out anything on TV or online, asking for community help?"

"A press release went out this afternoon," Navarro said. "We listed him as a person of interest, posted his photo, and asked if anyone out there has seen him. So far, nothing, but I'll keep you up to speed. What else do you have?" he asked Kit and Connor.

Kit sighed. "Other than the guard, our main leads involve

tracking the Chevy Suburban pulling an unwrapped trailer and hoping some of Brooks Munro's belongings ping on Bruce Goddard's robbery radar."

"We also have the threatening emails Munro received from his constituents," Connor said. "That fits the ME's multiple-hands theory."

Navarro slowly shook his head. "I don't think it was his constituents. Just my gut."

Joel raised his hand. "Same."

Sam nodded. "Me too. The blackmail makes all the sense, especially given the theft of the Ferrari. Someone wanted to claim that car because Munro had stolen from him. It's the only thing that makes sense."

"I wonder where Munro kept his cash," Connor said thoughtfully. "Weaver, the guy Munro ruined to win his last election, said that one of Munro's household staff claimed he had a safe where he took cash from to pay them. But the safe in his office was empty."

"We'll search the house again for another hiding place," Navarro said. "Let's call it a night. We'll all think more clearly on a decent night's sleep."

Kit was so tired that she didn't even argue. And when Sam offered to walk her to her car, she was grateful.

"You were good with Laura," Sam said once they'd reached her Subaru. "She can be . . . sharp-tongued."

Kit sighed. "Like I said, she wasn't entirely wrong."

"But she didn't used to be so bitter. I'm sorry she said those things to you. You were—and are—kind. End of story."

Kit found herself leaning into his shoulder. He was warm and safe and smelled so good. "Thank you, Sam." She realized what she was doing and pulled back. She was tired, which meant that it wasn't a good time to be leaning on anyone. She wasn't as clearheaded as she needed to be to take that step. "That means a lot coming from you."

He opened her car door for her, stroking his hand over her hair as she climbed behind the wheel. "Are you going to the boat or to McKittrick House?"

"Home. To Mom and Pop's."

"Good. Text me when you get there so I know you're safe."

She smiled up at him. "If you do the same when you get home."

"Of course. I pinkie-swore to be careful."

Kit was laughing as she drove away, her heart a little bit lighter.

234

CHAPTER ELEVEN

Kit brought her Subaru to a stop in her parents' driveway, which was already filled with Subarus. Mom's and Pop's vehicles were here. And so was Akiko's.

That could be good or it could be bad. Kit hadn't forgotten about Akiko's mysterious phone call from the woman claiming to have known her mother. She hoped there'd been no trouble on that front.

She started to get out of the car, then remembered her promise to Sam and opened a text window.

Am home. All safe.

A minute later she got the reply. *Same. Walking Siggy. Sleep well.*

Just a few words and she felt warm and . . . safe. Settled.

That was more than a little terrifying.

She got out of the car and locked her door. They weren't

usually a victim of crime way out on the farm, but everyone was on edge with Christopher Drummond's trial coming up.

A tall, broad figure stood on the front porch waiting for her, and Kit's heart settled even more.

"Hey, Pop."

"Hey, Kitty-Cat." He waited until she was on the porch before enveloping her in the best hug. He and Mom were expert huggers and were the only ones who hugged her without asking.

Kit loved that her brothers and sisters understood boundaries. Many of them shared her past and knew that forming attachments could be difficult.

Kit hugged him back, leaning into him longer than she usually did.

"You okay, Kit?" Harlan asked gruffly.

"Just tired."

"Your mom has a room all ready for you."

Kit pulled back to frown up at him. "I figured I'd sleep in my old bed." There were two twin beds in Rita's room, which had once belonged to Kit and Wren. And then, later, to Kit and Akiko. It was where she always slept when she came home.

"The other girls are bunking with Rita now. We rearranged the room to hold three twin beds."

"Is Rita okay?"

Harlan waffled his hand. "Mostly. But nights are hard and the other girls didn't want to leave her. So they've all moved in together. Mom's made their old room into a new spare room. You and Akiko will sleep there."

"Akiko's staying over?" Her sister rarely stayed over at Mom and Pop's house.

"Um . . . yeah." Harlan winced. "Something's going on with her, and Mom and I are worried. She came over and had way too much strawberry wine."

Kit's eyes widened. "Akiko got drunk?" she whispered.

Harlan nodded, his expression troubled. "Do you know what's going on? All she'd say was that she'd had to cancel tomorrow's charter because Paolo got the flu. She's never canceled a charter before."

"I know some of it, but she didn't give me permission to tell." Only to tell Sam, and he hadn't asked.

Harlan nodded once. "As long as one of us knows, I'm okay. And I'm glad it's you." He kissed her forehead. "Should we just keep that bed open for you? You seem to be staying over a lot more often these days."

"Oh. I didn't think of that. All this time you could have taken another foster. I'm hogging their bed."

"Hush. You are our child, Kit. You come when you need to. I'm glad you're here. I'm *always* glad you're here."

She leaned into him again. "Thanks, Pop. I'm always glad to be here."

He put his arm around her shoulders and steered her into the warm house with its unmistakable smells of home. Fresh laundry, lemon furniture polish, and apple pie. "Mom saved you some dinner. She was hoping you'd be back."

The house was quiet, the only downstairs light the one in the kitchen.

"Rita and the others went to bed already? And where is my dog?"

"Snickerdoodle is upstairs in their room, being spoiled. The girls are doing their homework. Tiffany has a test tomorrow and she's nervous, so they're helping her study. I keep hearing giggles, though, so I don't know how well they're studying. Akiko is in bed. She got . . . weepy."

Kit's eyes widened once again. "Akiko cried?"

Harlan shrugged helplessly. "I didn't know what to do, so

Mom got her upstairs and into bed. If she's awake when you go in, make sure she has some aspirin and some water. And maybe a trash can next to her bed."

Kit cringed. "If she barfs, I'll hold her hair back."

Harlan laughed, a deep quiet laugh that was as much a part of this house as the good smells. "I knew I could count on you. Betsy, Kit's here."

"I heard her drive up." Betsy linked her arm through Kit's and walked her into the kitchen. "*And* I saw you on the new camera. Who were you texting?"

"How did you know I was texting?"

"I didn't," Betsy said with a chuckle. "I suspected, but you just confirmed it."

Kit had to laugh. "You've been watching TV cop shows again, Mom."

"Yep." Betsy busied herself warming Kit's dinner. "So . . . who were you texting?"

There was a hopeful note in her voice that made Kit nervous. Kit knew what her mother hoped for—that Kit was texting "someone special." She didn't want to admit it, even to her parents.

Because it was terrifying. And what if it didn't work out?

What if it does?

Her folks had been with her every step of her life since she'd hidden in their barn as a twelve-year-old runaway. Surely she could pay them back with the news they clearly craved.

She drew a deep breath. "It was Sam."

Betsy grinned slyly. "I knew it," she whispered.

"Betsy," Harlan cautioned as he sat down, carving knife in one hand and some partially carved wood in the other.

"It's okay, Pop. I figure I owe you two some good news every once in a while."

Both of her parents stopped what they were doing and turned to stare at each other before staring at her.

"You owe us nothing," Betsy said. "Your private life is exactly that. Private. Now, if you want to tell me, I'm all ears. But if I ask and you don't want to share, then say so, and I'll let it go."

Kit smiled, inhaling when Betsy put an overflowing plate in front of her. Tonight had been Swedish meatball night and Kit was a total fan. "I know. But you do deserve to know when things are good. Not just when they're bad."

Harlan went back to carving. "So things are good with Sam?"

Kit chuckled. "Yes, Pop. He's asked me out on another date, for Saturday night."

Betsy took the chair opposite Kit and sipped on a cup of coffee. "And if you're working?"

"Unless I'm hip-deep in a crime scene, I'm taking time off for dinner."

Once again, her parents stopped what they were doing and stared at her.

Kit frowned. "What? I can be a grown-up, too."

Harlan went back to his task, a smile on his face. "We know. We raised you right."

"You did. Now let me eat. I'm starving." She pointed at Harlan's block of wood. "Whatcha making?"

"I don't know. I think something for Sam. Or Georgia or Eloise."

"Do one for the ladies first. They'll get cranky otherwise."

"Eloise never gets cranky." Betsy sighed. "And now we know why."

Kit laughed. "Pot brownies." The old woman was famous for them at the Shady Oaks Retirement Village. "She's very generous with her baking."

"Rita got her to share the recipe," Betsy said sourly.

"Rita's not gonna make pot brownies," Kit said with certainty. "She's just trying to keep you on your toes. Besides, I'll tell her to not even think about it."

"Thank you," Betsy said fervently. "This old woman's going to bed now. Can you put your plate in the dishwasher, Kit?"

"Of course. Thanks, Mom. Sleep well."

The words made her cheeks heat. Sam had said those same words. They were warm and lovely.

Harlan remained, quietly whittling as she finished her dinner. "Why are you really here, Kitty-Cat?" he asked when she'd all but licked her plate. "I want you to always come when you need to or want to. But is there anything bothering you?"

"This case," Kit confessed. "For a while we had too many leads, but our last one dried up tonight." She mimed slitting her throat.

Harlan grimaced. "That sucks."

"Especially for the victim," she said dryly. "And several of our suspects are being represented by Laura Letterman."

Harlan's shaggy gray brows shot up. "Sam's ex?"

"Yep. She doesn't like me."

"Well, that's not a surprise, Kit. You have the good man she threw away."

"I don't *have* him. I'm more just . . . I don't know."

"Dipping your toe in. I know. So does he."

Kit had been picking up her plate to put in the dishwasher, but she set it down. "How do you know that?"

"I asked him. He told me. It's called communication, Kitty-Cat."

She wanted to be irritated, but it was Harlan, so she only huffed. "You've been talking about me?"

"Only a little. Just making sure he knows to be patient. I don't want him to break your heart."

"Somehow I can't see Sam breaking anyone's heart," Kit said honestly. "If anything, I'll break his."

"Your heart is more fragile than you want to admit. I'm your father. I get to give Sam the speech."

Kit had to smile at him then. "I'm so glad you're my father."

Harlan dipped his head shyly. "Go take care of your dishes, then sit down and tell me about this case. You know I'm a vault."

He was. So was Betsy. Anything she said to either of them would never be repeated.

She obeyed, then settled back down in her chair to watch him carving the block of wood. It was soothing.

"Well, we have one suspect. All we know is that he's got a neckbeard. We don't even know if he really has one or it's just a disguise."

"Hard to get features if his face is covered in hair," Harlan agreed. "Smart disguise. No one even thinks about looking at the rest of his face."

"That's right. So far he's killed four people and maybe a fifth," she said, thinking of the guard shack guy. "And that's just this week. We're out of leads except for the fact that he used a trailer to steal the first victim's Ferrari."

"And Bruce Goddard hasn't been able to find it?"

"Nope. Nor the Rolex the first victim was wearing when he died. I want to believe the widow had nothing to do with it, but she was hinky, too. Says he hit her, so she ran away. That she planned to divorce him, but he died first."

"That could be true."

"It could be. Alicia Batra thinks more than one person killed the first victim. Like *Murder on the Orient Express*."

Harlan made a face. "That makes it harder on you."

"Yeah. And we don't even know where to start with the

possible perpetrators. The first victim was blackmailing a lot of people. Enough to buy a Ferrari and a Rolex. Enough to finance a wealthy lifestyle when his wife had him on an allowance."

"Ouch. That allowance had to have chafed."

"I know, right? But I keep wondering if we're starting in the right place. The wife—the illegitimate second wife who has an ironclad alibi—is rich enough to hire someone to do all this, to make it look all elaborate when it's really just a pissed-off wife."

"And the other three murders?"

"Loose ends. Snip, snip, snip."

"So what are you going to do next?"

"I guess we go back to the whiteboard and figure out what we're missing. What we need is the list of people he was black-mailing. That would satisfy the ME's multiple-hands-stabbing-him theory, even if I hate her theory with the passion of a thousand suns."

"But do you *hate* it, Kit?" Harlan teased, then he sobered. "If it was multiple people, how did they communicate with each other? How would they have known the others existed? It's not like someone tacks a postcard up on a bulletin board saying, 'Hey, I'm being blackmailed, how about you?'"

He chuckled, but Kit did not. "That's a damn good question, Pop. How would multiple people have communicated? It's likely to have been electronic, so there would be some data trail. Even if they met in person to discuss the details, they might have had phone calls or a group text to tell folks where they were meeting. I really need that list. I don't know where to start."

"How did he get the names of his blackmail victims?"

"He had a PI, unlicensed. He was the most recent body we found. The PI dug up the dirt, and the first guy who was killed—"

"You can say Brooks Munro, Kit," Harlan interrupted. "Everyone knows that's the case you're working."

"I know," she said with a sigh. "Munro made contact with the victims, and his admin—who's also his legitimate wife—collected the money."

"Where did she collect it? I mean, did she do it in person or was there a drop box? Did they pay her electronically by wiring funds or was it cash?"

Kit tilted her head. "It was cash," she said, "but as for where the money changed hands, she never really said. That was sneaky of her. Maybe Joel can include that in his plea deal arrangements."

"You'd support cutting her a deal?" Harlan asked, looking surprised.

Kit shrugged. "Sometimes it's the lesser of two evils. She's not a nice woman, and she knows more than she's telling. We didn't follow up on where her marks dropped their money, and that's on us. I'm going to text Joel right now and ask him to try to get that information as part of her plea agreement." She got to her feet and dropped a kiss on Harlan's cheek. "Go to sleep, Pop. You can whittle tomorrow."

He dutifully sheathed his carving knife and slid the block of wood into his pocket. "I was just waiting on you."

Kit hugged him again, hard this time, getting a grunt of surprise. "I love you, Pop. I don't say it often enough."

He stroked a hand over her hair, just as Sam had done earlier. "I love you too, Kitty-Cat. Always have and always will. Now make sure your sister has a barf bucket next to her bed."

"Will do, Pop."

Stopping in one of the bathrooms to grab an empty trash can, Kit slipped into the spare room and quietly set the can next to Akiko's bed. Her sister wore a serious frown, even in her sleep. Kit stroked her hair, hoping to get her to let go of whatever had followed her into her dreams.

Akiko stirred and stared blearily up at Kit. "You're here."

"I am," Kit whispered. "You're drunk."

"I was," Akiko said sadly. "Still am, li'l bit. Sorry."

"Hey, no judgments. But I am worried. Does this have to do with that call you got about your mom?"

Akiko nodded. "Was thinking about how she just *left* me on the steps of a firehouse, in a *box*. When I was really little, I was told that I'd had a photo of her, but it got lost somewhere. She put a picture of herself in the box with me."

Kit sat on the edge of the bed, continuing to stroke her sister's hair, unsure of what to say. It was unusual for Akiko to be so melancholy. "I never had anything of my mom's. I'm sorry you lost that picture."

"I don't know what she looked like. If I do meet with that woman, how will I know if she's telling the truth? Any pictures she shows me will be like a stranger."

"Maybe she has more than photos. If she's got hair, maybe we can do a DNA test."

"Thought about that. But how likely is she to have my mother's hair?"

"I don't know. But you *will* wait to call her back, right? Until I can go with you?"

"I promised I wouldn't go alone. Mmm. Feels good."

Kit continued to stroke Akiko's hair. It was long, black, and so silky. "You've always had the prettiest hair. I wished mine looked like yours when we were teenagers."

Akiko huffed a laugh. "I wanted blond hair like yours. You're pretty."

"You're prettier."

Akiko pinched her hard.

"Ouch! What was that for?" Kit asked, rubbing her arm.

"For not just saying thank you. Just say thank you, Kitty-Cat."

"Thank you," Kit said obediently. "You ready to sleep now?"

"You'll stay here with me?"

"Until I have to go to work in the morning."

"I got no work in the morning," Akiko lamented. "Had to cancel my charter because I'm too chickenshit to go out on my own."

"Not chickenshit. Smart is what you are. Say it with me. Smart."

Akiko giggled, sounding like the girl she'd once been. "Smart. Love you."

"Love you, too. Here." Kit got an aspirin from the bottle Betsy had left on Akiko's nightstand along with a bottle of water. "Take this. You'll thank me tomorrow."

"Can I thank you tonight?"

Kit leaned down and kissed Akiko's forehead. "Sure."

Akiko snuggled closer. "You kissed me. Is it my birthday?"

She'd meant the question in jest, Kit was certain, but it still stung.

Am I that stingy with my affection?

That had to stop. She was protecting her own heart and hurting those she loved in the process. *No more.*

"Not your birthday. Not yet. Go to sleep. I won't leave you."

"M'kay." Akiko rolled over and in less than a minute was snoring delicately, just as she'd done when they'd been McKittrick House roommates all those years ago.

Kit got in her own bed, immediately noting that Betsy had set out her old quilt. Betsy had made two back then, one for her and one for Wren. It was as close to a security blanket as Kit had ever had.

She snuggled under the quilt and took out her phone.

Her first text was to Connor. *We never found out from Veronica about where their marks would drop the money.*

Three little dots appeared before Connor's reply. *Shit. You're right. She said it moved, but we need the last few places. We can check surveillance footage if we know a few places.*

Yep, Kit answered. *I'll ask Joel to put it on his list of things to bargain for. Just wanted you to know.*

Let's focus on that tomorrow first thing. You okay?

Kit was startled at the question. Why wouldn't she be okay? *I'm good. You?*

At CeCe's. All is well.

Why did you ask?

Because Letterman was mean to you. Wanted to smack her.

Kit laughed softly, touched. *Thank you. I can handle meanness. Go to sleep.*

She texted Joel about the drop location, then sent an email to Navarro. Everyone was all caught up, but she wasn't done yet.

One more text.

Sweet dreams, Sam.

His reply was immediate. *You too.*

He added a heart emoji and Kit stared at it for the longest time before sending a heart back.

Now she could go to sleep.

San Diego PD, San Diego, California
Wednesday, January 11, 8:00 a.m.

"Thank you?" Kit said in surprise when a large chocolate cupcake was deposited into her hand as soon as she walked through Homicide's double doors.

Detective Kevin Marshall nodded with a wide grin. "You're welcome."

"So . . . someone solved a case?" she asked, dragging her finger through the cupcake's icing. She licked it off, humming in appreciation even though her mother's baked goods were a thousand times better.

These cupcakes had come from the bakery near the precinct and were the standard celebration food whenever someone closed a homicide.

"We did," Marshall said, then his grin turned sheepish. "Or you did. The Munro case is still open, of course, but we closed the Crocker case. The gun you found under Walter Grossman's body last night was a ballistics match for the gun that killed Jacob Crocker, William Weaver's PI."

Kit wasn't surprised. "I wonder if Munro ordered it or if Grossman took it on himself to kill Weaver's PI."

"Ask Veronica," Alf Ashton said, coming to stand with his partner. "She recognized Jacob Crocker's name, so she at least knew about him. We asked Joel to add it to the things he wants to get in her plea bargain."

"Joel's going to be busy," Kit said. "I hope Laura Letterman doesn't find out exactly how much we want to know."

"Joel's going to offer reduced prison time in exchange for her full cooperation," Marshall said. "So Veronica's attorney won't know the details until he starts asking questions."

"Letterman's pretty good." It hurt to admit, but it was the truth. "If I were Veronica's attorney, I wouldn't agree to full co-operation. I'd make everything à la carte."

Navarro walked up to them, coffee in one hand and a cupcake in the other. "Then I'm glad you're not Veronica's attorney. Solve this case fast, if you don't mind. The bakery cupcakes are okay, but I want something your mother baked."

Kit laughed. "Fine." But she sobered when she stopped to

study Navarro's face. He was frowning. Not his normal "every-thing sucks" frown, but the one he got when something in par-ticular was bothering him. "What's going on, boss?"

Navarro sighed. "Come with me." He left them, crossing the bullpen to his office.

"What did you do?" Marshall whispered.

"I don't know," Kit whispered back, racking her brain for what might be the problem.

"Close the door," Navarro said as he sat behind his desk. "And have a seat."

Warily, Kit obeyed. She set her cupcake on the corner of Na-varro's desk, her appetite gone. "What did I do?"

His smile was rueful. "Nothing. It's what you *might* do, and I need you to stop and think before you act."

"Okay." She folded her arms over her chest. "Let's have it."

"Christopher Drummond contacted the DA's office this morn-ing."

Kit had to breathe through a sudden rise of rage. "What did he say?" she asked, proud that her voice held steady.

"He says he has information about Brooks Munro," Navarro said. "He's willing to share if the DA drops all charges."

Kit was out of her chair before she knew she was even moving. Her fists clenched and her whole body was taut as a wire. "*No.*"

Absolutely not. That man killed Rita's mother. He raped Rita.

Over my dead body will that piece of shit walk free.

Navarro waved a hand, indicating she should retake her seat. "Sit down, Kit. No one wants to give that man air to breathe, much less a get-out-of-jail-free card."

Shaking from pure fury, Kit sat, but her fists remained clenched. "Are Joel and his boss considering that fucker's offer?"

Navarro shrugged. "Depending on what he has to offer, they

might be interested, but Drummond's up on a murder one charge. He only made bail because he's rich and has powerful friends, but still I think he'd have to have some pretty compelling testimony to get any concessions. Personal opinion? The best Drummond could even hope for would be life with parole."

"He *could* get twenty-five years with parole," Kit said, using every ounce of control she possessed not to fly out of Navarro's office and strangle Christopher Drummond herself. "That's the minimum mandatory."

"I know," Navarro said quietly. "And he might get that. This is his first offense and they have nothing more on him. He can claim he killed her in a fit of rage and he could even get his charges taken down to manslaughter. All of that could happen."

Kit closed her eyes. *Stay in control.* She couldn't have Navarro thinking that she was a loose cannon.

Breathe. She did so, then breathed again when she realized the voice in her mind was Sam's. *Breathe, Kit. That's the way.*

When she was calm, she opened her eyes to find Navarro watching her carefully. He nodded once. "You okay now?"

"Yes, sir." She unclenched her fists and gently shook her hands. "I suppose the best way not to give in to Drummond's demands is to figure out what he wants to tell us some other way."

"Exactly what I was thinking."

One more deep breath. "Will the brass want us to give Drummond a deal?"

"Not if we don't have to, but I'm getting pressure to solve this case."

"It's only been four days," she protested. "We're not water walkers here."

Navarro's lips tipped up. "They think you are. You've solved some big cases recently. You have their full attention."

"No pressure," Kit muttered.

Navarro shrugged. "You can handle it. What are you going to do?"

"I'm going to tell Connor first and we'll come up with a plan."

"Good answer. And then?"

Kit knew what he was asking. "I need to tell Rita. If she hears about this on the news, she'll freak. She's already terrified that Drummond will come after her to keep her from testifying."

Navarro frowned. "Has she received any threats?"

"Just a vaguely ominous letter. The writer said that he hoped she enjoyed being in *Alice in Wonderland*—that's the play her school is doing this year. Rita's part of the ensemble. He said he'd be in the front row."

"What a fucker," Navarro growled. "He's been watching her. Why didn't you tell me?"

"Pop told Joel before Christmas, but I just found out Friday night. Rita knows about it, though, so she's been what-iffing a lot. She's a teenager who's too intelligent for her own good and who was dealt a real shitty hand in life. She was eleven years old when she found her mother's dead body, sir. She's only fourteen now. She knows firsthand how rotten Christopher Drummond is and what he's capable of."

"What are your parents doing to keep her safe?"

"Pop's upped security at the farm. He's got a new home security system plus cameras and motion detectors." *He's also got a shotgun,* she thought, but no way would she offer that piece of information. "They're also getting a dog, which means I'll get Snickerdoodle back. I think Pop's picking up the new pup from the animal shelter today. And I've been staying there most nights."

Some of it was for Rita. *Some of it for me.*

"Until Drummond makes a move, that's all you can do," Navarro said, his voice heavy with regret. "Tell your father about

Drummond's request for a deal. Let him decide when the time is right for Rita to know. Can they keep her home from school?"

Kit wanted to say yes. She wanted to drive home and barricade them all in the warm house with its homey smells. She wanted to wrap her family in bubble wrap and never let them leave her sight.

But she couldn't do any of those things. "Keeping her home from school would have to be a last resort. She's finally found her footing. She's making friends and catching up from all the time she missed after her mother's murder. I don't want to undo her progress."

Navarro sighed. "This sucks, Kit. I'm not gonna lie."

"How long before we're pressured to make a deal with that piece of shit?"

Navarro shrugged. "I don't know. I'll push the decision out as far as I can. That's all I can promise."

"I appreciate it, sir. He might have nothing new on Munro."

"Then again, he might hold the key."

Kit sighed. "You're right. This sucks. They both served on the city council. How sad is it that two members are rotten to the core?"

"Pretty damn sad."

"Although Munro operated his blackmail scheme for eight years, according to Veronica. And even though it looks like Grossman murdered Jacob Crocker, we might not ever know if Munro was involved. A jury might see Munro as being worse than Drummond. Munro committed crimes for years, while Drummond killed his maid in a fit of rage after learning she was pregnant and unwilling to get rid of the baby. That he raped the woman isn't easily provable. He can say the sex with Rita's mother was consensual, and she's conveniently dead, so she can't refute him."

Navarro sat quietly, waiting. He knew Kit well enough by now to know that her mind was turning over all the possibilities.

"We didn't question any of the other council members yet," she went on, "because we didn't know what exactly Munro had done. Now we know there was blackmail and possibly murder. I hate to think any of the other members of the council are dirty. I guess we have to find out." She bit at her lip. "Unless there's another place Munro and Drummond intersect."

"Like?"

"I don't know. We're going to find out. Did you have anything else, sir?"

"No. Go forth, Kit. Figure this out."

"We will. I'll call Pop and then we'll get started." She looked through the window in Navarro's office door. "Connor's here, so we can get the party started. Is this something we can share with Marshall and Ashton? I'd like to get all hands on deck."

Navarro fully smiled then. "Look at you, being all cooperative." He faked wiping a tear from his eye. "My little detective, all grown up."

Kit huffed a laugh, then grew serious. "Thank you for telling me, sir. We will figure this out."

She left, making sure to take her cupcake with her.

CHAPTER TWELVE

Connor's expression was concerned when she sat at her desk. He rolled his chair closer. "You okay?"

"Not really." She told him what Navarro had shared, gratified when his face reddened with fury.

"Sonofa*bitch*. That was a righteous collar. Drummond needs to rot in prison for the rest of his fuckin' life. And now he's trying to weasel out of it? We can't let him do that to Rita."

Connor and his now-retired former partner had investigated Drummond for murder and made the arrest. He had a right to be angry.

He didn't even know about Drummond sexually assaulting Rita. The only other people outside the family who knew, other than Rita's therapist, were Sam and Navarro.

Sam had also respected Rita's decision.

Kit wasn't sure if Navarro even remembered Rita's quietly

spoken words about her assault by Drummond. It had been a confusing, terrifying scene the night Rita had been saved from a different monster, a serial killer who'd gone after Rita simply to hurt Kit. Navarro had been in shock that night and had taken leave soon after. That had been nine months ago and all of them had been picking up the pieces of their lives.

Rita included.

Which is why Drummond needs to be put away forever.

Kit forced herself to focus. "Let's figure out how Drummond could have learned of Munro's crimes, assuming that's what he wants to sell us in return for his freedom."

Connor frowned. "What if Drummond knows about crimes we haven't uncovered yet?"

"I don't know," Kit admitted. "But this calls for a brainstorming session." She waved over Marshall and Ashton. "Hey, guys?"

The two detectives were just as angry when Kit told them about Drummond, and even angrier when she explained that the man had already tried to intimidate poor Rita out of testifying.

"Let's go back to the whiteboard," Marshall said. "We don't know much about Drummond, but we gathered a lot of information on Munro that hasn't been important up till now. Let's see if any of it can help."

They filed to the conference room, Kit hesitating at the door. "I need to call my father. You guys go on in and get started. I'll join you in a few."

Connor squeezed her shoulder. "Let me know if you need extra security at the farm. I know a few people."

"I will. Thank you." She waited until she was alone in the hall before dialing her father's number. She thought she'd have to leave a message when the phone rang and rang, but he finally picked up.

"Kit?" His voice sounded hollow and there was a cacophony of barking dogs in the background. He'd gone to the shelter to pick up their new dog.

She'd hoped she could catch him at home, but this would have to do.

"Can you go somewhere quiet, Pop? This is important and I need you to hear me."

"Give me a minute." The barking dogs gradually quieted until they were replaced with the sounds of traffic. He'd gone outside. "What is it, Kit?"

"Okay, so I need you to be calm."

"I'm always calm."

He was not always calm. Not when it came to the safety of his children. This she knew from experience.

"Christopher Drummond called the DA's office. He claims to have information on Brooks Munro and wants all charges dropped in exchange."

Harlan drew a deep breath, then let it out. "You won't let that happen." The surety in his tone made Kit's chest grow tight with a combination of gratitude and anxiety.

Her father believed in her. But that was so much responsibility.

"I'm going to do everything in my power to make sure that man goes to prison forever. But for the moment, he's out on bail and can say and do what he pleases. We need to let Rita know, but I don't want her to be afraid."

"She's gonna be afraid, Kit."

"I know. I hate it, but I know. I don't want her to hear about this from anyone but us. Can you go to her? Tell her in person?"

"Of course I will. Has Drummond done a press conference or anything? Will it be online?"

"To my knowledge he has not."

"Then I have enough time to sign the papers for the dog."

That made Kit smile. "I think you do. Thanks for getting them a dog, Pop."

"He's a sweet thing. Giant schnauzer mixed with mastiff."

Kit blinked. "Whoa. That's a big boy."

"He will be. He's still young, but he has paws the size of dinner plates. Come by when you can and meet him. I brought Snickerdoodle with me today, and they get along like gangbusters."

Well, that was a relief. "Does he have a name?"

"Well, his former owners called him Killer, but I think the girls will want to rename him."

"I should think so. Be careful, Pop. Love you."

"Love you too, Kitty-Cat. See you later."

"If Rita needs me, I'll take off and come home."

"I know you will. I'll get the dog and then I'll take Rita out of school, just for today. Bye, honey."

Kit slid her phone back into her pocket. At least Rita's new dog would inspire confidence.

The three men looked up when she came in.

"Well?" Connor asked. "What did your father say?"

"Pop's going to take her out of school to tell her. He's just picking up their new *gigantic* dog from the shelter, so hopefully that will help soothe some of her fear." She sat next to Connor and began to scan all the papers on the table. "Where are we?"

"We've got all the background on Munro that Marshall and Ashton pulled together." Connor nodded to the two detectives on the other side of the table. "There's a lot of information here.

I pulled up my report on the Christopher Drummond investigation."

"So we cross-reference Munro's life against Drummond's and see where they intersect." She pointed to the papers on the table. "May I?"

"Of course," Marshall said. "We gathered so much information, we're having trouble seeing the forest for the trees, if you know what I mean."

"I know exactly what you mean." Kit began sorting the pages into piles. "We have Munro's personal life—Wilhelmina, his house, his missing Ferrari, his lawyer, his doctor, his accountant. We should definitely talk to his accountant. We need a warrant for Munro's books." She put those pages aside. "And this pile can be his council life—the threatening emails and his donor list." She stopped to review the names of the donors to Munro's campaign fund. "Do we know who any of these people are? I only recognize a name or two."

Connor took the page from her hands. "I know about ten of them. They're all members of the country club where my folks have a membership."

Kit looked over his arm to the list of names. "Is Drummond on there?"

"He wouldn't be," Connor said. "He wouldn't contribute to another politician's campaign, would he?"

"Actually, he is on there," Marshall said. "Go back to last year. He gave the max, as did his wife. Not a whole lot, considering how rich Drummond is, but he did contribute to Munro."

"Did Munro contribute to Drummond's campaign?" Kit asked.

"Let me check. I think we got a list of Drummond's donors too, when we were looking at him for the murder of Maria

Mendoza." Connor swiped and tapped the screen of his phone until he found the file he was looking for. "No, he didn't."

"That might not be weird in their world," Kit said, "but it feels weird to me. Can I see the list again?" Connor passed it over and Kit studied each name. "I recognize at least fifteen names, now that I'm really looking at them. They're all heads of companies around the city. I've seen articles about them over the years. I don't think I've met any of them, though." She stopped, her eyes frozen to a single name. "Tamsin Kavanaugh contributed to Munro's campaign."

"She did," Ashton said. "Why is that important?"

"Well, she gave the max. As did her mother and her father." She looked up at the three detectives. "First of all, reporters aren't supposed to be affiliated with any political party. That she was sleeping with Munro was bad, but she could claim that she wasn't and nobody could prove otherwise unless they took photos of the two of them in bed."

Connor shuddered. "Gee, thanks for that mental image."

"You're welcome," Kit said, not missing a beat. "But this here, *this* is a documented paper trail. She shouldn't have been donating anything to any candidate. She could get fired from her job with the online newspaper."

"Didn't think about that," Marshall muttered, sounding embarrassed. "Is there a second point to follow the first?"

Kit nodded. "Yep. Her parents are dead. Have been for twenty years, if she didn't lie to me about that."

Ashton frowned. "Why would she tell you that?"

"She interviewed me three years ago, when I was new to Homicide and had solved a cold case. She was trying to make me feel all chummy with her, like, 'Your sister was brutally murdered and my parents are dead, too. See, we're the same!'" Kit scowled. "Spoiler alert: we are *not* the same."

"She donated to Munro two years ago, so after she told you that." Marshall was typing on his laptop. "She didn't lie about it. Her parents are dead. She donated a couple thousand of her own money, but gave two-thirds of that in her dead parents' names? Why would she do that?"

Connor's eyes narrowed. "I wonder if the payment was the original entrée into Munro's orbit. Remember that Veronica tried to shake down Sam for an appointment with Munro."

"You're right," Kit said. "I wonder if the rest of these people also paid for appointments. Ash, can you write that question on the whiteboard since you're closest?"

"His handwriting sucks," Marshall said. "I'll do it."

"My handwriting is fine," Ashton said. "I just pretend it's not because those dry-erase markers give me headaches."

Kevin Marshall gave his partner the evil eye. "You suck."

"It's fair," Ashton said amiably. "But I don't have a headache now."

Kit chuckled. "Thank you, Kevin, for writing that down. Okay, back to this list. The names I recognized are those of rich dudes who own companies. They might be the country club names you know, Connor. Let's ID each name and figure out their relationship to Munro. But first, I want to sort the rest of these records. So we have his personal life, his council life, and . . ." She studied the next pages in the stack. "His social life, I think. There's his golf membership . . ."

"Member*ships*," Marshall corrected. "Munro belonged to six golf clubs and three country clubs around the city. Plus you'll find records of his vacations to play golf in Palm Springs, Pebble Beach, and Half Moon Bay."

Connor whistled. "Munro was spending a fortune on golf."

Ashton huffed. "He recently bought a custom-made set of clubs for almost eight grand."

Kit blinked. "For *golf clubs*? Damn, I will never understand rich people."

Connor shrugged. "Mine were much cheaper, if it makes you feel better." Then he frowned. "Wait a minute. Drummond had fancy golf clubs, too. I remember searching his golf bag, among all his other things, when we arrested him. They might have even played together. I wonder where Drummond was a member."

"Will a country club tell us who's a member?" Kit asked.

"It's unlikely without a warrant," Connor said. "They like to keep their membership roster private. But I bet my mom would know."

"Can you call her?" Kit asked.

"Sure." Connor tapped his phone, then put it on the table, with the speaker on. His screen said *Mama*.

"Aw," Marshall said. "He calls her Mama."

"Leave him alone," Kit said. "His mom's nice."

"What happened with Connor, then?" Ashton asked, but he was teasing.

"Hello, Connor," his mother said. "Shouldn't you be at work?"

Connor laughed. "I am at work, Mom. You're on speaker. I'm with Kit and two other detectives, Marshall and Ashton."

"Are those their first or last names?" his mother asked tartly.

Marshall chuckled. "Kevin Marshall and my partner Alf Ashton," he said. "It's nice to meet you, Mrs. Robinson."

"Call me Susan, please. Now, what can I do for you this morning? More gossip? Because that is totally my jam."

Kit's lips twitched at Susan's enthusiasm. "Yes, ma'am. We were hoping you could tell us which of the country clubs Christopher Drummond is a member of."

Susan sighed heavily. "Ours, unfortunately. The man is a pig. Which is mean to pigs. We thought so even before Connor arrested him for murder."

Kit glanced at Connor. "You didn't know Drummond was a member of your own country club?"

"It's not mine," Connor said. "It's my parents'."

"Connor hasn't been in a long while," Susan said. "Maybe just to play squash."

"I play squash at the athletic club, Mom, not the country club."

"Well, those are clearly different places," Ashton said dryly.

Connor flipped him the bird and continued. "So . . . how did I not know that Drummond was a member of your club, Mom? You never mentioned it when I was investigating him."

"You didn't ask. I figured it had come up in your investigation and you already knew. You know I'd never interfere in your work. But when you ask . . . well, that's different."

"What can you tell us about Christopher Drummond, ma'am?" Kit asked.

"He's always been an impossible chauvinist pig. That he killed that poor woman was not a surprise. Everyone knew he had a terrible temper. My husband and I avoided him like the plague."

"That was probably smart, ma'am," Kit said. "How long has he been a member?"

"Oh my. For ten years or more. Mostly played golf." She paused, then said, "Is this to do with your current investigation, Connor?"

"Yes, Mom. And you can say we're investigating Brooks Munro. Everyone knows. Why did you ask?"

"Because they used to play golf together, Munro and Drummond. And then they had some kind of falling-out. This was maybe four years ago—after Munro married Wilhelmina. Munro and Drummond wouldn't speak to each other. Drummond stopped coming to the club as often—which everyone was pleased by—and Munro joined somewhere else."

"Two somewhere elses," Kit said. "He was a member of three country clubs."

"Probably so he could schmooze," Susan said. "Munro was a thoroughly unpleasant man if you looked really hard, but on the surface, he had a lot of charisma. Even I thought he was a nice guy for a while. But I realized that he was just a blowhard and everyone knew he cheated on his wife. If you're looking for information, try his admin assistant. She was definitely doing him."

"Mom!" Connor said, shocked.

"I didn't say she was *effing* him, Connor. Give me a little credit for decorum."

"We know about Veronica," Kit said. "Was there anyone else he was intimately involved with?"

"Of course," Susan said. "The man could not keep his pants zipped. Give me a minute to think of the names of some of the women." Susan was quiet for a moment. "There were several, but the ones I remember were Estelle White, Juanita Young, and Trisha Finnegan. Two of them were divorced already. Trisha Finnegan's husband divorced her soon after her affair with Munro."

"Is there a reason you remember them specifically?" Connor asked.

Susan made a hesitant sound. "I got the impression that none of the three women actually *wanted* to be with Munro. I didn't know them well, but that was the gossip around the club. Maybe they were lured by his money. I don't know. But none of them seemed happy. Maybe they can tell you more about him."

"When was this, ma'am?" Marshall asked.

"At least two years ago."

"Thank you, Susan," Kit said. "You've been a huge help. Can you keep this conversation under your hat?"

"Of course. Give my love to CeCe, Connor. We're grilling steaks on Saturday. Be here at five, please."

"Yes, Mom."

Susan made kissing noises. "Bye, now."

Wincing, Connor ended the call and seemed to brace himself for the teasing. Instead, Marshall and Ashton only smiled.

"Your mom seems nice," Marshall said, taking the donor list back from Kit.

"And she approves of your girlfriend," Ashton added. "Good for you. My mother hated my girlfriend. Still does and we've been married for twenty-five years."

Kit chuckled. "So. Now we know Munro is an even bigger asshole than before."

"Hold on." Marshall frowned. "The three women he had affairs with are all on his list of campaign contributions, including the one who got divorced from her husband. They donated *after* he had affairs with them."

"Blackmail?" Kit asked.

"It's a place to start," Marshall agreed. "Although the two divorced women shouldn't have cared who found out they were sleeping with him. The married woman, yes, but not the divorced women. I wonder if Munro knew something else."

"I wonder if that's what Drummond knows," Connor said.

"I hope so," Kit said fiercely. "I'll be so happy to shove his kind offer down his fucking throat."

"We're right there with you," Marshall said. "What next?"

Kit sighed. "Let's find out who on Munro's donor list are also members of one of his country clubs. For now we'll focus on the one Connor's folks are members of, since that's where Christopher Drummond went, too. We definitely want to talk to the three women who had affairs with Munro. And I guess we need to add Tamsin Kavanaugh to that list, too." Kit scowled. "I hate that woman."

"We'll take Kavanaugh," Ashton offered. "We want you to

solve this case so we get your mother's cupcakes. If you get put on leave for breaking Tamsin Kavanaugh's nose, we don't get sweets."

Kit laughed. "Thanks, guys. Let's get busy."

Del Mar, San Diego, California
Wednesday, January 11, 10:00 a.m.

"Thank you for agreeing to see us, ma'am," Kit said as she and Connor sat on Trisha Finnegan's living room sofa.

The woman who'd had an affair with Brooks Munro was in her late fifties with a severe platinum-blond bob. She also resembled Wilhelmina. And Veronica. It seemed that Munro had a type.

Or maybe he chose women who looked like Veronica to assuage his guilt for cheating on her to get ahead in life. They might never know.

Trisha folded her perfectly manicured hands in her lap. "How can I help you?"

Her voice was steady, but her body language screamed anxiety.

Kit smiled, trying to relax her. "This is going to be an awkward subject, but we're investigating the murder of Brooks Munro and—"

"And you want to know if we had an affair," Trisha finished grimly. "If you call a one-night stand an affair, then yes. We did. If I could go back in time, I'd change everything about that night, but I can't."

"Just once?" Kit asked, surprised.

"Not the way you heard it, I know." Trisha wrung her hands

absently. "I was the topic of a lot of gossip at the country club." She eyed Connor warily. "I know your mother, Detective. She was kind to me after Munro."

"She was the one who suggested we speak with you," Connor confessed. "She seemed to think that you didn't want to be with Munro."

"Because I didn't," the woman said through clenched teeth. "He was a monster."

"What can you tell us, ma'am?" Kit asked, trying to be gentle. This woman seemed emotionally brittle.

Trisha stared down at her hands. "My husband and I were separated. I was at the bar at the country club that night, drinking too much. Munro seemed to care, like he wanted to listen." She exhaled heavily. "The next thing I knew I was waking up in my own bed and he was in the shower. We'd had sex, that much was clear, but I didn't remember anything about it."

"Do you think he drugged you?" Connor asked.

"I know he did," Trisha said with a bitter laugh. "He told me that he did."

Bold, Kit thought. "Did he blackmail you, ma'am?"

"Yes, but not because we had sex. My husband had his next wife all lined up by then, so he didn't care what I did or who I did it with. We had no prenup. I was always going to get half of our assets, so there was no reason for Munro to do . . . what he did. It wasn't like Munro telling my husband we had a one-night stand was going to make me get less money."

"But it wasn't just a one-night stand. Munro raped you," Kit murmured, realizing how Trisha had glossed over that fact.

Trisha jerked a nod. "Yeah, I guess he did."

"If it wasn't the sex, then what did he blackmail you about?" Kit asked.

Trisha closed her eyes. "When Munro contacted me later to give me the terms of the blackmail, he told me that I was a 'very chatty drunk.' I'd told him a secret I'd been holding on to for sixteen years, at that point. No one knew. No one. But all of a sudden Munro knew and that's why I paid him to keep quiet."

Kit wanted to ask what that secret was, but she felt like she was treading on thin ice with this woman. One wrong question and Trisha Finnegan would fall apart. "You donated to his campaign."

Trisha laughed again, the sound more hysterical than it had been before. "I did. That was how he started getting money from me. The first payment was to his reelection fund. He shouldn't have had one because he couldn't run again. He'd just been reelected to his second term. I told him this because, contrary to how it might seem at the moment, I'm not stupid."

Trisha was a retired schoolteacher. She'd won awards for exemplary teaching twenty years before. "You're far from stupid," Kit said.

"Thank you."

"What did Munro say when you told him that he shouldn't have a reelection fund?" Connor asked. "Because we've been wondering about that."

"He said he was going to run for state senate and to just donate the money without arguing or he'd tell my husband."

"Did it stop there?" Kit asked.

"No. It went on another three months."

Kit tensed. This could be what they needed to know. "How did he contact you?"

"Texts to a burner phone, supplied by him."

Kit nodded. "How did you make the payments?"

"Put the cash in a locker at the bus station the first time. Then at the gym another time. The third—and last—time, it was at a train station."

So the location did vary, Kit thought. Veronica hadn't lied about that. "The gym? Which gym?" Because that was weird. If Veronica was picking up the money, that meant she'd have to have access to the gym's locker room, which meant she was a member of that gym, too.

"The Beachside Athletic Club. That was a last-minute change. I was supposed to use the train station that time, but I was contacted and told to use my gym locker instead. That I should give them the combination to my lock. So I did."

That was the same gym Connor went to. Where he played squash, of all things.

"How did you manage to stop paying him?" Connor asked.

Another bitter laugh. "My husband finally served me with divorce papers. He cited infidelity, but not with Brooks Munro."

Kit looked around the room. There were framed photos on nearly every surface—all of the same young man. He looked like Trisha Finnegan and, in the most recent photos, he looked at least eighteen. She played her hunch. "He knew your son wasn't his biologically."

Trisha froze, then slumped back into her chair. "I've read you two are good detectives. I guess the media was right."

"It would have been a secret worth paying to keep," Kit said. "That's what you told Munro that night?"

"Yes. I don't know why I did, but I must have. I didn't want my husband to find out because I was afraid that he'd take it out on Tommy. Which he did. He cut Tommy out of his life, both emotionally and financially, and he'd been the only father Tommy had ever known."

"Salt in the wound," Kit said softly. "Munro drugged you,

raped you physically, then stole that secret from you against your will."

Trisha swallowed hard. "Yes. To all that. But I guess I got the last laugh when it came to Brooks Munro. Turns out, my husband had suspected for some time that my son wasn't his. He had a paternity test done on the sly as he was preparing the divorce papers. He divorced me and my son."

"How did your son feel about this?" Connor asked.

"He was devastated. Both with my ex-husband for disowning him and with me for lying to him all those years. I didn't find out I was pregnant until after we got engaged. I didn't want to believe Tommy wasn't his son, but as Tommy began to grow, I could see his biological father in his face, his eyes. His mannerisms. Tommy's biological father was a sweet man who died about five years ago, so Tommy will never know him. He's angry about that, too. He still speaks to me, but our relationship isn't the same. But that's on me, not Munro."

But the psychological damage from the rape and blackmail had to still be an issue for this woman. "Munro did enough, though."

Trisha sighed. "Yes, he did."

"Do you know who killed him?" Connor asked.

"No. If I did, I'd send them a thank-you card. Brooks Munro was a parasite."

"That seems to be a common opinion," Kit said. "Do you know if anyone else was being blackmailed?"

"I've always assumed so, only because he had the process down to a science. But that's not the kind of thing one talks about with other people."

"I suppose not," Kit said. "What about Juanita Young and Estelle White?"

Trisha shook her head. "I truly don't know. I did know them

a few years ago, but never well. Certainly never well enough to disclose such personal things with them and vice versa. The rumor mill said that they also slept with Munro. I don't know if he drugged them. You'll have to ask them. I dropped out of the country club scene after that. I just . . . couldn't go back."

"What are you doing now?" Kit asked, hoping the woman had been able to move forward.

"I was a teacher when I was younger. I loved my job back then, so I volunteer now with the school where I taught, tutoring at-risk kids. I also putter in my garden. I keep to myself, mostly."

"That's so nice," Kit said. "The at-risk kids, I mean. I do not have a green thumb so every garden begs me not to putter."

Trisha's smile was tentative. "Thank you. This was easier than I thought it would be. I've been expecting you since I read about Munro's murder. I figured anyone he was blackmailing would be a suspect. Am I a suspect?"

"Did you kill him?" Kit asked seriously.

"No. But when I'm not at the school volunteering, I keep to myself here at home. I have no one to vouch for my whereabouts."

Kit didn't think this woman had anything to do with Munro's death, but she did remember Alicia's multiple-hands theory. They couldn't rule Trisha out.

"You're not a suspect at this time," Connor said, saving Kit from answering. "But we're still investigating. If you think of anything that could help us, we'd appreciate it. Like the exact dates and places you made your money drops. It was a while ago, so we probably can't get security footage of those places anymore, but it's always worth a try."

Trisha got a notepad from a drawer in the lamp table beside her and scratched out a list. "It was more than two years ago, so I don't think these locations will do you any good, but there they are. My day was the second of every month."

"Your day?" Connor asked.

Trisha shrugged. "That's what Munro told me. That's when I figured he was doing this to enough people that he had to assign me my own day." She filled up a few lines of the notepad, then tore off the page and gave it to Connor.

"You're the first victim we've talked to so far," Kit said.

Trisha put the notepad away and folded her hands again. "Once you identify a bunch of us, we should have a support group."

Trisha said it lightly, like she was joking, but Kit thought that wasn't a bad idea.

It might have already happened. Multiple hands might have stabbed Munro. It all fit.

Trisha Finnegan didn't strike Kit as a person who was angry enough at Munro to stab him, but the man *had* raped her. Trisha might just be a very good actress.

"That's not a bad plan," Kit said, keeping her voice even when she wanted to immediately leave and begin looking for more blackmail victims. "Did you know that Munro had a kind of a dead man's switch? A list of his victims and their secrets that he'd make public if he died unexpectedly or violently?"

She frowned. "No, I didn't know that. He never threatened me with that. I always paid him."

Until she hadn't, Kit thought. "How did you tell him that your secret was no longer blackmail material?"

"I scheduled an in-person appointment with him, which meant dealing with his admin, who was a real bitch. Sorry." She grimaced. "This is bringing back a lot of bad memories."

"What did he say when you told him you were done paying him?" Connor asked.

She stilled, seeming to be thinking. "He didn't say much of

anything. Just . . . 'Okay.' But the look he gave me was terrifying. He was so angry. For a minute I thought he had a trapdoor in his office floor and I'd be fed to the sharks. But then he kind of cleared his expression and just said 'Okay,' and I left."

"He didn't warn you not to tell anyone?"

Trisha shook her head. "I'd already volunteered that I wouldn't when I was giving my spiel. I'd practiced and practiced it. I was so scared walking into that appointment. I didn't know what was going to happen. I didn't think he was violent, but I also hadn't thought he'd blackmail me. I just wanted to get on with my life. Looking back, I must have appeared pretty pathetic. I'd lost a lot of weight and my hair was falling out from the stress. I'd considered . . . you know. Ending things. Maybe he hoped I'd do myself in and he wouldn't have to worry about me."

"Did he ever retaliate in any way?" Kit pressed.

She started to shake her head, then sucked in a breath. "I had a car accident the following week. Hit-and-run driver. My car was totaled and I was badly hurt. I was even in a coma for a few days afterward. I didn't even think that it could have been Munro's doing. I was in a bad headspace back then and, honestly, my thinking was not ordered at all. Could that have been Munro's doing?"

"Possibly. Do you remember what the vehicle that hit you looked like?"

"No, I'm sorry but I don't. So . . . this tell-all list Munro supposedly had. Is it real?"

"We think he was killed for it," Kit said.

"Okay, then. Wow." Trisha hesitated, then shrugged. "I guess it won't be the end of the world for me if it's published. I pretty much cut myself off from the country club crowd, and the kids I tutor would probably think I'm 'fire' if they knew I'd once been blackmailed by a guy who was 'unalived.'" She used air quotes as she attempted to mimic her students. "What else do you want to know?"

"How much did you pay him?" Kit asked.

"Fifteen thousand dollars after my 'voluntary contribution.'" More air quotes. "Five thousand a month for those three months. Paid in fifties. Nonsequential bills."

"Not a small sum," Connor said.

"No, but like I said, my husband and I had no prenup. I got fifty percent of our property. It would have been a problem if I'd gone on paying. I can show you the record of my cash withdrawals from those months where I paid Munro. I thought if I ever did fall prey to his trapdoor with the sharks, I wanted to at least leave a paper trail in case someone cared enough to look for me."

Like Munro had, Kit thought. He'd chosen the joint account for his withdrawal of fifty thousand dollars. He had to have known that Wilhelmina would be informed.

She'd almost forgotten about that.

She wondered why he hadn't sent some kind of similar message to Veronica. Maybe they had no joint assets.

Something to check.

She glanced at Connor. "Anything else?"

"No, I'm finished."

Kit rose, Connor alongside her. "Thank you for seeing us, Mrs. Finnegan. Contact us if you remember anything else, even if it seems small."

CHAPTER THIRTEEN

Estelle White said she'd had an affair with Munro," Marshall said when Kit, Connor, and the other two detectives had gathered together to debrief their interviews.

She and Connor had shared what Trisha had disclosed, but neither of the other women who Munro had had affairs with had been as forthcoming. Juanita Young hadn't even let Kit and Connor into her house. She'd closed the door in their faces.

Ashton pulled four sub sandwiches from a bag and passed them around. "Estelle was lying," he said bluntly. "About the sex and the blackmail. She wouldn't look at us through the entire interview."

"She has three kids," Marshall added. "Oldest is fifteen. He wouldn't leave the room. I think whatever Munro had on her, she didn't want her kids to know."

"Thanks for lunch," Connor said. "We'll provide dinner if we're still working."

"We will be," Kit said glumly. "And yes, thank you so much for lunch. I always forget to eat."

"We know," Marshall said.

"We all know," Ashton added. "You work so many hours, you make the rest of us look bad."

Kit rolled her eyes. "Anyway. If you'd been able to get Estelle alone, do you think she would have been more honest?"

Marshall shook his head. "She was afraid. Even though both Munro and Grossman are dead and Veronica's in jail, she was terrified."

"I thought the same," Ashton said. "So we didn't get anything from her. Nothing like you got from Trisha Finnegan."

"Trisha had stopped paying Munro," Kit said. "And the thing he'd held over her head no longer had any power over her. The other women may still be paying. Or at least they were up until last week. If we have to, we can subpoena their bank records. Trisha volunteered to show us hers. Maybe the others made monthly cash withdrawals, too."

Marshall noted it on the whiteboard as a possible next step. "I've been thinking about the drop boxes that Trisha said she used. Lockers at the bus stop and the train make sense, but the gym? Why the gym? That meant whoever picked up the money that month had to have been a gym member to get access to the locker room, right?"

Kit nodded. "That would have been Veronica. Connor goes to the same gym and he confirmed her membership on our way back here after Juanita Young slammed her door in our faces."

Connor crumpled the now-empty sandwich wrapper and

lobbed it into the trash can. The man could inhale food so fast it made Kit's head spin. She was still eating.

"So . . . what about Tamsin Kavanaugh?" Connor asked. "Did you talk to her?"

"Only briefly," Marshall said, his expression darkening. "She said that she had indeed had an affair with Munro. She said that it was 'perfectly consensual' and that they'd both benefited. He gave her early access to any newsworthy items coming out of the council and he got a few complimentary articles in her paper. She said it lasted about three months. She admitted to making the donations. She said that's how she got access to Munro to begin with. She also said that she didn't know who'd killed him, that if she did, it would have been all over the internet by now. Then she asked us why we'd asked her about consent with Munro, and she got that gleam in her eye. We left soon after that. We didn't want to inadvertently give her a story."

"I get that," Kit said. "I knew she'd do anything for a story, but Munro? Ick."

"A lot of women liked his looks," Ashton said. "My wife thought he looked like Rock Hudson."

"Who?" Connor asked, and Kit elbowed him in the ribs.

"You know who that is. You're just trying to make Ashton feel old."

Connor grinned. "Did it work?"

Ashton laughed. "No, because I already felt old. You're way too late for that, young pup."

Kit's mind was racing. "Veronica didn't lie about the locations changing each month. What if she used the bus and train stations often? What if she used one of those locations in the last month? What if we get the surveillance footage from both places for the last month?"

"That is a lot of footage," Ashton said. "We'll need to ask for help."

"But it's doable," Marshall said. "You ask Navarro for more assistance, McKittrick. He likes you best."

"He really doesn't," Kit said. "But I'll ask." She called Navarro and he said he'd coordinate getting the footage and a team to review it. She turned back to the three men, who were stuffing themselves with potato chips. "Done. So we have one confirmed blackmail victim. I didn't get killer vibes from Trisha Finnegan. Did you, Connor?"

Kit wished they'd taken Sam with them. He was good at reading people. *But so are we. We survived before Sam was our psychologist.*

"I didn't. But she was also *very* cooperative."

"Too cooperative?" Ashton asked.

Connor shrugged. "Enough that we can't rule her out. Are you thinking about Alicia's multiple-hands theory?"

"Yeah," Kit grumbled. "Trisha suggested that if we identified more blackmail victims, they could have a support group. That made me wonder if a bunch of them did get together and plan their little *Orient Express* scheme."

Marshall wiped dust from the potato chips off his hands. "They'd need to have identified each other. That's kind of the beauty of Munro's plan. If he had multiple people with secrets to hide, nobody is going to talk about their secrets. They'd have no way of knowing if other people were in the same boat."

"And if there were more victims at the country club, they'd all have the funds to pay," Ashton added.

"Not everyone there is super rich," Connor said. "Trisha was paying five grand a month. That could break quite a few people in the club."

"Anyone file for bankruptcy lately?" Kit asked. "How could

we find out the state of the finances of each member? We'll never get a warrant for their financials. Not with what little we know."

"True." Marshall looked at Connor. "Would your mom know?"

"Maybe, but my dad's more likely to have heard something about specific finances. I'll call him." He dialed, then put his phone on speaker again.

"Connor? Is everything okay?"

"We're fine, Dad. Everyone's fine. I've got you on speaker. I'm with Kit and two other detectives, Kevin Marshall and Alf Ashton. We're working the Munro case. This is my father, Andrew Robinson."

"Nice to meet you, Detectives. Hi, Kit. What do you need?"

"We're focusing on the country club," Connor said. "Do you know of any members who've had recent financial issues?"

"Can't get a warrant, huh?"

"Haven't tried yet. Hoped to get some insider info."

"It would mean a lot, sir," Kit asked.

"Oh, I'll help you. I'm thinking. Hush now. My brain doesn't click into motion as fast as it used to." They were quiet until Andrew finally cleared his throat. "Okay. There are a few things I've noticed. Simon Daly recently sold his Maserati and bought a Cadillac. He took some grief for that because that Maserati was a damn fine car. He said he was streamlining his finances so that he could retire. I personally thought he'd likely made some bad financial investments. Then there's Hugh Smith. He recently sold his house in La Jolla for a place downtown. A lot less square footage and a lot less fancy. His wife was none too pleased and told *everyone* who'd listen. Your mother would probably have more details." He was quiet for another moment, then he sighed. "Then there's Earl O'Hanlon."

"He died, didn't he?" Connor asked.

"Killed himself."

Kit sat up straighter. "When was this?"

"Two months ago. Let me check my calendar. I went to his funeral." Twenty seconds passed with Andrew muttering to himself in the background. "Found it. His funeral was November eighth."

"Why did he kill himself?" Kit asked.

"He was broke. His wife thought he had another woman on the side and she'd left him to go live with her sister. His housekeeper went in for her final paycheck—because he'd had to fire all the help—and found him hanging in the great room. He'd been dead at least a day, from what I heard. He left a letter saying that he'd made some bad business decisions and couldn't see any way out."

"That's sad," Kit murmured. "Do you think he made bad business decisions?"

"I always thought Earl was a savvy businessman. He'd turned one small corner store into a chain of high-end grocery stores. He was rolling in money at one point. But we never talked about his personal finances."

"Was there anyone he would have shared his financial issues with?" Kit asked.

"Joe Rooney. The two were business partners for thirty years, up until Joe retired. If he told anyone, it would have been Joe. Earl's widow might know. But she's moved somewhere southeast. Mississippi or Alabama, maybe. Oh, your mother's coming, Connor. If you don't want her involved, we need to end this call now."

"If you think of more club members with financial problems, can you let us know?" Connor said. "Thanks, Dad. See you Saturday."

"You be careful, son."

"I will." Connor ended the call. "We have the names of three people who were hemorrhaging money. Earl O'Hanlon can't answer any of our questions, but his widow might. We just need to track her down."

"Or the friend," Kit said. "Joe Rooney. Do you know him, Connor?"

"I've seen him at a few country club events, but we've never really spoken. He's my dad's age, so our paths didn't cross. But we can talk to him."

"What about the other two?" Marshall asked. "Mr. Maserati and Mr. Ex La Jolla?"

"I say we bring them here for questioning," Kit said. "I doubt they'll be receptive to answering our questions in their homes. And if we don't get anywhere with them, we'll bring in Juanita Young and Estelle White and question them again. Maybe they'll be more forthcoming the second time around. For now, let's focus on the men. Connor and I will take Mr. Maserati and you two bring in Mr. Ex La Jolla."

"Otherwise known as Simon Daly and Hugh Smith," Connor said dryly. "I doubt either of them will just come in because we ask."

Kit shrugged. She didn't understand rich people, but she knew how to embarrass them into doing what she wanted. "Then we threaten to go to their place of business with a warrant tomorrow and tell their coworkers in a *very loud voice* that we're from Homicide and there to bring them downtown."

Connor nodded once. "That will work."

Ashton grinned. "This is going to be fun."

Kit studied the whiteboard. "We still have so many interviews to do."

Marshall was checking his notes. "We also still need to find the guard who was on gate duty the night Munro went missing. He was tagged in a social media post by one of his friends about six months ago. We've contacted the friend and are waiting for a call back. I'm not holding out a lot of hope on finding him alive. Let's get these guys in for questioning, and then Alf and I will pay a visit to the friend who made the social media post."

"Sounds good." Kit brushed the crumbs from her lunch into the trash can. "We should ask Joe Rooney to come in too, to ask him about Earl O'Hanlon's money troubles. We should talk to him before Simon Daly and Hugh Smith, in case he has information that might help crack the other two."

Carmel Valley, San Diego, California
Wednesday, January 11, 3:00 p.m.

Kit rushed into her parents' house, her heart pounding with fear. "What's wrong?"

She'd been with Connor, about to load Mr. Maserati, a.k.a. Simon Daly, into the back of their car when her father had called her to come home, a tightness in his voice she'd only heard a few times.

None of those times had been good. So she'd left Connor to bring Simon Daly in for questioning while she took an Uber to her car, which she'd left in the SDPD parking lot.

She honestly couldn't even remember the drive back. She'd been on autopilot.

Sam was waiting for her in her parents' foyer. He reached out to grip her shoulders, keeping her from running any farther. "Kit, wait."

Kit blinked up at him. "Why are you here? What's wrong? Where's Pop?"

"He's upstairs with Rita. She's physically okay."

Sam's calm voice allowed her to take a moment to breathe.

"Okay. What's wrong with Rita?"

Sam grimaced. "She didn't take the news of Christopher Drummond's deal well."

Kit closed her eyes, wondering how Sam had found out. "I meant to tell you, but we got busy and . . ."

Sam pulled her in for a hug. "It's okay, Kit. Just take a second to calm down. You can't help her if you run upstairs loaded for bear."

She huffed a laugh against his solid chest, her arms wrapping around his waist. This man was a rock.

He could be your rock.

Someday. Maybe.

"Okay, I'm calm now. Tell me what happened."

Sam let her go, tipping her chin up so that he could see her eyes. "Harlan picked up Rita from school, like he told you he would. He wanted to tell her about Drummond when they got home, but she was suspicious about being picked up early."

"Of course she was. She's smart."

"She is that. She didn't buy that your father was picking her up so that she could help him with the new dog."

Kit looked around her parents' living room. "Where is the behemoth?"

"Upstairs. He took to Rita right away. He and Snickerdoodle are on her bed with her." He sighed. "Your dad told her about Drummond in the car and she kind of lost it."

"I was afraid she would. I should have taken off work and told her myself."

"You're not her parent, Kit. You're a great big sister, though, and you did the right thing. The news needed to come from your father. But Rita panicked. She got out of the car and ran, right there in front of her school."

Kit closed her eyes again. "But she's not hurt?"

"No. Close call, though. She ran across the road and a car nearly hit her. I think your father nearly had a heart attack."

Kit's eyes flew up to Sam's, new fear icing over her heart. "For real?"

"He should see a doctor. I didn't like how pale he was by the time I got here. But right now, he seems to be okay and focused on Rita. Blames himself for botching the delivery of the news."

"He would. He always blames himself."

"Like father, like daughter," Sam said mildly. "Rita actually got him home. She saw him nearly pass out and that snapped her out of her flight mode. She called Akiko to come and get them. Akiko did so and signed out Tiffany and Emma, too. Brought them all back here. The way I heard it, Rita held it together until they were safely back home and then she lost it again. She started crying hysterically and packing her things to run."

"Who called you?"

"Tiffany and Emma. They should have called Dr. Carlisle, but they didn't think about it."

"They trust you. Is Dr. Carlisle able to see Rita today?"

"She'll be coming over as soon as she's done with her final session, but I really think you can help more than anyone else. That's why Harlan called you."

Kit nodded, trying to find her composure. "So Rita heard the news and . . . what? She thinks Drummond's going to get a deal from Joel?"

Sam grimaced again. "She thinks he'll get a deal from you."

"From *me*?" Kit stared up at him. "Why would she think that?"

"Um . . ."

Kit and Sam turned to find Emma standing in the doorway

leading to the kitchen. Kit went to her, giving her a hug that should have been warmer. It was tense and rigid, but Emma didn't seem to notice.

The teenager sank into the embrace and Kit drew another breath, her heart hurting when Emma started to cry.

These girls had been through hell.

And if Rita thought I was going to make a deal with Drummond? She had to be feeling so betrayed. Kit stroked Emma's hair and rubbed her back, all the things Harlan did when Kit was upset.

"Why are you crying, Emma?" Kit asked softly.

"I messed everything up. Pop McK is going to be so mad at me. Mom McK, too. They're going to make me leave. Pop almost had a heart attack, and it's my fault. Mom is going to hate me. And Rita . . . You have to help her, Kit."

"I will," Kit promised. "But let's help you first, okay? First of all, Mom and Pop will never send you away. Not unless you use violence, and I don't think you did that, did you?"

Sniffling, Emma shook her head. "No. I was just so stupid." It came out as a wail, and Kit went back to stroking Emma's hair.

"You are not stupid. Come, let's sit at the kitchen table and you can tell me what's going on, okay?" Kit put an arm around Emma's shoulders and, throwing a helpless glance at Sam, led the teenager to the kitchen.

Sam was ready with a box of tissues, and the three of them sat down. Emma mopped her face and shuddered out a breath. "Last night," she started.

Kit waited, but when Emma didn't continue, she gave her a gentle nudge. "Last night?"

Emma bit her lip. "I heard you and Pop McK talking."

Kit frowned. They'd been talking about Veronica Fitzgerald

and how she and Connor needed the money drop locations. "What did you hear, Em?"

"That you would make a deal with someone named Veronica. I didn't mean to listen. I just wanted some cookies because we were studying and—" She dropped her head into her hands and started to cry again.

"So I assume you told this to Rita?" Kit asked, trying to string the events together.

Emma nodded miserably. "We tell each other everything. And then today . . . when she heard about Drummond . . ." She looked up, her face blotchy from crying. "You won't let him be free, will you? Please, Kit. *Please.*"

"I will not make a deal with Drummond," Kit said firmly. "But I can see how Rita might think we would." She might have hoped that Rita would have trusted her more, but Rita was still a traumatized child. Kit remembered exactly how that felt. "You didn't do anything wrong. Listening in wasn't great, but you didn't mean to. And as for Pop, we will make sure he sees the very best doctors."

Her lungs wanted to freeze at the thought of losing Harlan, but she'd deal with that later. "They will not send you away, Emma. I know it's hard, but have a little faith. You'll see. I did so much worse and they never once even discussed sending me away."

Emma's nod was jerky. "Really?"

"Really." She reached across the table and squeezed Emma's hand. "Someday I'll tell you all about it, but let's get Rita back to okay first. Come on. Is everyone upstairs?"

"Yeah. Mom won't leave Pop, and Akiko is guarding our bedroom door in case Rita tries to run again. She already had to grab her once and push her back into our room. That's when Pop called you."

"Well, someone should have called me right away."

"We know you're busy," Emma said.

"Never too busy for you guys." Kit tipped up Emma's chin just as Sam had done hers minutes before. "Now dry your eyes and follow me." She met Sam's gaze. "Come with us?"

"Of course," Sam said.

The three of them climbed the stairs to find Mom, Pop, and Akiko camped out in the hallway. Someone had brought out some folding chairs and her parents were seated in them.

Akiko stood at the bedroom door in a soldier's stance, her grim expression softening when she saw Kit. "Hey, you."

Kit smiled at her sister. "Hey, yourself. I hear you're a bouncer today."

Akiko shrugged. "Fisherwoman, chef extraordinaire, bouncer. I can do it all." She glanced at their parents from the corner of her eye. "Add father wrangler to the list."

Kit turned her focus to Harlan, who was rolling his eyes. "I'm fine."

His color looked normal, Kit thought. She'd been standing next to her former partner Baz when he'd had a heart attack at a crime scene, and she didn't think she'd ever forget what he'd looked like.

Harlan looked like himself. A tired version, but himself nonetheless. She bent to give him a hug. "Why didn't you call me sooner, Pop?"

"Because I knew you'd be trying every trick in your book to keep Drummond from getting out of going to trial. I needed you to be working." He looked over her shoulder to where Sam stood on the stairs. "Thank you for explaining everything to Kit."

"I was happy to help," Sam said.

Kit looked over her shoulder at him. He really was happy to help. She wondered if he knew exactly how extraordinary he was. "You always do," she said, then kissed Harlan's forehead. "You, Pop, are seeing a doctor as soon as I get Rita straightened out."

He rolled his eyes again. "I know."

"I already told him," Betsy said. Her face was also pale, but Kit thought that might be from fright.

Kit gave her a hug as well. "I'll do my best to fix this. I'm sorry that Rita jumped to the wrong conclusion, but I get it."

"I knew you would," Betsy said. "Go on. Tiffany is in there with her, along with the dogs. There might be room for you, but there might not. It's pretty tight."

Kit chuckled. "Sam? Join me?"

He came the rest of the way up the stairs. "You can handle this yourself. You don't need me."

"Rita trusts you. Please. You too, Emma." She opened the door and found that, yes, the room was now a very tight fit. Two twin beds had been okay. Three twin beds, three teenage girls, two big dogs, plus herself and Sam made a crowd.

Kit left the door open, gesturing for Emma to go in first. The tension in the room was so thick that it was palpable.

Rita looked up, dread on her face. "Is Pop okay? I didn't mean to hurt him."

"Oh, honey." Kit shoved at the new dog until he got off Rita's bed with a huge doggy sigh. He was going to be enormous. He was already huge. But, once he was trained, nobody would mess with Rita or the other girls. "Pop looks fine, but we'll get him checked out. He's always had a healthy heart up until now. Mom makes him go for checkups every year, even though he grumbles. Hopefully he just got scared seeing you nearly become roadkill."

Rita winced. "Sorry. I shouldn't have run across that busy road. That was dumb."

"Don't be sorry. I get it." She scooted backward on the bed

until she and Rita had the wall at their backs. "Let's get the obvious issue out of the way first. I will move heaven and earth so as not to let that bastard Drummond get a deal. We've been working all day to figure out what he might know so that we can circumvent him completely. That means we'll go around him."

Rita scowled. "I *know* what 'circumvent' means, Kit."

Kit chuckled, relieved to hear some of Rita's natural snark return. "Good. It'll make your college entry exams a breeze."

"Did you?" Tiffany asked. She tried to look forceful, but Kit could see the scared kid she and Sam had met just months before. "Did you find a way?"

Healing happened slowly, Kit knew. Things might appear normal on the surface but she knew that each girl struggled with her fears every day. *I still do.*

"I think we may have. Once we're done here, I need to get back for a few interviews, but . . . yeah. We have a good lead. One I'm not going to tell you about, so don't even ask."

Three teenage mouths snapped shut in unison.

She looked at each of the girls in turn. "I'm not mad that you listened, Emma, but that was a private conversation between me and Pop. What else did you hear?"

"Just that sometimes cutting a deal was the lesser of two evils."

Kit suspected she'd heard more, but let it go for now. "Sometimes it is. With Christopher Fucking Drummond, it's not. Nobody I talked to today—on our side, anyway—wants to give that bastard a single fraction of an inch." She hesitated, then pulled Rita closer. Rita relaxed into Kit's side. "We know what he did, Rita." Kit wouldn't say that Drummond had raped the teenager. Not in front of the other two girls. "We will fight tooth and nail to make sure he goes to prison forever."

"They know. Tiff and Em. I told them what he did." Rita's swallow was audible. "What *else* he did."

Kit studied Tiffany and Emma and saw nothing but loyalty. And anger, but Kit figured that was directed at Drummond.

"Okay," Kit said. "Then I can be blunt. That he murdered a woman in cold blood is enough for a criminal trial. That he murdered the child she was carrying is also enough for a criminal trial. We don't need to bring in the fact that he assaulted you, not right now. If it comes to it and you're ready, we'll tell Joel. But know that you have time to decide if you want to come forward and press charges. Lots of time. That you haven't doesn't mean Drummond can go free for the murder of your mother. They'd be separate trials."

Rita looked to the door where Sam was standing. "Should I tell Joel?"

Kit couldn't blame Rita for wanting a second opinion. She'd trust Sam for the truth in the same situation.

Sam shook his head. "Not until you're ready. And if you're never ready, that's okay, too. Kit's telling you the truth. And nobody in this house blames you for not pressing charges."

"Even if Drummond gets off on a technicality?" Rita pressed, her voice cracking.

"Even then," Sam said in his soothing voice. The tension in the room began to drop, and Kit felt like she could breathe again. "Joel knows that Drummond has threatened you. He might be able to use that against Drummond when he goes to trial, because trying to intimidate you is against the law, too. For the time being, don't panic. Nothing is different now than it was yesterday except that Drummond is getting desperate."

"What do you mean?" Rita asked warily.

Sam looked to Kit. "That explanation's yours."

"He means," Kit said, "that if Drummond is offering to give us information on the case we're working, then he knows about a crime he didn't come forward about on his own. Depending on the crime, that could make things worse for him."

"Oh," Emma breathed. "It's because Munro was blackmailing people. Maybe Drummond was getting blackmailed, too."

"I thought you'd heard more than you let on," Kit said dryly.

"Sorry," Emma said with a wince. "But that's right, isn't it? If he knows about blackmail, maybe it's because he was being blackmailed, too. And if he was being blackmailed, he'd have to tell you all about that, and since he kept it a secret, that would be another crime you could arrest him for."

Kit's lips twitched. "You wanna be a cop, kid?"

Emma sat up straighter, preening. "Maybe. But I'm right, right?"

"You could be," Kit admitted. "But even if you're wrong, Drummond is getting desperate. That means we're doing all the right things. I would never take the easy way and let that asshole off for murdering your mother, even if he'd never laid a hand on you. But that he did that, too? I want him to rot in jail forever."

Rita let out a quiet breath. "Thank you, Kit. I'm sorry I caused so much trouble."

Harlan appeared in the doorway, looking like his normal self, much to Kit's relief. "You are never trouble, honey. This one?" He pointed to Kit. "She was trouble."

"Guilty," Kit said, giving Rita a small, affectionate shake. "Let's get a snack and then I have to head back. Connor's holding our leads in interview rooms until I can help with the questioning."

Rita exhaled. "I should have known you wouldn't let him go free."

"Have a little faith," Emma said, giving Kit a smile.

"I will." Rita slid off the bed and gave Sam a hard hug before hugging Harlan. "I'm sorry, Pop. I didn't mean to scare you."

Harlan kissed Rita's forehead. "Just don't do it again. I think I'll see that car narrowly missing you in my dreams for a long time. Your life is precious, Rita. Let's take better care of it, okay?"

Rita put her hands on her hips. "Like *you* will by going to the doctor?"

In the hallway, Akiko laughed. "Busted, Pop. I'll take you now."

Kit watched her parents, Akiko, and the three teenagers head downstairs. "Thank you for reassuring Rita," she said to Sam.

"It's not that she doesn't trust you," Sam said. "She does."

"I know. But she needed verification. She reminds me so much of myself. Pop never knew it, but I was ready to run after Wren died. I was going to investigate and find her killer. I'd even have killed him myself if I'd found him. Pop offering to help me find Wren's killer kept me here."

"I think he knew that when he offered. He's pretty smart."

"He probably did." It made Kit love her father all the more. "I was actually about to call you before Pop called me. You wanna come watch some interviews and tell me what you think?"

He smiled at her. "Sure. Who's in the hot seat today?"

"Mr. Maserati and Mr. Ex La Jolla." She chuckled at his confusion. "I'll explain when we get there. Suffice it to say that today I am grateful that Connor's family is loaded."

"I can't wait to hear about it. Is Laura representing them? Please say she's not."

Kit laughed out loud. "I truly hope not."

CHAPTER FOURTEEN

Joe Rooney sat at the interview table with his head in his hands. "I didn't know," he said sadly. "I didn't know that Earl was in such financial trouble. I would have helped him. We'd been partners for years, friends for even longer. But he never said a word."

Kit believed him. Joe's best friend, Earl O'Hanlon, had committed suicide because he'd lost everything. Clearly Joe Rooney was still grieving.

"I understand you two ran a grocery store chain together," Kit said. Connor and Sam were on the other side of the glass, observing. She thought Navarro might be back there, too. They'd agreed that Kit would talk to the man alone. Too many people might put him on the defensive and, as far as they knew, Joe Rooney wasn't involved in Munro's blackmail scheme.

Joe nodded. "Earl started it with one little corner store. I was his first franchise. We knew each other from college. Had been friends for years already when we joined forces. I retired first, mainly because my wife was diagnosed with MS. She needs more help these days. I didn't want to leave Earl in the lurch, but he urged me to retire. Said I needed to take care of my wife. So I did."

"And then?" Kit asked, because it felt like something was coming.

"Earl managed the company as a whole. I'd focused on sales because that was what I enjoyed. When I left, he brought in someone to take my place. Young fella, just graduated with his MBA. Son of another friend. I think that might have been when things started going sideways. I wish I'd paid more attention."

"It's possible that Earl didn't want you to know," Kit suggested. "If he hid it from you, there's no way you could have known."

Joe sighed. "That's likely. He was always a proud man."

"What about the new guy? What is his name and what did he do?"

"Louis Durant. He resigned about a year ago. He was hired to take over sales, but somehow he was also managing the financial end. Earl said that Louis was a real go-getter. Earl was letting Louis have more responsibility so that Earl could semi-retire. He said that Louis was making him money hand over fist. We played golf a lot more often at the club, because Earl had so much free time. I thought he was happy, and maybe then he was."

"That changed?"

Joe shrugged uncertainly. "He did get tense, but Earl was a worrier. At the time my wife was having significant MS flare-ups, and I was concentrating on her."

He sounded apologetic, so Kit gave him an encouraging

smile. "As you should have been. Do you think that Louis Durant resigned on his own, or did Earl force him to or be fired?"

"I don't know. I can give you the name of the HR manager. She might be able to help you. All I know is that all of a sudden, Earl was canceling our golf games. We went from playing two or three times a week to once a month and then never. I tried to call him, tried to find out what was wrong, but he told me that he was missing the office and that his semi-retirement had been a mistake. He didn't sound upset." Joe closed his eyes. "He didn't sound suicidal."

"Did he change his spending habits over the last year?" Kit asked.

"He must have. Darlene—that's his wife—thought he was cheating on her, that he was spending their money on another woman. I knew Earl would never do that. He loved his wife. But he wasn't the flowers and poetry type. He worked hard to provide for her, and I guess he figured that was enough. It wasn't for Darlene. She wanted his time. I should have said something, but I didn't want to get between him and Darlene."

"Did he sell a car or a house?"

"No, but he sold some stock. A lot of stock. That was after he'd semi-retired. Before he went back full time. At the time I thought it was part of his retirement planning. I figured he'd put it into his 401(k) or something. I guess you're insinuating that he didn't?"

Kit kept her voice gentle, like Earl was a victim and not a guilty party. She didn't think Joe would be happy if she insinuated Earl had done something nefarious with the proceeds from that stock sale. "We think he might have been being blackmailed."

Joe reared back, shock on his face. "*Earl?* For *what*?"

"We don't know. We were hoping you could help us find out."

Joe studied her for a long moment. "Munro," he finally said flatly.

"What about him?" Kit asked, keeping her tone conversational.

"Well, he's dead. You're homicide detectives, investigating his murder. It doesn't take a PhD to put it all together."

Kit couldn't refute that. "Did Earl spend time with Brooks Munro?"

"No. He couldn't stand the man." Joe frowned. "He did play golf with him once. I heard about it from one of the other club members who asked if Earl and I had 'broken up.' I had no idea what he was talking about until he told me that he'd seen Earl and Munro out on the links the Sunday before."

"About how close in time were the golf game and Earl's sudden sale of stock?"

Joe seemed to wilt where he sat. "Not long. A week? Maybe two. I didn't put it together. What could Munro have blackmailed Earl over? Earl was a straight shooter. He didn't cheat, not in business, not on Darlene. He paid his taxes and he was good to his employees. I don't know what Munro could possibly have had on him."

"Where did the sudden resignation of Louis Durant fall with respect to the stock sale and the golf game?"

Joe's face scrunched and he dropped his chin. "Not long after. A month or two. I can't believe I missed it."

"Your wife was sick, sir. She is your priority."

"I was a shitty best friend, though. Maybe he'd be alive today if I'd done something."

Kit wasn't touching his last statement. Life was full of maybes and she couldn't tell the man that he was wrong. "Could Louis Durant have done something illegal? Something that Earl would have been accountable for?"

"It's possible. I worried a little when Louis hit the ground running so fast. Not about illegalities. It was more my ego. I'd had that role for years and I'd never had those kind of results."

"Maybe because you're honest?"

Joe sighed heavily. "Maybe. How can we find out if Earl was being blackmailed?"

"Well, *we* aren't going to do anything. *You* are going home to your wife, who needs you. My partner and I are going to track down Mr. Durant. You can help us by giving us all the contacts we'll need. HR, Accounting, all the departments."

Joe pulled a pen from his pocket, his expression grim. "Hand me a piece of paper. I'll give you anything you need."

San Diego PD, San Diego, California
Wednesday, January 11, 6:00 p.m.

Well, Sam thought, at least he didn't have to look at Laura Letterman through the glass tonight. Simon Daly, also known as Mr. Maserati because he'd sold his sports car, had a male attorney who was currently trying to discourage Kit from the interview.

The other person of interest, Hugh Smith, a.k.a. Mr. Ex La Jolla after he'd sold his mansion in La Jolla and downsized to a condo in the city, hadn't yet been located.

Sam hoped Daly would give them something good or at least confirm that the club members were being blackmailed. Then they could be a little more certain that they knew the secret that Drummond had been hoping to trade for his freedom. Sam sure as hell didn't want Christopher Drummond to profit from his crimes against little Rita. Sam's heart still hurt at her fear. But she trusted them. She trusted Kit to do the right thing, so Sam sent up a prayer that Kit would be able to crack Simon Daly.

"You're wasting your time, Detective," the attorney said. "My client isn't going to tell you anything."

Daly's gaze was fixed on the table. His eyes weren't visible, but the man's body language screamed "guilty."

"That's okay," Kit said sweetly. "My partner and I have some information your client might find useful, though."

"He's toast," Navarro said with a chuckle.

"He is," Sam agreed.

Kit and Connor had teamed up this time, and Sam was looking forward to seeing what they could pry out of Mr. Daly.

"So," Kit said, her elbows on the table. "You sold your Maserati recently, Mr. Daly."

"Not a crime," his attorney said.

"Of course not," Kit agreed pleasantly. "But we're thinking you did do a crime, Mr. Daly, and you sold the Maserati to pay your blackmailer."

Daly jolted, the movement seeming to be involuntary.

"Oh yeah," Navarro murmured. "He did something, all right."

Sam agreed. "His shoulders just hiked up to his ears and, from the way his biceps just flexed, I'd bet he's clenching his fists under the table."

"My client doesn't know what you're talking about," the attorney said, as if he hadn't a care in the world. Except his left eye was now twitching. An unfortunate tell for an attorney.

Laura never would have allowed her face to twitch like that.

"Oh, I think you do, Mr. Daly." Kit still sounded so sweet. "And, just so you know, we've got a warrant in front of a judge so we can search your home and your bank records. I'm betting we'll find a bunch of cash, all fifties, nonsequential. Maybe in your safe or hidden in a shoebox, just waiting for your day to pay. Which day was yours, Mr. Daly? The first of the month? The fourth? The woman who paid on the second of every month has already shown us her bank records."

"Did she?" Sam asked Navarro.

"No, but she offered. Her secret was discovered by her ex-husband, so she had nothing to gain by continuing to pay Munro."

"Munro just let her go?"

"From what she said, yes. But he may have tried to kill her in a traffic accident, so we're not sure."

On the other side of the glass, Mr. Daly had grown more tense but remained silent.

Kit was smiling at Daly sunnily. "No worries, we'll figure it out. We're combing through surveillance footage at the most recent drop points. We'll find you on the recordings, Mr. Daly. Unless you sent someone else."

"He wouldn't have," Connor said to Kit, as if Daly weren't there. "That would be one more person who knew he had something to hide."

"True," Kit said. "So, the dead man's switch. Have you lost sleep this week, Mr. Daly, worrying about it?"

Daly looked up then, his glare glacial. But he said nothing.

"I bet you have," Kit said. "I wouldn't be getting a wink of sleep if I knew that Munro had a list with my name on it, just waiting to be shared with everybody in the event of his unfortunate demise."

Daly looked back down at the table, but his throat worked as he tried to swallow.

"It was a *very* unfortunate demise, too," Connor said. "His body was nearly unrecognizable. Luckily, he had that neck tattoo. His killer was angry."

"Or his *many* killers," Kit said, her smile slipping into something grim. "Did you help, Mr. Daly? Was one of those many stab wounds by your hand?"

Daly flinched again, which was very interesting.

"That's enough," Daly's attorney snapped. He stood up. "We're done."

"We're not," Kit said, all pleasantry gone. "Sit down, please." She waited until he'd done so. "Mr. Daly, that dead-man's-switch list is still out there. Several people have searched for it, but to no avail. Somebody found it, though. Of that we're pretty sure. Probably the person who cut off all of Munro's fingers and toes to get him to talk."

Daly swallowed again, his shoulders hunching forward.

"He's gonna puke," Navarro said blandly.

Sam hoped not. It looked like Daly was holding it together. But barely.

"Maybe not *all* his fingers and toes," Connor said. "Sure, they were all cut off, but I'm betting Munro caved after the first few and told his tormentors what they wanted to know. The rest were likely cut off just for fun."

Daly clamped his hand over his mouth.

"Trash can is behind you," Kit said.

The information was given just in time, because Daly grabbed the can and retched into it.

Sam grimaced. "I hate when they puke."

"Not my favorite thing, either," Navarro agreed. "At least he hit the can. Sometimes they miss."

"So gross," Sam muttered, feeling green just watching.

"Are his reactions legit?" Navarro asked.

"The puke is real," Sam said. "The rest, I'm not sure. He certainly knows about the list Munro kept. And I'd bet that it has been keeping him awake at night. He looks like he hasn't slept well in some time."

"That's what happens when you do crimes that get you blackmailed," Navarro said.

"He flinched when Kit asked if he was one of the people who stabbed Munro. If he wasn't, he knows who was."

Navarro sighed. "Damn. I hated that multiple-hands theory as much as Kit did, but it's looking viable."

"The thing is," Kit was saying, "just because Munro is dead doesn't mean you're off the hook. I'd expect a call or text or singing telegram from the guy who now holds the list giving you a new payday and a new drop location."

Daly closed his eyes, defeat in the movement.

"Yes," Sam whispered. "He's already been contacted."

"I think you're right, Doc," Navarro said.

"Was it a call, text, or singing telegram, Mr. Daly?" Kit asked cheerfully.

His skin pale and clammy, Daly just glared.

Connor slid Walter Grossman's mug shot across the table. "Know this guy?"

Daly's eyes burned as he stared at the mug shot but no words left his mouth.

Daly had met Grossman somewhere along the way. Now the man knew who had given Munro his secrets.

Connor's smile was feral. "If you're thinking of getting revenge on the guy who told Munro your secret, you're too late. He's as dead as Munro. Throat slit ear to ear." He produced one of the crime scene photos of Grossman's dead body. "Whoever has that list isn't afraid to spill blood. I'd recommend not missing any payments."

Daly still said nothing, but there was satisfaction in his eyes when he saw Grossman's body. He was glad the man was dead.

Kit turned to the attorney. "Tell your client that his cooperation could earn him a deal with the prosecutor. My partner and

I are not personally interested in whatever Mr. Daly did to get on that blackmail list, unless it was a homicide, of course. We just want to catch a killer who's put at least four bodies in the morgue since Saturday."

"Is my client under arrest?" the attorney demanded.

"No," Kit said.

"He's free to go," Connor added, and both attorney and client rose from their chairs. The attorney grasped Daly's elbow when the man swayed on his feet. "But if he's approached by a guy with a neckbeard, he should run as fast as he can as far as he can."

Daly's face went from pale to stark white and he sank back into his chair. "What?"

"Neckbeard," Kit said with the sunny smile. "He's killed several people. If he decides you're too big a liability—especially since you've been called in to see us—he might come after you." She wiggled her fingers in a wave, then mimicked a knife across her throat, ear to ear. "Ta-ta! Have a nice evening."

Daly didn't move and his attorney slowly sat beside him. "Simon?" the attorney asked quietly.

Daly shook his head. His mouth opened and closed but nothing came out.

The attorney looked at Kit and Connor. "I'd like to speak with my client privately, please."

Kit smiled and came to her feet. "Okay! Just tap on the glass when you're ready. We'll turn down the volume."

Sam was still shaking his head when the two detectives walked into the observation room. "Ta-ta?"

Kit chuckled. "It worked."

"You scare me sometimes," Sam said.

Kit's smile grew brighter. "Thank you."

"I'm not sure that was a compliment," Navarro said.

"It was, actually," Sam said.

Kit gave herself a shake. "Gosh. That cheerfulness really starts to chafe after a while." She turned down the volume of the speaker in the observation room, then stood at the glass. Her gaze was glued to Simon Daly and his attorney. "What do you think, Sam?" she asked, her voice back to normal.

"I think he recognized Grossman and he was glad the man was dead. Do I think Daly had a hand in killing Munro? Probably not. But you definitely got his attention with the mention of Neckbeard Guy. He knows him. Or at least he's seen him."

Daly and his attorney had turned so that their faces weren't visible to the observers on the other side of the glass, but Daly's body language now screamed fear and desperation.

"I also think he's going to give you something in just a few minutes," Sam said. "Maybe not what you're looking for. He's not going to cop to what he did to get blackmailed by Munro. He's not that desperate yet. But he'll probably tell you where he saw Neckbeard. He might even tell you about which group wanted Munro dead. He flinched when you said 'many killers.'"

"I saw that."

Sam wasn't surprised. "Figured you had. I don't know if he stabbed Munro, but I doubt it. If he did, he didn't know about the fingers and toes."

"I wonder what he did to get blackmailed," Connor murmured.

"What is his profession?" Sam asked.

"He owns an import/export business. Lots of shipping."

Sam grunted. "That's an open door right there."

They fell silent, watching Daly and his attorney have an animated conversation that they couldn't hear. Daly's fists were definitely clenched now. They were in full view, occasionally pounding on the table.

Finally, the attorney knocked on the glass.

"Showtime," Kit said.

She and Connor filed back into the room.

"My client is ready to talk, but he wants protection," the attorney said.

"From whom?" Connor asked.

The attorney gave him a cutting glare. "From this guy with a neckbeard, of course. That was your intent in mentioning him, wasn't it? To scare my client into a confession?"

Of course it was, Sam thought, but Kit was ignoring the attorney, her attention focused on Daly. "You saw him, Mr. Daly?"

Daly nodded. "He came to my office. Brought me a package. It was an Amazon package, so it could have been left on the stoop and he just picked it up. Never occurred to me that he wasn't the legit deliveryman. He stopped to chat. Asked how I was doing. Asked how my wife was. Said he'd heard she was under the weather."

"Didn't you find that suspicious?" Connor asked.

"No. Our normal deliveryman knows my wife. She works in the front office. Answers the phones and does the accounts. She wasn't there that day because she had a cold."

"Which day was this?" Kit asked.

"Monday."

Kit glanced at Connor. "Neckbeard didn't waste any time, did he?" She turned back to Daly. "How were you contacted about new payments?"

"Text on a burner phone. Same one as before."

That was not unexpected, but still good information to have. "When were you contacted by burner phone?"

Daly swallowed. "Sunday morning."

"What did Munro have on you?" Connor asked.

His attorney shook his head. "That's not on the table."

"How much were you paying him each month?" Kit asked.

Daly ground his teeth. "Thirty grand."

Kit whistled softly. "Wow. The other victim only paid five. What you did must have been really bad. What do you know about a group effort to kill Munro?"

"We want a deal," the attorney said.

Kit's smile was feral. "We'll call Joel Haley."

San Diego PD, San Diego, California
Wednesday, January 11, 8:00 p.m.

"Thank you for dinner, Betsy," Ashton said, handing her the plate he'd completely cleaned of a heaping stack of chicken and waffles. "This sure beats a burger and fries."

"Of course it does," Betsy said, clucking over them like the mother she was. "My Rita loves breakfast for dinner, and she had a bad day today so she got to pick what we ate. It wasn't any trouble to make enough for you all. Sam? Another helping?"

Sam patted his flat stomach. "Oh no, ma'am. I couldn't eat another bite. But thank you."

"Kevin? Connor?"

"No, ma'am," both men said.

"I'll have another helping," Navarro said, almost pouting.

Betsy laughed. "I was getting to you." She dished out another helping onto Navarro's waiting plate. "And don't worry. There's still enough for all of you to take some home for breakfast tomorrow."

Kit gave her own cleaned plate to her mother with a kiss on Betsy's cheek. "Thanks, Mom. You're the best."

Betsy leaned into Kit, her shoulders relaxing on a sigh. "You all are doing your best not to give that Drummond an opportunity to go free. I would cook for all of you for a million years."

Kit snorted. "Don't tell them that. They'll take you up on it. We should probably take a plate to Joel. He's been wheeling and dealing with that lawyer for two hours now. Not about Drummond, Mom," Kit added when her mother frowned. "Someone else. I promise."

Betsy smiled, relaxing once again. "Well then, I'll be going. Have a productive evening."

All the men stood, and Connor reached for the bags in which Betsy had brought the food. "Let me walk you to your car, Betsy. It's dark outside."

Kit knew that Connor would be able to get her to accept the envelope of cash the detectives had filled to defray the cost of the food. And if Betsy wouldn't take it for the food, Connor planned to tell her it was a donation to McKittrick House, to help care for Rita, Emma, and Tiffany, since the state's foster stipend was meager, at best. Either way, Betsy would be recompensed for her generosity.

When Connor and Betsy had departed through Homicide's double doors, Navarro dug into his third helping. "I hope you never leave Homicide, Kit. We'll miss your mother's cooking. Has Joel contacted you yet?"

"Not yet, and I've been watching my phone." She rolled her shoulders, trying to work a kink out of her back. She'd been thinking about the conversation she'd had the night before with Harlan. "If Munro's murder was a group effort, how did the participants communicate with each other? We need to get Daly's cell phone records."

"He could have used a burner," Marshall said.

"Maybe," Kit agreed. "But he wasn't clever enough to fly beneath Munro and Grossman's radar. They must have had an inkling that Daly had done something they could blackmail him for. I'm hoping that means Daly wasn't clever enough to use a burner."

"Ever the optimist," Navarro said, using his last bite of waffle to clean his plate before popping it into his mouth. "Don't lose that, Kit."

"Doing my best, sir. But back to the group effort. They had to have communicated with each other somehow—either cell texts, emails, or calls. And either on their own phones or burners. But I'm still surprised they'd get their hands dirty. Daly is a wealthy man. I'm assuming the others on that blackmail list are also wealthy." She turned to Sam. "Do you think Daly would have killed Munro with his own hands?"

"Hard to say. My gut says no, though."

"Mine too." Kit bit her lip, thinking. "I keep thinking about the Ferrari. If a group stabbed Munro, did they share the car, too?"

"Maybe Neckbeard got the Ferrari," Ashton said, "because he took the risks. He was the face—albeit bearded—of the group."

"Maybe," Kit murmured.

"But your gut says otherwise?" Sam asked.

She nodded. "But it doesn't mean a thing without proof." Her phone buzzed with an incoming text from Joel. "Which maybe we'll get soon. I'll text Connor to meet us in the observation room."

They found Joel standing on the observation side of the glass, watching Daly and his attorney. He turned when they filed in, his eyes lighting up at the covered plate in Kit's hands.

"For me?"

Kit gave him the dinner. "Compliments of my mother. So where are we?"

"Starving," Joel muttered. He took the plate to one of the chairs and began to eat. After a few mouthfuls, he blew out a breath. "I missed lunch. Thank you. We're going to put Daly and his wife into a safe house until we have Neckbeard in custody or until the threat is diminished."

"That could be a long time," Navarro said.

Kit frowned. "You said we were unstoppable."

Navarro winced. "And you are. I'm just saying these things sometimes take time. Sometimes years. We don't have the personnel to guard him for years, Joel."

Joel sighed. "Then I hope Kit's righter than you are. You can't ask Daly about what he did. You can ask him about the blackmail plot and the plot to assassinate Munro."

"It was a multiperson effort, then?" Connor asked warily.

"I don't know. That's all I got."

"You were in there for two hours," Kit said. "That's all you got?"

Joel scowled at her. "I was *trying* to get you more. Daly zipped his lips and wouldn't say another word, so I finally gave up and wrote the deal as is."

"So wait," Marshall said. "If we're not allowed to ask Daly about his crime, doesn't he know it'll come to light anyway once we get to Neckbeard and that list?"

Joel sighed again. "It won't matter. I've granted him transactional immunity."

Kit sucked in a surprised breath because that was a super big deal. "What?"

"What the fuck?" Ashton asked at the same time.

The others made similar noises of stunned surprise.

Normally Joel only gave immunity for future prosecution resulting from whatever evidence the suspect provided. Transactional was more like blanket immunity. He couldn't be tried for any crimes related to Munro's murder or the blackmail.

"I know, I know." Joel rubbed his temples. "I've worked with

Daly's attorney in the past. He's good and he's honest. He assured me that Daly's information was worth it, and that the crime he was being blackmailed for would only get him five to ten, max. The blackmail was mostly so that Daly's customers didn't find out what he'd done because he'd lose his business. I've made sure to include that if Daly was responsible for any assault, murder, any physical harm to any human, that the deal is void." He looked from Kit to Connor. "So make this good, Detectives."

"Now the two hours this took makes more sense," Sam said kindly. "Finish your food, Joel. And take two of these." He pulled a bottle of pain reliever from his pocket. "You'll feel better."

And there went Sam again, making people feel better.

"Thanks, bro." Joel took the pills, then returned his attention to Kit and Connor. "Do you have a list of questions for him?"

Kit handed him her phone. "These so far. Mostly how they communicated with each other, who did what, and where they did it. We still haven't found the trailer. Or that damn Ferrari."

Joel scanned the list. "These are all permissible questions. Good luck."

San Diego PD, San Diego, California
Wednesday, January 11, 8:35 p.m.

Kit and Connor took seats across the table from Simon Daly and his attorney. Daly appeared pale but resolute as he stared Kit in the eye defiantly.

"We have a deal in place," Kit said. "How long were you blackmailed by Munro?"

"Three years," Daly said. "Started out as ten grand a month, went up to twenty in year two and thirty in year three."

"Steep," Connor noted. "How did you afford it?"

Daly gave Connor a *duh* look. "I'm richer than your parents by a factor of ten. I could afford it."

Connor didn't look offended. "Yet you sold your Maserati."

Daly lifted a shoulder. "By the end, I was getting a little short."

"Short in money, temper, or both?" Kit asked.

"Both," Daly admitted. "But I did not kill him. I never laid a hand on him."

Kit watched his face carefully, grateful that behind the glass, Sam was doing the same. Never hurt to have another pair of eyes. "But you know who did."

"I know who talked about it," Daly said. "I never thought they'd do it."

"Who is they?" Connor asked.

Daly slid a sheet of paper across the table. "Names."

Okay, then, Kit thought. Maybe the transactional immunity had been worth it.

She leaned over to read the nine names along with Connor. To her disappointment, Christopher Drummond was not on the list.

But several of the names she did recognize, either from news coverage on them or their companies or from Munro's list of campaign donors. Six men and three women. All movers and shakers, as Ronald Tasker had claimed.

And, lo and behold, both Juanita Young and Estelle White were two of the three women. They'd been the women who, according to Connor's mother, had slept with Monroe. They'd also been the women who'd either slammed their door in the detectives' faces or denied everything when they'd been interviewed.

They're going to have to talk to us now.

"Do you know any of them?" she asked Connor, knowing he'd recognized at least the two women's names.

"I've personally met six of them. All are members of the country club." Connor looked up at Daly. "How did this transpire? How did this group come together?"

Daly exhaled quietly. "It was after Earl killed himself. We were shaken, all of us. But we didn't know about each other then. We suspected, of course, that Munro had several of us on his blackmail list, but we didn't know who. It's not something you shout out loud, like 'Bingo.'"

Kit thought of her father saying that they didn't tack a postcard on a bulletin board but somehow had communicated. "Then how did you find out about each other?"

"It was Hugh Smith." Daly pulled a handkerchief from his pocket and wiped his brow. "He was paying attention at Earl's funeral when the rest of us were not. Hugh heard Earl's wife tell his wife that there was no money left, that Earl had drained their accounts. She was all but penniless and was going to have to move in with her sister. Maybe even get a job."

Oh, the horror, Kit thought, then gave herself a mental smack. Earl O'Hanlon's widow was nearly Betsy's age. Starting over at that stage of life would be terrifying. Especially for a woman who'd never worked outside her home.

"So what did Hugh do?" she asked.

"He investigated because he had a hunch that Earl was also paying Munro. We never knew for sure, but it certainly looked like it. Hugh got his hands on Earl's bank statements and saw that he was withdrawing forty thousand dollars every month. Out of everyone on the list, that was the highest amount. That anyone was willing to admit, anyway."

"Do you know what any of the others did?" Connor asked.

Daly shook his head. "All we knew was that we were being blackmailed. It seemed Munro was hunting his victims at our club."

Munro had been a member of three country clubs. Kit wondered how many victims he had at the other clubs, then filed the thought away for later. "Did Hugh Smith bring you all together?"

"Yes. He started checking out our finances. He's the head of security for one of the military contractors at the naval base at Coronado. I guess he had the means to get our account statements and portfolios."

"When did you first meet?" Kit asked. "And where?"

"The first meeting was one week after Earl's funeral. We gathered in Hugh's home office. He said it was bug-free and soundproofed, so no one would hear us."

"Did you know why you were meeting?" Connor asked.

"No. We were all . . . stunned. At first, we were furious with Hugh. I'm still furious, if I'm being honest. But after he let us speak our piece, he said that together we could bring Munro down. Of course no one wanted to go to the police."

"Of course not," Kit said dryly. "So what did you decide to do?"

"To kill him," Daly said with no inflection whatsoever.

"But *you* didn't," Connor said. "If you didn't, who did?"

"I don't know. I attended only two meetings. After we decided that we'd kill him in that first meeting, we met again because Hugh had contacted a hit man."

Ah. This was closer to what Kit had expected. She didn't think that a group of rich people would get their own hands dirty. "Who?"

"I don't know. Hugh said he got a creepy feeling about the guy, so he didn't press him for a contract."

A creepy feeling about a hit man. Imagine that.

"Do you think Hugh talked to the hit man personally?"

Connor asked. "Because that sounds riskier than I can see Hugh Smith being."

One side of Daly's mouth lifted in a sardonic smile. "I thought the same thing, that Hugh had an underling talk to the hit man, but I don't know for sure. I left after that. I wanted no part in their scheme."

"They just let you . . . leave?" Kit asked, making sure her disbelief fully registered.

"We aren't hoodlums, Detectives," Daly snapped. "What were they going to do? Kill me?"

"Someone killed Munro," Kit said calmly, choosing not to snap back. "Someone in your circle seems to be fully capable of murder."

"Which is why we're here," Daly's attorney interjected. "My client fears for his life."

"As well he should," Kit said soberly. "Give me a moment, please."

Not moving from her chair, she constructed a group text to Navarro, Sam, Kevin Marshall, Alf Ashton, and Connor.

Could Hugh Smith be Neckbeard?

Maybe came Marshall's immediate answer. The man hadn't been home when they'd knocked, but they had his driver's license information. *He's 5-10, average build, average weight, just like Neckbeard.*

But Neckbeard had spoken to Daly. Had asked about his wife. Surely Daly would have recognized Smith's voice.

Kit showed her phone to Connor and Joel, then returned her attention to Daly. "So Mr. Smith might have asked an underling to find a hit man. That means at least one more person knows about the plot."

"I know," Daly said grimly. "Smith is a fool. We all wanted to make Munro suffer, but none of us are thugs."

The jury was out on that. "How did you communicate your meeting places?"

"Hugh called us on our normal cell phones, but he used a burner. The fucker. Can't trace anything back to him. He's got us over a barrel, but his hands stay clean."

If Hugh Smith was Neckbeard, he had them all over a barrel anyway, since he would have access to Munro's list. But if he wasn't . . .

That Marshall and Ashton hadn't been able to find Hugh Smith took on a darker meaning. Whoever had killed Munro, be it an individual or a group, could possibly be tracked through Smith, assuming Neckbeard knew about him. Hugh Smith was an unfortunate loose end.

She sent another text to the group. *Can we send someone to do a wellness check on Hugh Smith? Break down his door if you have to.*

Already on it came Navarro's reply. *Uniforms should be arriving at his house any minute.*

"Did Smith say how he found the hit man?" Connor asked.

Daly shook his head. "He didn't say, we didn't ask. I don't know what he does in his day-to-day security job, but I assumed he had less-than-savory connections."

Kit scanned the list of Daly's names again. "How well do you know the others on the list?"

"Some better than others. I'd call two friends, three acquaintances, and the others are just people I nod to at the club or on the green."

"Was Hugh Smith a friend?" Connor asked.

"Acquaintance. If that. Bert Ramsey and Henry Reese are friends. Or they were. After this, I don't think any of them will be speaking to me again."

"You might have saved their lives," Connor said seriously.

"They won't see it that way," Daly muttered.

"Could any of the men on this list have been the person who spoke to you on Monday?" Kit asked.

Daly appeared to be honestly taken aback. "What? Like, in disguise?"

"Yes, sir," Kit said, managing not to roll her eyes. "In disguise."

"I . . . I don't know. I don't think so, but . . ." Daly frowned, his fear reappearing. "I just don't know."

Kit believed him. Mostly. "Did the others meet again?"

"I don't know. I blocked Hugh's burner on my cell phone and never got any further communication from him or any of the others."

"When was your last payment to Munro?" Kit asked.

"My day was the twenty-fifth of the month. Last month I got the twenty-sixth because my day was Christmas."

"Where did you drop the thirty grand last month?" Connor asked.

"In a locker at the gym."

Again with the gym locker. Like Kit would even leave her phone in a locker, much less thirty thousand dollars. *Rich people, for heaven's sake.*

"Did you ever wait to see who came to pick it up?" she asked.

"No." The word was snapped and final.

Okay, then. "Was Christopher Drummond being blackmailed, too?"

Again, Daly appeared shocked. "Drummond? He has enough trouble without being blackmailed, too."

Kit smiled at him. "Not an answer, sir."

"I don't know," Daly said bluntly. "I wouldn't be surprised if he was. I do know that Munro and Drummond used to be . . . well, not friends. I don't think they had any actual friends. But

Drummond canceled his membership from our club quite some time ago. Long before Earl committed suicide and Hugh Smith took it on himself to get revenge against Munro."

"Did anyone talk about Munro's Ferrari?" Connor asked. "Like how they might have wanted it or thought that Munro didn't deserve it?"

"None of us thought he deserved it and none of us wanted it. It was a flashy car and that's how he intended it." Daly shrugged carelessly. "He was new money. Liked to flaunt it. In reality, he was a nobody who married way above his station."

Above his station? How very Downton Abbey.

"He was a city council member," Kit offered.

Another careless shrug. "Big fucking deal. Munro thought it was, though. No one I knew liked him. We tolerated him at best. Sometimes he could be useful if we wanted something special for our businesses from the city. But otherwise, we didn't have anything to do with him. No one invited him to any parties. He was a useful pariah."

"Did you want to kill him, sir?" Kit asked.

Daly just shook his head and said nothing.

"Were any of these other people on the list in favor of Hugh Smith's hit man?" Connor asked.

"I don't know. I only know that I wasn't."

"Did anyone speak up?" Connor pressed. "Or did they simply leave like you did?"

"A few people were in favor of a hit man during the first meeting, but that could have been emotion talking. My emotions do not control me, so I didn't feel the need to say anything."

Connor slid the list back to Daly. "Can you put a check mark by the names who were favorable?"

While Daly did so, Kit's phone buzzed with an incoming text from Navarro.

Hugh Smith is dead. Throat cut. Missing a finger. Safe open and empty. He's been dead at least a day or two.

Kit exhaled. She was not shocked. When she showed her phone to Connor, he didn't appear shocked, either.

So Hugh Smith was not Neckbeard. *Damn.*

"How did the man with the neckbeard sound, Mr. Daly?" Kit asked.

"I remember a deep, gravelly voice. He might have had a twang. But I really only remember the beard. It was a medium brown and came down his neck and went down under his collar."

Kit nodded once. "Thank you, sir. You're the only one we've met who's survived meeting him. Hugh Smith is dead."

Daly's face went frighteningly pale, his swallow audible. "Hugh?"

"Yes, sir," Kit said. "We may need more information as our investigation continues. Please don't try to escape your safe house."

Daly mopped his face, now drenched with sweat. "I won't."

CHAPTER FIFTEEN

It had already been a very long night.

Kit rubbed her temples as she stood in the observation room looking through the glass. They'd brought in everyone on Simon Daly's list, excepting Hugh Smith, of course.

Smith was in the morgue.

Their interview rooms were full, with a few of the people being held in conference rooms until space was cleared. At this point, every name on the list had lawyered up, their attorneys arriving wearing suits and looking awake.

Unlike us. Kit and Connor were tired and she knew that Kevin Marshall and Alf Ashton were as well. But they were going to power through, conducting at least the preliminary interviews while they still had each suspect separated to keep them from comparing stories with the others.

Kit and Connor had already interviewed Estelle White, who continued to deny that she'd been blackmailed by Munro, but there had been desperation in her gaze. Estelle had also denied being in Hugh Smith's home and had denied participating in a discussion about hiring a hit man.

The woman had lied about everything. Even the threat of an examination of her financial records hadn't been enough to break her. But Estelle was terrified. It was easy to see.

At this point, Estelle—and all the others who'd been interviewed so far—were counting on their comrades to keep the secret. If one went down, they all went down. If no one spoke, nothing could be proven, especially with Hugh Smith being dead.

The five surviving male suspects on Simon Daly's list didn't even have the courtesy of having different body types. Every one of the five was around five-ten, with an average weight and average build.

Any one of them could be Neckbeard.

Or none of them.

The man currently in the interview room was Peter Shoemaker. Shoemaker was forty-five, married to the same woman for twenty years, and a father of three. His oldest was a college freshman in San Francisco and his twin daughters were eight years old.

He had been a high school English teacher in an exclusive private academy for years but had recently transitioned into administration. He'd been an assistant principal for the past three years. Shoemaker looked nervous.

His attorney was an older man who appeared bored with the whole proceeding.

"You okay?" Sam asked quietly from behind her.

"Tired, that's all." She sent him a smile over her shoulder. "I've been worse." Then she caught the aroma of coffee. "For me?"

He handed her a travel mug that looked familiar. "You and everyone else. I called your mom."

Kit's heart melted. "You did?"

"She made me promise to call her if you needed anything, so I did. I went to McKittrick House to pick it all up. There's sandwiches, cookies, and an entire urn of coffee. Should keep you going most of the night."

"Thank you, Sam. You're too good to us."

He just smiled and tapped the end of her nose. "Now get in there and make him talk."

"If Estelle is any indication of how this will go, it's not looking good."

Marshall joined them at the glass. "Juanita Young confirmed the blackmail."

Kit's brows went up. "She did?"

"She did. Juanita's lawyer heard about Daly's deal and wants the same. Juanita says her 'alleged' crime would probably be a misdemeanor and the statute of limitations has run out."

"But she continued to pay Munro," Sam said. "Why?"

Marshall made a face. "Juanita said it was because Munro threatened to tell her boss and make sure that she never got hired again. Her job requires she be bonded and she could lose her license if she's caught. She has no idea how Munro found out she'd ever been accused by a client of wrongdoing, unless he'd asked her ex-husband, who would have been glad to spread rumors. She's not copping to the crime or any knowledge of the hit man plot, only to paying the blackmail to protect her job. Her day was the twelfth of every month and she paid five Gs. She said most of her ex-husband's alimony and child support payments went to Munro. She didn't admit to knowing about the dead-man's-switch list, but she knew. Ashton and I both saw her flinch. She knew about the hit man too, even though she vociferously denied it."

Kit tucked that away in her mind for later. "We can tell Shoe-maker that she told us all about the hit man. We can even say that we know the hit man's name. The only one who knows for sure how far Hugh Smith took his inquiry was Hugh Smith. And he's not around to call me a liar."

Connor entered the observation room, a cup of coffee in one hand. "You ready to roll?"

"Yep. You lead this time." Kit arched her back. Her muscles were too damn tight. Next time Akiko was free, Kit was asking her for a massage. Her sister had trained to be a massage therapist, using that income to save for her boat. Now she was a full-time charter boat captain, but she could still bring Kit's recalcitrant muscles to heel. "I'm ready as I'll ever be. I hope I don't have to be cheerful. I don't think I've got that much energy left."

Connor finished his coffee and followed her into the in-terview room.

"Mr. Shoemaker, I'm Detective McKittrick and this is my partner, Detective Robinson," Kit said as she and Connor sat across from him. "We have some questions for you."

"I gathered that," Shoemaker said. His body language was nervous. He was sweating profusely, despite only wearing a short-sleeved T-shirt. His knee bounced and his fingers drummed on the tabletop. Kit wanted to tell him to stop because it was an-noying, but a nervous suspect often blurted out things he'd later wish he hadn't.

"We're hoping you can help us with an ongoing investi-gation," Connor said, taking the lead as they'd agreed.

"How?" Shoemaker sounded wary.

"Ask me your questions," his attorney said. "Not him."

Connor just smiled at the attorney and returned his attention to Shoemaker. "You were being blackmailed by Brooks Munro."

Shoemaker's mouth fell open, the color draining from his face. "What?" he whispered.

"Say nothing, Pete," his lawyer said firmly. "My client admits to no such thing. Why are we here?"

"Because you, Peter," Connor said, still ignoring the attorney, "were listed as being part of a plot to hire a hit man to murder Brooks Munro since you, and others, were being blackmailed. We're obtaining warrants for your home, business, phones, and financial records as we speak. Murder for hire is a very serious charge. Now, the way this works is that whoever gives us information first gets the best deal. You're already third in line behind your murder-for-hire compatriots. Tick tock."

"This is ridiculous," the lawyer snapped. "Is my client being arrested?"

"Not at the moment," Connor said. "But we suggest you stay and listen to what we have to say," he added when the lawyer stood up and gripped Shoemaker's shoulder. "It could save your life, Peter."

"What does that mean?" the lawyer asked angrily.

"It means," Kit said, "that whoever killed Brooks Munro also killed at least one of the people involved in the murder-for-hire plot. Hugh Smith is this killer's fifth victim. That we know of."

The lawyer sat back down.

Shoemaker licked his lips nervously. "Hugh's dead?"

"Throat slit," Kit said. "Ear to ear. Lost a finger, too. His killer wanted the combination to Smith's safe, and I don't think Smith was initially cooperative."

Shoemaker covered his mouth. "Oh God."

Please don't throw up. "Trash can's behind you," Kit said in a bored voice.

Connor leaned forward, elbows on the table. "So . . . your compatriot told us about the murder-for-hire plot in exchange for protection. Not sure if that deal's still available, but we can ask the prosecutor nicely."

Shoemaker closed his eyes. "Oh no," he whispered.

"Pete?" his lawyer warned. "We discussed this. They can't prove anything. If they could, they'd have arrested you already."

"That's what your compatriot said, Pete," Connor said. "Until we told him that Hugh Smith was dead. Then he changed his tune. Look, unless what you did to get blackmailed was a homicide, we aren't interested in the details. We want whoever killed Brooks Munro and four other people. We don't want you to be number six."

Shoemaker swallowed hard, then whispered something in his lawyer's ear.

The lawyer shook his head. "Goddammit, Pete." He blew out a breath. "Okay, what are you offering?"

"Nothing," Connor said, "until we hear what it is he has to say. We already have some information." He turned to Pete, who suddenly appeared terrified. "If you can't provide anything new, no deal."

"How will we know if Pete has anything new to offer?" the lawyer demanded. "What do you already know?"

"Nope," Kit said coldly. "You first, Mr. Shoemaker."

Shoemaker's hand fell away from his mouth, dropping limply to the table. "We didn't do it."

"Didn't do what, Peter?" Connor asked.

"Didn't hire a hit man. We talked about it. Maybe fantasized about it a little, but we never followed through."

Connor seemed relaxed, as if discussing the weather, but Kit knew he was alert and on edge. They both were. "Why not?" he asked.

Shoemaker's laugh was mirthless. "Because we're not killers. My God, this is a nightmare."

"Start at the beginning," Connor said sympathetically. "When did Munro begin to blackmail you?"

"Two years ago. I . . . cheated on my wife. That's all I did."

Kit wasn't so sure about that, but she remained silent.

"And Munro found out?" Connor prodded.

"Yeah. I don't know how, but he did. Said he'd tell my wife if I didn't pay him. It was two thousand dollars a month. That was most of my paycheck. I'm an assistant principal, for God's sake."

"Your wife has the money?" Connor asked. "I seem to remember seeing her name in one of the country club's newsletters."

Once again, Kit was grateful that Connor was rich.

"Yes," Shoemaker said bitterly. "She's always had the money and has never loosened the purse strings. Her parents are obscenely wealthy and my wife has a trust fund. We have a prenup and if she found out I'd cheated, I'd lose everything. I wasn't willing to lose everything, so I paid Munro what he asked for."

"For two years," Connor said.

Shoemaker nodded. "Yes."

Kit made an impatient gesture. "And then?"

"I paid him and paid him and paid him. I thought there might be others getting blackmailed, but I didn't know for sure. I wouldn't have told them about my situation even if I had known. I didn't want anyone to know. And then Earl O'Hanlon killed himself. I suspected that he'd been bankrupted by Munro, but again, I didn't know for sure. Not until I got a call from Hugh Smith. He used a burner phone but called us on our cell phones.

He couldn't be touched, but he'd left a trail straight to us. He said to come to his house if we didn't want our secrets shared."

"So you went?" Connor asked.

"Of course I did," Shoemaker snapped. "I know what Smith did for a living. I know he was some high-ranking security guy. I figured he was going to start blackmailing me, too. But that's not what happened."

"What *did* happen, Mr. Shoemaker?" Kit demanded, not having to fake her annoyance. This guy needed to get on with it. She and Connor still had several interviews to do.

"There were others there."

Kit drummed her fingers on the table. "How many others?"

Shoemaker turned to her. "Look, I'm trying here, okay? Stop the—" He mimicked her drumming fingers. "You're making this worse."

Kit drummed her fingers once more before folding her hands on the table. She'd rattled him. Excellent. "How many others, Mr. Shoemaker?" she asked.

"Nine, I think." Shoemaker closed his eyes, his mouth moving silently. Then he nodded and opened his eyes. "Nine. Including Hugh Smith. I can give you their names."

Connor slid a legal pad and pen across the table. "Write."

Shoemaker did, stopping to take deep breaths when his hands shook so hard that the pen ripped the paper. Finally, he'd listed the names.

They were the same names that Daly had provided.

"So what happened when you were called to Hugh Smith's home?" Connor asked.

"He said that we'd all been victims of Munro's blackmail. He said he didn't know what we'd done and wasn't interested in finding out, only that we work together to make Munro stop. 'By any means necessary.'" He used air quotes. "Those were his exact words. We discussed how to do that without giving our-selves up to the police. My issue wasn't going to bring jail time, but I got the impression that the others would be in legal trouble. Mine was only a case of my wife finding out and cutting me off financially."

Poor baby, Kit thought. Having to bear the consequences of his actions. *So sad.*

Shoemaker ran his fingers through his hair. "It was insane. We were sitting around talking about killing a man. About hiring a *hit man*, for God's sake."

"Who brought up the hit man?" Connor asked.

"Hugh. He said he knew a guy who knew a guy. I just wanted to go home."

"Why didn't you?" Kit asked.

Shoemaker's eyes flashed. "Because first Munro held my life in his hands, and then Hugh did. I didn't want him to either blackmail me or tell my wife."

Ah. A possible discrepancy. He'd said that Hugh didn't know what they'd done. "Do you think he knew why everyone there was being blackmailed?"

Shoemaker looked startled. "He said he didn't. It's possible he knew why, although I don't know how he could have. But him just telling my wife I was being blackmailed would be cata-strophic, even if he didn't know why."

"Okay," Kit said. "Who was on board with the hit man?"

Shoemaker hesitated. "I don't want to say."

Kit shrugged. "Then we're done."

"Detective," the lawyer snapped. "He's doing his best."

Kit leaned forward, so happy to be the bad cop. "He *isn't* doing his best. He's protecting his friends."

"They're not my friends," Shoemaker said bitterly. "Not a single one of them is my friend. They only cared about themselves and they never spoke to me at the club. My wife was part of the social circle, but I wasn't. I don't play golf. I don't dance. I am an assistant principal. I was beneath them." He paused to suck in a deep breath. "Sorry. It's just that the club put me on Munro's radar. I didn't even want to go after he started blackmailing me, but my wife insisted. She's part of that world. I'm not. That's why I had an affair. I was just looking for affection that didn't come with a price tag."

"Who was on board with the hit man, Mr. Shoemaker?" Connor asked, repeating Kit's question.

Shoemaker closed his eyes. "Fucking hell." He took another deep breath. "The women. Especially Juanita. Hugh was gung ho, of course. One of the other men, too. Bert."

Bert Ramsey, Kit thought. One of Daly's friends. "What happened then?"

"We took a vote. Everyone voted for the hit man. I left and didn't even get to my car before I was throwing up. It was a nightmare. It *is* a nightmare."

Kit bet Shoemaker wished he hadn't cheated on his wife. She wondered if the "affection without a price tag" was worth the price he was paying now.

"And then?" Connor asked.

"I went home. Went to work. Tried to forget it had ever happened. Tried to believe it was just a bad dream. That lasted a week, and then Hugh called us back to his house. He said we needed to organize. When we got there, he said that the hit man he'd considered hiring was 'hinky.' That was the word he used. Hinky and creepy. He got cold feet and didn't go through with it. Said he knew that sometimes undercover cops posed as hit men and he didn't want to go to jail for that, too."

"Smart," Kit observed. "And then?"

"We talked about other ways to get back at Munro, to make

him stop. We talked about finding a way to expose his dirty business dealings in the city council. We all knew he was dirty."

"Did you come up with an idea?" Kit asked.

"Not a good one. Hugh mentioned the Agatha Christie novel *Murder on the Orient Express*. That we could all stab Munro and none of us would know who'd truly killed him. I couldn't take any more. I left. I figured murder was a lot worse than being financially cut off. I decided to take my chances that Hugh wouldn't tell my wife because then his crimes would be exposed, too. I didn't hear anything more from any of them. The next thing I knew, I was reading online that Munro was dead."

"What did you think happened to him?" Connor asked.

"Honestly? I figured Hugh had found a hit man. Or that he and the others had done their own *Orient Express*. All I know is that I wasn't involved in Munro's death."

"Did you know about the dead man's switch?" Kit asked. "The list he threatened to make public were he to die unexpectedly?"

"I didn't until Hugh mentioned it. I always paid Munro. Like clockwork. I never missed and was never late, so I guess he didn't think he had to threaten me."

"Have you received instructions for this month's payment?" Kit asked. "In the last few days, I mean."

Shoemaker flinched. "Yes. I got a text to my phone on Sunday. My day is the seventeenth. I'm to take the money to a locker in the bus station."

"So you knew that request couldn't have come from Brooks Munro," Kit said. "Since he was dead by then."

"No, I guess not. So what happens next?"

"We'll keep you, pending corroboration of your story."

Shoemaker frowned. "What does that mean?"

"It means," Kit said, "that we'll be searching your home, office, phone, and financial records just like we said we would when we started this interview. It's being recorded, so you can watch it for yourself if you want verification."

Shoemaker started to rise from his chair, but a menacing look from Connor had him sitting back down. "You're going to search my house?"

"Yes," Kit said. "You are involved in a murder-for-hire plot, Mr. Shoemaker. You should have come forward immediately after it happened. Like it or not, you're part of a conspiracy to commit murder."

"But I didn't *do* anything!"

"That remains to be seen," Kit said. "You didn't report it, though, and that makes you look really bad, sir."

"But . . . but now my wife is going to know."

Kit shrugged. "That's not our problem."

Shoemaker's eyes narrowed, fury clear on his face. "You—"

"Peter!" his lawyer interrupted. "That's enough. We'll get a deal. You've clearly given them a lot of information they didn't have before. We will get a deal."

Shoemaker slumped into his chair. "This is a nightmare."

Kit glanced at Connor and saw his nod. He was also done.

She pushed to her feet. "Yeah, well, this killer's five victims would agree with you that this is a nightmare. *If* they were still alive to do so. Sit tight. We'll be back."

They left Peter Shoemaker with his head in his hands.

San Diego PD, San Diego, California
Thursday, January 12, 12:45 a.m.

"Well?" Navarro asked. "What did you think?"

"Yeah, Sam," Kit said, closing the observation room door. "What's your opinion?"

Sam continued watching Peter Shoemaker, who'd begun to shiver despite the warmth of the interview room. The man pulled his head from his hands and was nervously pulling on his blazer. Mopping his sweaty brow, Shoemaker stuffed a handkerchief into his coat pocket, tugged his sleeves into place, then dropped his head back into his hands.

"I'm not sure," Sam admitted. "He definitely hates his wife."

Navarro snorted. "I got that."

Sam sighed. "Paying most of your salary to a blackmailer seems like a lot of trouble to hide an affair from your wife, but I suppose the stakes are high."

"The Shoemakers have a big, expensive house in La Jolla," Kit said, coming to stand next to Sam. "They're loaded with a capital 'L.'"

"They're old money," Connor said. "At least the wife is. Shoemaker himself grew up in Chula Vista. I believed him, I think. And I'm really glad he managed not to puke."

That bothered Sam. "Was he actually going to, though? He didn't look like other people I've seen vomiting because of stress. They get a glassy, panicked look in their eyes, but Shoemaker didn't. Maybe he only *thought* he should be sickened by Hugh Smith having a finger chopped off."

"You could be right," Kit said. "I think the thing that bothers me is how all the people we've talked to assure us that their crimes either wouldn't require jail time or, if they would, it would only be a few years. Or the statute of limitations has run out. We just have their word on that since only Munro, Grossman, and the killer—or killers—have seen the list."

Sam nodded. "That bothers me, too. It's like, *Um yeah, I was blackmailed but it wasn't for anything that bad. Trust me. But I still paid the money every month.* I wonder what Peter Shoemaker's wife would have to say about his affair. I wonder if she knows."

Kit watched Shoemaker through the glass. "We'll ask her when we search his house."

Sam turned to her, surprised. "You weren't bluffing about that?"

Kit gave him a wink. "I was, but Shoemaker just confirmed Daly's murder-for-hire tale. We have enough to search his home and the homes of everyone on that list."

"That was nicely done," Navarro said. "I almost believed you myself. How many more people do you need to interview?"

Kit glanced at her phone screen. "We brought in eight, and Connor and I just interviewed two of them—Estelle White and Peter Shoemaker. Marshall and Ashton interviewed Juanita Young and they're in with Henry Reese now. We each have two more. Bert Ramsey is next on our list."

"Bert's the president of an insurance company," Connor said. "Not *old*, old money, but his family's owned businesses in the city for decades. He was also one of Simon Daly's friends. I guess we'll see if their friendship will stand up to Daly's narcing on him. You want me to be good cop, Kit?"

"Please. I still have hives from being so sweet with Daly."

Sam chuckled. "You do not." But he wanted to check every inch of her skin to make sure. Kit in cop mode was hotter than hell.

"Maybe not hives," she allowed. "But it's like a coat that's two sizes too small. Come on, let's move to the next interview room. Bert Ramsey awaits."

Sam followed them, taking his place by the glass, next to Navarro, who'd been moving back and forth between the interviews Kit and Connor were conducting and those by Marshall and Ashton. Once they'd completed all the interviews, they'd gather to debrief.

"Bert Ramsey is the same size as Shoemaker," Sam said,

studying the man at the interview table. Who was the same size as Neckbeard.

Who was the same size as all the men in the group. They were all physically average in nearly every way.

Bert Ramsey was in his early fifties and appeared to be in good shape. His hair was cut severely, shaved on the sides and short on top, reminiscent of the Marine he'd once been.

Sam wondered where the man had served, in what capacity, and what he'd seen. He wondered if he'd come home hardened to life, or if he'd always been calm, cool, and collected in the face of what most people would consider a highly stressful situation.

Bert Ramsey was regarding the glass mirror as if he could see who watched him and was completely unimpressed.

"He's very chill," Sam said.

"Faking it," Navarro said.

Sam wasn't so sure. This was what he'd expected when they'd begun to interview the rich and somewhat powerful. This cool indifference. This lack of concern that the law could touch him.

Bert Ramsey radiated those vibes.

So had Brooks Munro. Sam could still see the man's smirk as he'd propositioned Sam to declare Ronald Tasker unfit for trial.

"I guess we'll find out," Sam murmured as Kit and Connor took their seats.

"Hello, Mr. Ramsey," Kit said. "I'm sorry to have kept you waiting."

Sam leaned closer to Navarro. "I thought she was going to be the bad cop."

A small smile played over Navarro's lips. "Just wait."

"This is my partner, Detective Robinson," Kit said. "Do you know why we brought you in tonight?"

Ramsey just stared at her.

His attorney, a well-dressed woman about half Ramsey's age, frowned. "I've advised my client to say nothing."

Kit smiled indulgently. "So did all the other attorneys. But their clients were convinced to say many things." She turned to Ramsey. "You're the CEO of a privately held insurance company. You specialize in healthcare."

"Get on with it, Detective," the attorney said in a frigid voice.

Kit ignored her, her attention still on Ramsey. "You hold people's lives in your hands. That must make you feel powerful. Do you give them money for treatment or not? Do you allow them to live or let them die?"

"It's not that simple," Ramsey said, but there was a light in his eyes. One that said that yes, he did hold people's lives in his hands and that, yes, that made him feel powerful.

"Sir," the attorney murmured. "Please."

Ramsey looked at the woman as if she too were a bug. "I know what I can and cannot say, Miss Fremont."

The attorney's frown deepened, but she didn't say another word.

"Why do they even bring attorneys?" Sam asked. "They never listen to them."

Navarro chuckled. "Neither did you, when you were sitting where they are."

Sam scowled. "Not a good memory, Lieutenant."

Navarro abruptly sobered. "I'm sorry, Dr. Reeves. That was uncalled for."

Mollified, Sam grunted. It had been uncalled for.

It had also been true. When Sam had been a suspect for murder, he'd naively trusted that the system wouldn't let him down because he was innocent.

It hadn't, but that was because he'd been investigated by Kit McKittrick. She'd kept an open mind, determined to find the real killer and not throw Sam under the bus for her convenience. Kit's partner at the time had been prepared—and happy—to arrest him, though.

Sam had forgiven Baz, mostly because the man had a passion for getting justice. Now they were friends, but Sam no longer believed that the justice system was fair to everyone.

Bert Ramsey was flicking invisible lint from his five-thousand-dollar suit. He had not looked at Kit since basically dismissing his attorney.

Kit and Connor remained silent, waiting for something. Sam wasn't sure what.

Until Ramsey finally glanced at Kit before setting his gaze on Connor. "Am I being arrested, Detective?"

"Probably," Connor said with a genuine smile. "Sorry, Bert. I know this is inconvenient. But that's kind of what happens when you decide to participate in a murder-for-hire scheme."

Ramsey's only reaction was a slight twitch of his eye. There and gone before Sam could blink. He wondered if Kit and Connor had seen it.

He shouldn't have wondered.

Kit set her elbow on the table, resting her chin on her fist. "We have corroborating statements placing you in the middle of negotiations for murder for hire, Mr. Ramsey. So, yes, we will be arresting you. Charges will follow after we've finished searching your home."

One side of Ramsey's mouth quirked up in a smirk similar to Munro's. "I imagine you have a search warrant."

"Of course," Kit said. "So, why did you go to Hugh Smith's home, Mr. Ramsey?"

Ramsey stiffened. "I was invited. I had no idea why. When I found out, I left."

"Sir," his attorney whispered.

Ramsey didn't even look at the woman. "His security cameras will show that I was there, Miss Fremont."

"They did," Kit said. "We got the footage while processing the scene of his murder."

Ramsey stilled. For a moment he didn't even breathe. Then the smirk returned, but it seemed more fragile now. "Who would do such a thing, Detective?"

Navarro made a displeased sound. "He thinks he's clever."

Sam agreed. Luckily Kit was far cleverer.

"Maybe *you* did," Kit said. "Hugh Smith knew you were being blackmailed."

Ramsey's expression didn't change. "He told you this?"

Kit shook her head. "No, sir. The first time we encountered Hugh Smith in person, he was too dead to speak to us. Throat was slit ear to ear. Nasty business." She settled in her chair, getting comfortable. "Thing is, he's the fifth victim killed exactly this way. Do *you* own a knife, Mr. Ramsey?"

The attorney shoved her legal pad into her bag. "We're finished here."

"No, we're not," Kit said, her focus still on Ramsey. "Your client has been accused of conspiring to murder Brooks Munro. Two separate individuals have specifically mentioned Mr. Ramsey in connection with encouraging the contracting of a hit man."

"I did no such thing," Ramsey said smoothly. "Whoever said so is lying."

"We'll check your financial records, sir," Kit said. "Will we find regular withdrawals in cash around the same time every month?"

Ramsey looked almost amused. "No, you won't. Because blackmail never happened. Murder for hire never happened."

Kit sighed. "You have a separate account for such transactions, then. One we're not going to find easily. I hate when this happens. But we will find it, Mr. Ramsey. I promise you this. If I have to upend your life and put it on display for every Tom, Dick, and Harry in San Diego to see, I will find it."

Ramsey's eyes had narrowed, ever so slightly.

"Bingo," Navarro murmured.

"Check the Caymans," Sam said dryly. "Maybe he banks at the same place that Veronica and Grossman did."

On Kit's side of the glass, Ramsey said nothing, maybe finally listening to his attorney.

"Why was Munro blackmailing you?"

No answer.

Kit slid a photo of Walter Grossman across the table and Ramsey's nostrils flared.

"Okay," Kit said. "You know him. He was Munro's PI. He managed to dig up a lot of dirt on a lot of people. Unfortunately, he too was a loose end." She then showed Ramsey the photo of Grossman with his throat cut wide open. "This is what he looks like now."

Not a single flicker of emotion whatsoever crossed the man's face.

"Wow," Sam murmured. "He's a sociopath for sure, but that doesn't mean he's a killer. He could just be a CEO with an ironclad stomach."

"He is very good," Navarro murmured back. "That's a hard photo to see."

Sam shrugged. "He was a Marine. Maybe he's seen his share of dead bodies."

"So have I," Navarro said. "But I still had a reaction to Grossman and Hugh Smith and even Munro. Bastard that Munro was, I couldn't look at his mutilated body and not feel some degree of . . . disturbed."

"Where did you meet this man?" Kit asked, tapping the

photo of Grossman. When Ramsey said nothing, she remained calm. "Mr. Ramsey, there were ten people in Hugh Smith's living room that night. Now there are nine, because Smith is dead. Smith was missing a finger, by the way. I don't think he was forthcoming with the combination of his safe until his killer chopped it off. That had to have hurt. A lot. Munro was missing all his fingers and all his toes in addition to twenty-five stab wounds and the mutilation of his genitalia. Whoever killed them isn't fooling around. They've also killed some innocent people who have been unfortunate enough to get in their way. Now, I imagine this doesn't alarm you because you have bodyguards. Our police officers met them when they brought you in for questioning. Apparently, they're former Marines, just like you."

Ramsey narrowed his eyes to mere slits. "Not a *former* Marine, Detective. I'll be a Marine long after you've been demoted back to walking a beat."

Kit smiled. "Some days, walking a beat would be a blessing. I hate sitting at a desk. My point was, Mr. Ramsey, that of the ten people in that room, nine are left. Three have already named you as co-conspirator with Hugh Smith. With your military background—and bodyguards—I'd imagine you'd have resources at your disposal. Resources who might know hit men. That you and Hugh Smith were conspiring together isn't a huge stretch. You certainly had the motivation, as you were also being blackmailed."

"I was *not* being blackmailed. I don't know where you're getting your information, Detective, but I've done nothing that would put me in a position to be blackmailed."

"Munro's dead-man's-switch list would beg to differ."

Another twitch of Ramsey's eye, again so fast that Sam nearly missed it.

Kit's smile grew. "You know about the list. Three of your nine compatriots said that Hugh Smith mentioned it at your first meeting. I imagine paying blackmail was very hard for you at first. You're a powerful man. Who was Brooks Munro to demand anything of you? He was some upstart nouveau riche asshole who drove a fancy car and lived off his wife."

"He's breathing harder," Sam murmured.

"He is," Navarro confirmed. "She's getting to him."

"Wilhelmina isn't even his real wife," Kit went on. "He was married to his admin, Veronica. I'm sure you met her. You were on Munro's calendar last year. Nobody got an appointment with Munro unless they went through Veronica. They've been married for thirty-some years. Their whole San Diego existence was one big scam." Kit sighed. "And you fell for it. Too bad. If you'd dug a little, you could have been blackmailing him instead of the other way around."

Ramsey's breathing had grown harder and faster, but his expression had gone neutral.

"You do understand how deals work, right, Mr. Ramsey?" Connor said helpfully. "The first to the trough get the best consideration. There are three people ahead of you and our partners in this investigation are speaking to another one of the surviving nine. You could be fourth or fifth if you don't jump on the bandwagon soon."

"I don't need to make a deal," Ramsey said, clearly seething. "I have done nothing wrong."

"Well, I guess that's for a judge and jury to decide," Kit said. "I can see it now, splashed on every newspaper in the country." She waved her hand as if seeing the headlines. "'CEO convicted of murder for hire. Sentenced to twenty years.' You'll be an old man when you get out, sir. And Munro's killer will still be out there, walking free. Spending *your* money. Your three compatriots are getting deals that grant immunity for whatever they did to get blackmailed. You can, too." She pulled another piece of paper from her folder. "This is a list of the people who plotted Munro's death. The first one we received, actually. But it's identical to the others."

It was a slight stretch. There were no "others," plural. Only Daly and Shoemaker had given them lists. But it was just a small fib.

Kit pushed the list Simon Daly had given them across the table. "Take a look, Mr. Ramsey. Recognize the one name *not* on this list?"

Ramsey didn't look at the page immediately, but after about thirty seconds, his gaze dropped to read it, as if he couldn't help himself.

His mouth immediately tightened, a muscle in his cheek clenching as he ground his teeth.

Kit's smile was genuine. "I see you recognize who is not on the list. Your friend gave you up, Mr. Ramsey. Simon Daly got an *excellent* deal from the prosecutor. As my partner said, you know how this works. The quality of your deal is dependent on what you can offer us that we don't already know. Tick tock, Mr. Ramsey."

Ramsey's fist clenched on the tabletop.

"Sir," his attorney warned, putting a hand on his shoulder. "Not a word."

Ramsey shook her hand off. "What was my *friend's* excellent deal?"

"Transactional immunity," Kit said with a grimace. "As a cop, I hate to see that happen. But sometimes you gotta break eggs to make an omelet, am I right, Detective Robinson?"

"You're right, Detective McKittrick."

"Daly won't have to serve time for his crime?" Ramsey asked. "For whatever got him blackmailed?"

Kit didn't blink. "That's what 'transactional immunity' means, *sir*. Now, the question is, are you going to serve time for your crime *and* the murder for hire? Because that's a lot more years, *sir*."

Ramsey's composure broke at last. "You're a disrespectful bitch," he snarled.

Kit shrugged. "I've been called so much worse. *Sir*. This is what's going to happen next, because I don't know about my partner, but I'm losing patience with you, and we still have several more interviews to do. Hopefully with people who are more cooperative than you are. We don't really need you. If you continue to claim your innocence, we'll arrest you, search your *everything* and then you'll probably get out on bail, because you're richer than I'll ever be on a cop's salary."

Ramsey's smirk was back.

"But I really hope you have good bodyguards," Kit went on. "Because you're a loose end. Whoever killed Munro—assuming you didn't have a hand in stabbing him twenty-five times and cutting off his fingers and toes—seems hell-bent on permanently silencing anyone who could identify him. Eventually, *should you survive*, you will go to prison for a long time. No bodyguards there, unless you make some friends real quick. And eventually, *should you survive*, we will find that dead-man's-switch list and know what you did. I will personally make sure you're prosecuted to the fullest for that as well. Those are the facts, sir. You can still save yourself."

Ramsey's expression went cold as he hesitated. "Who else told you I was involved?"

Kit shook her head. "Can't tell you that, *sir*. See, I'm not an expert boardroom negotiator like you are, *sir*. I'm just a cop, making one one-hundredth of what you make. You talk or you don't. You get a deal or you don't. It's really up to you."

Ramsey's eye twitched again, his expression growing dark

and thunderous. "I did *not* participate in the murder-for-hire plot."

Kit's expression remained neutral, but Sam could see that her body had subtly tensed. Only those who knew her would even recognize it for what it was—satisfaction. She knew she had him now.

"Who did?"

"Sir," Ramsey's attorney said loudly.

Ramsey swatted at her, not taking his eyes from Kit. If looks could kill, Kit would be dead where she sat.

Sam hoped Ramsey never got free.

"Hugh Smith. It was all Hugh Smith. Juanita Young said she knew someone if Smith's contact didn't pan out. I tried to get him to stop."

"How?" Kit pressed. "How did you try to get him to stop?"

"The guy Smith was talking to was an undercover cop. Anyone with eyes could have seen it."

"So you witnessed Hugh Smith talking to the hit man?" Kit asked carefully.

"Smith wore a wire to the meeting. I was listening. I told Smith to leave, that something was off. I was right. The man was an undercover cop. I checked him out later. Juanita gave Hugh her guy's name and he was legit. I checked them both out. If anyone killed Munro, it was Juanita's guy. She probably even helped him. I think they were sleeping together."

"Juanita and Hugh Smith?" Connor asked.

"No." Ramsey shot him an impatient, angry look. "Juanita and her hit man. If you want names, I'll give you names. After I have a deal."

Kit nodded once. "I'll call Joel Haley, the prosecutor. You might have to wait. Mr. Haley is having a busy night."

CHAPTER SIXTEEN

Kit sent a mental thank-you to her mother for the large urn of coffee and food she'd sent to sustain them. This had been one long night. She needed to go home, sleep, and shower, but she had the feeling that none of those things were going to happen for a while.

She refilled her mug and joined the others at the conference table, taking a seat between Connor and Sam. The whiteboard was looking pretty full. She was going to have to reorganize it after this meeting.

Navarro tapped the table to get everyone's attention. Marshall and Ashton had interviewed all their suspects, and Joel had joined the team after negotiating deals all night long. And then there was the captain, who'd come in especially for the debrief.

So . . . no pressure at all.

"We've finished interviewing all nine of the people involved in the plot to hire a hit man to kill Brooks Munro," Navarro said.

"We have two names of hit men," Joel added. "Bert Ramsey gave us the real hit man associated with Juanita Young and the fake hit man who Ramsey had correctly identified as an undercover cop. Real hit man is Jason Goodman and the UC cop is Kirk Torrence. You'll need to contact Torrence's handler, because his cover has been compromised."

"Shit," the captain muttered. "I know Torrence. He's been very useful to us in his undercover capacity. But he's been UC for a while, so it was nearly time to bring him back, anyway. I'll take care of that. How did Bert Ramsey identify him?"

"He wouldn't say," Joel said. "He's got a horde of bodyguards and some connections in the security world. We might be able to squeeze him further later, but that wasn't my priority tonight."

"I understand," the captain said. "You've all had a long but productive twenty-four hours."

Considering it was nearly dawn, that was a true fact. They were running on coffee and adrenaline.

"We still don't know if the hit man did it," Kit said. "The ME's theory of multiple participants in the murder itself has yet to be disproven."

"Do you think any of them could have stabbed Munro?" the captain asked.

Kit looked at the other detectives, who all gave her the nod to take the lead. "I think Simon Daly could have, sir," she said. "I definitely think that Bert Ramsey could have. The man didn't blink at the sight of Walter Grossman's body."

"Grossman was Munro's PI?" the captain asked.

"Yes, sir," Kit said. "According to Veronica, only Munro and Grossman knew who was on the list."

"And I don't think Veronica is lying about that," Joel said.

"She'd be able to negotiate herself a sweeter deal if she knew and she hasn't done that yet."

"Sam?" Navarro asked. "Your take?"

Sam rubbed the back of his neck. "I definitely agree that Bert Ramsey is capable of stabbing a man. He's a cold-blooded sociopath. But I'm not sure he did stab Munro. Like the others, I don't think he'd get his hands dirty. I don't think that any of them would have participated in the murder-for-hire scheme if Hugh Smith hadn't ambushed them all by inviting them to his house."

"Could one of the nine have killed Hugh Smith?" the captain asked. "I'd be mad as fuck if someone outed my blackmail situation like that."

"Possibly," Kit said. "We're still waiting on the ME to give us a tighter window on Smith's time of death. Right now, it's going to be difficult to get airtight alibis on any of them because they'd have to account for every moment of two full days. They were likely all alone at one point, so . . ."

"Got it," the captain said.

"I've got two of my detectives searching for Jason Goodman, sir," Navarro said. "The hit man associated with Juanita Young."

Ashton smirked. "Juanita Young offered him up on a platter like a Thanksgiving turkey, affair or no affair."

"That made my job easier, for sure," Joel said.

"Ours too," Navarro said. "She told us exactly where to find him. I've sent people to pick him up. Hopefully we'll have news on that front soon."

"What about this 'Neckbeard' character?" the captain asked, using air quotes.

Connor sighed. "He's infuriatingly average. We have video of him, but he's either covered in more facial hair than Sasquatch or wearing a hoodie and a mask. We have no clear photo of his

face. From a body-type standpoint, every one of our male suspects could be him. Hell, half the men in this room could be him.
We just don't know. At this point, we need to check the alibis of
the nine suspects for the time during which Munro was abducted and then tortured."

"Each agreement requires them to cooperate with the police,"
Joel said. "I kind of hope they don't because I need a shower after
negotiating all those deals. I'd like all of them to break their deals
just so I don't have to follow through with them."

"Did everyone get a deal?" the captain asked, frowning.

"No. The last three we talked to didn't have anything new."
Joel huffed a weary laugh. "They were very angry that they were
last. Kind of like when you're at the back row of the airplane and
all the good dinner choices are already gone by the time the
meal cart gets to you."

Kit slid a plate of sandwiches over to Joel. "You're making
food references. Eat something."

Joel grabbed a sandwich. "Thank you. I'll be honest with
you. They're all going to get out on bail. We have them for conspiracy to murder Munro, but the real evidence is only what
they've said about each other. We have no physical evidence yet.
The finger-pointing will be compelling at trial, but I don't think
a judge is going to give us a no-bail option at arraignment. These
are 'pillars of the community,' and a lot of them donate to the
various judges. They'll be back at home by five p.m. today."

"Can we at least get their passports taken?" Kit asked.

"I'm sure as hell gonna try. They're definitely flight risks. But
I can't make promises. We should plan to have them watched as
soon as they're out on bail. Especially Bert Ramsey. Simon Daly
negotiated a safe house for himself and his wife, so he'll be
where we can easily find him, but none of the others got protection. None of them asked for it."

"That's telling," Marshall murmured. "They don't want to be under surveillance."

"Well, they're gonna be," Navarro said grimly. "I'll set that up. Thanks for the heads-up, Joel."

Joel waved at him, having filled his mouth with a huge bite of his sandwich. He closed his eyes and moaned, a pitiful little sound.

"Anyone have anything else?" the captain asked.

"The tan Chevy Suburban," Sam said. "The one that the landscaper saw Neckbeard driving. Has there been any success in tracking it with an unwrapped trailer?"

"I've got a team analyzing all the traffic cams," Navarro said. "They've tracked two that may be the same Suburban/trailer combo. One was last seen on 163 and the other was on the 8."

"State Route 163 runs north," Connor said with a frown. "I-8 runs east. Which way did he go?"

Navarro shook his head. "They're still working to figure out where the vehicles went from there. They disappear, then re-appear. The vehicles aren't where my team expects them to be if they use normal traffic patterns."

"He's doing it on purpose," Kit said. "To muddy the waters."

"It's working," Navarro muttered. "But we're not giving up."

"Sir, what about Christopher Drummond?" Kit asked. "We're not still entertaining his offer, are we?"

The captain gave Navarro a questioning stare and Kit winced. "Sorry, Lieutenant," she murmured.

Navarro waved her apology away. "I told you that Drummond offered to exchange information for a deal," he reminded the captain. "I also told you that we didn't want to allow it."

"I remember," the captain said. "I also remember telling you to find out what he knows."

Kit swallowed, the food she'd eaten taking a nasty roll in her stomach. But she trusted Navarro. He'd had her back on numerous occasions.

He'd also heard Rita quietly confess to having been assaulted by Drummond.

"He murdered a woman in cold blood," Navarro said evenly. "That is not something we want to reward."

The captain looked displeased. His mouth was set as if he planned to further discuss this with Navarro later.

Kit cleared her throat. "Captain? We now know who was involved in the plot to kill Brooks Munro, in part because of Drummond's offer. We weren't looking at the country club connection before that. It makes sense that the country club set was the information he wanted to trade. Every one of the nine people we talked to tonight is implicated by Munro's dead-man's-switch list. And when we find the list, my bet is that Drummond is on it, too."

Navarro nodded. "I'm thinking the same thing. If the country club/blackmail connection is what Drummond intends to offer, he wouldn't have known unless he was being blackmailed, too. Whatever we find on that list, we can use to charge him with later. If he's given an immunity deal, he could include any past crimes included in this case. I'd rather wait until we find the list and not immediately give away an opportunity to get Drummond for something more."

More than the murder of Rita's mother. More than the rape of a child. Either should have been enough to put Drummond away forever, but Kit knew that wasn't how the system always worked.

Evil people knew how to get away with their crimes. Especially smart, rich evil people.

The captain considered Navarro's words. "That makes sense.

All right, then, I can be patient. I guess Drummond isn't going anywhere for the time being. He needs us at this point."

"His attorney called my office all day yesterday," Joel said, having wolfed down a sandwich and taken another. "Asking when we're going to sit down and discuss this with his client. I told the attorney to back off, and my boss is in agreement. We don't want to give Drummond the time of day if we don't absolutely have to. We believe that Drummond is responsible for making a threatening overture toward his victim's fourteen-year-old daughter and we want to get him for witness tampering too, if we can. Giving that man a deal is the last thing we want to do."

Kit briefly closed her eyes, relief washing over her. *Thank you, Joel.*

"I didn't know he'd been in contact with the child," the captain said in a quiet, furious way that made Kit wonder if Navarro actually had disclosed the rape that Rita wasn't yet ready to report. *If she ever is.*

"Not with the victim's daughter personally," Joel said. "She received an anonymous letter that—understandably—made her believe that she was being watched. I think it was Drummond and my boss agrees. Drummond is scum, plain and simple. I'd rather give immunity to a million Veronica Fitzgeralds than one Christopher Drummond, and that's only because Fitzgerald doesn't know exactly who's on the list and what they've done. Munro and his PI knew and now they're dead. If the PI had survived, I wouldn't want to give him a deal, either."

"Understood," the captain said. "Where is Veronica Fitzgerald now? Is she out on bail yet?"

Joel shook his head. "Given that both Munro and Grossman are dead, her attorney and I agreed that she'd be safer in protective custody, so she'll remain your guest until things are settled."

The captain nodded. "I concur with what you've all said. This is good work, people. I know you've been working nearly round the clock on this and we appreciate it. Just . . . try to work faster."

"And on that note," Navarro said, "go home and get some rest while you can. Simon Daly and his wife are already in a safe house. The remaining eight will be out on bail soon, so you're going to have to hustle to get the evidence to bring them down."

San Diego PD, San Diego, California
Thursday, January 12, 6:30 a.m.

Kit found herself stumbling as she walked to her Subaru, which was parked in the employee lot. She hadn't been so tired in a long time.

Getting soft.

No, not true. She'd just gotten used to what it felt like to take care of herself. For the longest time, her life had been only work, eat, sleep, and repeat. Occasionally she'd break to have Sunday dinner with her family. In the past nine months she'd gotten better about prioritizing. This wasn't the first time she'd gone twenty-four hours without sleep during that period, but it didn't happen nearly often enough anymore to become the norm.

Her bed at McKittrick House beckoned. Mom and Pop would have the girls off to school by the time she got home. She could cuddle up with her dog and get some rest before it all started again.

"You."

Kit spun around at the voice, filled with venom. And she froze.

"You," she repeated, her heart beginning to hammer. Not from fear, but from fury.

Christopher Drummond loomed over her, his toes not even an inch from her own. He was a tall man, and he used that height to try to intimidate her.

"You're responsible," he hissed, his breath foul. He smelled like whiskey and desperation.

"For what?" she asked calmly, sliding her hand into her pocket for her cell phone. She'd get help quickly enough by contacting 911. She was in the SDPD parking lot, for fuck's sake.

If she could activate her recording app, even better. But for now, she needed to get help before this escalated. She tapped the side button on her phone five times. It was a powerful thing, being able to contact 911 without dialing. She'd never had to use it before but was glad she'd set it up.

Her other hand moved to her service weapon. She released the safety latch on her holster and gripped the gun's handle firmly. She didn't want to fire her weapon at Drummond unless it was to save her own life.

So much paperwork was required after firing one's service weapon.

Drummond poked her chest with his finger, hard enough to hurt. "I was gonna get a deal, but *you* got in my way."

"Not my call, Mr. Drummond. Take it up with the prosecutor."

"He's in with you. Probably sleeping with you, you bitch."

Kit took a measured step back. Drummond stepped forward, still in her space. "I need you to move away, sir," she said politely.

He was baiting her into taking action against him and she

wasn't going to do that. Not when he could muddy the waters of his case by screaming that she'd assaulted him, which she figured was his intent.

"You go back in there and tell that fucker Haley to call me. And his news better be good."

"I'm not telling Joel Haley anything. *Sir*," she added, making her tone as sarcastic as she could muster. At least she wasn't tired any longer. Adrenaline was surging like a flood-swollen river. "You murdered a woman in cold blood *and* assaulted her child. I'm not lifting a finger to help you. You've earned whatever horrible things happen to you from here on out. Have a good day. *Sir*." He reached out and gripped her arm, faster than she'd believed him capable. He was strong, too. She'd have a bruise later. "Release me. Now."

Drummond tugged her into him, his face close enough that their noses nearly touched. "What did you say?"

Kit blinked at him, feigning innocence. "What do you mean?"

There were cameras all over the place. Surely one of them was capturing this moment. Hopefully with audio.

"What did the little whore say I did?"

"You mean the child of the woman you murdered?"

"I didn't touch that kid. Whatever she said I did, she's lying."

But once again, he sounded desperate. Desperate and oh so guilty.

Please be recording, cameras. Please.

"That's for a jury of your peers to decide, Mr. Drummond."

"She never said I touched her. My lawyer would have told me."

"Did you? Touch her?" That Kit wasn't clawing his eyes out or filling him with bullets made her proud of her own self-control. *You motherfucker. Touching my little sister. I will* end *you.* But she'd do so legally.

She needed Rita to see that the justice system did work.

His iron grip on her arm tightened, and he hauled her even closer until the front of her body was up against his. "I didn't fuck her. If she says I did, she's lying."

His fetid breath filled her nostrils. *Do not gag.*

"I never said you 'fucked' her, sir." The words wanted to stick in her throat, choking her. "I only said you assaulted her."

His grip tightened even further and she had to bite the inside of her cheek to keep from wincing. "She's a liar," he snarled.

Kit's fingers flexed on her service weapon. She'd have to stop him soon. "We'll see what the DNA says."

It was a long shot. Rita had never told her any details of the assault and Kit had no idea if there was any physical evidence of the act, as Rita hadn't told anyone at the time it happened.

But Kit was certain that there'd been no rape kit. Drummond didn't know that, though.

He blanched. "What?"

"I said, we'll see what the DNA says. You *do* know about DNA, right? It's the hard evidence that proves you killed Maria Mendoza." Rita's mother's skin cells had been embedded in the crevices of the signet ring that he'd worn the night he'd beaten her to death.

Connor had been responsible for that investigation shortly before they'd been partnered up. *Thank you, Connor.*

Drummond took a step back, still holding her arm. "You're lying," he said, his voice uncertain. And scared.

She smiled up at him. "Whatever makes you feel better. Next time you rape a child, use a condom."

"*I did,*" he gritted out as his free hand balled into a fist and headed for her face.

But she saw this one coming. Catching his arm and simultaneously wrenching her own free, she spun him around and kicked his legs out from under him.

Drummond fell to the pavement with a thud hard enough that she might have felt sympathy if she hadn't hated him so much.

"You're under arrest for assaulting a police officer," she said as she cuffed him. "And hopefully for a whole lot more."

He was cursing a blue streak when she jerked him to his feet. Kit just let the insults roll off her. And wished to high heaven that she'd been able to record the entire exchange.

"Nice," a familiar voice said from the shadows behind her car. Sam stepped out, clutching one of her mother's Pyrex baking dishes in one hand and his cell phone in the other. The cell phone was pointed straight at Drummond.

She grinned at Sam, hoping that he'd recorded everything. "Were you going to hit him in the head with the dish?"

Sam shrugged. "If I had to. I figured you had things under control, but I had your back. Just in case."

"You got it all on video?"

Sam's smile was feral. "Every word. Even 'I did.'"

Drummond began to struggle, but Kit just kicked his legs from underneath him again, dropping to kneel on his back, her knee in his kidney.

Sam looked equal parts exultant and pained, the latter most likely at the memory of the time she'd done the same thing to him.

Luckily Sam had more than forgiven her.

"He's not as smart as I thought he was," Connor said, casually approaching as he reholstered his gun. "I didn't think you'd get him to admit to anything."

"Me either," Kit confessed, "but he's drunk and maybe even high. Not a good combination."

Marshall and Ashton were close behind Connor. "That was awesome," Ashton said. "Better than television."

That her colleagues had had her back was reassuring. She'd been certain that she'd been all alone.

Connor yanked Drummond to his feet and the three men escorted him back into the building. "Go home, Kit," Connor said over his shoulder. "We'll get him in a holding cell until we can fill out the paperwork. Hopefully by then he'll be sober and fully able to appreciate what he just did to himself."

Sam tapped his cell phone as the detectives walked away. "Just sent the video to you and Connor and to my cloud account." He set the Pyrex dish on the hood of Kit's Subaru. "Did he hurt you?"

She shrugged. "Nothing I can't handle. I was hoping to at least get him for assaulting a cop. Didn't dream he'd actually say anything useful."

Sam gently pushed back the sleeve of her jacket and, using the flashlight on his phone, checked her arm where Drummond had grabbed her. Sam's jaw tensed. "It's red already. You need ice."

I need you. Because once again this man had come to her aid. Even though she could have dealt with Drummond on her own, having had Sam with her made her too warm and happy.

She leaned into him, resting her forehead on his chest. "Thank you."

His arms came around her, snug and safe. "You forgot to take your mother's dishes and the coffee urn. I was bringing them out to you when I saw him grab you. I texted Connor and then started recording."

"After you grabbed Mom's dish to bash him on the head with."

His chuckle rumbled up from his chest. "Don't have a gun. Had to make do." He inhaled deeply, his voice changing. Becoming shaky. "You scared ten years off my life."

"I had him under control."

"I know. It's the only reason I didn't hit him myself. But you still scared me. What if he'd had a gun?"

"Kevlar."

"Doesn't protect everything." He exhaled, his shoulders sagging. "I know you're careful. But . . ."

"I know," she whispered. Then she pulled back far enough so that she could meet his eyes. Those lovely green eyes behind the Clark Kent glasses. As usual, they were open and honest and said a million things that she couldn't parse right now. "Thank you. For having my back. And for trusting that I could handle myself. But especially for recording everything. It will make a huge difference."

"If they can use that to get a guilty plea out of that miserable sonofabitch, then Rita can report the crime without having to testify in court. Not at that trial at least."

She'd still have to testify at Drummond's murder trial, but Kit believed that Rita could handle that. Especially if the man was being punished for the sexual assault.

"Thank you," she said again, then lifted on her toes to kiss him. Just a quick one, but it still made him smile. "You're my knight in shining armor."

"Wielding my trusty nine-by-thirteen baking dish."

She wanted to laugh, but she found her eyes stinging instead. "I think I'm having an adrenaline crash."

"Then let me drive you home."

She wanted to say no. But he was right. She shouldn't be behind the wheel of a car right now. "Okay."

La Jolla, San Diego, California
Thursday, January 12, 12:15 p.m.

"Wow," Kit breathed as Connor drove them up the winding driveway to Peter Shoemaker's home.

The house itself was spectacular. Up on a hill, the house was done in an old Spanish hacienda style, but with a literal twist. The house wound around itself, creating a spiral effect.

"The entire back side is semicircular," Connor said. "All windows. Backs right up to the bluffs. The views of the ocean at sunset are breathtaking."

Kit rolled the car window down a few inches and was immediately met with the sound of crashing waves and the smell of salt water. "How do you know what the back looks like?"

"I googled it," Connor said. "It was featured in a magazine about fifteen years ago. The Shoemakers have lived here for ten years, so they weren't the owners then. But I can't imagine that they changed much. This house sold for twenty mil. When you spend that much, you don't want a fixer-upper."

Kit swallowed hard. "Twenty million dollars?"

"Yep. You ready to meet the wife?"

They'd come to both search Shoemaker's home and question Aylene Shoemaker about her husband's alibi. He'd told Joel that he'd been with Aylene on Wednesday after school when Brooks Munro had been abducted, at school the next two days, then at home with her again the next two evenings. They'd already confirmed that he'd been at school all day from Wednesday through Friday, but the rest of the time was still in question.

They were checking alibis of all nine participants in the murder-for-hire scheme, but as Kit had predicted, getting the location and activities for all nine was proving difficult. Hopefully Peter Shoemaker's wife would be able to back her husband up. They'd at least be able to cross his name off their list.

Kit wished that Sam could be with them today, but he'd had clients that morning and an afternoon of volunteering at New Horizons. He had to be exhausted. At least she and Connor had been able to sleep four or five hours. Sam couldn't have gotten more than an hour's sleep before his day had begun.

They crested the hill and Connor tapped the car's brakes. "Whoa, whoa, whoa. What the hell?"

Kit's thoughts of Sam evaporated at the scene before them. A police car sat alongside a Rolls-Royce in the circular driveway in front of the home where two uniformed officers were restraining an older man. The man appeared to be in his mid to late sixties and he was shouting and fighting them.

Kit and Connor hurried to the action, showing their credentials. "What's the problem, Officers?" Kit asked.

"This man was trying to break into the house," one of the uniforms said.

"I was not!" the man thundered. "I *bought* this house. My daughter lives here. I'm trying to get in there to check on her, but my key isn't working."

Kit held up her hands, hoping to both reassure and quiet the man. "What's your name, sir?" She glanced at the officers. "Can you let him go? Don't run, sir. We want to help you."

Because she'd had a sudden shiver at the thought of this man coming to check on his daughter. From his age, Kit was guessing that his daughter was Peter Shoemaker's wife.

The man yanked out of the officers' grips and turned to face Kit. "I'm Duncan Tindall."

"He is," Connor confirmed in a quiet whisper that only Kit could hear.

Even Kit recognized that name. Duncan Tindall was one of the wealthiest men in Southern California.

"Thank you, sir. I'm Detective McKittrick and this is my partner, Detective Robinson. Tell me what's happened."

Tindall drew a shaky breath and let it out. "My daughter Aylene isn't answering my phone calls. She *always* answers my calls. My twin granddaughters are staying with us for a few days and they wanted to talk to their mother, but she didn't answer their calls, either. Something is wrong."

"Do the children live with you?" Kit asked.

"No. My daughter asked me to keep them for a few days. She and my son-in-law wanted some time alone before the spring semester got busy."

"And you have a key to the house?" Connor asked.

Tindall glowered. "Yes, I have a key. I bought this damn house!"

"I'm so sorry, sir," Kit said, hoping she sounded placating. "We didn't mean to insinuate anything. You say your key no longer fits?"

"It doesn't. I was trying the windows when these . . . *men* accosted me."

The uniforms gave Kit and Connor identical unimpressed looks. "We were assigned to make sure no one entered who wasn't authorized," one of them said.

Tindall's eyes narrowed. "Why?" The single word was filled with a combination of outrage and fear.

"Your son-in-law was brought in last night for questioning," Connor told him.

Tindall's outrage seemed to deflate, shock taking over. "For what? Pete's a fine man."

A taxi pulled up behind them and none other than Peter Shoemaker got out of the back seat. He waved the taxi away and started toward them, a wary expression on his face.

"Why are you here, Dad?" Shoemaker asked, ignoring Kit and Connor.

"Why doesn't my key fit in the lock?" Tindall demanded. "And why were you brought in for questioning?"

"I'd hoped I'd be able to talk to Aylene about this in private first. Why are *you* here, Detectives?"

"To search your house and to talk to your wife," Kit said. "We're confirming alibis, just as we said we would. Sounds like we all want to talk to Mrs. Shoemaker."

"Tindall," Tindall corrected. "She kept her maiden name."

Which seemed to bother Peter Shoemaker if his frown was any indication. "Your key doesn't work because Aylene changed the locks," he said. "There were reports of a prowler around, so she wanted to be careful." He pulled a set of keys from his pocket and gave one to his father-in-law. "Here you go. Now, why are you here, Dad?"

"Aylene isn't answering my calls. She didn't answer when the girls called, either."

Shoemaker stilled. "She didn't answer when I called, either. I thought she was mad because I didn't come home last night." He started for the front door at a fast jog. "She was mad when I left."

"Did you tell her where you were going?" Kit asked, following closely behind because the shiver down her spine had grown to full-blown dread.

Something was wrong.

"No. She was already in the bathtub when . . . when I was summoned. I figured I'd only be an hour. Two tops. I told her to enjoy her bath and I'd be home soon." Shoemaker's hands shook as he tried to get his key into the lock. "And then . . . after . . . I didn't want to have to explain anything to her over the phone."

"Explain *what*?" Tindall demanded. "Dammit, Pete. What's going on?"

"In a minute, Dad." Shoemaker sucked in a breath and blew it out, trying to calm himself. "I need to get inside."

"Let me," Connor said, taking the key from Shoemaker's hand. It slid into the lock and easily turned.

Kit looked up and froze. *Oh shit.* The camera pointing at the door had been covered with black spray paint.

"Detective," she murmured, pointing up when Connor looked over his shoulder.

Connor looked up, his eyes closing briefly before he returned Shoemaker's keys. "We're going to need you to stay out here for a few minutes, Mr. Shoemaker, Mr. Tindall. Please."

"No!" Tindall shouted. "I want to know what's going on!"

"And we'll tell you as soon as we know," Kit assured him. "Officers?"

The two uniformed officers took their places in front of the door, barring entry to the two men, who were both freaking out.

Kit and Connor took the stairs at a run, the elegant staircase more than wide enough for them both at the same time. The seven bedrooms were clear, but when they entered the primary bath, they stopped in their tracks.

"Motherfucker," Connor muttered.

Yes, Kit thought. *Motherfucker.*

Because Aylene Tindall lay in the immense bathtub, the water a dark brownish red. Her throat had been slit. Ear to ear.

Kit took a step back and called it in to Dispatch while Connor called CSU. She then called Alicia Batra to retrieve the body, finishing her call as Connor was dialing Navarro. He put Navarro on speaker.

"What?" Navarro asked flatly when he picked up.

"Shoemaker's wife is dead," Connor said. "Throat slit, same as the others. And the front door camera's been painted over."

"Goddammit." Navarro sighed. "I'll add additional protection to the families of the other seven. Seems like Simon Daly asking for protection was timely."

"Maybe too timely," Kit said. "I guess it depends on when Aylene Tindall was killed."

"She's Shoemaker's wife?" Navarro asked. "Christ, this is a nightmare. She's the heiress to one of the biggest fortunes in

Southern California. The mayor has been on my back for days and this is just going to make things worse. Keep me posted as you know more."

Kit couldn't rip her gaze from the dead woman in the tub. "She was Peter Shoemaker's alibi, sir. Now we can't ask her anything."

"I know. Have you done any other alibi confirmations?"

"So far Estelle White's alibi has checked out. Shoemaker was our second visit. We haven't talked to Marshall and Ashton about their afternoon."

"Juanita Young's and Henry Reese's alibis also checked out," Navarro said. "Kevin and Alf just reported in. I'll send them to check out Bert Ramsey's alibi next. We can check Simon Daly's last, since he's in a safe house and isn't going anywhere for now. The one woman and the other two men haven't posted bail yet, but they will within the hour. Joel was able to get the judge to confiscate all their passports."

"Unless they're like Veronica and have fake ones," Kit said.

"I've got local airports—including charter services—on BOLO. If they try to flee the country, we'll pick them up. Everyone has police presence at their homes and workplaces. We're telling them it's to keep them safe, and after Aylene Tindall's murder, they might even believe us. Stay there at the scene and take statements. I'll keep Kevin and Alf on alibis. You can pick up any of the ones they didn't get to once the Shoemaker scene is secured. I'll send people out to check on the immediate families of the remaining seven."

Seven, Kit thought, mentally counting them. Of the ten, Hugh Smith was dead. Simon Daly and his wife were in a safe house. Peter Shoemaker's wife was dead. That left seven suspects' families to check. Good. They couldn't let anyone fall through the cracks.

"Do we know where Hugh Smith's wife is?" Kit asked.

"Visiting their grandchildren," Navarro said. "She's in Baltimore now, and she's been notified of his death. She's on her way home."

"Aylene Tindall and Peter Shoemaker have three children," Connor said. "One's in college in San Francisco. We'll get the location and have someone inform her as well."

Kit was still staring at Aylene Tindall's body. "Why kill Shoemaker's wife? Was it a message? And if so, what? He said he was making payments to Munro. He said he would have continued making payments to Neckbeard, if Hugh Smith hadn't outed them all. He said his only crime was cheating on Aylene."

"He said a lot of things," Navarro muttered. "They all did. And I'm betting a lot of it was lies to either get a deal or to try to make us forget to investigate what they did to be on Munro's list. Or both."

Kit sighed. "We need to tell her father and her husband. They're outside."

Navarro's sigh echoed her own. "Get to it, then."

Connor turned for the bathroom door. "I'll do it this time. It's my turn."

"Wait." Kit lightly grabbed Connor's hand before he ended the call with Navarro. "Check on Wilhelmina Munro as well. If Neckbeard's starting to kill family members, he might go after her and Rafferty, her caretaker."

"Didn't they go back to Boston?" Navarro asked.

"No. She said that even though she wasn't going to bury her husband—because Veronica gets to do that, being the legal wife—she's going to stay until we finish our investigation. I told her it could be a while, but she's rented a condo in the city. I'll text you the address."

"Thank you. Stay safe, both of you." Navarro ended the call.

Connor exhaled. "Let's do this."

They headed down the stairs, able to hear both Shoemaker and Tindall shouting at the cops on the other side of the closed front door. Kit and Connor slipped through, not giving the two men a chance to enter.

Connor exhaled again. He really hated doing notifications, Kit knew, but no one liked them. And it was his turn.

"Your wife is dead, Mr. Shoemaker," Connor said as compassionately as he could. "You can't go in until the forensics team and medical examiner are finished and we've cleared the scene."

Shoemaker just . . . collapsed. Fell on the concrete front porch on his ass and didn't even react to the pain of the fall. He looked like he'd been unplugged. His body sagged and he leaned back against the front wall of the house.

"This is all my fault," he whispered.

Tindall had gone an alarming shade of white. *"What?"* he asked soundlessly, the word forming only on his lips.

Kit took his arm and escorted him to a porch swing that gently swayed in the ocean breeze. "I'm so sorry, sir."

He slumped onto the swing and stared up at her. *"How?"* Again the word was soundless.

"She was murdered, sir."

Closing his eyes, he mouthed *murdered* but said no more.

"Can we call someone for you, sir?" Kit asked. "Your wife?"

He nodded, still silent. Then his eyes opened and Kit saw the glazed look of shock. "Kennedy. I need to tell her."

"Who is Kennedy?"

"My granddaughter. She's at college." He fumbled for his phone, but Kit stayed him with a gentle touch to his wrist. "Let's make sure someone's with her when you tell her, okay? Like a friend or a dorm roommate. Maybe her residential advisor."

Tindall nodded numbly. "The girls. How am I going to tell them?" Tears welled in his eyes. "Why would someone hurt my Aylene? She was good. Kind."

"I don't know," Kit said honestly. "We're going to find out."

He nodded again, then went still. Then rigid, sitting up so abruptly that the swing nearly dumped him. "What does this have to do with Pete? Why was he questioned?"

Kit glanced over at Peter Shoemaker, who still sat on the concrete, rocking himself. His mouth continued to move and Kit thought he was saying, over and over, that it was all his fault.

"I can't give you all the details right now—we're still figuring things out," she added when Tindall opened his mouth, undoubtedly to object. "But your son-in-law was questioned because we believe he was being blackmailed."

Again Tindall looked lost. "Pete? For what?"

Kit was nearly certain that Peter Shoemaker had done far more than cheat on his wife. The message Neckbeard was sending was graphic: pay or else. And, relative to the sums the other blackmailees were paying, Shoemaker's two thousand a month didn't seem enough to murder a woman over. "I'm not sure. Like I said, we're just getting started on our investigation. But we will find out."

A muscle clenched in Tindall's jaw. "So this really is Pete's fault?"

"Well, no, sir. It's the fault of whoever's been killing people over the last week."

Tindall stared at her again, and then clarity seemed to hit him. "Brooks Munro. You're McKittrick. You're investigating the murder of that slime bag Brooks Munro."

"Yes, sir."

"Then *he's* responsible?"

Kit wanted to say that Munro couldn't be responsible for Aylene's murder, as he'd been dead for around a week. But that wasn't what Tindall was asking.

She answered as best she could. "It's related. I'd tell you more if I knew." Mostly true. "Can I ask you a few questions? I know this is awful timing, but . . ."

"Of course," Tindall murmured. "She was my baby. My only child."

"I'm so sorry. Your daughter and son-in-law, did they seem happy together?"

He nodded. "Yes, they did. Pete treated her like a queen."

That was interesting. Peter had said some awful things about his wife the night before. "Did your daughter work outside the home?"

"She worked from home, managing our family's foundation. We give a substantial amount to charities around the city."

Kit had read that in the news over the years. "So money wasn't tight."

Tindall shook his head. "No. She had a trust fund and minimal expenses. I paid for nearly everything so that she could do the charity work and Pete could teach school. They give back."

Kit smiled sadly. "She sounds utterly wonderful."

"She was," Tindall whispered. "How am I going to tell the kids?"

"It's not easy," Kit said. "Not to tell and not to hear. I can give you the name of a good psychologist who specializes in childhood trauma due to crime. She's helped my family."

He lifted his eyes, so filled with pain and shock that they hurt Kit's heart. "You lost someone?"

She couldn't tell him about Rita, so she gave him the answer that anyone who'd read an article about Kit would already know. "My sister. We were fifteen. We never caught the guy who did it, but we *will* catch whoever killed your Aylene."

"Thank you, Detective." Duncan Tindall lowered his face to his hands and began to weep.

CHAPTER SEVENTEEN

Kit slumped into her desk chair and frantically searched her drawer, sighing in relief when she found the Snickers bar she'd left there for just such an occasion. It was king-sized, but still not big enough for the amount of stress she needed to assuage.

"You're not okay," Navarro said, perching on the edge of her desk. "So I won't even ask."

"Good," Kit said through a mouthful of chocolate and caramel. She swallowed the first bite and put the candy aside, because Navarro wanted an update. "Alicia Batra said the bathwater fucked with Aylene's body temperature, so TOD's not clear. Sometime between seven last night and seven this morning. Her husband said she was in the tub when SDPD showed up to bring him in for questioning and that was at nine fifteen last night, so that narrows the window a bit."

"When did we pick up the other suspects?"

"Between nine and midnight. So any of them could have done it if TOD is on the earlier side." She flung her arms wide. "Or none of them could have done it. We don't know!"

Navarro remained silent, patiently waiting for her outburst to subside.

Kit took another huge bite of the candy bar and crossed her arms over her chest as she chewed. "I'm sorry," she said when she'd finished the entire king-sized bar. She checked her drawer, but there was no more. "Dammit."

Navarro pulled another Snickers bar from his jacket pocket. "I bought the party pack. Have one of mine."

"Thank you. I'm going to save this one because I haven't had food today and the sugar's gonna make me sick if I have any more."

Navarro rolled his eyes and pulled a wrapped sandwich from his other pocket. "I figured you wouldn't have time to eat. Marshall and Ashton brought a bunch of Cuban sandwiches from the corner deli."

"You are a prince among men," Kit said and dug in. "Connor's taking a break. He needed to go home to CeCe for a little while. Probably a better way to decompress than me eating a party pack of Snickers bars."

"Probably," Navarro said mildly. "When is he coming back?"

"Soon. He said he just needed a hug."

Navarro's lips twitched. "I heard you got a hug this morning after nailing Drummond to the wall."

She remembered the way Sam had held her as her adrenaline had crashed. "I did. Got something to say about it?"

"Nope. If I say it's a good thing, you'll leave Sam just to be contrary. And if you leave Sam, your parents will have my hide. And I like your mom's cooking."

Kit chuckled. "Everyone does." She sighed and sobered. "Mr.

Tindall—*the* Duncan Tindall—was distraught. He had to tell his wife and grandchildren. The oldest daughter is flying home as we speak. Tindall sent his personal assistant on the company jet to pick her up and bring her home. I mean, private planes aren't great for the environment, but at least she doesn't have to endure a plane ride while her world is falling apart."

"She's not much older than you were when Wren died," Navarro noted.

"She's seventeen. First time away from home. The twins are only eight. I gave Mr. Tindall Dr. Carlisle's number. She's done so much for Rita."

Navarro squeezed her shoulder, just a brief touch. "You've got a good heart, Kit. Don't get too hard-nosed."

"Trying." She rubbed her hands over her face. "So are Wilhelmina and the others okay?"

"We're still checking. Of the seven remaining suspects, we've confirmed that five of their families are alive and well. The Dalys are in protective custody and I spoke with Hugh Smith's wife personally. I'm expecting news on the remaining two families in the next hour."

"Okay. Why kill Peter Shoemaker's wife? Why her? Why now?"

"Maybe he intended to kill more people but hasn't gotten around to it yet."

"Maybe. I keep thinking that Peter Shoemaker's sin is much worse than simple adultery. Why else would Munro even bother blackmailing him? Two grand a month? I mean, that's a lot of money for me. That's a lot of money for most normal people. But for someone with Shoemaker's money?"

"You're assuming he had access to her trust fund."

"True. She kept her name and he said she kept a tight hand on the funds. But Aylene's father said that they were happy together. Shoemaker really seemed to hate his wife, but his father-in-law said he treated her like a queen."

"And now his alibi can't be corroborated."

"Right." And that made her wonder about what else Shoemaker had done. He was the right size to be Neckbeard and his was the only family member of the ten co-conspirators who'd been targeted. "Were the rest of the alibis corroborated?"

"As much as they can be. There's still some work to do on a few of them, but everyone seems to have been where they said they were."

They both turned when the Homicide double doors opened and a young woman walked in. Kit sucked in a breath, recognizing the woman's face from the photograph on Duncan Tindall's phone.

"That's Kennedy Shoemaker," Kit murmured. "She must have come straight from the airport."

Kennedy was pulling a suitcase behind her. Her face was red and blotchy, her eyes swollen. She was still crying, wiping her face with a tissue that had seen better days.

Kit stood. "Miss Shoemaker. I'm Detective McKittrick. Would you like to sit down?" Kennedy nodded and took the chair next to Kit's desk. "This is my boss, Lieutenant Navarro. How can we help you?"

"I'm not Miss Shoemaker. I'm Kennedy Tindall. Or I will be by the end of the month."

Kit sat down, studying the young woman. She had the sweetest face, but her words had been sharp and venomous. "Why?"

"I don't want anything to do with my father."

Okay. Kit leaned forward, her instincts setting off every alarm in her head. "Why, honey?"

Kennedy swallowed hard and looked Kit right in the eye.

"He sexually molested me from the time I was nine years old until I got out of the house in August for college."

And there it is. She glanced up at Navarro. "Much worse than adultery," she murmured.

"Indeed." He smiled gently at Kennedy. "Thank you for telling us. You've had a long trip. Can I get you some water or coffee?"

Fresh tears filled her eyes. "Yes, please. Water is fine. I've cried so much that I have a headache." She fished a bottle from her purse. "It's just Advil," she said defensively.

"Then you'll need something to eat with it." Kit held out the sandwich. "I'll split it with you."

Kennedy shook her head. "I think I'd throw up. But thank you. You're very kind."

Navarro returned with a bottle of water. "Can you tell us what you know, Kennedy?"

"I will. But first . . . my grandfather said my mom was murdered because my father was being blackmailed. Is that true?"

Kit nodded. "We think so, yes."

"That was why you said that incest was worse than adultery. He was being blackmailed for adultery?"

"He said he was," Kit said. "Your statement puts that in doubt."

"You had doubt to begin with."

Smart cookie. "Yes, I did. You said the abuse started when you were nine?"

"Yes, ma'am. My mom was pregnant with the twins. She had a difficult pregnancy. She was older and she was on bed rest for most of the time."

"Your father started touching you." Kit kept her voice calm when inside she wanted to scream.

"Well, he started touching me before that. The actual sex started when I was nine."

"Did you tell your mother?" Navarro asked gently. Still, Kennedy flinched.

"No, I didn't. My father told me that if I told my mother, she wouldn't believe me. That she'd send me away to boarding school and I'd be all alone."

Sonofabitch. "Do you think your mother would have?"

"Maybe? When I started to tell her once, she cut me off. Said that I was being dramatic, so I didn't say any more. But if I had told her, I know it would have hurt her. She loved him with all her heart, even when he hurt her feelings."

"How did he hurt her feelings?" Navarro asked.

"He'd leave for a weekend here or there. He was cheating on her. I knew that and I think she did too, but she loved him. Maybe more than she loved us. I don't know. Maybe if I had told her what he did, she would have sent him away." Her shoulders heaved in a sob. "I'll never know now."

"The woman your grandfather told me about would have loved you," Kit said softly. It might not have been true, but it was what the young woman needed to hear right now.

Sniffling, Kennedy dabbed at her eyes with the soggy tissue. Kit gave her the box from her desk and Kennedy took one with a nod of gratitude.

"It wasn't all the time," Kennedy went on. "My father, I mean. He waited until my grandparents took the twins for a sleepover and then . . . he'd come into my room. I think he put something in my mom's bedtime tea because she always slept through it, even when I yelled."

"For help?" Kit asked.

Kennedy shrugged. "And because it hurt."

Beside her, Navarro took a long breath through his nose, but said nothing.

"Can we ask a few questions about your parents?" Kit asked. "How was money? Did they both have enough? Did they argue?"

"They never argued, not that I heard. Not even when he'd disappear for a weekend. Mom just cried and made excuses for him. As for money, there was always enough. I guess, in that, we were lucky. My dad handled all the bills, so Mom never worried about it. He said he didn't trust an accountant with their finances. That was how people got ripped off."

Also made it so that his wife would never know how much he was paying Brooks Munro, Kit thought. So much for Aylene keeping a tight hand on the family purse strings. "How did you get away?"

"I applied to colleges outside of San Diego. I wanted to be far away from him, but I didn't want to be too far from my sisters. They're only eight."

Kit regretted having eaten that entire Snickers bar. "Do you think he'd molest them, too?"

"You believe me?" Kennedy whispered.

"I do. That's why I asked about your sisters. Are they safe?"

She shrugged again. "I FaceTime them every week. My roommate laughs at me for being homesick, but it's not that."

"You're checking on them," Kit said.

She nodded. "I've seen photos of me before and after. I was so happy before, but after . . . my eyes were just dead. Y'know?"

"Yes," Kit said simply. "So you figured you'd be able to see the signs in your sisters' eyes if he started abusing them?"

"I thought so, yes. That's why I came in today. I couldn't keep the secret anymore." A sob rose in her throat and her voice broke. "My mom's gone, but now that means he'll be alone with the girls. I can't allow that."

"I understand. You're brave, Kennedy."

She shook her head. "If I'd been brave, I would have taken up for myself years ago."

"You were a child. A child being abused and manipulated by her father. The person who should have been making sure the world never hurt you, yet he was hurting you in the worst possible way."

Kennedy dropped her chin, her shoulders shaking as she cried. She seemed so alone. And Kit knew she had to do something. Even if it made her feel like she was wearing a coat two sizes too small.

"Do you want a hug?" Kit asked softly. "No worries if you don't. But you look like you could use one."

Not looking up, Kennedy sobbed harder. But she nodded. So Kit opened her arms and pulled the girl close. "I'm so sorry," she whispered into Kennedy's hair. "I'm so sorry this happened to you."

"Will you make him pay?" Kennedy asked as she cried.

"I will do everything in my power to do exactly that." She glanced up to see Navarro staring at her curiously, his eyes bright with unshed tears.

He patted Kit's shoulder and went to his office. Kit just held on to Kennedy, figuring the young woman would pull away when she got tired of the hug.

Kit wasn't sure exactly how hugs worked, but that made sense to her.

She looked up when Connor came through the double doors. He too stared at her like she was a stranger. Then he approached cautiously.

"You okay?" he asked quietly, and Kit became aware of how often he asked her that.

"I am. This is Kennedy Shoemaker, soon to be Kennedy Tindall. She's just given us some very valuable information."

Kennedy pulled away then, glancing up at Connor.

"This is my partner," Kit said. "Detective Robinson. He's a good guy."

Kennedy nodded. "I need to go to my sisters. Do I need to sign anything for you?"

"If you could write out a simple statement and sign it, we'd appreciate it. Now, while everything is fresh in your mind."

Kennedy scoffed. "Like it ever disappears."

Hopefully it would someday. Or maybe just not be the first thing she thought of every morning when she woke.

"I already wrote out my statement on the plane," Kennedy added. "I can email it to you now. You can print it and I'll sign it."

Kit was impressed. "Thank you, Kennedy. Do you think your grandparents will believe you? Do you expect trouble from them?"

"I think they'll be okay, once they're over the shock. That my father's blackmail led to the death of my mother will be in my favor."

"Okay." Kit gave Kennedy her business card. "Send your statement to me at this email. And, trust me, honey. You are very brave."

"Thank you," Kennedy whispered.

New Horizons, San Diego, California
Thursday, January 12, 6:30 p.m.

"Dr. Sam?"

Sam turned his gaze from the window of his office at New Horizons, immediately feeling a smile curve his lips at the sight of Emma in his doorway. "Emma. How are you? How is Rita?"

That Rita's understandable meltdown had happened only

twenty-four hours before seemed impossible. It had been a very long night and an even longer day. But he was nearly finished with his volunteer shift at the shelter and could soon go home and finally get some sleep.

"She's okay. She stayed home another day." Emma's smile was fleeting, but real. "Mom McK's orders. Can I come in for a minute?"

"Of course, Em. Please, sit down."

"I hope I'm not bothering you."

Sam took the chair beside her. It was much less threatening than having a desk between them. "You could never bother me. What's on your mind?"

Emma was studying his face. "You look tired."

"I am, a little. But not too tired to hear what you have to say."

"Look, I'm new here and I know that I haven't earned the right to—"

"Emma," Sam interrupted, because he wasn't going to let her continue that train of thought. "You don't have to earn rights here. We value you—your time, your empathy. Your brain, because you are so smart."

Emma blushed. "Tiffany's smarter."

"Tiffany is a little more street smart, perhaps, but she was on the street longer than you were. She had to be street smart to survive. You are both highly intelligent young women. And I think that you see things adults might miss."

He had the satisfaction of knowing he'd hit the target when Emma straightened, confidence filling her eyes. "The kids talk. The new kids, I mean. Not so much around you, but around Tiff, Rita, and me? They talk." She blew out a breath. "I overheard something two nights ago at McKittrick House that I shouldn't have listened to."

"Kit's conversation with Harlan?"

She nodded. "I didn't mean to. Honest."

"I know. Kit knows that, too." And Sam figured that Kit would be a lot more careful where she discussed cases with her father in the future. "She's not mad at you, you know."

"I know." She was quiet a moment, but that was Emma's way. She thought first, then sometimes spoke. Her best friend Tiffany was the opposite. Thoughts flew from Tiffany's brain through her mouth with no filter. "I heard Kit say that the killer has a beard. Like one that goes all over his face and down his neck."

Sam stilled, because this wasn't what he'd been anticipating. "Yes. It's frustrating because that's the only feature on this man that people remember."

She grimaced. "That's what makes a good disguise."

"Do you know anything about this man, Em?"

"Not me. But one of the girls—one of the new girls—she does. She was just telling some of the others that if they went back on the street and started . . ." She hesitated. "Well, you know . . . hooking."

"I know some of the kids sell their bodies, Em. I hate that for them, but they're doing it to survive. No judgment. Not from me."

She relaxed a little more. "I didn't think so. Well, this girl was telling some of the others that when they left and went back on the street to be careful. There was this guy with a beard like that. A neckbeard?"

Sam realized he was holding his breath. Quietly he exhaled. "Yes. That's what it's called."

"She said not to go with him. That girls go with him and they don't come back. It's probably nothing and I'm probably being stupid, but . . ."

"You are not stupid," Sam said firmly. "You are so smart. And like I said, you see things we don't see. And hear things, too. When did she tell you this?"

"It wasn't me personally. She said it to a group and I was there. But it was just now. Like five minutes ago. The neckbeard thing caught my attention."

"See? You're observant. Can I talk to this girl?"

Emma's sigh didn't bode well. "She's here, but she's twitchy."

"Like on drugs?"

"Maybe, but I don't think so. More like she's so used to being watchful that she can't stop. More than the rest of us. I wish she could come home with me, but Mom and Pop McK are full up."

"Like I said, you are smart and empathetic. A lot of kids who've been on the street like you were would only be thinking of themselves. You're looking out for others."

Her smile became a little brighter. "Kit looks out for other people, too. She was like me, once."

Another Kit worshipper. They all saw Kit as a superwoman. And they were right. "She was like you." He remembered what Kit had shared with Connor, about the foster father she'd had to stab with his own letter opener because he'd planned to assault her. "She had Harlan and Betsy to guide her. Just like you do."

"And you," Emma said loyally. "You're the reason Tiff and I are safe now."

That made him warm inside. "You just made my day, Em. Let's see if this girl can give us any information on Mr. Neckbeard, and maybe we can make Kit's day."

Emma was on her feet in a second. "She's in the common room."

"If she doesn't want to talk to me, we aren't going to force her to," Sam warned.

"I know. But maybe she will."

Sam followed Emma into the New Horizons common room, a cozy space with murals on the walls painted by the teens. There was a TV with video games, a small library, and an area for arts and crafts. Sam was always surprised at how many teens he found painting or drawing in the craft corner.

This room was the heart of New Horizons.

The teens watched as Sam entered. He knew most of them, but there were a few girls in the conversation pit who he didn't recognize.

One of them, a sharp-edged girl of about sixteen, rose slowly when she saw them coming. "You narced on us," she hissed to Emma.

For a moment Emma cowered, but then she held herself tall. "I did not. That's not why he's here."

The girl crossed her arms over her chest in a gesture of defiance, but Sam saw the scared kid beneath. "I'm Dr. Reeves, but everyone calls me Dr. Sam."

"The shrink," the girl said, clearly unimpressed.

"Guilty as charged," Sam said lightly. "I'm not here to get anyone in trouble. I'm hoping you can help me."

"How?" the girl said, tensed in suspicion.

"Emma heard you warn the other girls about a guy with a neckbeard."

The girl gave Emma a narrow-eyed sneer. "You did narc."

Sam held up his hands. "No, Emma was helping me with a case I'm working on."

The girl's sneer softened to a scowl. "What case? Are you a *cop*?" She said the word like others might say "serial killer."

"No, but I work with cops. I'm a police psychologist. Some people call me a profiler."

"Yeah?" The girl tried not to look interested, but there was a gleam in her eye.

"Yeah. So, there's this guy who we're looking for. He's got a neckbeard, just like you saw."

"Lots of dudes have neckbeards," the girl said dismissively.

"True, and the guy you saw may have no relation to the guy I'm looking for. But . . . what if he does? What if you could help us crack a case?"

The girl tilted her head, watching him. "What do I have to do?"

"Can you describe him for me?"

She sighed long-sufferingly. "He has a neckbeard."

"I got that part. Is he tall, short? Fat or thin? Did he have tattoos?"

The girl's face crunched as she considered. "He was totally average."

Sam's flicker of hope grew. "How did he sound?"

"Deep voice. Like . . ." She pursed her lips. "Almost like Darth Vader but without the . . . you know." She exaggerated breathing in and out.

"Oh, oh," one of the other girls said. "Like Simba's father in *The Lion King*. That was the same actor."

"Yeah," the first girl grudgingly agreed. "Like that."

"James Earl Jones," a third girl said. "That's the actor's name."

"Then that's what he sounded like," the first girl said.

"Can you tell me your name?" Sam asked. "Doesn't have to be a real one. But it would be nice if it were."

"Why?" The girl went back to being suspicious.

Emma giggled. "The night we met Dr. Sam and Kit—that's his girlfriend—Tiffany thought they were sus. She said our names were Jane and Janey."

The first girl guffawed, then slapped a hand over her mouth, looking appalled that she'd laughed.

Sam's lips twitched, both from the memory and the thought of Kit's face if she'd heard Emma calling her Sam's girlfriend. If Sam had his way, that would be true, but Kit wasn't ready for that step yet. "It took Tiffany a bit of time to trust me with their real names. I had a feeling they weren't really Jane and Janey."

"Dawn," the first girl said. "I'm Dawn."

Sam smiled at her. "Hi, Dawn. I appreciate you talking to me."

Dawn shrugged as if Sam's appreciation meant nothing, but she was standing a little taller than she had before. "Whatever."

"So this guy is average, but his voice is deep. Any tats?"

"Didn't see any."

"Eyes?"

"He had two."

Sam let himself laugh at that. "Good for him."

Dawn's lips curved, just a little. Then she scowled some more. Kit would like this girl, Sam thought.

"He has a rash, I think," one of the other girls offered. "I'm Amy," she added shyly.

"Hi, Amy. Why do you think he has a rash? Did you see one?"

"No, but he, like, did this. A couple of times while he was talking prices with us." Amy pushed two fingers under the cuff of her long-sleeved shirt and rubbed her wrist. Then she tugged her sleeve into place. "That's why I didn't get into his car, honestly. I didn't want to get a rash."

"When did you see him?" Sam asked.

"Two weeks ago," Dawn said.

"About that," Amy agreed. "He was on the corner a few blocks from the high school in El Cajon."

"That's really helpful," Sam said, taking out his phone. He jotted notes to himself, then looked up to find the girls watching him. "Just taking notes. I'm old, y'know."

"You kind of are," Dawn said, her sympathy clearly a sham. There was also challenge in her eyes. She was trying to see if she could provoke his temper.

Sam chuckled. "I can't argue against facts. Did you see what he was driving?"

Let it be a tan Chevy Suburban.

"Big car," Dawn said thoughtfully.

"An SUV," Amy corrected. "Like a tan color."

Yes! Neckbeard's Suburban was tan-colored. Sam wanted to fist-pump the air, but then Amy swallowed and tears filled her eyes. "One of our group got into the SUV with him and didn't come back."

Sam's heart squeezed painfully. "I'm so sorry, Amy. Who was it?"

"Daniella," Amy said. "She hadn't been with us long. Her not coming back scared the shit out of us. It was why we came here."

Dawn nodded. "She was really young. Thirteen, fourteen."

And you're oh so old at what . . . sixteen? Sam's heart squeezed again. "Dammit," he muttered. "I'm glad you're here, all of you. But I'm sorry your friend didn't come back."

"Is she dead?" Amy whispered.

Sam thought of the bodies he'd seen, their throats slit. But this might not be the same Neckbeard. "I don't know. But I will ask my friends in SDPD to check this out."

Dawn scoffed. "Like that'll work. Nobody cares about us, especially not cops."

"Kit does," Emma said, her loyalty returning with a vengeance. "She's a cop. Her parents are our foster parents."

"Good for you," Dawn said sarcastically. "So some cop with a heart of gold is trying to help the runaways. Big deal."

"She was a runaway, too," Emma said. "Grew up in foster care. She ended up with the McKittricks and now she's got a career. She *cares.* They all *care.*" Her voice broke. "The McKittricks saved my life. Tiffany's and Rita's, too. They're adopting

Rita. They adopted Kit. And, maybe someday, they'll adopt Tiff and me, too."

Dawn's eyes shifted from sarcasm to a childish vulnerability laced with a hopelessness that broke Sam's already battered heart. "Good for you," Dawn said huskily. "I mean, really."

Sam had to help these kids. He wondered if Harlan and Betsy could handle a few more. If they couldn't, he'd find someone else. A good place for Dawn, Amy, and the third girl, who watched them with wide eyes.

Dawn cleared her throat and tossed her hair back. "Anyway, that's all we know. Hope it helps."

"Me too." He wanted to ask them if they'd come to SDPD and sit down with a sketch artist, but he knew that would send them running. "If I get some pictures of this guy, maybe some video, can you have a look? Maybe tell me if he looks familiar? Sometimes seeing a person move triggers a memory."

Dawn shrugged. "Sure. Whatever."

"You'll stay here tonight?" Sam pressed. "Don't go back on the street?"

Another shrug. "It's cold out. We get a hot meal here and a clean bed. We'll stay another night."

Relief swamped him, partly because he did need their help but mostly because they wouldn't be on the street tonight. "Thank you." He turned to Emma. "And thank you."

Emma's smile was brilliant. "You're welcome."

Sam started for the door. "I'm going to go now. I'll be back as soon as I can."

"Tell Kit I said hi," Emma singsonged with a giggle.

"I will."

After cleaning his desk and locking his office, Sam headed to his car and placed a call to Harlan McKittrick.

"Sam. Is everything okay?"

"Yes, sir, everything's fine. How are you? What did your doctor say about your little heart blip yesterday?"

"My EKG was one hundred percent fine and you can ask Akiko if you don't believe me. I even brought a copy of the results to Betsy because I knew she was scared. I'm fine. What's really on your mind, Sam?"

Just ask. The worst he can say is no. "Look, I know you've got three fosters right now, but I was wondering if you had room for a few more."

There was a creak in the background, like Harlan had sat in a chair. "Talk to me."

CHAPTER EIGHTEEN

Stunning view, isn't it?" Connor murmured as he approached Duncan Tindall's house.

The mansions were large and bright white against the blue sky, all with twenty-million-dollar views of the Pacific Ocean. Kit would never understand how much money the rich spent on real estate.

"It really is." Kit's phone buzzed in her pocket, distracting her from the view. "It's the boss." She glanced behind them at the young woman who was quietly crying. Kennedy Shoemaker had given them a detailed statement with approximate dates of her father's abuse in the early years, but specific dates starting about three years before. They couldn't have asked for much more. They had an arrest warrant for Peter Shoemaker in their hands. It was for rape, but Kit hoped they'd found Neckbeard, too.

Why else kill Aylene Tindall, if not to shut her up?

Kit answered Navarro's call but didn't put the phone on speaker. "Yes, boss?"

"We have another body."

Kit's heart sank. "Who?"

"Bert Ramsey's wife."

Well, shit. That blew Shoemaker being Neckbeard out of the water.

Kit opened her mouth and closed it again, trying to come up with something to say that wouldn't alarm their passenger. "When?" she finally asked.

"We found her a half hour ago. She's been dead eight hours, give or take an hour or two."

It hadn't been just Peter Shoemaker's wife. And Shoemaker couldn't have killed Ramsey's wife. He'd been in court up until six hours ago. They'd seen him arriving at his home. And he had truly appeared to be in shock when they'd told him that Aylene was dead. "And the protection detail?"

Dammit. Kennedy had just lifted her head and was watching Kit, her expression intense. *Girl's too damn smart.*

"They checked the house when she didn't answer the door, but didn't find her. Her body was found by Bert Ramsey when he got home from his arraignment. She'd been hidden in the pool, under a tarp."

"Spray paint?" Kit asked.

"Why are you talking in half sentences?" Navarro asked, then caught on. "Oh. You have Kennedy Shoemaker in the car. Got it. Yes, the security cameras were all spray-painted over. One camera caught a guy in a hoodie wearing a Halloween hockey mask, just like with Munro and Shelley Porter at the body shop. I'll let you know when I have more information."

"Can you tell Connor what you told me?"

"Sure."

Kit handed Connor her phone and waited. Connor's jaw clenched as he listened, and then he nodded. "Got it. Thank you, sir."

Kit took her phone back, told Navarro they'd let him know when they were headed in with Shoemaker in custody for rape, then ended the call.

"What was that about?" Kennedy asked. "Someone else is dead?"

Kit considered lying but decided against it. She wanted Kennedy to trust her. "Yes, but I can't divulge details. We have to notify families first."

"Oh. I guess that makes sense. How do you do this every day? Deal with people like my mom getting murdered?"

Kit twisted around in her seat so that she could see the young woman. "It's not easy, but when we solve a case, when we get justice for the dead, it's worth it."

Kennedy nodded, then cleared her throat. "I tried to record him."

Kit twisted around again. "Your father?"

Another nod. "He took my phone at night. Told my mom it was because I was texting too late and my grades were suffering. He said he told all the parents at his school to take their kids' phones at bedtime. Mom bought his bullshit. She always bought whatever he was selling."

Kit had wondered why a smart girl like Kennedy hadn't tried to get proof of the abuse by her father. Now she knew. "He just didn't want you to be able to reach out to anyone or to get evidence against him. Abusers isolate you."

"I know. I've read all about it. He did that to my mom. She hardly ever left the house unless she was going to see my grandparents. She told them that she was having lunch with friends or going to the club, but she hardly ever did."

"Did your father go to the country club?"

"Oh yeah. He loved it there. I don't know why. He took me once and I hated it. I didn't know if they were like my father or not."

Maybe not sexual abusers, but many of the other country club members had been hiding secrets, just like Peter Shoemaker. And Peter had lied about that, too. He'd said he hated going to the club, that the members paid attention to his wife but not to him.

"Do you want us to wait with you while you tell your grandparents about your father?" Connor asked. "We can do that. We can put your father in cuffs and have the officer on duty outside keep him in the cruiser until you're ready for us to go. Or if you're more comfortable with just Detective McKittrick, I can wait outside with your father."

"Really?" In that moment Kennedy sounded so young. "You won't be mad?"

"Not at all," Connor said gently. "This is a very personal story and I get that you'd be more comfortable with a woman listening."

"It's not that. Well, yes, it is that," Kennedy said. "But not mostly. I'm worried my father will get away. I'd be more comfortable if one of you was watching him."

"I'll be happy to do that," Connor assured her.

They parked behind the police cruiser and waved to the officers sitting inside. The house was immense and, like the Shoemakers' house, backed up to the bluff. Kit's eyes widened. To the *very edge* of the bluff.

"Wow, that's close to the edge," Kit murmured. "Don't the houses usually sit back a bit?"

"Normally, yes, and this one probably did at one time, but erosion happens."

"It's a little scary during windstorms," Kennedy said, "but otherwise we just have a great view." She blew out a quiet breath. "I guess I'll be staying here from now on when I come home."

The door opened and a woman in her sixties rushed outside as the three of them got out of the car. Her hair was falling from its bun and her eyes, like Kennedy's, were red and swollen. This, Kit thought, would be Aylene's mother.

"Kennedy Shoemaker! *Where* have you *been*? Your grandfather and I have been worried sick. You just . . . *disappeared*."

Kennedy winced. "I'm sorry, Nana. I told Grandad's assistant that I was coming straight home when she put me in the cab, but I needed to stop at the police station first. I didn't realize it would take so long."

Mrs. Tindall gave Kit and Connor disapproving looks. "Why are you harassing my granddaughter? And on a day like this?"

"No, Nana," Kennedy protested. "I went to them. We need to talk."

Mrs. Tindall put her arm around her granddaughter's shoulders. "I know, baby. It's a horrible day."

"Um . . . Nana? I think it's going to get worse before it gets better."

Mrs. Tindall stopped abruptly. "What's going on, child?" She looked over at Kit and Connor. "You've delivered her. Thank you. Now, please leave. We're grieving."

Kit hadn't expected to be so summarily dismissed. "We can't leave just yet, ma'am. We need to speak with your son-in-law."

Mrs. Tindall shot them another, even more disapproving look. "He's asleep. Our doctor had to give him a sedative. You may return when he wakes up."

"Mrs. Tindall," Connor said authoritatively. "This is not a courtesy call. We must speak to your son-in-law. Go wake him up. Now, please."

Mrs. Tindall looked like she'd tell Connor off, but her granddaughter interceded. "Please, Nana. It's important. I'll explain. And I'd like Detective McKittrick to stay with me for a few minutes."

Kit hoped that was all it would take. The woman's husband was far more approachable and less . . . rich sounding.

"Then come in," Mrs. Tindall said. "I'll go wake Pete."

Kennedy's jaw clenched. "Yes. Please do that." She led them into the living room, where she settled on a sofa, patting the seat beside her. "Detective McKittrick?"

Kit took the place beside her and nearly moaned at the feel of the buttery soft leather against her skin. Okay, now *this* was a rich person's toy that she could appreciate. She was going to have to fight not to curl up and take a nap.

"Pete?" Mrs. Tindall's voice carried from upstairs. "Pete? Peter? Where are you?"

"Shit," Connor muttered, then took the stairs at a run. A few minutes later, he was back, fury snapping in his eyes. "He's not here."

Mrs. Tindall followed at a much slower pace, wringing her hands. "Where could he have gone? That poor boy. He's devastated right now and may be wandering all alone somewhere. He was sedated. He might not even know where he is. He sleepwalks sometimes."

Kennedy's face was ashen. "That's how he explained to my mother when she caught him wandering the hall near my bedroom. He said he was sleepwalking because he took Ambien. She believed him. He never took the pills. He just pretended to."

Kit squeezed Kennedy's hand. "We'll find him. Try to breathe."

She wished Sam were there. He was so much better at getting people to breathe when they were freaking out. "Mrs. Tindall, did Mr. Shoemaker know Kennedy was coming home?"

"Yes, of course. We told him that we sent the company jet for her."

"I told him I'd tell," Kennedy whispered. "I told him I'd tell if anything ever happened to Mom, because it wouldn't matter anymore."

Which was why he couldn't stay. With his wife dead, there was nothing keeping Kennedy quiet. "Stay here, honey," Kit said. "I'll be right back."

She followed Connor outside, ignoring Mrs. Tindall's sputtered outrage.

"How could he have escaped?" Kit asked Connor. "The back of the house butts up right against the bluff. That's a two-hundred-foot drop."

"Closer to three hundred," Connor muttered, motioning for the officers to come talk to them.

The uniformed officers got out of the car. "We've been here the whole time," one of them said. "Nobody left."

"Well, he's fucking *gone*," Connor snapped. "How could you have lost him?"

"We didn't," the other officer insisted.

"Unless he can fly, he had to come out this way," Kit said logically.

"He rappels," Kennedy called from the doorway. "Check the back for a rope."

And, sure enough, there was a rope hanging from one of the bedroom windows.

"I don't understand any of this," Mrs. Tindall said imperiously once they'd regrouped in the living room. "What is going on?"

Duncan Tindall had joined them, sitting next to his wife on a love seat. "Yes, Detectives, what is the meaning of this? We are having a family crisis here and Pete's missing. What are you doing to find him?"

"Trust me, sir," Kit said. "We will find him. We posted a BOLO for him—that's 'be on the lookout,'" she added when Mrs. Tindall looked confused. "He took off on foot after rappelling down the cliff behind your house. Where could he have climbed back up to street level?"

Unless he'd had access to a boat. *Dammit. He could be anywhere.*

"The nearest trail to the top is about a mile down the beach," Duncan said. "Why would he do that? Go out through the window?"

"It's what he does," Kennedy said woodenly. "It's how he'd get past Mom's security system. She didn't monitor the back because she believed it was inaccessible."

"He's escaped like this before?" Kit asked.

Kennedy nodded. "He thinks it's fun. Exhilarating, he says." Tears filled her eyes. "He's supposed to go to jail."

"And he will," Kit murmured. "Did your mom know about his rappelling?"

"I don't know. If she did, I don't think she knew he was doing it at our house."

"Did he keep a rope with him?" Connor asked.

Kennedy shrugged. "He had a lot of camping equipment in the back of his car. Ropes and other things. He could have kept a harness, too."

"What is going on?" Duncan demanded. "What's this about rappelling? About escaping?"

Kit took Kennedy's hand. "It's time now, honey. Tell your grandparents."

Kennedy squeezed Kit's hand so hard that it hurt. "Nana, Grandad . . ." She trailed off, looking helplessly at Kit.

"You want me to start?" Kit asked, and Kennedy nodded. "Okay." She turned to the grandparents. "This may be difficult to believe, but I need you to listen to Kennedy. Women don't make claims like this for fun. This is serious. Kennedy's father has been sexually molesting her for years." Mrs. Tindall's mouth opened and she covered it with her hand. Mr. Tindall didn't blink, just stared at Kit. But they hadn't yelled yet, so she kept going. "She didn't tell her mother because her father convinced her not to. He told her that her mother wouldn't believe her and she wouldn't love her anymore."

"This can't be true," Duncan said, blustering. "There's some mistake."

Kennedy lurched to her feet, but she kept hold of Kit's hand. "You think I'm *lying*?"

"No, no." Duncan backpedaled. "Of course not, but Kennedy, surely you see that this is impossible. Your father loves you."

"My father started raping me when I was nine years old," Kennedy said coldly. "You believe me or you don't. I'm tired of keeping secrets for this family. You want proof? I'll call Dr. Mac-Namara at the clinic in El Cajon. He's got my records from the time I got chlamydia."

Mrs. Tindall gasped. "Your mother would have known!"

"Not that I got an STD. My father took me to a free clinic. Gave a fake name. Said if I told the doctor the truth, he'd tell my mother, who'd think I was a whore. I was twelve, Nana." She dropped back to the sofa, like a marionette whose strings had been cut. "Didn't you wonder why I always wanted to stay here when Mom was out of town? Didn't you wonder why I never had any dates?" Her voice was rising with each question. "Didn't you wonder why I never smiled?"

Duncan was pale. "Your mother said you were being treated for depression."

"Because that's what my father told her," Kennedy said wearily. "Every word Detective McKittrick said is true. That's why I went straight to the police station. The girls . . . I couldn't let it happen to them, too." She stiffened. "Where are they? Where are the girls?"

"Upstairs watching a movie with headphones on," Connor said. "They're here." He smiled at Kennedy. "They're safe."

Kennedy sagged, leaning into Kit's shoulder. "I couldn't let him hurt them."

Kit stroked Kennedy's hair. "I know." She met the grandparents' shocked gazes. "If you believe her, she can stay here. If you don't, I'll find a place she can stay while we investigate Peter Shoemaker for the rape of a minor."

"For the *repeated* rape of a minor," Connor said.

Mrs. Tindall burst into tears and ran from the room. Duncan appeared to be numb. "I can't believe it," he whispered, then seemed to realize what he'd said. "I believe you, Kennedy. You don't lie. You've never lied. But this . . . it's hard to accept."

"I know," Kennedy said sadly. "But it's true. My father is a monster and I hate him."

"That's why you insisted on going away to college," Duncan said, still talking as if he were in a dream. A nightmare. "Pete didn't want you to go. He asked me to talk you out of it. To forbid you. He said you were too wild to go away on your own, that you wouldn't take your medication and you'd become suicidal."

"I was suicidal for a while, before I went to college. I won't go back to him, Grandad. I won't."

"Okay," Duncan said. He looked at Kit. "What should we do?"

"Counseling to begin with," Kit said, giving Kennedy's hand

another squeeze. "Do you still have the name of the therapist I gave you, sir? She can help, both with the grief and the abuse. And . . . let Kennedy heal. She's already taken an enormous first step. Reporting your abuser is terrifying, sir. That's why it's so crucial that you believe her."

"I do. My wife does, too. She's just . . . this has been an awful day."

"I know," Kit said. "We're going to leave you now. Kennedy, why don't you say hi to your sisters. I think it'll make you feel better."

She went upstairs, giving Kit a grateful smile.

Kit turned to Duncan. "Who sleeps in that room where the rope is hanging from the window?"

"That was Aylene's room," he whispered, and his tears began to fall again. "He can't scale the side of the house if we remove the rope, right? Can he get back in?"

"We don't know," Connor said. "Call your security company. And change your alarm codes." Connor stood and Kit joined him. "We're sorry for your loss," Connor said quietly. "I know it's not much, but it's all we can say."

"I don't care what you have to *say*," Duncan said angrily. "Find Pete. That's all you have to *do*."

Kit followed Connor to the department car. They'd gotten Kennedy to her grandparents safely. Now they had to find her sonofabitch father.

"I wonder if he groomed kids who came to him as the assistant principal," Connor murmured as he started the engine.

"I thought of that," Kit said. Her cell buzzed and she checked the caller ID. "Navarro again."

"Maybe they found Shoemaker," Connor said hopefully.

"Your mouth, God's ears." Kit accepted the call and put

Navarro on speaker. "Here with Connor, sir. Did you find Shoe-maker?"

"No," Navarro said with disgust. "But I do have some good news. The team tracking the Suburban and the trailer has tracked them as far as the Descanso exit off the 8. They've checked extensively and the Suburban and trailer have not been seen east of Descanso. That's exit 40 off I-8, heading toward Julian. I want you to go to Descanso and start knocking on doors. Ask to see security footage taken by local businesses."

"On our way," Connor said. "We'll keep in contact."

Kit ended the call and mapped the route. "Let's do this."

San Diego PD, San Diego, California
Thursday, January 12, 7:45 p.m.

"It might not be the same guy," Navarro cautioned as he sat in Connor's desk chair and rolled himself over to where Sam sat at Kit's desk, staring at her monitor.

"I know, but I need to check." Sam signed into the department's server, careful not to touch any of the files stored on Kit's computer. He'd asked to use his own laptop—he'd even stopped by his apartment to get it after walking Siggy—but Navarro told him that he'd need special software to access the department server, and to use Kit's computer.

Navarro pointed at one of the files. "That's the recording that came from Ace Diamond's camera that he put at Jennifer's Body Shop. Thank the good Lord for jealous boyfriends."

"Yes, indeed."

"Haven't you seen this?"

"Not yet. Kit was going to show it to me and we kept getting pulled in other directions." Sam clicked on the video, wincing when Neckbeard tossed Shelley in the back of the Ford truck without a care. "Have you found the Ford yet?"

"Possibly. We found one yesterday that had been reported stolen. It's the same make, model, and color, so maybe it's the same truck."

"No fingerprints, I assume?"

"None that don't belong to the woman who reported it stolen. Who is seventy-five years old and about five feet five."

"The girls tonight said the guy they saw drove a big tan SUV."

"Promising," Navarro murmured.

Sam rewound the Ace Diamond video and watched it again. Then he saw it. "There." He froze the frame. "See how he tugs at his sleeves? The girls said he did that, too." He rewound and rewatched. "And there. He's scratching the inside of his wrist." It was a tiny movement, easily ignored if one wasn't looking for it. "It's the same guy."

"I hope so," Navarro said, frowning. "We can put surveillance at that street corner, in case he comes back looking for another young girl."

Sam was frowning, too. "I've seen someone do that recently. The sleeve-tugging thing. I'm trying to remember who. Damn, I hate it when I can't think." He needed to get some sleep.

"Wait," Navarro said, something odd in his tone. "Our murderer likes young girls?"

"The girls at New Horizons said the girl he took away was thirteen or fourteen, so yeah. Young."

Navarro grabbed the mouse from Sam's hand. "Sorry. We need to see something else."

Sam watched as Navarro found whatever he was looking for.

"Here," Navarro finally said. "This one."

Sam froze as the video started. It was one of the interviews Kit and Connor had done the evening before. "Peter Shoemaker?"

Whose wife had been murdered sometime between seven last night and seven this morning. Her throat had been slit. Kit had texted him shortly after discovering the woman's body.

"Yes. Kit and Connor went to pick him up this afternoon for the rape of a minor."

Sam's stomach rolled. "Who?"

"His daughter," Navarro said grimly, fast-forwarding the recording. "She came straight from college to tell us what he'd done. Started on her when she was only nine years old. She hadn't told before because she feared her mother's reaction."

"But now her mother's dead," Sam said quietly. "Let me guess. Other children in the home?"

"Got it in one. Twin girls, eight years old. Watch." Navarro hit play.

On the screen, Peter Shoemaker was putting on his jacket after Kit and Connor had left the room. He shook his shoulders, then tugged on his sleeves.

Right after scratching the inside of his wrist.

Peter Shoemaker was Neckbeard. Peter Shoemaker, who had killed seven people—Munro, Shelley Porter and her mother, Walter Grossman, Hugh Smith, Aylene Tindall, and Lila Ramsey.

"I missed that last night," Sam said numbly.

"We weren't looking for that last night. I need to call Kit and Connor."

"But . . ." Something wasn't right. "Bert Ramsey's wife was also murdered, but that was this morning. Wasn't Shoemaker still in jail then?"

Navarro paused, his finger hovering over Kit's name on his cell phone. "He was. Or at least he showed up in a taxi just as Kit and Connor were arriving to confirm his alibi with his wife, just after noon."

"His wife was his alibi, which can no longer be confirmed or denied," Sam said.

"Exactly. Wait." Navarro dialed another number, put the phone on speaker.

"Courthouse. Can I help you?"

"Yes, this is Lieutenant Navarro, Homicide Division. What time was Peter Shoemaker released today?"

"Let me check, Lieutenant."

They waited several minutes in a tense silence.

"Lieutenant?" the courthouse clerk finally said. "Peter Shoemaker was released on his own recognizance at ten thirty this morning."

"Thank you," Navarro told the clerk. "You've been very helpful." He ended the call and looked up the addresses of Bert Ramsey and Peter Shoemaker.

"Ramsey and Shoemaker only lived a few miles from each other," Sam said. "And Shoemaker was released early enough that he could have killed Ramsey's wife before returning to his own house in a taxi."

"The ME said Mrs. Ramsey hadn't been dead long. Yeah, Shoemaker had time."

"He killed Lila Ramsey so that his own wife's murder wouldn't stick out as unusual," Sam said, feeling pity for both women. "But weren't they supposed to have uniformed officers following the accused from the courthouse after they made bail?"

"They were." Navarro checked a list on his phone, then dialed another number, once again putting it on speaker. "Dispatch, please patch me through to Officer Damon Johnson." He waited, drumming his fingers on Kit's desk. "This is Lieutenant Navarro. You were assigned to follow Peter Shoemaker when he left the courthouse today."

There was a brief hesitation. "Yes, sir. We were. And we did, but he got a ride from his lawyer, who lost us. So we went right to his house and waited outside until he got home."

"You didn't put that in your report," Navarro said coldly.

"I'm . . . No, sir. We didn't. I'm sorry, sir."

"Yeah, me too," Navarro snapped. "Report to me at oh eight hundred tomorrow. Do not be late." He ended the call and muttered, "Bert Ramsey's wife is even sorrier that you didn't do your fucking jobs. I wonder if Shoemaker told his attorney to lose his tail. We're going to have to add him to the investigation."

"But you know where Peter Shoemaker is, right?" Sam asked. "Those officers are still guarding him, aren't they?"

"No. Shoemaker was gone when Kit and Connor went to pick him up for raping his daughter. He's been in the wind for hours now." He dialed Kit, then frowned. "Voice mail," he said.

Sam got an uneasy feeling. "A man who killed seven people is running around free?"

"Nine people," Navarro said grimly. "Marshall and Ashton finally found the guard who admitted Munro's killer into his neighborhood. He was with his girlfriend, at her house. They're both dead."

Sam swallowed bile. "Where are Kit and Sam now?"

Navarro checked the time. "Past Descanso by now."

"Why are they there?" Descanso was a town east of San Diego off Interstate 8, about an hour away.

"My team checking traffic cams found the tan Suburban pulling an unwrapped trailer. Last seen on the 8 just before the Descanso exit. Depending on how far Kit and Connor got, they might be hitting patchy cell service."

"They need to know that Neckbeard is Shoemaker," Sam said, lurching to his feet. "They don't know that he was out of court in time to kill Ramsey's wife. Let's go. Now."

Navarro had also risen but was frowning at him. "Stay here, Doc. This isn't your responsibility."

The hell it wasn't. Kit was his responsibility. "If you leave me here, I'll only follow you. Wouldn't it be better to know where I am?"

Navarro rolled his eyes. "You would follow me, wouldn't you? Then let's go. We'll take my car. We can use the flashing light."

Lake Cuyamaca, California
Thursday, January 12, 8:40 p.m.

"This feels pointless," Connor said. They'd been driving for a while and the sun had gone down. There were no streetlights along this stretch of road and Kit thought they might be searching for a needle in a haystack.

State Route 79, the road Navarro's analysts thought the Suburban had taken from I-8, ran through some truly beautiful countryside. But it was very rural, mostly state parkland and nature preserves.

"We're at least on the right track," she said, earning a sigh from Connor.

"I know. But it still feels like we're just throwing spaghetti at the wall."

That was fair.

They'd stopped in Descanso, asking if anyone had seen the tan Suburban pulling a trailer, and had gotten a lot of shaking heads. But one gas station owner had allowed them to view his security footage and they'd caught the Suburban pulling a plain, unpainted trailer on Wednesday evening of the week before.

That was the day that Brooks Munro had been abducted from his home, so they were on the right track. But the gas station's camera hadn't picked up the Suburban coming this way in the days since, so Kit didn't have much hope that they'd find their killer. At least not today.

She and Connor had decided to keep looking.

Kit had tried to call Navarro to let him know, but there was no cell signal, so she'd sent a text instead. That hadn't gone through, either.

The gas station owner had been charitable, offering them water and the use of his landline. Kit's call had gone to Navarro's voice mail, so she'd left a cryptic message, aware of the gas station owner's intense interest in her call.

He didn't seem like a bad sort, just super curious. And something of a gossip.

They'd been driving along the eastern edge of the Cleveland National Forest and were close to the town of Julian, where State Route 79 continued, another highway branching east.

"Well, at least now dumping the body in Anza-Borrego makes sense," Kit said. "At Julian, a new highway starts up. It's one of the routes into Anza-Borrego. From Julian it's only about an hour to where Sam and I found Munro's body."

"Then that does make sense. Kind of." Connor frowned. "But why drive an hour to dump Munro there when there's literally hundreds of square miles of forest close by?"

"I don't know. I can't help but wonder if he really wanted Munro's body to be discovered. At least at some point. Maybe not as quickly as we found it. It's bothered me that he didn't bury it."

"Sam thought the wind was too heavy for the killer to see that night."

"Maybe. But to just leave the body there? On top of the sand?" Kit shook her head. "He's been so methodical in everything. He planned to use Norton Landscaping as his entrée into Munro's neighborhood. He planned where to get the wrap done. He planned to use Shelley Porter's addiction against her, to tempt her with cash that he never intended to pay so that he could get the trailer. No money trail. He's killed seven people without leaving any forensic clues behind. Not a print, not a hair. He's been one step ahead of us all this time, but he doesn't bury the body?"

Connor sighed. "Well, now that you put it that way . . ."

"Also, I don't know how many people hike and camp in the forest this time of year, but this is a busy time for Anza-Borrego. The days aren't too hot and the nights aren't too cold. Tons of people go there at night to stargaze."

"So it's a tourist draw this time of year. Someone at some point would have noticed the body lying on top of the sand."

"Yeah. It was partially covered but still clearly recognizable as a body. But where he could have gone from here last Wednesday is anyone's guess."

"The next town is Julian. We can stop there and ask around. My parents have friends who own vacation homes up there, so if it's a bust, we can at least stop at one of their houses and use a phone. Maybe even internet."

"I don't want to go too far and possibly pass where he took the trailer."

Connor lifted his brows. "And how do we know how far is too far?"

Kit sighed. "I don't know. If I were bringing someone out to the middle of nowhere to torture and kill them, I wouldn't want to be too close to a town. People are nosy."

"They are. But unless you have a better idea . . ."

Kit sighed again. "Let's stop at the next gas station and check their security footage. If that's in Julian, so be it."

"But your gut says he won't be in Julian."

Kit shrugged one shoulder. "Not *in* Julian. The town doesn't even have eighteen hundred people. Too many people would remember him—either as Neckbeard or whatever he really looks like. But you're right. We don't actually have a choice. Too bad it's after hours. I bet a mail carrier would know who lives behind the trees."

The trees weren't thick, at least not around this side of the forest. But they were dense enough and the surrounding hills high enough to hide a trailer behind.

"I bet a lot of these areas don't get mail service," Connor said. "They have to use a PO box at the post office in Julian."

Kit shuddered. "That makes me nervous, being that far from civilization."

Connor chuckled. "Civilization is in the eye of the beholder. Many of the land parcels up near Julian are under a hundred acres. It's not like they have to travel for days in a horse-drawn buggy to get to a town."

"Still. No mail service?"

"If it makes you feel better, they probably still get UPS deliveries. Amazon too."

Kit turned to look at him. "Yeah? I wonder if we could talk to the local drivers. They might have seen something. They're on the road all the time."

"Not a bad idea. Let's figure it out when we get to Julian."

"Or we could take one of these driveways and ask a resident."

Connor winced. "I'd prefer not to get shot today. It's rural and isolated enough that residents don't get regular visitors, and it's dark outside, but what the hey. Let's give it a try." Connor flicked on the high beams. "Watch for driveways. They won't be obvious."

Kit kept her eyes peeled for any kind of break in the brush along the roadway. And then another set of headlights came toward them.

Kit crossed the fingers of both hands. "Be an Amazon truck. Please be an Amazon truck."

Connor laughed. "You're impossible."

"I'm an optimist." She watched as the vehicle drove past. "Turn around."

"Not an Amazon truck, Kit."

"But it *is* a tow truck. Maybe they've seen something. The driver might be on this road a lot."

Connor heaved a heavy sigh and pulled onto the sliver of a shoulder, doing a three-point-turn. "Better hope nobody comes along and T-bones us."

Kit crossed the fingers of both hands again, making Connor laugh once more.

They got turned around and pursued the tow truck. Connor flashed his high beams, but the truck didn't budge.

Finally, Kit put the flashing light on the roof of the car and the tow truck slowed to a stop.

Both Kit and Connor got out of the car hands up to show that they weren't armed. Their guns were holstered.

The driver rolled down his window. "What's the problem?" he asked gruffly. "You need assistance?"

"No," Kit said. "Or at least we don't need a tow. I'm Detective McKittrick and this is Detective Robinson. We're with San Diego PD."

The driver gave them a long, assessing look. "Kind of far from home."

"A bit," Kit agreed. "We're looking for a specific vehicle that may have come this way last week."

The tow truck driver gave them an incredulous look, like they were insane but he wasn't about to say so. "Which vehicle?"

"A tan Chevy Suburban," Connor said. "He was pulling a trailer."

He took out his phone and showed the driver the photo he'd taken of the gas station owner's feed.

The driver shook his head. "Haven't seen the trailer, but there's a Suburban driving this road sometimes. Usually on the weekends. He had a flat once and I changed his tire."

"What did he look like?" she asked.

"Average, I guess. Except for his beard. Looked like Bigfoot. Nice fella, though. Tipped me big for changing his tire and paid cash for my spare. He didn't have one with him."

"Do you know where he lives?" Kit asked, trying not to hold her breath.

"Nope." The driver scratched the back of his head. "Or maybe . . ." He thought some more, then shrugged. "It was along this road somewhere. Between here and Julian." He squinted out his windshield. "I followed him for a while, just to make sure he was okay. He pulled over, waved me to go on. I guess he was nervous about a stranger following him."

"Then how do you know it was between here and Julian?" Connor asked.

"Because I got another call for a tow and had to turn around. Never passed him. I'd say he pulled into one of these driveways within no more than five miles from here. If that."

"Thank you," Kit said. "We appreciate it." She gave him one of her business cards and Connor did the same. "If you think of anything else, please let us know."

The driver nodded soberly. "I will."

"Thank you." Kit had to force herself not to dance a jig. "Have a good evening."

She waited until she and Connor were back in the car before gloating. "Optimism for the win!"

Connor laughed, turned the car around, and started driving again. "Keep crossing your fingers. It seems to be working."

CHAPTER NINETEEN

This isn't creepy as fuck," Connor said sarcastically, because it was, indeed, creepy as fuck out here in the woods.

They'd turned into three driveways searching for the Suburban. That the trailer might still be with it was a long shot, but Kit was going to remain optimistic.

And it had finally paid off. The fourth driveway was unmarked, without even a signpost bearing an address. The driveway itself was over a mile long, winding through trees that weren't dense enough to be a forest, but still dense enough to create a feel of absolute darkness.

A light fog had crept in, not as a bank but as sinewy fingers twisting through the trees. Shadows seemed to lurk on the edges of the dirt driveway, and even their high beams only allowed them to see a few feet in front of them.

Anything could be out there. Or anyone.

Creepy as fuck.

And they were there in the middle of nowhere with no cell phone signal. She checked her phone again. Still nothing.

"Oh my God," Connor whispered, slowing the car to a stop.

Because illuminated in their headlights was the trailer. There was no sign of the Suburban. About fifty feet away sat a small cabin, maybe five or six hundred square feet and rustic. It was dark, the whole area seeming to be abandoned.

"We should have brought a sat phone," Kit muttered. "We need to call for backup."

"Let's take a quick look around and then head into Julian. We can get help from the sheriff's office there." Connor drew his weapon, grabbed a Maglite, and got out of the car. "If he is here, he now knows we're here, too. I don't want him to get away."

On high alert, Kit followed Connor to the trailer.

"Fucker," Connor breathed as he shined the light into the empty trailer.

Kit grimaced at the sight of the blood. It was dried and brown and covered the floor, the walls, and even the trailer's ceiling. She swallowed hard. There was an old table in the middle of the trailer with a vise at its head and restraints at the four corners. She thought of the dents in Munro's skull. Blood covered the table as well.

There were fingers and toes littering the floor, like garbage. This was where Brooks Munro had been tortured.

"Two sets of tire tracks," Connor said, sweeping the trailer's floor beneath the table with the light. "There was a car in here before the table was brought in. Those tire tracks are about the width of a Ferrari. I wonder if it's here. Behind the cabin, maybe."

"We can come back and check," Kit said. "One of us can stand on the main road, while the other goes to Julian, just in case he's here and tries to run. But I don't want to be standing here. We've got no cell signal and there's no cover."

"Yeah," Connor agreed, but he did one more sweep of the interior. "There's also a set of single tire tracks. He had a motorcycle in here. And Sam's rehab contact had said Neckbeard was holding a motorcycle helmet."

"Connor, let's go. Now." Kit turned for the car, hoping he'd follow. She understood Connor's desire to catch Neckbeard—whoever he was. But being here without backup was just plain stupid.

Reluctantly, Connor stepped back from the trailer. "We need to clear the cabin."

"We need backup." Kit's instincts were firing on all cylinders.

He frowned at her. "You're normally the one to go charging inside."

Yes, she was. Was she growing soft?

Get out of here.

The voice in her head would not be silenced. "I'll charge inside once I have backup. Let's go."

She was two feet from the car door when the first shot rang out, followed by a loud thump and a grunt of pain. Immediately she dropped into a crouch. A second shot was followed by Connor's vicious, breathless curse.

"Connor?" she called, trying to stay calm.

For a moment there was no reply. "I'm . . . hit," he called back, the sound of his breathing between words louder than the words themselves.

Kit's heart dropped into her stomach. "Shit, shit, shit." She crawled around the front of their car to where Connor lay flat on the ground staring up at the sky, one hand pressed to his upper thigh. The other hand still clutched his service weapon.

She looked around and saw no one. The shooter—presumably Neckbeard—was somewhere behind the tree line. She pulled Connor between the back of the trailer and the front of their car, then leaned over him. "How bad?"

"First shot . . . here." He let go of his leg to touch his chest, leaving bloody fingerprints on his white shirt. "Vest stopped the bullet. But it hurts to breathe."

Not good. The vest kept the bullet from piercing the skin, but it didn't stop the bullet from breaking ribs or even puncturing a lung.

"How bad is the leg?" She pulled a pair of gloves from her jacket pocket and tugged them on. Her pocketknife was next. She closed Connor's fingers around the Maglite. "Hold the light. I need to see." She looked up and around, expecting to see the killer standing over them with his rifle pointed at their heads. But they were alone in the three-by-six-foot space.

As gently as she could, she cut the fabric away from Connor's thigh. The fabric was already heavily wet with blood.

"It's bad," Connor gritted out. "Bleeding a lot."

"I think he hit an artery. I need to get you out of here." She pulled her belt from her pants and slid it under his leg, fastening and tightening it. The makeshift tourniquet was the best she could do. "Can you walk?"

Connor tried to push himself up, his face contorting in pain. "Can't even stand."

"Then I'll drag you." She hooked her arms under his and dragged him to the edge of their safe zone. She stopped at the last minute, turning her head to search for the shooter.

Another bullet whizzed past her ear, and she dropped to cover Connor's body with her own. "Motherfucker," she snarled.

If she hadn't stopped to look, that bullet would have killed her.

"Just go," Connor said, clenching his teeth. "He's over by the cabin. Crouch behind the car and run into the woods. It's less than a mile to the main road."

"Not leaving you."

Think, Kit. She needed to get Neckbeard away from the cabin, needed a clear sight line. Then she could take him down.

"You need to run, Neckbeard!" she yelled. "Did you think we came without backup? You have about two minutes before the road is blocked in both directions."

How he'd get away was unclear, unless he had the motorcycle— or the Ferrari or the Suburban—stashed around the back of his cabin.

"Liar!" a voice called back, gravelly and deep. Like Simon Daly said the deliveryman who'd inquired about his wife had sounded.

"I heard you say you needed backup," he added. "Don't lie to me."

Shit.

Kit leaned down to whisper in Connor's ear. "I'm going around the trailer, try to draw him out. If he stays in that cabin, we're sitting ducks." And no one was coming to help them. "Stay here."

"Help me sit up," he whispered back. "I want to be able to see him if he comes through the cabin door. I can cover you from here."

Kit helped him sit, wincing at the faces he made. But he didn't cry out or moan. He was quiet in his pain.

Kit got down on the ground, propelling herself around the trailer with her elbows. It helped that the ground was wet. The slick mud eased her way.

When she got to the front of the trailer, she took a minute to breathe. *In and out.* That she could hear the words in Sam's voice gave her a little comfort.

"You might as well run while you can," she shouted. "We

actually do have backup on the way. I called my lieutenant, told him exactly where we were going. Lots of people saw us coming this way, so there will be a shit ton of cops here soon. Considering you've killed a shit ton of people, I'd run if I were you."

"Throw your gun away," Neckbeard yelled back. "Both of you. Then we'll talk."

Kit inched her way to the front edge of the trailer. She could see the cabin from here. The front door was open, but all she could see was blackness. "Not gonna happen, Mr. Neckbeard. Come on out and I won't kill you."

Neckbeard laughed. "You won't be killing me," he said, his voice no longer deep and gravelly. It was melodious, almost like a song. "You'll be too dead."

Kit wondered if there really were two men. Multiple hands. "Who's your friend?"

"And they say you're so smart."

A glimmer of movement from the cabin caught Kit's eye. Not from the front door where the man's voice was coming from, but from the window on the far left. A light had been turned on, throwing a figure into silhouette.

Kit blinked in shock. It looked like a girl, and she was trying to open the window. She pushed and pulled, finally pressing her face to the glass in a silent cry for help before disappearing from the window.

The light in the window went out.

Shit, shit, shit.

He had a hostage. The girl couldn't be more than twelve or thirteen.

And then Kit realized.

Peter Shoemaker.

Shoemaker had raped his daughter from the time she was

nine years old. Kit didn't know who the girl in the window was, but it made sense that the man would go after other girls now that Kennedy had left the home. "Shoemaker, it's over. I've talked to Kennedy. I know what Munro was really blackmailing you over."

There was a beat of silence. "You don't know anything."

It was a third voice, neither deep nor melodious. He sounded like the assistant principal they'd met the night before.

Kit ran through the facts in her mind. She'd questioned Shoemaker as the killer until Bert Ramsey's wife turned up dead. Shoemaker would have been in court at the time of Mrs. Ramsey's murder.

He could still have an accomplice. Or . . .

Or he hadn't been in court at the time. He'd arrived in a taxi just after Kit and Connor had stopped at his house to interview Aylene. Conveniently timed. And it had also been convenient that no one could get in to discover his wife's body until he'd arrived to look shocked.

Did he think we wouldn't look at what time he was released from court?

He probably had thought so, because they *hadn't* double-checked. They'd accepted his arrival at face value.

"You shouldn't have run away, Peter," Kit called. "If you'd stayed at your in-laws' house, the worst you would have been charged with is sexual assault of a minor. Now we've got you on seven murders."

"Nine," he shouted. "And it's going to be eleven when I'm done with you two."

"I don't think so. The longer we stand off, the more time my boss has to get here. I really did call him not too long ago and told him where we were searching."

"You didn't call him. No cell signal. I heard you say so."

"I called him from a gas station. Used their landline. You're trapped."

"So are you." The front door slammed, leaving them in silence, the only sound the rain now falling on the trees.

Kit watched the cabin, squinting into the darkness. He might come out the back, but she should see him approach.

And she did, but not until it was too late. A figure dressed in black slunk around the rear of the cabin. Kit fired twice but didn't think she'd hit him.

She ran back to where Connor sat, now shirtless. He was still sitting up, one hand clutching his gun, the other pressing his shirt to his wound.

"If you don't bleed out, you'll catch pneumonia," Kit muttered.

"How'd you know it was Shoemaker?"

"He's got a young girl in there. I saw her through the window. You can't see from here. I think our best bet is to get into the car and drive like hell. If he's in the woods next to the cabin, he can't get a good shot if we stay on the driver's side of our car."

"We're letting him go? No way in hell. He's killed *nine people*, Kit. We can't let him kill any more."

"I won't let you be the tenth."

Connor closed his eyes. "Fucking hell. You're so goddamned stubborn."

"Stop arguing. We're wasting time. Come on." She hooked her arms under his and started dragging him out of their little safe zone. Which wouldn't be safe if Shoemaker was walking around with a goddamned rifle.

The roar of a starting engine cut through the air and Kit froze where she crouched, her breath sawing in and out of her lungs because Connor really did weigh a ton.

A moment later, the Chevy Suburban they'd been hunting hurtled around the cabin, passing the trailer and their department car. Kit flung herself over Connor, expecting more bullets to fly.

But none came. Instead, the Suburban raced down the driveway and out of sight.

"He's gone," Connor fumed. "We let him get away."

"You're bleeding out," Kit snapped, but her heart was still in her throat. "I need to check on the girl, to see if she's still there. If he took her, we might never find her."

"Then go, goddammit."

"I will, but first I'm going to get you into the car." She dragged him to the rear door on the driver's side, helped by him pushing with his uninjured leg. She repositioned her hold, putting his arm over her shoulder. "Now up. Use your good leg to boost yourself."

Connor did what she asked and was finally lying on the back seat, his brow covered in sweat. He was pale, his skin clammy.

He'd lost a lot of blood and the clock was ticking. She needed to get him to a hospital or . . .

No. She wasn't going to think about that. Kit eased his legs out the way of the back door and closed it.

Crouching low, Kit slid behind the wheel, her gun still in her hand. She was going to drive them right up to the cabin and then check on the girl.

But she froze when more shots cracked the air. The car rocked as three additional bullets hit it. Two shots later and the car listed to the passenger side.

Two of their tires were gone.

Shoemaker had come back.

She wondered how many bullets he had in his magazine. Could be ten, could be a hundred. Either way, she cursed herself for not knowing that Peter Shoemaker was a marksman.

She'd been snowed by his "I'm just an assistant principal"

persona and now they were trapped. No, not trapped. She'd get them out of here.

More shots to the back of the car had her cursing.

He was moving again. She'd taken too long. She put the car in reverse and gently pressed the gas, her head only high enough to see over the steering wheel. If they got stuck in that mud they really would be trapped.

Another shot hit the driver's window and it spiderwebbed, the bullet leaving a hole. Stopping the car, Kit ducked her head, knowing she'd never navigate that winding driveway if she couldn't see. Especially with two flat tires.

Another bullet hit the window, lower this time. If she hadn't ducked, she'd be dead.

The window wouldn't take a third hit.

But she wasn't going to die. Nor was Connor. Not today at least.

"You okay, Connor?"

"Yeah." It was barely a whisper.

"Good. I'll be back."

She was going after Peter Shoemaker.

Kit wasn't sure if Connor had lost consciousness or he knew it was pointless to argue, because he said nothing as she maneuvered over the center console to the passenger side and slid out that door. She crawled back into that sweet spot between their car and the trailer before poking her head up to see where he'd gone.

Then froze once more at the feel of cold steel against the side of her head. A handgun. He was armed with more than one weapon.

"Throw your gun away, Detective," Peter Shoemaker said. "And stand up."

Fucking hell.

Outskirts of Julian, California
Thursday, January 12, 8:45 p.m.

"They've stopped," Sam said, staring at his sat phone. Navarro had told him how to track the GPS on Kit and Connor's department vehicle through the SDPD server, and Sam had never been so relieved to see a little blue dot on a screen.

They'd watched Kit's car meander up State Route 79, stopping for ten minutes here, fifteen minutes there.

Then the two detectives had stopped, turned around, stopped again, then turned back around. That had been twenty minutes ago.

Since then, the two detectives appeared to have been checking driveways. They'd gone up and down three driveways before coming to the fourth. It was a much longer driveway than the others.

"Thank God you brought the sat phone," Navarro said. "I haven't had a signal in miles."

"I hike the deserts, often alone. Just me and Siggy. A lot of the places we go don't get good cell coverage at all. Pays to have a sat phone in your gear."

Gear he'd grabbed from the back of his RAV4 as he and Navarro had hurried to Navarro's department vehicle. He also had water, power bars, a headlamp, and the night-vision goggles his parents had given him for Christmas. He never figured he'd use them, but his mother had made him promise to include them in his backpack.

Now he was glad he had them with him. Just in case.

"I'm sure they're fine," Navarro said. "This could be just a nice drive into the countryside. But I don't like that we haven't heard anything since Kit left that message."

Sam didn't, either.

Kit had called Navarro from a gas station, leaving him a voice mail that they'd seen the tan Chevy Suburban pulling a trailer on a security camera feed. The trailer had passed by on Wednesday night, about two hours after Munro had been abducted.

Since then, neither Sam nor Navarro had heard anything.

Sam had a bad feeling about this situation, but he usually did when he thought Kit was in danger. *She can take care of herself. She always does.*

"Have they left that property yet?" Navarro asked.

"No. They've been there for two minutes now. In all the other driveways, they immediately turned around."

"They might have found something, then. Can you call the sheriff's office in Julian? We might need backup."

Sam dialed the number and put it on speaker.

"San Diego County Sheriff's Office," a woman said. "How can I direct your call?"

"This is Lieutenant Navarro, San Diego Homicide. We've got two detectives searching for a suspect's vehicle along State Route 79. A colleague and I are en route to provide support. Requesting backup."

"Location?" the woman asked.

Sam gave her the coordinates. "Sorry, we don't have an address."

"No problem. I'll get someone out there as soon as I can."

"Thank you," Navarro said. "We've got nine people in our morgue. We think we may have found one of the killer's hiding places."

"Oh," the woman said. "That's the Munro case in San Diego. I'll make sure this is put at the highest priority."

"Thank you," Navarro said again, then nodded to Sam.

Sam ended the call and went back to the GPS tracking screen. "They're still there. We'll be there in three minutes."

Navarro stepped on the gas. "Less than that."

They were silent until Sam saw the driveway. It was unmarked and he would have missed it had he not watched the blue dot that was Kit and Connor's car turn that way. "There."

Navarro slowed to turn, and then they both froze at the sound of rapid gunfire.

"Shit," Navarro hissed, flooring the car.

Which lasted for all of ten seconds. The driveway—if that was what it really was—wound dangerously through the trees, and the car's back tires slid on the wet dirt. Navarro swerved so that they didn't plow into a tree.

"Dammit." Navarro was white-knuckling the steering wheel.

More shots were fired and Sam had to fight not to be sick.

She's okay. She has to be. Connor too, of course.

But Kit. She was Sam's. Or she would be someday.

Let her be okay. Please.

Navarro drew a breath and began more carefully navigating the curvy road. The shots grew louder.

"If we keep going," Sam said, "he'll know we're coming."

"That might make him stop."

"Or it might make him desperate."

Navarro scowled. "I'm getting out. You wait here for the sheriff."

That felt like a bad plan, but Sam wasn't going to argue with the Homicide lieutenant. He was unsurprised when Navarro reached into his coat and drew his service revolver from its shoulder holster. He was surprised, however, when Navarro pressed the gun into Sam's hands.

"But you need this," Sam said.

"I wear a double shoulder holster, so I've got two handguns, and there's a rifle in the back. You know how to use that?" Navarro pointed at the gun.

"I do. I practice with Connor at the range."

"Good. Use it to defend yourself if you have to. Just . . . don't shoot anyone."

Sam wanted to ask why Navarro was handing a gun to him if he wasn't allowed to shoot anyone with it, but he bit his tongue. "You want to take the sat phone?"

"Keep it in case the sheriff's office calls."

Navarro took off, leaving Sam sitting alone in the car.

More shots cracked the air and Sam's stomach clenched.

He couldn't just sit here.

He *wouldn't* just sit here.

Climbing across the console of Navarro's car, Sam got behind the wheel and searched for the EV mode button. Navarro's vehicle wasn't a Toyota like Sam's, but it was a hybrid. Switching to the electric motor would allow him to approach silently.

He found the switch and put the car in drive, navigating the winding road while watching for a glimpse of Navarro, Kit, or Connor.

Instead, he came up upon the tan Chevy Suburban, parked diagonally across the road, blocking his path. He couldn't get through.

And Kit and Connor wouldn't be able to get out.

Shoemaker was here and he'd trapped them.

Grabbing the sat phone, his hiking backpack, and Navarro's handgun, Sam left the engine running and jogged through the woods. And then his steps slowed.

There was the trailer.

And there was Kit and Connor's car. The driver's-side window was shattered.

Sam had to force his feet to keep going, staying just inside the tree line. His heart was beating so hard, he felt dizzy. And when he got closer, he was so glad he had kept going.

Kit was slowly standing. It was so dark that he only knew it was her because of her blond ponytail, which was in the hands of a man dressed in black. It had to be Shoemaker, but it was too dark to see anything clearly.

Sam ran to the side of a rustic cabin, dropped to his knees, and, as silently as he could, searched his pack. *Thanks, Mom,* he thought as he found the night-vision goggles he'd thought were such a joke. Slipping them on, he slowly stood, taking in the scene, staying in the shadows.

Shoemaker stood behind Kit, his gun to her head, his finger on the trigger.

No, no, no. Sam looked around, frantically searching for Navarro.

Oh. Sam shuddered in relief. There he was. The lieutenant had come through the trees on the other side of the cabin.

Navarro was focused on Shoemaker, who'd dragged Kit a few feet into the open. She'd been wedged into a small space between Shoemaker's trailer and her department car but was now standing, her arms at her sides. Her hands were empty.

Shoemaker had forced her to drop her gun.

Sam could see the expression on her face. Stoic and defiant and . . . resigned. She thought she was about to die. Panic closed Sam's throat and he had to drag air into his lungs.

Shoemaker yanked Kit's head back by her hair, exposing her throat. Her head was right up against Shoemaker's chest. "I wish we had more time together," Shoemaker said, his voice carrying in the quiet of the night. "Although you're a bit old for my taste."

"So sorry," Kit said, her breaths sounding choppy. Then her expression changed, her vision zeroing in on where Navarro stood with his rifle. "Wait," she blurted. "Tell me something first."

She knew help had arrived and, in true Kit fashion, she was stalling, giving Navarro time to set up his shot.

"Why?" Shoemaker asked, looking over his shoulder.

Sam moved deeper into the shadows. Navarro did the same.

"Because I'm curious," Kit said. "And you're going to kill me anyway. Was it just you?"

"Of course it was just me," Shoemaker said with contempt. "You're supposed to be so smart."

"I didn't think there were multiple doers," Kit said. "Maybe I'm smarter than you think. Did you make all those different stab wounds because you were trying to throw blame on the others?"

"No. I was trying to make each of them think that the others had gone through with it. No one was going to come forward because they'd have to explain how they knew. Foolproof way of keeping everyone quiet."

"Why not let Juanita Young's hit man boyfriend do the dirty work for you?"

"And let him get his hands on Munro's list? Until Hugh Smith brought us all together, I didn't know how many people Munro was blackmailing, but once I did . . ."

"You knew you could recoup what you'd paid him."

"And a helluva lot more."

"Now you can't."

"Sure I can. I still have the list, and all you have is a bunch of he-said-they-said. And you don't know what they actually did to get on the list to begin with, so they won't go to jail for that. They'll walk free. Just like me. They can wire me the money when I get to where I'm going."

"Which is?"

"Somewhere very far away. Enough questions. You're done."

"*Wait*. My parents." Her voice cracked and Sam didn't know if her emotion was real or feigned. "I won't get to say goodbye."

"Neither did any of the others. Now down on your knees. Unlike Munro, yours will be quick."

Sam's panic rose higher. He couldn't watch Kit die. Why wasn't Navarro shooting?

Sam glanced the lieutenant's way to see that he was repositioning the rifle he held, moving a few feet to his left. Navarro didn't have a good line of sight. He couldn't safely shoot while Shoemaker had Kit in that position. He might either shoot Kit or cause Shoemaker to pull the trigger.

Either way, Kit would be dead.

They needed a distraction.

"Hey!" Sam yelled, before he knew he was going to do it. "Hey, Shoemaker, you fucking sonofabitch!"

Shoemaker spun, taking Kit with him, but at that moment, his gun was no longer pressed to her head.

Kit's eyes widened at the sight of Sam, and then her eyes narrowed. She was *pissed*. But she was smart and she dropped to her knees.

Shoemaker was swinging his gun back up to Kit's head when someone fired. Startled, Sam turned to look at Navarro, who looked equally stunned.

It was then that Sam noticed the window in the back seat of Kit's department car was partially rolled down, a gun resting on the window's edge.

Connor. That the detective wasn't getting out didn't bode well. He had to be hurt, and his injuries had to be bad or the man would have been running to Kit's side. But for a long moment, no one moved.

Shoemaker had dropped to the ground, falling to his side, one hand clutching at his hip. But he wasn't dead and he hadn't dropped his gun. Kit was twisting in the mud to grab her gun, but Shoemaker was already pointing his weapon at her again.

Sam didn't even pause to think.

He lifted Navarro's handgun, pulled the trigger, and shot Shoemaker in the head.

The sound of the gun firing left his ears ringing, but Sam swore he heard other shots going off as well. Shoemaker didn't move after that, his gun hand open, his weapon on the ground beside him.

Ripping the goggles off, Sam ran to Kit, making sure she wasn't injured before kicking Shoemaker's gun out of the way. Just in case the man tried again.

But . . . Shoemaker would not be trying again. Ever.

His head was . . . not there. Blood and brain matter were everywhere.

I killed a man. I just killed a man.

But Kit was alive. She knelt in the mud, her gun in her hands, which had started to tremble. "Sam?"

Sam dropped to his knees at her side, not looking at what was left of Peter Shoemaker. "I'm here. Are you hurt?"

"No. But Connor is."

Navarro had run to join them. He took one look at the scene before him, then gently took the gun from Sam's hand.

"You okay, Sam?" he asked.

I killed a man. "Yes," he said aloud. "I'm fine."

I'm not fine.

Kit climbed to her feet and held her hand out for Sam. "You're not fine," she said knowingly. "But you will be. You guys saved my bacon. Thanks."

It's worth not being fine. Kit's still breathing.

Navarro grunted. "That's worth the paperwork I'll have to fill out for having our civilian consultant kill a suspect."

"I'll give my statement later," Kit said, handing her weapon to Navarro.

Standard operating procedure, Sam thought. She'd fired it and there would be paperwork.

He'd fired, too. Bile rose to burn his throat. He hadn't just fired.

He'd killed a man.

"Connor's hurt bad," Kit said. "I need to get him to the hospital." She ran to the back of her car and cursed. "He's unconscious. Goddammit."

"Connor fired the first shot," Sam said. "The one that hit Shoemaker in the hip."

"Then he saved my life." Kit swallowed hard and glanced at Navarro, who'd joined her at her car. "He's bleeding out. We have to get him help."

"Get him to Julian," Navarro said. "Use Sam's sat phone to call the police. They're standing by to provide assistance. Ask them to get a medevac to meet you there. They don't have a hospital, but hopefully they can get a doctor to meet you there as well to do . . . whatever they can do. I'll stay here with the scene. Have them send me backup ASAP."

"But we can't get out," Sam said. "Shoemaker left the Suburban parked across the driveway. Your car is just behind it, Navarro."

"Then I'll drive as far as I can," Kit said, "and then you and I, Sam, can transfer Connor to Navarro's car. I don't think this car would get us far anyway."

The tires were flat. Sam could see that now.

If we'd been a few seconds later . . .

"Come on, Sam," Kit said gently. "I think you're in shock. Come with me."

Kit put him in the front passenger seat of her car as the numbness washed over him.

I killed a man.

Not just him. *But I helped.* He stared at his hand that had held the gun. It was empty now. But he'd fired. *I shot him in the head and he's dead.*

Kit put the car in gear, rolling down the window to call to Navarro, who'd stepped away from the car. "Boss, there was a girl in that cabin. She might still be in there. I think Shoemaker abducted her, too."

"Daniella," Sam mumbled. "Her name is Daniella."

"I'm gonna want to know how you know that," Kit said. "And how you all came to save the day. But later." She began slowly driving down Shoemaker's long driveway, the car barely limping along.

I killed a man.

But then Sam looked at Kit, who held on to the steering wheel like it was a life preserver. She was pale and trembling, but still fierce.

And still breathing. She was alive.

I killed a man.

And I'd do it again.

CHAPTER TWENTY

Sam was not okay.

Kit studied him in the hospital's elevator, just as she had all through today and the day before as they'd done endless debriefings and finally a press conference. They'd sat for hours with Navarro, the San Diego sheriff, and the SDPD brass, who'd talked and talked and talked.

Sam had replied every time he'd been spoken to. He'd been articulate and composed. But Kit had known him long enough and well enough to know that Sam Reeves was not okay.

She'd found him staring at his hands, his gaze unfocused as conversation had gone on around him, and she'd known where his mind had gone. To that moment he'd pulled the trigger.

For me.

Killing someone was a trauma. Even a bastard like Peter

Shoemaker, who'd deserved a bullet to the head and so much more.

It was traumatic for the cop. Or, in this case, the police psychologist.

He'd done it to save Kit. Knowing this made her want to turn back time and tell him not to shoot. That she'd do it. That Navarro would do it.

That even Connor would do it.

Because they'd all shot Shoemaker there in the woods. Kit had dived for her gun as soon as Shoemaker had gone down after Connor's first shot had hit the bastard's hip. She'd seen Shoemaker aim for her again and she'd shot without even thinking.

Navarro had shot him with his rifle—and that was the shot that had blown Shoemaker's head apart like a smashed melon.

Connor had even managed to fire again, hitting Shoemaker in the chest. Connor had lost consciousness right after that, and Kit was so glad he was going to be okay. They'd gotten him to the medical center in Julian just in time to be airlifted to the hospital in San Diego with a level one trauma unit.

That Connor had needed a level one trauma unit still freaked Kit out. But Connor was out of the woods. He'd be okay.

Kit glanced up at Sam as they exited the elevator in the ICU ward. He was pale and seemed shaken. She reached out and grabbed his hand, giving it a squeeze. "You with me, Sam?"

He looked down at their joined hands, then met her eyes. "Yeah. I'm with you." His hand tightened around hers, just enough that she couldn't let hers drop away.

Which she'd been about to. But he needed her and she wasn't going to let him down.

"He looked pretty good when I was here last night," Kit said, speaking of Connor. "CeCe was with him, and his parents, too."

The nurses had made an exception to the two-visitor rule.

"I know," Sam said. "I was here yesterday, too. After they were done grilling me."

After he'd finally been released with the knowledge that he wouldn't face any legal consequences from his actions. He'd been prepared to do so, had that been the case, and had said several times that he had no regrets about pulling that trigger.

But he was a civilian, not a cop, and Kit had been unsure what the repercussions of Sam's part in Shoemaker's death would be. So far, they'd kept it from the press. The SDPD had said that they would not be releasing any statement about his involvement and they suggested he not as well.

Sam had been good with that. He hadn't fired that shot to get attention. Despite his Clark Kent glasses, he had no desire to be a Superman.

Even though he really was.

Kit paused at the doorway to Connor's room, poking her head in. "Hey," she said quietly.

Susan Robinson came to her feet with a smile on her face. "Kit. And Sam. I'm so glad to see you."

The woman enfolded Kit in a hug, which Kit was expecting, as she'd gotten a similar hug the night before. Kit patted Susan's back awkwardly, but it was worth it because Sam's lips were twitching.

He knew hugs were difficult for her.

Finally, Susan let her go, grabbing Kit's hands in an extension of the hug. "You saved my son's life."

Kit almost hadn't. It had been close. But she'd done her best to get him to help as soon as she'd been able to. "He saved mine, too."

"Let her go, Mom," Connor said from the bed. "We talked about this."

"Pssh," Susan said, waving her son's objections away, but she let Kit go and turned to Sam.

Leaving Sam in Susan's capable hands, Kit turned to Connor. "You look better."

"I am better. They're going to let me go to a regular room tomorrow."

"Good." Kit moved closer, examining his face more closely. His eyes were brighter, his skin less sallow. "Thank you," she murmured.

That night in the woods, he'd dragged himself to a sitting position in the car's back seat, and Kit couldn't imagine how he'd managed it. And then he'd fired at Shoemaker. Twice. He'd get a medal for this. Kit wouldn't rest until she made that happen.

"You should've left me," he said, his tone logical. "Glad you didn't, though. Not sure when I'll be back at work."

"Navarro's giving me a temporary partner. I made sure he knew it was *temporary*. I want you back."

Connor's grin brightened his whole face. "Yes! I finally replaced Baz the Magnificent."

Kit snorted, even though she felt a little bad for making Connor feel like he'd had to earn his place with her. "Baz is not magnificent. And you didn't replace him. Nobody could. But I do kinda like having you around."

"Aw." Connor faked wiping a tear from his eye. "I'm overwhelmed by your deluge of love."

"I'd hit you if I could," Kit said dryly. "Where's CeCe?"

"I made her go home to get some rest. She was beat. Dad drove her home. You just missed them. So tell me everything. Mom won't let me watch the news."

"Because it's all awful," Susan said, taking the chair next to Connor's bedside. "That horrible Tamsin Kavanaugh is getting so much screen time, doing interviews, talking about her 'time with Brooks Munro,' like it was some kind of fated love story."

"I saw that interview," Sam said, standing next to Kit. "It really was awful."

"Tamsin Fucking Kavanaugh," Kit muttered darkly.

Connor chuckled, then winced. He had a broken rib and his lung had collapsed from the blow of the bullet. But the vest had saved his life. Kit's belt had done the same with his leg, the tourniquet holding back most of the flow until they'd gotten him to the medical center in Julian.

"Did you find the Ferrari?" Connor asked.

"We did," Kit said.

She and Sam had rejoined Navarro back at the scene after seeing Connor off in the medevac. They'd discovered many gruesome things that Kit was still mentally processing. Shoemaker had kept fingers and toes and other body parts in jars in that little cabin. "The Ferrari was in a large shed behind that ratty cabin. The shed even had lighting—floodlights mounted on the ceiling that were powered by a generator. When the switch was flipped, they all came on and illuminated the Ferrari like it was a museum piece."

"A souvenir," Sam said. "He kept Munro's Rolex, too."

"What about the gold bracelet Veronica left in the glove box?" Connor asked.

"It was there, too," Kit said. "CSU found it. The bracelet was just one item in a bunch of jewelry she was arrested for stealing. Bruce Goddard found out that it had been stolen twenty years ago from a dead woman's jewelry box in Tulsa. The rest of the jewelry was recovered in pawn shops at the time. We think Veronica and Munro used the money to finance their new start in San Diego."

Connor frowned. "And the girl? The one you said was in the cabin?"

"Daniella," Sam said. "She's here, in this hospital. We're going to see her after we're done with you."

"Why was she there?"

Kit grimaced. "Shoemaker's daughter wasn't enough for him, so he apparently picked up homeless teenagers off the street."

And had been doing so for a very long time.

"Three of Daniella's friends ended up at New Horizons," Sam said. "They were instrumental in my figuring out that Neckbeard was Shoemaker. One of the girls—Amy—saw him itching the inside of his wrist, then pulling down his sleeve. I'd seen Shoemaker do that after you two had interviewed him at SDPD. Turns out he was the director of the drama program at the school where he taught. He was apparently good at doing different voices."

"And looking shocked when told his wife was dead," Kit added.

Connor sighed. "He sure fooled me. I never questioned that he'd come straight from court on Thursday afternoon. How did he manage to kill Bert Ramsey's wife? Didn't he have a tail?"

Kit scowled. "His lawyer lost the tail after he picked Shoemaker up from court an hour and a half earlier. The lawyer claims he was just pissed at the SDPD and wanted their eyes off his client. He seemed shocked to learn that Shoemaker was a killer. And all the other things. The lawyer is being investigated, and the cops that didn't report that they'd lost Shoemaker are being disciplined."

"As they should be. That lawyer could have had a hand in killing us both. He needs to be disciplined and so do those two cops." Connor hesitated. "Is the girl—Daniella—okay?"

"She will be," Kit said. "Eventually." *We hope.* "Shoemaker was . . . brutal with her."

"God," Connor breathed. "I'm glad we killed him."

Susan exhaled carefully. "Me too."

"Same," Kit said. "Because there were . . . more. More bodies."

Sam leaned his shoulder into Kit's, a show of support. "Daniella said he bragged about how many girls he'd taken and showed her where she'd end up," he said. "There are a lot of graves behind that cabin."

Connor sagged back into the pillow, closing his eyes. "And he was an assistant principal. Working with children."

"I know," Kit said. "But he's not anymore."

"Good," Susan said fiercely. "That poor girl. What will happen to her?"

"She's only thirteen," Kit said. "A runaway. No father, mother is an addict." It was, unfortunately, all too common a story. "She'll go into the system."

Susan's jaw tightened. She said nothing, but Kit could see the woman's mental wheels turning.

"Talk to my father if you're interested in fostering," Kit said. "Mom and Pop have been doing it for years. They'd take Daniella, but they're truly filled up. Six is the state limit."

Connor had been looking at his mother, but now turned back to Kit. "Six? I thought they only had Rita, Tiffany, and Emma."

"Now they have Dawn, Amy, and Stephie," Sam said, a true smile curving his lips. "They were the girls who were living on the street with Daniella. Her not returning after getting into Shoemaker's Suburban was what prompted them to seek shelter at New Horizons. Emma championed them to Harlan, and he and Betsy couldn't say no."

"Not that they ever would," Kit said fondly. "I found Pop cleaning out a storage room last night. He said he had to have somewhere for his 'grown-up kids' to stay when they came home. That's me and Akiko, mainly, but others come home to visit from time to time."

"Those girls will need things," Susan said. "Clothes and school supplies."

"The state gives foster parents a stipend, and Mom and Pop have money set aside. A lot of us former fosters give them cash every month for the new kids, and that helps. But if you also want to help, by all means let them know."

"I'll talk to him," Susan promised. "About many things."

Kit smiled at her. "Thank you."

"How's Rita?" Connor asked. "Is she okay now that Christopher Drummond is going to be charged with her assault?"

Sam's smile grew bigger. "I think she's watched that video I took of Kit knocking Drummond on his ass about sixty million times."

"Sam is her knight in shining armor," Kit said, only half teasing.

"And you are her idol," Sam added. "I'm always stunned that you can take down men twice your weight."

"You are nowhere close to twice my weight," Kit said, remembering taking Sam to the floor of his condo the night they'd met. "Connor, on the other hand, weighs a freaking metric ton, even if he *says* he's only one eighty-five."

"I'm dense," Connor said, then grimaced when Kit started laughing. "You're not allowed to laugh. I'm hurt. I *saved* your *life*."

"Yeah, well. I thanked you for saving my life. I'm not going to do that again."

But she would, and Connor's little smile told her that he knew that, too.

"Did you get confirmation about what Drummond wanted to trade for a deal?" Connor asked. "Was it the country club blackmail scheme or did he know something more?"

Kit shrugged. "His attorney told Joel that they had nothing more to offer, so we're assuming it was the blackmail. Drummond has finally shut his damn mouth."

Connor's scowl was impressive. "We wanted to shut it for him permanently after he ambushed you in the parking lot, but that would have meant paperwork. What about Munro's money? Did you ever find his stash?"

Kit rolled her eyes at that question. "Yeah, we did."

Connor's brows lifted. "Why do you sound like that?"

"Because I'm embarrassed. You will be, too. Wilhelmina took it. She found it before we got to Munro's house the night we did the notification."

Connor's mouth fell open. "Wilhelmina? What the fuck?" He winced. "Sorry, Mom."

"It's okay," Susan said, looking equally shocked. "Wilhelmina stole from Brooks Munro? What the fuck?"

Connor choked and his mother just patted his hand.

"CSU did a scan of Munro's floor and found a very well-concealed safe under the hardwood floorboards. Remember we thought it didn't look like Veronica had searched his home office? She confirmed that she'd left it a mess when I talked to her yesterday. However, when Wilhelmina was cleaning up the mess, she found the lever that popped up a board, revealing the safe. The combination was Veronica's birthday. So Wilhelmina more than 'suspected' that Munro and Veronica were intimately involved when she talked to us that first night. She outright knew they'd been having an affair for years. We think she guessed that Munro would choose a combination that was related to Veronica."

"But why?" Susan asked. "Were her millions not enough?"

Kit shook her head. "She doesn't have millions. Not anymore. Wilhelmina's lawyer for the family trust fought hard for a few days to keep from sharing her financial statements, but Marshall and Ashton were finally able to get the warrant. Remember the little sculpture in Wilhelmina's rental condo? The one you thought was worth twenty-five grand?"

"Yes," Connor said. "And was I right?"

"About that, yeah. But remember how I contacted the condo's owner to ask about it when we were driving back to the station after talking to Wilhelmina, and I had to leave a message? The owner finally called me back, but I wasn't in the office, so the call was routed to Kevin Marshall. Turns out, the sculpture did *not* belong to the condo owner. He said he'd seen it in Munro's house when he'd visited Wilhelmina there. She'd told him that her husband had bought the sculpture, that it was Munro's."

"So, that she'd taken property from the house was cause for suspicion," Connor said slowly.

Kit nodded. "Exactly. The theft, plus the fact that she'd lived with a blackmailer, indicated that she might have had motive to kill Munro as well, but it was the theft that tipped the scales in our favor. Marshall and Ashton got the financial report right about the same time that you were getting shot. Turns out that Wilhelmina's dead broke."

"What?" Susan gasped.

Kit nodded. "Looks like Munro took a lot of Wilhelmina's money and some bad investments ate the rest. So we got a warrant for the condo she's renting and we hit the jackpot. Seems Wilhelmina had stolen a fair amount of the artwork he'd owned, mostly items that were small enough to transport in the trunk of her rental car. She'd already filled it up before we arrived last Saturday night."

"How much did she get from Munro's safe?" Connor asked.

"Over six million dollars, all in fifties, all nonsequential," Kit said. "Munro apparently didn't believe in banks, on or offshore.

Wilhelmina had it packed in suitcases when we arrived at the condo with our warrant. You remember when I pointed out that fifty on the floor in her rental?"

"She said she'd given it to Rafferty for groceries."

"She lied. That was part of the haul. She and Rafferty had been counting the cash when we knocked on her door."

"Wow." Connor shook his head. "I guess she can argue that the artwork was jointly hers since they were married. Or she thought they were."

"Well, Laura Letterman isn't letting Wilhelmina get away with anything. She's filed on behalf of Veronica to get it all back. But neither of them will get to keep any of it. It's all going to go into a victims' fund. Not everyone Munro victimized were people who had done blackmail-worthy things. Some were people he'd forced to donate to his campaign in exchange for meetings with him."

"What an asshole," Susan said, and Connor choked again.

"Mom."

Susan just patted his hand. Her smile was bright, but it seemed fragile. Brittle even. Seeing her son nearly die had shaken her, understandably. She wasn't okay, either. But she would be.

"What about the hit man?" Connor asked. "The real one, not the undercover cop."

"He's gone," Kit said. "He crossed the border into Mexico about a week before Munro was killed. For now, he's in the wind. But we did find Veronica's bank account. Walter Grossman's, too. Both in the Caymans. But most of their money was in a safe in Veronica's house there. Veronica kept an accounting of the cash she collected from victims and doled out to Munro, and he in turn to Grossman. Her having an affair with Grossman meant Veronica was sharing the numbers, so he knew exactly what he was owed. For what it was worth, the three seemed to be honest with each other."

"How nice," Connor said sarcastically.

Kit grinned. "The ledger she kept was in her safe, along with the cash. The police in George Town had to get a warrant to search and then find a safe cracker. They just let us know about that money two days ago, but everything was out of control and Navarro didn't see the message until yesterday." She paused, going through the list of debrief items in her mind. "Oh. We checked the guard shack's security feed and found a motorcyclist driving out of Munro's community early Wednesday morning, then back on Wednesday afternoon. The times lined up with when Shoemaker's school was in session. We figure he used the trailer to transport both the Ferrari and the motorcycle out of Munro's neighborhood. The guard noted the motorcycle's reentry in his logbook on Wednesday afternoon, said the guy claimed to be with Norton Landscaping and had come to help his partner clean up after he'd been working all day." She sighed. "After the guard had seen him at least twice that day, I guess Shoemaker figured he was a major loose end."

"And Munro's list?" Connor asked quietly.

"Haven't found it yet," Kit said with a frustrated sigh. "CSU has searched the Suburban, that horrible cabin, and some of Shoemaker's house. The house will take longer to search because it's so immense, so we still might find it."

"Could he have buried it outside the cabin?" Connor asked.

"We thought that, so we got a team out there with ground-penetrating radar to check, but there were no buried boxes or anything like that."

Just eighteen graves.

Eighteen girls.

Alicia Batra and the other MEs had a busy time ahead of them, identifying the remains. They had no idea exactly how long Shoemaker had been killing girls, but it had been years based on the condition of the corpses. Kit had already promised that she'd help connect physical descriptions to missing persons. They'd probably been homeless teens. Girls that no one was searching for.

At least we found Wren's body. There had been some closure there. But seeing all the corpses had rattled Kit to her core. *That could have been me. I could have been one of those girls on the street, trying to survive. Had it not been for Harlan and Betsy . . .*

Sam grabbed her hand and gave it a squeeze. "Hey," he murmured, like he knew where her mind had gone.

He probably did. He'd been there at Kit's side when the team with the GPR had discovered the first body, and he and Kit had waited until all the graves had been located.

It had only seemed right.

"We should probably be going," Sam said. "We'll let you rest and come back tomorrow, okay?"

Connor was watching Kit carefully. "How many, Kit? How many graves did the GPR team find when they were looking for the list?"

"Eighteen," she whispered.

Connor's exhale was heavy and sad. "I'm sorry we couldn't save them."

"You saved Daniella," Sam said. "And Dawn and Amy and Stephie. They won't be on the street because of you two."

"And you too, Sam," Connor said. "I think I need to rest now. Get out of here." But it was said with affection.

Kit gripped Connor's hand. "Thank you," she whispered.

"You said you weren't going to say that again, but I knew you would," he boasted.

To make her smile, Kit knew. And it worked. Kind of.

Kit pointed two fingers at her eyes, then at Connor. "Tomorrow. I'll be back. And when you're back to snuff, I'm not pulling my punches."

"Bring it," Connor called as they left his room.

Kit's shoulders sagged when they were out in the hall again. "And thank you, Sam."

He brushed a lock of hair from her cheek, the tender gesture squeezing her heart too hard. "For what?" he whispered.

She pursed her lips, her eyes welling with tears she didn't understand. "For . . . everything, I guess." She wiped at her eyes angrily. "I have no idea why I'm doing this. I don't cry."

"It's leftover emotion," Sam said, "and very normal. You carry a lot on your shoulders. Sometimes a valve has to be opened so some of that pressure can escape. Tears are good."

"Let's go see Daniella." She straightened her spine and forced herself out of her comfort zone. For Sam. "Mom's making pot roast tonight. Wanna come to dinner?"

He smiled and she knew she'd made the right move. "As long as I can stop and get Siggy. He's been locked in his crate a lot this week."

"Of course Siggy is welcome. The girls will love him and he can play with Snickerdoodle and Petunia."

"Petunia? Who's—" Sam blinked. "Wait, that new monster dog is named *Petunia*?"

Kit laughed, glad the tears seemed to be gone. "Yep. Even though he's a male dog. The girls said they shouldn't be 'constrained by gender norms.'"

"Okay, but . . . *Petunia*? He's immense."

"Gonna get immenser," Kit muttered. "He got into Mom's flower garden and came running up to the girls with a mouthful of winter pansies. Mom wanted to be mad, but the dog was too cute with a bouquet of flowers sticking out of his mouth." She smiled, affection for the teenagers warming her chest. "I figured they'd name him Pansy, but the girls thought the flowers were petunias at first and the name stuck." She fished her phone from her pocket and showed Sam the photo her mother had texted.

The giant dog stared up with soulful eyes and a mouthful of purple blossoms.

Sam laughed, such a sweet, welcome sound. "Oh my God, that's hilarious."

"It really is. Luckily pansies aren't toxic to dogs, so the big doofus is just fine. The girls—" Kit stopped when her phone buzzed in her pocket. Caller ID listed Susan Robinson. "Susan? Is Connor okay?"

"It's me," Connor said. "My mother was laughing about me calling myself dense and I told her that I worked out and CeCe liked my dense muscles."

"He's okay," she told Sam. "Connor, what do your dense muscles have to do with me?"

"Because I get them at *the gym*," Connor said. "See if Peter Shoemaker uses a gym. See if he uses *my gym*. Veronica had their victims leave thousands of dollars in cash in a gym locker. Maybe that's where Shoemaker put the list."

"Hey, it's worth a try. I'll do that right now." She ended the call and dialed Navarro. "Can we find out where Shoemaker went to the gym?" she asked, bypassing greeting him when he answered.

Sam's expression showed instant understanding. Kit liked that about him.

"The list," Navarro breathed. "I'll get on that now. I'll call you when I have a warrant."

"Thank you," Kit said, ending the call. She smiled up at Sam. "Let's see Daniella and hopefully we can eat some pot roast before we search."

The Beachside Athletic Club, San Diego, California
Saturday, January 14, 9:15 p.m.

They did, in fact, have time for Betsy's pot roast before Sam and Kit headed over to the gym where Shoemaker worked out. The mood at McKittrick House had been boisterously happy and slightly chaotic, with six teenage girls and three dogs running around.

The newest girls were happy and they'd all given Sam big smiles. That had done some good for his soul. He'd killed a man, yes, but he'd helped these girls to get off the streets and into one of the best homes possible.

It was balance, and Sam appreciated that.

Harlan had pressed something into Sam's hand as they were walking out the door—a carving of Sam on a horse, wearing armor and holding a sword. It was a thank-you for Sam's part in saving Kit's life and currently rested in Sam's pants pocket.

Kit had her good-luck charm—the cat-bird figurine. Now Sam had one as well.

The nice family evening complete, he and Kit were back at work. But this might be one of those balance things again. The awful things Sam had seen balanced by the triumph of truly solving the case.

It had taken a few phone calls for Navarro to figure out where the man had a membership, and it turned out that Shoemaker had had three. Two were gyms he'd joined in the last week.

No shock there. Shoemaker would have needed access to all the places where Munro had done business with his blackmail victims. Navarro had gotten warrants for all of them.

But they'd started out at the gym where he'd had his membership the longest. It was the same athletic club where Connor played squash.

"It would be nice to find it at the first place we looked," Kit said.

Sam shook his head as they passed by the gym's front desk, heading for the locker room. "Except this isn't the first place you've looked. You've searched his house, his office at school, his in-laws' house, all his vehicles, and that cabin."

"True. I honestly thought he'd have hidden Munro's three-ring binder in the Ferrari. It's where I would have put it. Oh good. Navarro's here. Let's do this." She and Sam followed Navarro into the locker room, where a uniformed officer stood guard by one of the lockers.

"I figured you two should be here when we opened it," Navarro said. "Connor should be here too, but we can show him the video." He pointed to CSU's Sergeant Ryland, who held a camera. "Ryland's going to video the whole thing as evidence."

"It's like Al Capone's vault," Kit said. "Except hopefully this one isn't empty."

"Hush," Navarro said seriously. "Don't jinx it."

Kit mimed zipping her lips closed. "Do you have a key?"

Ryland produced a set of bolt cutters. "You want to do the honors, Lieutenant?"

"Sure would." Navarro cut off the lock, then stood back. "Kit?"

She pulled on a pair of disposable gloves. "My heart's racing."

But she was exhilarated. Sam could see it in her pretty blue eyes.

She drew a deep breath and pulled open the locker, Ryland standing behind her so that he could capture the whole thing on video. "Wow," Kit said, staring into the locker. "He actually worked out here?"

Because it was filled with stinky shoes and exercise clothes.

Kit began removing them, placing each into evidence bags as

she verbally cataloged each item for the recording. "More shoes, more shorts," she muttered. "A tennis racquet, a racquetball racquet, and . . . what is this?"

"That, Kit," Sam said, "is a squash racquet."

She gave him an indecipherable look before returning to the locker. "Some very smelly socks and . . . gross, a jockstrap." Then she made a sound of satisfaction. "One gym bag." She set it in an evidence box and unzipped it. Then reached in and pulled out a three-ring binder. "Bingo."

Navarro came to stand on her left as she opened the binder. Sam stood on her right and held his breath.

"Oh my God," Sam whispered as he scanned the first page. "Ronald Tasker said they were movers and shakers, but . . . oh my God."

"Indeed," Navarro murmured. "Shit. This is going to cause big waves downtown. There are politicians, CEOs . . ." He grimaced. "A few cops, even."

Munro had been quite organized. There was a column for the name of his victim, the date on which the crime—or crimes—was committed, the nature of the crime, the date the blackmail began, and the amount of the payment.

Kit flipped through the pages, her eyes wide. "There are more than sixty names on this list. And only a few have lines drawn through them."

One was Hugh Smith, the man who'd outed his fellow black-mailees. Another was Earl O'Hanlon, the man who'd committed suicide after Munro had drained him dry. Another was Trisha Finnegan, the woman who'd informed Munro that she was no longer going to pay him after her ex-husband had discovered her indiscretion.

"Drummond," Kit said, reading the man's name with satisfaction. "He was paying twenty thousand a month." Because Rita's mother wasn't the first woman he'd killed. Munro was blackmailing Drummond for the murder of the housekeeper he'd hired before Maria Mendoza. "He was probably hoping Joel would give him transactional immunity if the list became public."

"There's Shoemaker," Sam said and Kit paused in her page turning. "He'd been paying Munro for more than four years."

"Incest, kidnapping, sexual assault, and sexual battery," Kit read. "Munro knew that Shoemaker was kidnapping and raping girls, that he was raping his own daughter, and he didn't report him. He profited from it."

I'm so glad he's dead. That they're both dead. Sam would remember the words on that page the next time he felt the tiniest bit guilty for his part in killing Peter Shoemaker. That man deserved to die. Sam only wished he'd suffered more.

"It also appears," Kit went on, "that Shoemaker was paying Munro more than anyone else on this list. His payment was fifty grand a month. That's how much Munro took out of his bank account the day he disappeared, because Shoemaker demanded it from him."

That left Sam a little breathless. "Fifty thousand dollars a month for four years . . ." He quickly did the math. "That's two million, four hundred thousand dollars."

Kit turned to meet Sam's gaze. "I'd feel like Munro owed me a Ferrari, too." She closed the binder and dropped it into a large plastic evidence bag. "I think my brain has enough to process tonight and I feel like I need a million showers. I didn't want to know that so many people in this city were this evil. Is it okay if I go home now, boss?"

Navarro's smile was gentle. "Of course. You and I can go over this list on Monday. I imagine Joel Haley and his boss will want to be involved."

Kit pulled off the disposable gloves and dropped them in another evidence bag, just in case there was any trace evidence transferred from the locker's contents to her gloves.

"Come on," Sam said. "I'll drive you home now."

She and Sam were quiet until they were back in Sam's RAV4. "Just . . . give it to me straight, Sam."

He fastened his seat belt and looked over at her. "What?"

"Do you play squash?"

He laughed. "And if I do?"

She sighed, long and loud. "Then I guess I'll have to stop giving Connor a hard time for being a snobby squash player. Do you?"

He laughed again. "Twice a month since summer. Sometimes Connor and I bowl, too."

"Connor told me about the bowling a while back. Are you any good?"

"At squash? Not awful. Not in Connor's league, but I can hold my own. Why? You want to play with me?"

She lifted one brow. "Are you flirting with me right now?"

"Depends. Is it working?"

She smiled at him then, a sweet, shy smile that made him warm all over. "Yeah. It is. We had a date tonight, but we missed it."

"We've been a little busy. I figured we'd go next week."

"Or tomorrow night."

Sam reached over, trailing a fingertip over her cheek. "Tomorrow night."

"Your place. I don't want to go to a noisy restaurant, and Mom and Pop's is going to be crazy for a while."

"You want me to cook on our date?"

"No. I'll bring the food. I won't cook it either, so you're safe."

He swiped nonexistent sweat from his forehead. "You had me worried there for a minute."

Still smiling, she shook her head. "Take me back to Mom and Pop's, please. I need to help with the new girls."

EPILOGUE

This is nice," Kit said as she set her bags down on Sam's kitchen counter.

He'd hoped she'd think so. "I thought we should have a nice table for our date."

He'd set the table with his grandmother's china, his own crystal, and a vase with a single small sunflower. Kit didn't seem like a roses kind of woman. And the sunflower had made him smile.

She beamed at him, and for a moment he was thunderstruck. She was genuinely happy to be here. He'd been scared that she'd insisted on this date out of obligation.

"Thank you," she said. "Dinner is compliments of Akiko. She caught the fish and cooked it." She started unloading the bags, releasing amazing aromas. "Bluefin tuna. There's some rice, too. And green beans almondine. We're going fancy tonight."

Sam sat on one of the bar stools and watched her move. She was fluid, graceful. She'd left her blond hair down and it was soft and framed her face perfectly.

And he was totally biased. But that was okay. She was here, in his home, and he'd been a nervous wreck all day. Every surface had been cleaned and recleaned and sanitized. Every pillow plumped at least twice.

He'd even made his bed with clean sheets, even though he was certain they were far from that point. But a man could dream, couldn't he? Nine months ago, she'd told him they couldn't even be friends and now, here they were. Having dinner. Together.

A real date.

"I didn't think bluefin tuna were biting right now," Sam said, taking an appreciative whiff of the dishes she was setting on his counter.

"They're usually not, but Akiko took this charter group really far out. One of the clients caught a super cow."

"What's a super cow?"

"A fish over three hundred pounds. It was pretty exciting, honestly."

"You were there?"

Kit nodded, her smile going a little tense. "Yeah. Akiko is . . . well, she's a little on edge lately. Hasn't been comfortable taking charters out alone and her usual first mate still has the flu. I didn't want her to have to cancel another charter, so I went with her."

"Why is she on edge?" Sam had noticed a change in Akiko. She had seemed more preoccupied and anxious over the past week, but he'd attributed it to the trouble with Rita and Christopher Drummond.

Kit sighed. "She said I could tell you if you asked, so I'm not breaking a confidence. A woman claiming to have known her mother called her and asked for a meeting. We're going in two weeks."

"We?"

Kit shrugged as she plated two servings of Akiko's offering. "She's nervous about it and so am I. It feels . . . wrong, somehow. Which is probably just me being paranoid like usual, but I made her promise to wait until I could go with her. She called the woman yesterday, but the woman's out of town for the next two weeks. So . . ."

"You have good instincts and I'm glad you listen to them. I'm also glad Akiko listens to them, too. It's good that you two have each other."

"It is. We weren't close at first. I didn't want her at McKittrick House."

"Why not?"

"She took Wren's bed, and Wren hadn't been gone that long."

"Ah. That makes sense." Kit had been grieving her sister. She'd been fifteen years old and hurting. "But you're very close now."

She smiled. "We are. Sisters in every way but blood. She's always had my back and I've had hers. If you're impressed with that move I do, taking down men twice my weight? Thank Akiko. She taught it to me."

"I'll definitely thank her, then."

She took a final dish out of another bag. "Cheesecake. This one I bought. Mom was mad at me for not asking her to make something, but she was busy today getting the new girls ready to start school tomorrow. I didn't want to stress her out."

"She can make dessert for our next date."

Kit grinned. "Okay."

She seemed almost buoyant. If he didn't know better, he'd wonder if she'd been drinking. But Kit rarely drank and never when she was going to be driving. "You're in a good mood," he said tentatively.

"I know. I woke up this way." She sounded genuinely bewildered by this.

Sam laughed. "I'm glad. It's just . . ."

"Abnormal?" she asked, but she didn't seem irritated.

"A little. I kind of like sassy Kit."

"Good, because this good mood won't last long. They rarely do."

That was something that Sam hoped to change.

"What did you do today while I was playing first mate to Akiko?" she asked.

"I cleaned the condo," he said with a self-conscious laugh. "And Siggy and I took a walk to the comic book store."

Kit turned from the fridge, where she'd put the cheesecake. "Ronald Tasker's comic books. I should have known you'd remember."

"I promised. And he did give us some valuable information."

Kit sighed. "And he has another family in LA."

That was the secret he'd kept, the one that Munro had blackmailed him over. It had been noted in Munro's three-ring binder. "Yeah. That would be hard for his daughter to forgive."

Kit pushed a lock of hair behind her ear. "Anyway. Nonwork topics. This bluefin tuna is ours because the guy who caught it lives in New York City. He got his picture taken with the fish, but he didn't want to take it all home with him. Akiko offered to ship it, but the guy doesn't even like fish."

"Why'd he go on a fishing trip, then?"

"It was a bachelor party. Most of the group were from somewhere else. Even the groom lives in LA."

He pulled her chair out for her and she beamed at him again. It was amazing how a smile from Kit McKittrick could make him feel ten feet tall. He sat beside her, still stunned that this evening was happening at all. "Then why have the party here?"

"Bride's family is local and they wanted to throw a big country club wedding." She shuddered. "I've had enough of country clubs for a while. But again, nonwork topics. The guy said that Akiko could have the tuna, and she was over the moon. We filled her freezer, Mom's freezer, and the freezers of most of our brothers and sisters. When she brought that fish to Mom and Pop's, I thought the girls' eyes were going to pop out of their heads. They'd never seen a fish that big. Most people haven't. It took all of us a long time to clean and chop up that fish."

"I'm glad they got a new experience. And I'm glad I get to eat it without having to do any work."

Kit chuckled. "And I didn't have to cook anything, so I'm happy, too."

"You must be tired. You had a long day." But she was still here. She hadn't rescheduled.

"I should be, but I'm not. I get a jolt of energy when I close a case, especially a big one. You ready to eat?"

Sam took a bottle of champagne from the ice bucket. "I know you're not a drinker, but we can have a little."

She smiled at him, and he felt like he'd already drunk the whole bottle, his insides all bubbly. "Just a half glass for me."

He filled it all the way, anyway. "You have to get the nose-tickling experience of a full glass of champagne."

She gave him a doubtful look. "If you say so."

He held out his glass. "To second second dates."

She laughed and tipped her glass to his. "And no murders."

"Definitely." He watched as she took her first sip, her eyes widening.

"Oh. This is good. I've never liked champagne before."

"This is the good stuff. It was a gift from my boss, and I've been saving it for a special occasion."

She dropped her gaze to her plate, her cheeks pinking up. But her smile was real. Shy, but real.

And so damn appealing. Everything about Kit McKittrick was so damn appealing.

She looked up and found him staring at her. Her cheeks became an even darker pink. "What?"

"You're pretty."

She rolled her eyes. "I'm just me."

"And you are pretty. Just say thank you, Kit."

Another eye roll, but she looked pleased. "Thank you."

He stopped staring and began eating the dinner Akiko had prepared. "This is delicious."

She hummed. "It really is. I should learn to cook, but between Mom and Akiko, I don't have to."

"Must say I'm jealous."

"You don't have to be. Mom would cook for you every single day if you asked."

"While tempting, it's not exactly practical. I'm not a terrible cook. My father taught me a few recipes."

"Not your mom?"

Sam chuckled. "No. My mother is an amazing woman, but she is a terrible cook."

They continued eating in a companionable silence until Sam couldn't eat another bite. "I want to eat more, but I'm stuffed."

"I know." Kit arranged her cutlery on her empty plate. "Akiko is a goddess in the kitchen."

He leaned back in his chair. "I'm curious about something, but I'm afraid to ask."

Her brows went up. "Okay. I'm kind of afraid to hear the question now. But go ahead."

"That night I heard you telling Connor about those awful foster homes."

Her eyes shuttered and he wanted to pull the words back. But if they were going to have any kind of relationship, he couldn't be walking on eggshells around her.

"And?" she asked warily.

"I wanted to know if they were punished. If they were still allowed to foster kids."

Her expression smoothed out immediately, and he was so relieved. "Pop took care of them. He met with the social worker who'd moved me from house to house, who'd refused to report the stabbing with the letter opener as an act of self-defense. It was in my record for everyone to see. It made me look like a little psycho, which Pop knew I wasn't. He didn't like the woman's attitude and he . . . well, she got fired soon after. Turned out I wasn't the only kid she was shafting."

"Good. And then?"

"And then a better social worker took her place. The letter opener guy was denied a foster license after that and the reason was put in *his* permanent record."

Sam lifted his glass, which he'd refilled. Kit was still working on her first glass. "To Harlan McKittrick."

She smiled and touched her glass to his. "Best father ever. The second incident, where I put sleeping pills in the foster father's whiskey? I kept that a secret for *years*, but Mom and Pop had known all along. That new social worker told Pop that she'd looked into that guy, too. I got Wren out, but the next girls who were placed there weren't so lucky. The new social worker believed the girls, and that guy served time and is now a registered sex offender."

She hadn't shared the part about sleeping pills with Connor, and Sam wondered why. He wondered if this was what she'd been hiding. But he wasn't going to ask. She'd tell him or she wouldn't. Either way, he was happy to be by her side. "Excellent."

She tilted her head. "That was it?"

"Yes. I figured they were no longer foster parents because I didn't think you'd let that go on. But I'm even happier knowing it was Harlan who made sure they were punished."

"He and Mom are the best."

Sam considered telling her that his parents wanted to meet hers, but he figured that would scare her and he wasn't ready for the evening to be over yet. He rose and held out his hand. "I'll do the dishes later and return Akiko's stuff to her. Let's sit on the couch for a while."

She swallowed hard and let him pull her to her feet. "Okay."

She was clearly nervous and he didn't want her to be. He cupped her cheek in his palm, gratified when she leaned into his touch. "To talk. And maybe have some dessert."

She closed her eyes, still leaning into his palm. "That's a little boring, don't you think?"

He slowly drew in a breath, hoping he'd understood. "What would liven things up?"

"Something like this?" She slipped her hand behind his neck and drew his head down.

And kissed him.

It had been only a week since she'd last kissed him, but he felt like it had been twenty years. He made a little needy sound that might have embarrassed him if she hadn't echoed it, rising on her toes to get closer. Sam kept one hand on her face and slid the other down her back, drawing her to him, elated when she allowed it.

The kiss went on. It wasn't hot, not yet. Nor over-the-top passionate. Not yet.

This was a learning kiss. Sweet, yet far from simple. His body responded, but he could control himself. For her. Always for her.

Finally, she eased her heels back to the floor, her eyes opening to lock on his. "You are a very good kisser, Sam Reeves."

His heart stuttered in his chest. "I'll be better with practice."

Her lips curved. "I bet you will be."

Sam had leaned in to kiss her again when someone knocked on his door. Hard.

No way. No freaking way.

Sam's head whipped around and he glared at the door, willing whoever it was to go away, but the kiss ruiner knocked again, even harder.

Kit sighed. "You'd better get that."

Sam was halfway to the door, grumbling under his breath, when his caller knocked a third time. "I'm coming, dammit! Keep your pants on."

He heard Kit give a little snort-giggle as he opened the door and frowned. "Navarro?"

Lieutenant Navarro stood there, his fist poised to knock a fourth time. He looked around Sam and blew out a relieved breath when he saw Kit. "Can I come in? It's important."

Sam stepped aside, his mind going a mile a minute. Had the police changed their minds? Would he be held accountable for the shot he'd taken at Peter Shoemaker?

Sam closed the door and walked over to where Kit stood. She too was eyeing Navarro nervously.

"What's going on, sir?" she asked.

Navarro gestured to the sofa. "You should sit down."

She shook her head. "What's going on? Tell me. Is it my father? My mother? Rita?"

"No, no." Navarro lifted his hands in a placating way. "They're fine. I'm surprised they're not here yet. I figured they'd rush over when they finally told me that you were here with Sam." He glanced at the table, at the pretty china and the bottle of champagne. "I'm really sorry."

"Why?" Kit asked, the single word coming out sharp and almost deadly.

Navarro squared his shoulders. "I've spent all day going through Munro's dead-man's-switch list. The three-ring binder."

"I know what it is," Kit said, without a note of inflection in her voice.

"There was . . . is a blackmail 'victim' on the list." He used air quotes. "His crime was murder."

Kit never moved a muscle. Her face seemed frozen in a neutral expression. Sam moved behind her, putting his hands on her shoulders. "Just spit it out, Navarro," he said. "You're scaring her."

"He's pissing me off," Kit snarled.

Navarro briefly closed his eyes. When he opened them, they were filled with sorrow and trepidation. "This murderer threw his victim—a fifteen-year-old girl—into a dumpster."

Like Wren had been, more than sixteen years ago.

Kit stiffened. "What?" she whispered.

Sam led her back to one of the dining room table chairs and gently pushed her to sit. That she followed without complaint was testament to how shocked she really was. "Who?" Sam asked. "And when?"

"It's a fake name. A few of the names are fake. I don't know why, not yet. He's listed as John Smith. He's been paying Munro for five years. Ten thousand a month. He might have nothing to do with Wren. He might be another sick bastard who treats his victims like garbage. But I didn't want you to come in tomorrow and see this. Not with everyone around."

Kit was staring off into space, her eyes unseeing. Sam ran his hand over her hair, resting his palm on the side of her neck. She didn't move. Didn't react at all.

"Kit?" Navarro asked, coming to crouch in front of her. "Say something. Please."

She swallowed. "Thank you for telling me."

That was all? Sam thought she'd be furious with the man who'd killed a girl and thrown her body in a dumpster. With Munro for knowing it was happening and not telling the authorities.

With Navarro for being the bearer of bad news.

But she didn't get mad. She was just . . . numb.

Sam bent to kiss the top of her head. "Come on, Kit. I'll take you home. To McKittrick House. Your parents will need you and you need them."

She nodded, rising to begin gathering Akiko's things.

"I'll do that later," Sam said, gently taking her hand. "Come now. Let's go to Harlan and Betsy."

"Okay." She walked to the front door like a zombie, but then turned to Navarro. "We're reopening Wren's case?"

"Yes. I'm giving it to Marshall and Ashton."

Kit nodded once. "Okay. Thank you."

"I'm sorry, Kit," Navarro said again. "I'm so sorry." He did look sorry. He looked devastated. "We'll find this guy and, even if he had nothing to do with Wren, we will make him pay."

Kit's lips firmed and her eyes grew sharp again, making Sam breathe a sigh of relief. "You'll keep me up to date with every step of the investigation?"

"As much as I'm able," Navarro promised. "I'll see myself

out." He paused as he passed Kit, still standing by the door. "I didn't tell your parents. I only got them to tell me where you were. I needed to tell you first."

"We'll tell them," Sam said.

Navarro left and Sam turned Kit so that her head was close to his shoulder. But she didn't lean in. She didn't move at all. He didn't put his arms around her. He thought she seemed too fragile for that at the moment. But he did rest his cheek atop her head.

"I'm here for you. I have your back. A lot of people do."

Kit nodded. "If I find him," she murmured, "I will kill him."

"And if you kill him," Sam promised with complete sincerity, "I'll help you hide the body."

She hiccuped, half laugh and half sob. And then the dam broke and she leaned into him, sobbing like a child. "I miss her. So much."

"I know."

"I'm going to find him, whoever did this. And I'll make him wish he had never been born."

"I know. I believe in you, Kit McKittrick."

After a few minutes, the sobs had quieted and she lifted her head, her pretty face streaked with tears. "Thank you, Sam. I'm . . . glad you were with me. I . . . needed you."

For some people, that wouldn't be a huge declaration. For Kit, it was everything.

Sam pulled her close and wrapped his arms around her. "I'm glad I was with you, too. I won't leave, Kit. Not unless you ask me to go."

Her arms came around his waist and she held on. "I'm not a good bet."

"Too bad. I've already made up my mind. If you want me, I'm yours."

"I should tell you no. I shouldn't be selfish and keep you. But . . . yes. I want this. I want you. In my life. Don't go. Please, don't go."

"I won't. I promise."

And Sam Reeves always kept his promises.

ACKNOWLEDGMENTS

The Starfish—Christine, Sheila, Cheryl, Brian, and Kathie. As always, thank you for the plotting and for all your help when I get stuck. Love you all.

Erin Dougherty for helping my characters find their way around San Diego. You are like sunshine, so warm and bright.

Andrew Grey for being my word-count buddy. Thank you for cheering me on!

Martin Hafer for taking such good care of me while I'm writing. Sarah Hafer for finding my mistakes before everyone else can see them.

Beth Miller for proofreading the galleys. I appreciate your fresh eyes.

To Robin, Liz, and Jen for your support for this series!

As always, all mistakes are my own.